Praise for *Dying Declaration*
and previous novels by Randy Singer

"An exp'... *ing Declara-*
tion, S ... and com-
pelling

— ... *ba,*

"Rand ... n the first
page a ... medicine,
and c ... ont pages.
Singer ... at clarifies
the dil

"Rand ... t's a joy to
read. I ... xploration
of the ... ntinues to
challe

"This ... hat is dis-
turbin ... w you in,
keepi ... and what
will h ... ding."

"An a ... eat action
with

"Legal thrillers seem to have found a home with CBA readers, and Singer once again adds a strong voice to this growing genre in the evangelical Christian market."

— *Publishers Weekly*

"In this second book by Randy Singer, he again paints an intriguing and thought-provoking look at issues that are hot buttons around the country. He pulls us into the storyline with believable characters, as well as a few we know from his first book, *Directed Verdict*. Hold on to your seats; this one will be a ride!"

— *Christian Library Journal*

"...[A] legal thriller that matches up easily with the best of Grisham."

— *Christian Fiction Review*

Praise for *Directed Verdict*

"*Directed Verdict* is a well-crafted courtroom drama with strong characters, surprising twists, and a compelling theme. Randy Singer's novel is engaging, memorable, and highly significant."

— RANDY ALCORN, author of *Deadline, Safely Home,*
and *Edge of Eternity*

"There is plenty of room in evangelical Christian fiction for fresh voices, and debut novelist Singer is a promising one."

— *Publishers Weekly*

"A riveting courtroom drama..."

— *CBA Marketplace*

"This is the best legal thriller I've read. Highly recommended."

— *Church Libraries*

DYING
DECLARATION

RANDY SINGER

DYING
DECLARATION

A NOVEL

WATERBROOK
PRESS

DYING DECLARATION
PUBLISHED BY WATERBROOK PRESS
2375 Telstar Drive, Suite 160
Colorado Springs, Colorado 80920
A division of Random House, Inc.

Scripture quotations are taken from the *King James Version* and the *Holy Bible, New International Version*®. NIV®. Copyright © 1973, 1978, 1984 by International Bible Society. Used by permission of Zondervan Publishing House. All rights reserved.

The characters and events in this book are fictional, and any resemblance to actual persons or events is coincidental.

ISBN 1-57856-776-9

Library of Congress Cataloging-in-Publication Data

Singer, Randy (Randy D.)
    Dying declaration / Randy Singer.— 1st ed.
        p. cm.
    ISBN 1-57856-776-9
        1. Attorney and client—Fiction. 2. Children—Death—Fiction. 3. Conspiracies—Fiction. I. Title.
    PS3619.I5725D95 2004
    813'.6—dc22

                                                                              2003026774

Printed in the United States of America
2004—First Edition

10 9 8 7 6 5 4 3 2 1

For Keith and Jody.
At the heart of this book is a special relationship
between a brother and sister.

Writing it has made me even more grateful for ours.

CHAPTER 1

She looked pitiful.

She was a plain woman with a prominent nose and an everyday face, made even less memorable by her refusal to wear makeup. She had stringy black hair, puffy eyes, and skin blotched with red marks where she had nervously clawed at her neck. She made no effort to stop the tears from running down her cheeks and dripping on Joshie's head. She hugged him closer to her chest, rocking gently in the recliner and humming softly, stopping the motion only to wipe her child's forehead with a cool, damp washcloth.

She placed the washcloth back on the arm of the worn recliner and kissed Joshie on the cheek. She felt his little body twitch back and forth in a way that mimicked the rocking of the recliner. She resumed her rocking. The twitching stopped.

The little guy was so hot. Motionless, almost lifeless, except for a quiet moaning. His pain was her pain. And it was doubled by her helplessness, her inability to stop the relentless march of the fever or to combat its devastating effect.

She could no longer bring herself to take the temperature of her youngest child, still four months shy of his second birthday. The last reading, taken two hours ago, registered 103. It was probably higher now. It would make no difference, because she couldn't do anything about it. And so she cried. And rocked. And prayed.

⊷ ⊰◊⊱ ⊷

Thomas Hammond had not left his knees for half an hour. He formed an odd picture, this burly man with the round scruffy face, bulging forearms, and callused hands slumped meekly on his knees—the posture of humility. This was spiritual warfare, and it was a battle that Thomas intended to win. He prayed in the master bedroom at the other end of the double-wide trailer from Theresa, next to his bed, his head buried in his massive hands.

"Take this fever from us. Spare my son, Jesus." He said the words aloud, barely audible but soaked with intensity. Over and over again the same simple requests. The story of the persistent widow filling his thoughts. *If I pray long enough. Hard enough.* "Increase my faith. Save my son. Don't punish him for my mistakes." He tried bargaining with God—he'd promise *anything.* "I'll go anywhere, Jesus. Do whatever You want. Serve You with all my heart. Just gimme this one thing. Don't punish Josh—"

"Dad!" It was five-year-old John Paul, his oldest son, the one that Thomas had nicknamed "Tiger." The boy called from his bedroom down the hall.

"Your Word says You are slow to anger, abounding in love, full of grace and mercy." Thomas stopped, the whispered words sticking in his throat. At this moment, it didn't feel like he served a God of mercy. He felt the anger rising, the frustration of unanswered prayer. And then he felt the guilt. Could his anger be the one thing holding back God's healing hand? "Show Josh your mercy—"

"Hey, Dad!" The call grew louder now. Persistent.

"Just a minute, Tiger." Thomas ran his hand through thinning hair and reluctantly rose. He trudged down the hall to the boys' room and wiped his eyes with the back of his hand. It was important to be brave.

He opened the door and let the hall light illuminate the cramped quarters that Tiger proudly called his own room, though he shared it with Josh. Tiger sat straight up in bed, clinging to his tattered blankie, his bright blue eyes wide open.

"Keep it down, Son. You'll wake up Stinky."

"Stinky" was Tiger's seven-year-old sister. She had earned her nickname when she was still in diapers. Thomas would talk to her while he changed her, wrinkle up his nose, and pronounce her "Stinky." The name stuck, and Stinky became a term of endearment. But it was a name that only family used, and only around the house. Others called her Hannah.

"I can't sweep, Daddy. I got some bad dreams…again."

Thomas sat down heavily on the bed and rubbed Tiger's ragged blond hair. "Well, they're over now, 'cause I'm here." He knew what Tiger needed to hear, and Thomas took some comfort in the routine that on other nights could be aggravating. "I'll beat that old bogeyman up one side and down the other," Thomas growled. He could see the slightest grin beginning to form on the young boy's face. He tickled Tiger's ribs and watched the grin grow. "Now just lie down and think your happy thoughts."

"I did," said Tiger. "But then I went to sweep. Daaaaddy?" Tiger drew out the name for maximum effect, then looked up with his best puppy-dog eyes.

"Yeah, buddy?"

"Will you lay down wif me?" Tiger scooted over in his small bed to give his dad some room. They had done this many times before. Thomas's large frame would never quite fit on the small portion of the bed unoccupied by Tiger. But Thomas would try. He would balance himself half on the bed and half off, with one hand on the floor propping himself up, telling Bible stories until he heard the heavy breathing of a sleeping boy.

"Not tonight, Son."

"Please, Dad, jus' one story!" Tiger whined. "Tell me 'bout Abe-ham and his son and how God got them a goat."

Thomas grinned. He could hardly resist the little guy even on normal nights. Tonight he craved the comforting routine of telling bedtime stories and watching Tiger's eyelids grow heavy. But tonight he also knew how badly Theresa needed him. And his prayers for Joshie were not yet finished. God had not yet answered.

"I can't right now, Son. I gotta go check on Mom and Josh again. If you're still awake when I come back, I'll tell you the story of Abraham."

"Okay," said Tiger cheerily. The kid obviously had no intention of sleeping.

Thomas kissed him on the forehead, pulled the covers up around his neck, then turned and walked toward the door.

"Daddy?"

"*What?*" The word came out sharper than Thomas expected. He stopped walking, a little ashamed of himself for taking it out on Tiger.

"I'm firsty."

⊷ ⊰✢⊱ ⊶

A few minutes later, Thomas joined his wife in the small living room. His stomach churned as he paced the stained carpet, watching helplessly as his wife continued her vigil—rocking, wiping Josh's brow, humming, and praying. She ignored Thomas.

"Is the fever breakin'?" he asked at last.

Theresa shook her head.

"Have you checked in the last few minutes?"

"Why should I?" Her voice was cold, her face etched with worry. The pressure of believing in things unseen was taking its toll.

Thomas walked behind the recliner and began rubbing her shoulders. He felt the gnarled and knotted muscles of her slender back, and he penetrated them with strong fingers, trying to massage out the tension. It didn't leave.

"When is the last time you checked?" he persisted.

"Two hours ago."

"Don'tcha think we oughta check again?"

"Only if we intend to take him to the hospital if it's still high." She turned her head and looked behind her at Thomas, pleading with large hazel eyes. She stopped rocking. Joshie didn't move.

Thomas avoided his wife's eyes, bowed his head, and shook it slowly. He walked from behind the chair and knelt in front of her. He placed his big hands on Theresa's legs.

"Just have faith," he said softly. "God'll heal 'im."

Theresa snorted at the suggestion. "I've got faith, Thomas. I've had faith. But he's getting worse... Don't you dare lecture me about faith." Her voice had an edge that Thomas had never heard before.

Joshie moaned. His little body jerked for an instant, then he curled tighter into a ball, snuggling against his mother's chest.

"You want me to call Pastor Beckham and the elders? They could git over here and anoint him with oil again, pray for him—"

"I want you to call an ambulance," she demanded, her voice quivering. "God sometimes works through doctors. How can you just kneel there and let your son suffer while you do nothing?"

"Theres—"

"Here," she sniffed as she thrust little Joshie out toward her husband. She held the child in outstretched arms, like a sacrifice. "You hold him. You look at your son, and you tell him why he has to die just so you can prove to the world how much faith you've got." She held him there for a moment, her youngest—her *baby*, then turned her head away.

Words failed Thomas. He reached out and took his son, pulling him against his own chest. He felt the heat radiate through his son's pajamas.

Holding the boy gingerly, Thomas rose to his feet. Only then did he notice, out of the corner of his eye, Stinky and Tiger standing in the doorway to the living room. They were dressed in their pajamas, holding hands. Tiger still clung to his blankie; Stinky held her favorite baby doll.

He turned to face the kids, wondering what they had heard. Tiger's bottom lip trembled, and his eyes were moist and big. Stinky looked confused, fighting heavy eyelids, her blonde curls shooting in every direction.

"Is Joshie gonna die?" she asked.

CHAPTER 2

He leaned forward and put his back into it, pulling the large green plastic trash can down Atlantic Boulevard. The trash can had built-in wheels on the bottom, but he still strained against the load, his lean cable-like muscles glistening with sweat. It was a typical June night in Virginia Beach—sweltering hot with suffocating levels of humidity.

He was quite a sight, this young black man with the square jaw, intense brown eyes, and electric white smile. And he drew more than his share of stares, even on a sidewalk lined with lunacy. But he was used to it, and he felt like a natural part of the cacophony of personalities that made Atlantic Avenue hum. There were skateboarders, punk rockers, rednecks, beach bums, surfers, and sunburned tourists. They wore baggy shorts, bikinis, obscene T-shirts, tank tops and visors. They sported every color and cut of hair imaginable. His own cut, a close-cropped flattop that accentuated his angular features, added nothing unusual to the mix.

He had walked more than a half-mile from the parking lot, but he had a few more blocks to go. He wheeled his contraption past a hip-hop band, with their baggy pants, boom box, speakers, and amps. This was their corner, and they had gathered a small crowd in a semicircle, clapping and gyrating. The boys were rapping, and the boys were dancing, just plain getting down, dreadlocks flying everywhere.

"Yo, Rev," said the man with the mike.

The man pulling the trash can stopped, pointed a finger at his hip-hop friend, and smiled. "'S'up, dog."

"We gonna bust a little freestyle for the rev," announced the man with the mike. Without missing a beat, he started a new line. "B-boys in the front, back, side, and middle. Check out my b-boy rhyme and riddle." The b-boys—the break dancers—let loose as the crowd pulsed in approval. "Rev teach the black book smooth as butt-ah, but po-lece and white folk dis the broth-ah."

The man with the trash can smiled and nodded, soaking in the energy from the brothers. Pleased, the singer attacked his impromptu rap with more vigor, each line growing worse than the one before, feeding off his own angry energy. After a few wholesome lines about the rev, the lyrics degenerated into the more familiar fare of sex, drugs, and the next punk to get whacked. When the rev had heard enough, he thumped his chest and pointed at the man. "Peace out," he said.

The brother nodded back, continued his rap uninterrupted—more vulgar than before since the rev was now leaving—and the man with the trash can moved on down the street.

By the time he hit his favorite intersection, his T-shirt was already sporting sweat stains under the arms and a thin line down the back. He pulled a handkerchief from the pocket of his cargo shorts and wiped his brow. People passed him on every side. He smiled and greeted the tourists as he started unloading.

"Praise God, Brother. How ya doin'?"

No answer.

"God bless, sir."

A strange look.

"What's happenin'?"

"Hey, man." Finally a response, a returned smile. The preacher handed the man a tract.

"Stick around," said the preacher. "We're gonna have church."

The tourist walked away.

Charles Arnold reached into the trash can and unloaded his wares. A karaoke boom box. Two large speakers. A well-worn Bible. A tangled web of cords. A microphone and a twelve-volt Wal-Mart car battery.

He hooked up the juice, popped in a CD, and transformed his trash can into a pulpit, his corner into a church.

"It's time to get our praise on!" he said into the mike, half yelling, half singing. The gospel tunes blared from the boom box, the cheap speakers distorting the sound. Charles started singing and swaying to the rhythm. The tourists cut him a wide berth.

"He's an on-time God—oh yes He is… He's an on-time God—oh yes He is… Well, He may not come when you want Him, but He'll be there right on time… He's an on-time God—oh yes He is…"

The crowd grew slowly but steadily. Charles pumped the volume of the music and raised his voice to match. He placed an empty coffee can in front of his trash can pulpit. The can was labeled TITHES AND OFFERINGS. There was not a penny in it.

Some people stopped to sing. Others gawked. Motorists drove by and yelled encouragement or insults.

He swapped high-fives with tourists passing on the sidewalk and interspersed his singing with "God bless you, sirs" for those who ignored him. He smiled at everyone. And he shrugged when the teens drove by in their souped-up cars and hurled their insults.

A few stragglers stopped. The crowd grew. A couple of young girls started singing along and dancing off to the side. He grabbed one by the hand and brought her up front to share the mike. Her friends followed, and soon he had a choir. Drivers blew their horns as they passed. A few turned up their stereos, but Charles's speakers drowned them out.

The tithes and offerings started rolling in.

Then a robust older woman with shorts too tight for her age, a painful sunburn, and a great voice started bellowing a solo. "Amazing Grace." The anthem of the street. He noticed smiles in the front. The nodding of heads. The soloist's husband had tears in his eyes. It was time to preach.

Charles thanked the lady. The crowd gave her a huge hand.

"You're probably wondering why I called this meeting," Charles began. A ripple of laughter. "Tonight, I want to speak with you about the sinfulness of man, the faithfulness of God, and the forgiveness of Christ. You are here not by *my* appointment but by *divine* appointment. This could be the most important night of your life."

He worked the crowd as he talked—pacing, shaking hands, letting his voice rise and fall in rhythm. He warmed to his subject, and the passion began to flow.

"You're crazy, man," two kids yelled from the back as they walked by.

"It's called the foolishness of the Cross," he responded into the mike. "Is it crazy to be out here preachin' on this street corner when I could be out par- tyin' at the next one?" A few in the crowd shook their heads no, a few "tell its" drifted up. The kids stopped and looked.

"Is it crazy to get high on Christ when I could be trippin' on crack?"

"No sir, brother," said a voice in the crowd.

"Is it crazy to trade in the rotting riches of this world for a heavenly hookup in paradise?"

"It ain't crazy!" a different voice.

"He is no fool who gives what he cannot keep to gain what he cannot lose."

"Amen, brother."

Charles had a few supporters in the crowd, but the skeptical teens were not impressed. He could see the smirks forming on their faces. They brushed him off with a wave of the hand, snickering as they walked away. "That boy is skitzing," one muttered.

Charles shrugged and returned to the faithful. He regained his rhythm, and the crowd swelled by a dozen. Most of the newcomers regarded him from a distance with bemused curiosity. But a few—there were always a few—crowded closer. They egged him on with their amens and uh-huhs and tell-its right on cue—the preacher and crowd in a spontaneous sermon dance. Synchronized emotions rising and falling.

Charles was in his glory. He was so focused that he didn't see the squad car pull up behind him, didn't even know it was there until he sensed the crowd disconnect as they looked past him, over his shoulder. The faithful shuffled back.

He turned just in time to see the boys in blue lug themselves out of their car and lean against the hood, arms folded, scowling at the street preacher. The older man, the one who disembarked from the driver's door, was a middle-aged guy with a severe-looking face—white pockmarked skin that had not recently seen the sun, sagging jowls, and a scar on his left cheek. He stood at least six-two, reminding Charles of a large oak tree, the kind that adds a ring of girth to the midsection with each passing year.

The younger man mimicked his partner's scowl but without the same intimidating effect. On his less-worn face, the frown morphed into a maddening frat-boy smirk, making it hard to take him seriously. This officer had pumped his share of iron, his tight blue uniform straining against bulging biceps and massive pecs. He looked like the kind who had wanted to be a cop his whole life, the kind who lived for nights when a black man might try to resist arrest.

Charles fought hard to suppress the feelings welling up inside. The po-lece…tic tacs…PO…looking down their nose at this black street trash. He felt the full weight of the nation's racial divide bearing down on him. He felt a powerful urge to lash out at these men verbally, to strike at those who were dissing him with their smug and pompous looks. But he also knew it was just what they wanted, an irrational black man starting something.

Charles Arnold had been there before.

"Take for example the boys in blue back here," he said in a friendly tone as he walked toward them. "If they catch you speeding, they give you a ticket. And it's no defense to say that everyone else is going faster. Right, men?"

No response. Stone faces.

Charles turned back to the audience. "It's the same way with God. It's no defense to say that others are worse than we are. This is not a competition. For *all* have sinned and fallen short of the glory of God. And *all* means *all*…"

Suddenly the volume died. Charles turned to see the hand of the weightlifter on the control knob, the snide smirk still on his face. The older man, leaning against the hood of the car, motioned Charles over with his finger.

"Excuse me a minute," said the street preacher to his retreating audience. "I believe I'm being paged."

CHAPTER 3

Thomas Hammond gently placed Joshie back in his mother's lap, then walked across the living room and knelt down in front of his other children. He put his beefy arms around both Tiger and Stinky and gave them a hug. He leaned back on his knees to talk with them.

"Joshie's not gonna die," he said. "He's been kinda sick for a couple of days, but there were a lot of people in the Bible who were sick too, and Jesus healed 'em. We've just gotta keep prayin'. Does that make sense?"

Both little heads nodded. Stinky's curls bounced up and down.

"Are we going to take him to a doctor?" Stinky asked.

"Honey, you know what we believe about doctors," replied Thomas firmly. "We pray to Jesus instead."

"Was Jesus a doctor?" asked Tiger.

"No, Tiger," Thomas frowned at his son. "Who told you that?"

"Jesus healed people," said Stinky helpfully. Her big eyes sparkled at her dad.

He opened his mouth to respond, to give her the rote answers that had been drilled into him at church. But the words never formed.

He had been strong, even stubborn. He had been full of faith and prayers for three long days. Seventy-two agonizing hours. His mind flashed to the story of Abraham. Called by God to sacrifice his own son—something that God had no intention of allowing Abraham to do. Then, at the last moment, as Abraham raised the knife to slay his son, God stepped in and provided another sacrifice.

Was God now calling Thomas to the hospital? It went against the grain of everything he had learned at church. It seemed so unlike God, but so did Abraham's call to sacrifice his son. If Thomas obeyed, would God miraculously intervene and heal at the last minute? Perhaps even on the way to the hospital or just before a doctor saw the child? Maybe so. Maybe God was testing him even now.

Maybe God was calling him to Tidewater General Hospital.

While Thomas wrestled with his thoughts, Tiger and Stinky fidgeted in front of him. Thomas could read the anxiety in their faces, the concern for a baby brother as listless as a rag doll.

"Get your cowboy boots on, Tiger. Stinky, get your sneakers. We're not just going to one doctor. We're going to a hospital that's chock-full of doctors." Thomas saw their eyes light up, and he smiled. "Joshie's gonna be all right."

Stinky threw her arms around her dad's neck. Tiger went racing down the hallway to find his cowboy boots, the only thing he would wear on his feet in public these days.

"Awright!" he yelled. "We're going to the hopsicle."

⋅—⋅ ☰✦☰ ⋅—⋅

Behind Thomas and Stinky in the living room, Theresa pulled little Joshie against her chest even tighter. She placed her cheek on his forehead and felt the intense heat of the fever. She glanced up, her eyes filled with tears.

"Thank You, Jesus," she whispered.

CHAPTER 4

The older cop leaned against his car while Charles stood obediently before him, the microphone dangling in Charles's right hand, as the preacher endured a lecture on permits and noise ordinances. Charles glanced down at the guy's name badge—Thrasher. *Probably fits,* thought Charles.

Out of the corner of his eye, Charles noticed his small crowd beginning to scatter. The die-hards would stay, but the curiosity seekers were leaving fast. Thrasher seemed to notice as well and took his time. He drew his words out slowly and stopped occasionally to spit on the sidewalk, building up a nice little pile of foamy white saliva.

"Preacher Boy, you know the noise ordinance. You been talked to 'bout this before." Thrasher paused, spitting another bull's-eye on top of the others. "You got no permit for that sound system, and you're disturbin' the merchants. Why can't you get that through your nappy little head?"

Nappy little head. The veins started pulsing in Charles's neck. He tried to concentrate on the little pond of spit but couldn't keep from thinking about the Beachfest riots, where thousands of African American college students, in Virginia Beach for spring break, had fought against the beach police. It took years to sort out the brutality. This guy had probably been there.

Stay calm. Stay focused.

"Officer, I'm just out here making the beach a better place." He paused, raising his eyes from the sidewalk to the cop, waiting for the man to blink. "Are you a believer, sir?"

The weightlifter moved next to Charles, violating his space, trying to intimidate. Charles took a lateral step and froze the weightlifter with a sideways stare.

"Buddy, we're not gettin' into that," snapped Thrasher. "You can preach till your lungs fall out, but you crank up that sound system again…and we'll impound the system as evidence and take you into custody. And I guarantee ya, you'll do some time, Preacher Boy."

Charles sighed. *The stupidity of these guys.* "Don't tell me I'll do time, Officer. You think just 'cause I'm a black street preacher that I'm *stupid?* I've got First Amendment rights—"

Thrasher lunged from the car in a flash—quick moves for a fat guy. He stuck his nose in Charles's face, and the weightlifter inched closer, moving just behind Charles's shoulder.

Thrasher lowered his voice to a threatening growl, emphasizing each syllable. "Don't give me that garbage… Don't tell me your rights." The man blew out a hot and putrid breath that recoiled Charles. "You pack up and go home, or you're gonna have a heap of trouble. You got that?"

"Hey, leave the man alone." A voice drifted up from what was left of the small crowd.

"Yeah, he ain't hurtin' nobody." Another bystander.

"Are you telling me I can't preach out here, even without my sound system?" Charles kept his voice measured as he spoke.

"I'm telling ya, if you know what's good for ya, that tonight you'll just pack up and go home." Thrasher still spoke slowly and simply, as if addressing a child. But Charles could see the man was losing control, didn't like the crowd turning against him. "And I'm also tellin' ya, that if you know what's good for ya, you'll never bring that contraption out here again unless you have a permit." The officer raised his eyebrows and nodded, a signal that he was done lecturing and it was time for Charles to go.

"That's what I thought you were saying," said Charles evenly. He turned, walked around the weightlifter, then stooped down next to his karaoke boom box. He looked back over his shoulder at the cops, took a deep breath, punched the Play button, then stood up and started singing with the CD. "He's an on-time God, oh yes He is…"

It was apparently the moment the weightlifter had been waiting for. He stepped over and jerked the mike from Charles, tossing it to the ground. He wrenched both of Charles's arms behind his back, farther and harder than necessary, and slapped on the cuffs. As the few remaining crowd members jeered, the weightlifter wrenched the cuffs tight enough that they threatened circulation, and then began reading Charles his rights.

"You have the right to remain silent. You have the right to an attorney. Anything you say can and will be used against you in a court of law…" As he spoke, he shoved Charles into the back of the squad car, banging Charles's head against the doorjamb. Meanwhile, the cop named Thrasher dismantled the sound equipment and stuffed it in the trunk. They would confiscate it, all except the trash can, as evidence for their case.

"You guys are pigs, man. Leave 'im alone," said a goateed man as he watched Charles get manhandled.

The muscled officer pointed at him like a championship wrestler calling out his next foe. "You shut up or you're next," he warned.

"I'm scared," said the man. Then he turned and walked away.

⊷ ⫞⬧⊱ ⊶

They had been riding in the squad car for several minutes, with Charles working hard to maintain his cool. Thrasher was driving and radioed in the report, talking about Charles in the third person—the "perp" this and the "perp" that, as if Charles were a big-time drug dealer. Charles's head ached from where the muscled officer had banged it against the doorjamb.

"Uh…guys, you've got these cuffs on too tight," Charles shouted through the bulletproof glass that separated him from the officers. "I mean, it's not like I'm a flight risk or anything…"

"Shut up!" barked the weightlifter, turning sideways in the front passenger seat to glare back at Charles. "You've done enough talking for one night."

"Oh, so now the First Amendment doesn't apply in the squad car either? Is that it? Virginia Beach is a Constitution-free zone now?"

"The reverend back there thinks he's cute," said Thrasher to his younger partner. "I think he's cute too. His type look particularly cute when they've got chains or cuffs or Dobermans on 'em."

The officers guffawed. Charles swallowed the urge to spit on the glass. No sense giving these guys an excuse to bruise him up.

"Hey, Tubby, what's the charge?" Charles yelled to Thrasher. "You guys ever think about telling a man what he's been charged with?"

"Public ugliness," responded Thrasher. The officers laughed again, then

Thrasher turned serious. "Look, Reverend, you were out there blatantly thumbing your nose at the noise ordinance. We were gonna cut you a break and just give you a warning. But you couldn't take a hint. So…now we've got you for resisting arrest as well."

"That's ridiculous," Charles protested. "No way that'll hold up in court."

Thrasher raised his palm and glanced in the mirror. "Don't tell us how to do our job," he shouted over his shoulder. "You do your job out there on the street—but leave the sound system at home next time—and we'll do ours."

"It's not my job," responded Charles. "It's my ministry."

"You mean the reverend is gainfully employed?" mocked the weightlifter. "A taxpaying citizen—now that changes everything."

"Where do you work, boy? KFC?" Thrasher snorted.

"I teach," said Charles.

"A teacher," grinned the weightlifter. "Imagine that, teacher by day, preacher by night. Maybe we should call him prof. Where you teachin', Prof?"

"Regent Law School," answered Charles.

CHAPTER 5

This was one of the reasons that Thomas Hammond avoided hospitals like the plague. He had no health insurance, just a strong faith in miracles. And now they would make him feel like a criminal.

"Occupation?" asked the intake clerk. She sat on the other side of a large Formica countertop. Thomas juggled Tiger on his knee, while Stinky stayed in the waiting room watching television.

"Self-employed."

"Insurance?"

"None."

"Excuse me?" she stopped writing, looking up from her paperwork for the first time, an eyebrow raised in condemnation. "You have no health insurance?"

"No, we'll pay for it ourselves."

She shook her head slightly, disapprovingly, her lips pursed. "Who is your child's primary-care physician?"

"He doesn't have one," said Thomas defensively. He watched the look flash on the lady's face again. She made no effort to hide it. She might as well have said the words. *White trash.*

"Maybe this wasn't such a good idea bringing him here," mumbled Thomas.

"Why in the world would you say that?" asked the bureaucrat as she reached in her top right drawer and pulled out a stack of Medicaid forms.

⊷ ⋇⊠ ⊶

Dr. Sean Armistead stopped outside Emergency Intake Room 4 to study the assessment from the triage nurse. He always studied the chart before talking to a patient, even on nights like tonight when they were crazy busy. Armistead wanted to know what he was up against. A doctor should exude confidence; patients always felt better if a doctor knew what he was talking about right from the beginning.

He had been working since three in the afternoon and, in addition to the usual parade of ER illnesses, had already been in emergency surgery twice. A knife fight and a shooting. Virginia Beach was rapidly becoming big-city America.

The surgeries had wreaked havoc on his already crowded ER schedule. Now he and his partner had them stacked up and waiting. This one had better be quick, and the chart had better be perfect. He had no time for anything less.

Time of admission: 9:04. It was now 9:30. The patient had been waiting a few minutes, but that was unavoidable. *Patient's name: Joshua Hammond. Age: 20 months.* He glanced down to the patient complaint section of the chart. *Pt w/ fever 106, ↓ activity, –playfulness, generalized achiness, n, v, x 3 days, sore and distended abdomen.*

This child was in acute distress.

The temperature of 106 would have been taken rectally, and rectal temperatures were always a degree high. Still, even a temp of 105 was in the danger zone. The kid had no energy, no zip. According to the note, he showed decreased activity and negative playfulness. He hurt all over—thus the notation for generalized achiness—but was particularly sore and swollen in the abdomen. This kid had been nauseated and vomiting for three days. Three days! *What kind of parent would allow these symptoms to persist for three days before seeking medical help?*

Just from reading the chart, Armistead formed a working diagnosis. Peritonitis. Poison in the system. Not literal poison but just as deadly. It could lead to a total breakdown of the nervous system and vital organs as a result of a severe bacterial infection. In this case, a likely culprit was the appendix, possibly ruptured and spewing the contents of the intestines into the abdominal cavity and ultimately the bloodstream of tiny Joshua.

It would not have been life-threatening on day one. Or even day two. But now, with Joshua lethargic, running a high-grade fever, an elevated pulse of 118, dangerously low blood pressure, and a respiratory rate of 28, there were no guarantees.

Armistead knew what to expect. They would open the child up to remove the appendix and find all kinds of inflammation caused by pus and fecal matter in the lining of the abdomen. He had seen some bad cases of peritonitis straggle into the emergency room, but none this bad. The child was hypotensive and in acute distress. Three days fighting a losing battle against the bacteria had taken its toll.

Armistead tucked the chart under his right arm, shook his head, and prepared to enter Intake Room 4. He pushed open the door and extended his hand to a mother who had waited three long days before bringing her dying baby to him for help.

He forced himself to smile.

━ ━ ≡◆≡ ━ ━

Theresa looked up as the door opened.

"I'm Dr. Armistead, how are we doing here?" the doctor asked, pleasantly enough.

Theresa was sitting on the examining table with Joshie on her lap. Her son was listless and lying on his left side against her, knees pulled up to his chest. Theresa shook hands with Dr. Armistead and did her best to return the doctor's thin smile.

He was younger than Theresa expected. And shorter. He had receding light blond hair, sharp cheekbones, penetrating eyes, and a prominent jaw. His smile displayed rows of perfect white teeth and created quite a contrast with the narrow gray eyes that stared intensely out from behind small wire-rimmed glasses.

His impeccable presentation, ramrod posture, and pressed lab coat made Theresa self-conscious of her own appearance. She had not thought about how miserable she looked until this very moment, confronted with a doctor who exuded confidence and composure.

"Not real well," Theresa admitted. "He's been running a fever for a couple of days, and now he's pretty…lifeless, I guess." She grimaced at her own choice of words. Something about Armistead intimidated her, made her feel inadequate.

He bent down and started poking at Josh. He checked ears, nose, and throat. He took Josh's pulse himself and confirmed a 116. He put a cold stethoscope on bare skin and listened to the lungs.

"Rapid respirations, difficulty breathing," the doctor confirmed. He put pressure on the lower right abdomen and elicited a moan.

"Hey, buddy," Armistead said as he poked and prodded. "Can you tell me where it hurts? Does this hurt…? How 'bout this…?" Joshie winced at times and remained stoic at others. "Man, you're a tough little guy." He rubbed Joshie's head, tousling already disheveled hair, and then looked over Joshie's head and directly at Theresa.

"When did you first notice the fever?"

"Um…it seems like maybe three days ago."

"You know we've got a pretty elevated fever here. One-oh-six rectally. Anytime that fever gets up over a hundred and two you ought to get him checked out, okay?"

"Yes sir. It was only about a hundred and three earlier today. I tried everything I knew to keep it down."

Armistead scribbled a few notations on the chart. He stopped for a moment and glanced at Theresa, said nothing, then went back to writing.

"How long has he been listless and lethargic like he is now?"

"That just started today, maybe yesterday… I mean, whenever he runs a fever he's not himself, you know, but it was just this morning that I noticed we couldn't get any reaction out of him at all."

Theresa stared down at the top of Joshie's head, unwilling to look at the doctor with the accusing eyes.

"I think we've got a case of appendicitis here," continued Armistead, studying the chart. "He hurts in all the right places. We should have a CBC and a urinalysis done just to get a read on the white blood cell count and to rule out other possibilities." He was writing again, mumbling more to himself than Theresa. "I don't know why she didn't suggest that lab work already; I'd like to have it in process by now."

He then turned back to Theresa, replacing his plastic smile with a frown. He pulled up a stool in front of her so they were sitting eye to eye. "Appendicitis is not generally life-threatening at Joshua's age if it's treated soon enough," he lectured. The absence of emotion made the words even more condemning. "But when a child's appendix bursts, it spews poison into his system. If that goes untreated long enough, it can lead to peritonitis and ultimately to septic shock. It can affect the circulatory system and central nervous system if the cause of the peritonitis is not treated.

"Joshua is showing classic signs of septic shock. We'll probably have to operate as soon as possible. But first we've got to try and resuscitate him with some IV fluids, start him on some antibiotics, and build up his strength for the operation. Once we get the fluids and drugs in him, you and I will talk again about the risks of surgery. But believe me, the risks of not having surgery, of not treating this problem, are infinitely greater."

Armistead stopped and let the silence linger. The unspoken accusation hung in the air and screamed for an answer. It was obvious that this doctor had no intention of speaking until Theresa answered his charge.

Why? Why had she waited so long?

"Our church teaches that healing comes from the hand of God, not the hand of man." She spoke softly, feeling the depth of her own guilt while holding Joshie and patting his back. "My husband and I knew we should come earlier, but we also knew that our church would forbid it. These last few days have been incredibly hard…" Her voice trailed off. She had said enough.

Armistead let the punishing silence remain a bit longer. At last he spoke. "These last few days have been hard not just for you and your husband but for Joshua as well. A burst appendix is extremely painful. With today's medical advances, no child should have to live through the pain of an untreated ruptured appendix for three days. But you're here now, and it was right for you to come. Let's try to help Joshua with the pain and get him back on the road to healing."

He tousled Josh's hair again and stood up to leave.

"Will he be okay?" Theresa asked. It was more of a plea than a question.

"We'll do our very best," promised Armistead. "Nurse Pearsall will be with you shortly."

And with that, he picked up the chart and left.

In the hallway Armistead quickly scratched out his diagnosis and orders. *Dx: Appendicitis, w/ onset of peritonitis and sepsis. R/O urinary tract infection. Prep for surgery. Orders: CBC, UR, antibiotics and hyperal.*

He needed to prepare Joshua for surgery, build the child's antibodies, and rule out any other potential causes of lower right abdominal pain, such as a urinary tract infection. All of this was basic stuff. Emergency Room Medicine 101.

But it was the order he did not put in the chart that gave Armistead reason to pause before moving on to the next patient. Should he keep this child at Tidewater General or order a transfer to Norfolk Children's Hospital?

Conventional wisdom dictated a transfer. Norfolk Children's Hospital specialized in pediatric care and surgery. They had all the latest technology and the certified specialists who could pull a child through even the most difficult cases. And from everything Armistead could tell, Joshua would be a very challenging case, the sepsis potentially affecting all the major organs.

Just from a pure liability standpoint, which was no small factor, it would make sense to transfer the kid to a hospital like Norfolk Children's, a hospital with the premier reputation for pediatric care in southeast Virginia. But Armistead personally believed its reputation was not justified. There were good surgeons at Tidewater General, better than most at Norfolk Children's Hospital. And he hated the thought of transferring this kid to those prima donnas at the big city hospital who would later take all the credit for saving a child that the doctors at Tidewater General couldn't handle.

And what if the specialists at Norfolk Children's lost the child? They would certainly blame it on the half-hour or so that Joshua sat in the ER examining room before being seen. After three days of total neglect, the hotshots in Norfolk would say it all came down to that extra half-hour. Or they would find something else to nitpick, something about Armistead's orders, something about the transfer.

No, there was no sense in transferring this patient. Armistead would keep the kid here. Joshua would get virtually the same level of treatment, and Armistead would not open himself up to all the second-guessing.

Transfers took time, and this patient didn't have much time. Putting aside all of his resentment for the place, putting aside all of the arrogance of the Norfolk Children's doctors, looking at it solely from the vantage point of the best interest of the patient, it still made sense.

They would operate here. No way would Armistead order a transfer to the same hospital that had five years ago rejected him for its residency program. Twice.

CHAPTER 6

Whoever designed emergency room waiting areas obviously knew nothing about kids. Tiger had already been told three times by his dad to sit still, each time louder than the last. He had really tried. But the magazines for kids had simply failed to keep his attention, and so his running around the room had earned him a long stretch of sitting in the same chair. Worse, despite some rather loud noises generated when Tiger cleared his throat, his dad seemed to forget all about Tiger being confined to the chair. The possibilities for getting up anytime soon seemed pretty dim.

Just when Tiger was about to give up hope, a chance for escape presented itself when his dad stepped into the men's bathroom. Tiger looked left and right, ignoring the accusing looks from Stinky, then decided to get up from his seat and take advantage of the momentary lull in supervision to test the operation of the automatic doors at the ER entrance.

Step on the pad, the doors open. Jump off the pad, the doors close. They seemed to be working fine.

"You're a-posed to be sitting down," warned Stinky, nervously eying the door of the men's room.

But Tiger had not exhausted all the options. Jump on quick and off quicker, and you can get the doors to open and close only partway. In fact, just a tap from the heel of a cowboy boot would send the doors springing open. What power! What fun!

Open…close…open…close…

"Tiger!" Dad was out of the bathroom. He didn't sound happy.

Without catching his dad's eye, the little guy scampered quickly to his seat and hopped up in it. Stinky started furiously reading her magazine. As usual, Tiger was on his own.

For a long moment Tiger just sat there looking down. He sensed a large shadow hovering over him.

"Doggone it," huffed the shadow. "Didn't I ask you to stay in your seat?"

Even while looking down, he could sense the other two families in the emergency room watching this showdown. They were probably thinking that the little pistol would finally get what he deserved. They didn't know they were the only thing saving him.

"Yes sir," came his squeaky reply. His voice never worked just right when he was in trouble. Tiger was scared but thought he would probably get by without a spanking. After all, this was a public place, and Dad didn't usually spank in public, not with others watching. And sometimes, if Tiger was especially lucky, Dad would forget all about the need for a spanking once they got home.

"Then why did you disobey and git outta your seat?" It seemed the shadow had a point.

"I dunno," said Tiger. It felt like a good idea at the time. In hindsight, he was starting to have second thoughts. "Sorry, Dad."

"Well, you've done earned yourself a time-out, young man."

And without another word, Tiger climbed out of his seat in the middle of the room, pulled a chair into the corner, and turned it facing the wall. He climbed into it and scooched back so his feet and cowboy boots were swinging freely. He was secretly relieved; it could have been a lot worse.

Then he heard a few soft words of pity from the others in the room, and it almost made him smile. "Aw…" whispered one of the moms. "He's sooo cute."

But cute wouldn't get him off time-out any faster, that much Tiger knew for sure. And so he simply stared at the wall and began serving his sentence. He was a repeat offender; he had been in for worse. He could do this time standing on his head.

In fact, he thought, *that's not such a bad idea. If I could just slide forward far enough, lean down, get my hands on the floor…*

— ⊷≒⊶ —

Across town a first-time offender wondered if he would make it through the night.

Charles Arnold had been fingerprinted and booked. They took his mug shots, one from the front and one from each side. The deputies took his cargo shorts, T-shirt, socks, and sneakers and replaced them with a bright orange jumpsuit and slippers. He felt like…well, he felt like a criminal. He supposed that was the whole point.

A deputy grabbed Charles's arm and yanked him down a tight and dingy hallway, ignoring the catcalls from the jail cells they passed. At the end of the hallway, the deputy opened the door of a large holding cell, shoved Charles inside, then backed away and swung the heavy door shut. It closed with a solid clang.

"Have fun, Professor," said the deputy as he disappeared back down the hallway.

Charles took a quick inventory of the rough-looking bunch. About a dozen men. Most of them younger than Charles. A handful of blacks, a handful of whites, a couple of Hispanics. Tattoos, dreadlocks, and scowls seemed to be in vogue. The cell was segregated, blacks on one side, whites on the other. The two Hispanics took up residence close to the whites.

The odor hit him first. And the thought that his own oily, slick sweat, brought about by the suffocating humidity of this place, now contributed to it. The cell reeked of unwashed and grungy men—the stench of defeat, frustration, and anger.

The inmates regarded the new fish with looks of disinterested disdain. Nobody spoke for a few moments as Charles shuffled to the African American side of the cell. It was moments like this that Charles wished he were a darker member of the darker nation. For these men, his light brown skin might trigger less than full-fledged membership among the brothers, making him an outcast on both sides of the cell.

"What you in for?" asked one of the brothers. He was a wiry young man, no more that eighteen or nineteen, Charles guessed, with a grotesque network of bulging veins and tattoos covering every inch of his exposed forearms.

"Cop killin'." Charles decided to make a good first impression.

"You bustin' me? You didn't pop no 5-0."

"Thought about it," responded Charles, taking a few steps toward the black side of the holding cell. He touched closed fists with one of the brothers. "So they Rodney Kinged me for resistin' arrest."

"Shut up, woman. Don't need no comics in here."

Woman?

The deep voice belonged to a huge brother in the back. He stood up slowly and walked toward Charles. Charles was six-one but gave up at least three inches and a hundred pounds to the guy. Even in a jumpsuit, the man looked buff. He had broad sloping shoulders, massive hands, and a huge forehead that hung like a cliff over his eyes. He sported a buzz cut and a scruffy mustache that merged into a close-cropped Fu Manchu. Despite the dimness of the cell, his gold tooth glistened when he spoke.

Charles didn't like the implications of the nickname. And nobody had to tell Charles that this man was the de facto leader of the holding tank. He stood just a few feet away, his hands clenching and unclenching.

"Now...whatcha in for...woman?"

Woman. Fear gripped the preacher's brain. He had never been in prison before, but he knew all the stories. *Woman.*

God help me, he prayed under his breath. Simple, quick, fervent.

"I told you, bro. Resistin' arrest and violatin' a noise ordinance." As the words came out, Charles was struck with how wimpy the charges sounded. "I'm a street preacher," he added, hoping this felon might at least have some respect for a man of the cloth.

Hoots and whistles came from the white boys in the cell, followed by some vulgar comments. They were clearly not impressed.

"Pop 'im, Buster," suggested one of the blacks. Charles was amazed at how quickly alliances shifted in this place. A few of the brothers stood up, and others started forming a circle for the outside ring of a fight. "Guard your grill, bro," someone suggested.

Charles had no intention of guarding his grill. The last thing he needed was a fight with the block of granite in front of him. What had he done to agitate this guy?

"Shut up," growled the man they had called Buster. He was talking to the other men in the cell but staring straight at Charles. There was instant silence. Buster moved a few steps closer, within striking distance. Charles tensed, ready to duck and dodge and weave, if necessary.

"If you a street preacher, why they callin' you professor?"

Good question, thought Charles. *Maybe this guy's smarter than I thought.*

"I teach constitutional law at Regent Law School," said Charles, putting on his best air of professorial authority, despite his nervousness. "I teach law students how to spot and exploit violations of constitutional rights. You know, like Johnnie Cochran."

The name of Cochran evoked the desired awe among some of the felons in the cell. But Buster just furrowed his huge brow, still looking skeptical.

"And I'm Judge Ito."

Charles fought back panic and rose to his full professorial stature. He calmly looked the big thug right in the eye, but stayed on the balls of his feet, ready to duck if necessary. At least this time the big gorilla had not called him a woman.

"The Fifth Amendment of the Constitution guarantees criminal defendants the right against unreasonable searches and self-incrimination. It applies to the states by virtue of the due process clause of the Fourteenth Amendment," Charles spit the words out rapidly, confidently, like a computer, all the while keeping a wary eye on his new nemesis. "Rights like Miranda warnings are actually the outgrowth of case law by the Supreme Court, in particular, the case of Miranda versus Arizona, decided by the Supreme Court in 1966, with the majority opinion written by one of my all time favorites, Justice William Brennan, may he rest in peace." Charles paused to catch a breath. He saw the confusion in Buster's eyes.

"You any good in court?" Buster asked, still clenching and unclenching his fists.

"Only the best teach. The others do what we train them to do."

"If you train the public defenders, I wouldn't be braggin'," said one of the longhaired white kids from the other side of the cell.

Buster shot the kid a glance, and Charles sensed a chance to reconfigure alliances. After all, this guy Buster *was* a fellow member of the darker nation.

"They're only as good as the cases they get," Charles said to the white kid.

Buster unclenched his fists. "The cops violated my rights."

"Word up," said one of the brothers standing in the outer circle. "Mine too."

Buster shot him a glance, and the man shot his palms up—*I'm backing off.*

"Look," lectured Charles, who now had the undivided attention of everyone, "I don't have time to litigate every constitutional violation that ever occurred. I'll bet 5-0 dissed half the brothers in this room." There were nods and murmurs of agreement. "But if you give me some time and space, I'll interview those of you who think you may have a constitutional claim. I can't promise anything, but if you've got a case, I'll help your public defender and maybe even handle a motion to suppress hearing."

Several heads nodded. Buster's was not yet among them.

"Let's start with you," suggested Charles.

Buster stuck out his jaw and then slowly nodded his head. "'At works for me." He glanced around the cell at the other men.

"Give the prof some room," Buster ordered, and the men who had been standing in a circle around Buster and Charles returned to their earlier spots. Charles and Buster then huddled in a corner of the cell while the others eavesdropped, pretending not to listen.

By the time he completed the interviews, Charles had determined that only one of the men in the cell had a case that deserved Charles's constitutional expertise. That man was Buster, who had, according to Charles, been the victim of a gross disregard of constitutional rights by the V-town po-lece.

Charles knew he would hate himself in the morning if he actually took a role in Buster's defense. He had participated in the defense of a few criminals during his six years as a law school professor, but they all had credible claims of innocence. The prospect of putting Buster back out on the street repulsed him. But not nearly as much as the thought of trying to survive the night without Buster as an ally. And Charles took comfort in the fact that there was actually little chance of springing Buster early.

Buster said he had been innocently cruising the main drag in V-town, the inmates' slang for Virginia Beach, alone in his Cadillac Escalade SUV with tinted windows. He drove a few laps around the block, then pulled over to the curb where a couple of young African American men joined him in the car. After another lap around the block, he dropped them off at the same place where he had picked them up.

For this innocuous conduct, the cops had pulled him over and begun their harassment. They accused Buster of selling drugs and ran the serial number on his vehicle. They ordered Buster out of the car and then claimed they had seen some small baggies with a white powder substance in plain sight sticking out from under the front seat.

Not true, said Buster. He assured Charles that the drugs were tucked safely away in the glove compartment and trunk. He was not a fool, Buster said, and he knew better than to leave the drugs in plain sight.

It was Buster's third offense, and he was looking at serious time under Virginia's "three strikes and you're out" sentencing guidelines. He had already spent three years of his life in jail on drug charges and was not looking forward to spending the next decade behind bars. "I'm a changed man," he told Charles. "I learned my lesson this time. You get me outta here, I'll make like Mother Teresa."

Charles listened intently to Buster's story, nodded his head a lot, and made guttural noises of sympathy as Buster shared his tale of woe. When Buster was finished, Charles wondered aloud whether the police could justify the stop in the first place.

"Sounds like racial profiling to me," Charles murmured. "How they gonna justify pulling you over in the first place if not for racial profiling? Truth is, they see a black man in a nice car, chummin' with a couple of black kids, and they automatically assume you're a drug dealer."

"But what about dem findin' da brick?" asked Buster.

"If they didn't have reasonable suspicion to stop you in the first place, then the crack becomes fruit of the poisonous tree, and the judge will throw out the charges. I'm not sayin' it'll happen; in fact, it's a long shot. But it's possible."

Buster smiled, and the gold tooth gleamed. "Fruit of the poisonous tree," he mumbled, nodding his head in approval. "I like dat. Fact, 'at's real good. Fruit of the poisonous tree."

After Charles had heard the less meritorious claims of the other inmates, he and Buster returned to the corner of the cell and quietly entered into a pact. Charles would represent Buster on the constitutionality of the stop, nothing more. Buster's public defender would handle the rest of the case. In return for the professor's help, Buster agreed to take care of Charles during the professor's brief stint behind bars. Sensing that Buster really wanted his help, Charles decided to push for one thing more.

"Think you could get a few of the brothers together for a Bible study on Saturday night?" whispered Charles. "I'll come lead it."

Buster furrowed his massive brow, and the eyes hardened.

"Think about it," whispered Charles quickly. He sensed that was the best he could do at the moment. "Might give us some extra time to talk about your case."

They sealed the deal with a soul handshake and announced to the other inmates that Buster had a new lawyer. You could hear some mumbled cursing as the others realized that the fix was in. But no one dared complain out loud.

That night Charles slept on one of the few mats in the holding cell. Just before he fell asleep, he cracked an eyelid and snuck one last glance at his protector. Buster sat nearby, eyes open, arms crossed, and a scowl on his gnarly face—just daring anybody to bother the well-earned sleep of his prized new constitutional lawyer.

CHAPTER 7

They had not heard anything for almost two hours, and it worried Thomas. He was tired of the sterile ICU waiting room, the yellow plastic furniture, and the two-month-old magazines. He had seen at least two other families come and go since midnight, yet here he sat, knowing nothing and fearing the worst.

The operation had started at 11:00 but had not gone well. Dr. Armistead came by at 12:30, very businesslike, to inform them that the appendix had been removed but that Joshua was not yet out of the woods. He referred to multiple system failures or something like that. Thomas had not been allowed to see Josh. Armistead mentioned consulting with some kind of liver or kidney specialists. How those organs got involved, Thomas did not know. But it didn't sound good.

Was God punishing him for taking Josh to the hospital? Had Thomas failed in his ultimate test of faith? If Josh didn't pull through, would there be anyone to blame except a father who abandoned his deeply held beliefs when the pressure was on? How could God honor such flimsy faith?

For the last hour Thomas had been beating himself up as he wrestled with these questions in prayer. He still had no answers and no sense of assurance that Josh would be okay. More than anything else, he just wanted to be with Josh and resented the doctors for keeping him away from his own son.

At least Tiger had finally run out of gas. He was sound asleep on the couch, mouth wide open and clinging to his blankie. Stinky had curled up on Thomas's lap and also slept soundly. She was getting heavier by the minute, but Thomas was not about to put her down. He found security in the warmth of her touch.

Theresa was not sleeping. She was up and down, roaming the hallways and pacing the waiting room. She would alternate between unjustified optimism and unwarranted pessimism. Right now, she was just sitting and staring. It had been at least five minutes since she had speculated about why they had not heard anything for so long. It had been fifteen minutes since she had stopped an ICU nurse in the hallway, pressing for information that was not forthcoming.

What else could they do but wait?

Though Thomas and Theresa had been glancing at the doorway for most of the night, Armistead somehow entered unnoticed. When Thomas caught Armistead in his peripheral vision, the doctor was already standing a few steps inside the room, in his white lab coat, looking grim. Thomas knew. Even before Armistead spoke, Thomas knew.

Theresa jumped out of her seat, moving toward the doctor.

"How's he doing?" she asked.

Thomas tensed but did not move. He didn't want to shake Stinky from his lap.

"It's not good," said Armistead evenly, professionally. "We did everything we could, but he didn't make it, he just—"

"No!" screamed Theresa. *"No! Not my Joshie…"* She collapsed on the floor, head in her hands, her words drowned out by her own sobs.

Thomas stood and placed Stinky softly in the chair. Stinky woke, looked confused, and blinked the sleep out of her eyes. "What's the matter?" she asked.

"It'll be okay," Thomas mumbled as he tried to absorb the unthinkable. A numbness washed over him. He sat down on the floor next to Theresa and wrapped his arms around her. She buried her head on his shoulder.

Tiger, who had been startled awake by his mother's scream, rubbed his eyes and hopped down from the couch. He walked quickly toward his mom and dad and shot a mean glance at Dr. Armistead. He took his special blankie, his comforter, and spread it across his mom's shoulders. Then he reached out and hugged his mommy's neck. Thomas embraced them both in a three-person hug. In a flash, Stinky joined them and made it four.

"Is Joshie okay?" Stinky whispered into her daddy's ear.

Thomas couldn't find the words or the heart to tell her.

CHAPTER 8

State law required that he report suspected child abuse. He had no choice in the matter. And so, after working a double shift, Sean Armistead reached for his cell phone while driving home, called directory assistance, and got the number for the Virginia Beach Department of Child Protective Services. He stayed on the line as the directory-assistance computer dialed the number.

It did not surprise him to hear the answering machine kick in. He did not really expect anyone to be at the office at 7:00 a.m. on a Saturday morning. He left a message, then speed-dialed another number. He counted three rings before it was answered.

"Hello," said a gruff female voice at the other end. The voice belonged to Deputy Commonwealth's Attorney Rebecca Crawford.

"I thought you'd be at the office by now. You're slipping."

"Sean?"

"Your friendly neighborhood doc with your weekend wake-up call."

"Fat chance. I've already finished my workout. It's almost lunchtime for me, Doc."

"You've got to get a life."

"I've got one—remember? I put the guys behind bars that you stitch up and throw back out on the streets."

As he listened to her on the phone, she crystallized in his mind. Thirty-eight and fighting the years with every ounce of her strength. Short, blonde hair with a layered cut, the roots beginning to turn brown. Tanned skin abused by too many long summers in the beach sun. The first signs of wrinkles had been ironed out with a facelift at age thirty-five. She had never admitted it to Sean, but he had his sources. She was not a natural athlete but worked hard to whip her body into shape, with fairly impressive results. She was only five-five, with big bones and a slow metabolism. She had to stay disciplined to keep off the weight.

Her face would be described by most as handsome but not stunning.

The angles a little too sharp, the eyes a little too narrow, the cheeks a little too hollow. Regardless, it worked for him. She always applied her makeup with precision, hiding every flaw and accentuating the positives. And her mouth was truly beautiful—full lips, always covered with dark lipstick, and straight white teeth. You found yourself staring at her mouth when she talked, the way you did with Julia Roberts. Armistead had been mesmerized by her mouth on more than one occasion, a trait he was sure he shared with many jurors.

"So what's up? You don't call at seven in the morning to chat."

Armistead smiled to himself. All business. He loved it.

"I think I've got an interesting case for you. High stakes. Big publicity. Sympathetic victim."

"I'm listening."

"A two-year-old child died last night in the emergency room because his parents refused to get medical help for a ruptured appendix for three days. We did everything we could to bring him around, but it was too late. Plus, though I can't prove it yet, I think the parents might have abused this child and their other two kids as well—a five-year-old boy and a seven-year-old girl."

Armistead paused, allowing the magnitude of his favor to kick in. "I thought you might be interested," he said.

"Interested," replied Rebecca. "You could say I'm *interested.*" She sounded energized. "Meet me at the office in an hour. I'll need an affidavit."

"I'll be there," he promised.

There was silence for a brief moment. "What's the kid's name?" Rebecca asked.

"Joshua Hammond."

"What did he look like?"

This strange question caught Armistead a little off-guard. Honestly, he couldn't much remember. "Typical two-year-old. Blond hair, I think, pudgy… Why is that important?"

"It's not, really. I just like to put a face with my files. On a murder case, I usually tape a picture of the victim to the inside cover of my trial notebook. Helps me remember what the case is about."

This side of Rebecca surprised him. It also shamed him a little. He couldn't remember what this kid's face looked like if his own life depended on it. The thought that a ruthless prosecutor had more compassion than he did was disturbing.

"Maybe you should tape your own picture there," Armistead suggested. "This case is about getting *you* a promotion."

She huffed. "You're such a jerk sometimes."

That's better. *That's* the Rebecca he knew. Combative, biting...irresistible. "I'll make it up to you later," he promised.

⊷ ≖♦≖ ⊶

Rebecca took a quick shower and threw on a pair of tight-fitting jeans and a loose-fitting tank top. Birkenstocks with no socks. She applied liberal amounts of blush, eye shadow, lipstick, and mascara in near record time. She layered on the deodorant and perfume. She was on her way in thirty minutes.

She formulated a strategy during the twenty-minute drive from her condo. She would talk to Child Protective Services on Monday. She could have a grand jury indictment by Tuesday. She would have an arrest warrant issued for the parents on Tuesday evening and request an arraignment and bond hearing for Wednesday morning. She would charge them with criminally negligent homicide, requesting a huge bond. She would seek a foster home for the children while the parents were behind bars. Even if the parents made bond, she would ask that it be conditioned on foster care for the kids pending trial on the theory that the best interest of the children required caregivers who would seek appropriate medical help.

She would pull the kids into her office and get some powerful videotaped statements before shipping them off to the foster home. She had cut her teeth on domestic-violence cases. She knew how to work the kids.

She would alert the media and promise exclusive interviews. And she would handle everything herself.

She thought about Sean's comment, and the anger seeped in. This case wasn't about her. Like every other case, it was about justice. She would be the voice for an innocent two-year-old kid who never had a chance. He died because of uncaring parents, just as surely as if they had slit his tiny throat themselves. Sure, they would come to court and cry about how much they loved their baby. But Joshua was dead. And no amount of crying could change that. Rebecca believed he would never rest in peace until those responsible had been brought to justice.

If doing her job on this case resulted in a promotion, so be it. It was about time Virginia Beach had someone heading up the commonwealth's attorney's office who cared about the victims. Career politicians had been running the place long enough.

She had labored for twelve long years in this depressing office. She had patiently waited the last five for Commonwealth's Attorney Harlan Fowler to retire or get a judicial appointment. It was not going to happen. She had to take matters into her own hands now.

She was planning a run against her boss in November. She would make an announcement two months from now—in August. Sean had nearly perfect timing. She could indict the parents, demonize them in the press, and not have to worry about a trial until after the election.

Finally, the break she needed. The one she deserved.

She glanced at the clock and pulled into a 7-Eleven. She had a few extra minutes and was in the mood to celebrate. She grabbed some coffee with two creams and a glazed donut. She turned up her nose as she walked past the yogurt.

⋯ ⋲✦⋺ ⋯

They hauled Charles Arnold before the magistrate on Saturday morning. He was still sporting his orange jumpsuit. The commonwealth's attorney never attended bond hearings on a misdemeanor. The arresting officers represented the interests of the state.

"Case number 04-3417," announced the clerk. "Commonwealth versus Charles Arnold."

Charles stepped up to the magistrate's bench. Officer Thrasher, the beefy cop with the pockmarked face, stood to his left. The deputies who had escorted the prisoners from the holding cell stood casually behind him. Everyone in the courtroom looked bored.

"You are charged with violating a noise ordinance and resisting arrest," said the magistrate without looking up. "You're entitled to a lawyer on the resisting-arrest charge. Can you afford your own lawyer, or do you want to see if you can qualify for the public defender?"

"Excuse me, Your Honor," interrupted Thrasher. "We're dropping the resisting-arrest charge and have no objection to a PR bond."

Charles expected as much. They had no basis for resisting arrest. They just wanted him locked up for the night. Teach him a lesson. Respect the boys in blue.

"I'm assuming the defendant has no objection?" The magistrate glanced up at Charles.

"I suppose not," said Charles. "But Judge, they kept me locked up all night on a baseless charge, they processed me like a felon, and now they just waltz into court—"

The magistrate held up his palm, and Charles stopped midsentence. "Look, buddy, even if all that were true, there's nothing I can do about it. I'm here to set bond, and the captain has generously offered you a personal recognizance bond. You get to go free as long as you sign a statement promising to appear on the trial date. It doesn't get any better than that, pal, and I've got a lot of other folks to process."

"Okay," said Charles reluctantly. "But when is my trial date?"

"I set it for the first Tuesday of next month," said Thrasher. "I'll be in court that day on a number of other matters anyway."

"That's a month away," complained Charles. A month of ribbing from his summer-school students. A month of explaining his innocence to everyone he knew.

And what if his ex-wife found out? He could hear her *tsk, tsk, tsk*ing him now. She'd find a way to blame it on him and the cops at the same time. She'd tell him to call the NAACP, countersue for a civil rights violation, show a little spine. No, he didn't need this charge hanging over his head for a month. The sooner he could get it behind him, the better.

"I want the first available trial date."

The magistrate grunted. It had probably been awhile since a defendant asked for an early trial date. "You got anything sooner?" he asked Thrasher.

The officer checked his black book. "Well, actually, Judge, I'm in court this Wednesday morning. I'm just not used to defendants who are released on a PR bond being so anxious to get back to court."

The magistrate chuckled. "Me either." Then to Charles. "Does Wednesday at 9:00 a.m. work for you, Mr. Arnold?"

"Yes sir."

"Very well, then, gentlemen, this case will be heard Wednesday morning. And, Mr. Arnold, if for any reason you don't appear, I'll have a warrant issued for your arrest. Is that clear?"

"Crystal clear, Your Honor."

"Call the next case," ordered the magistrate.

On the way past the holding cell, Charles noticed Buster standing against the front of the cell, holding the bars in each hand, pressing his face against the steel. Charles stopped and moved closer.

"You bustin' out?" asked Buster.

"I'm ghost," said Charles. "Already got the resisting-arrest charge dropped."

"I told you he was good," Buster said over his shoulder to the other inmates. "Cash money." He turned again to Charles, lowering his voice. "Don't forget about me, man."

"I won't," said Charles. "I couldn't if I tried."

They grabbed hands through the bars, another soul handshake. Charles sensed the man's guarded desperation and decided to take another run at the Bible study.

"See you next Saturday night?" asked Charles.

Buster hesitated for just a moment. "Might as well," he mumbled. "I ain't goin' nowhere."

"Seven o'clock," said Charles. He turned quickly to leave before Buster could change his mind.

CHAPTER 9

What are we going to do with all this food?" asked Theresa Hammond as she busied herself in the kitchen. "Everyone at church has just been incredible."

Thomas sat in his favorite recliner in the living room. The kids were in bed. It was Tuesday night, the night after Joshie's funeral. And it was like they had entered into an unspoken pact not to talk about Joshie's death. Every time Thomas tried to bring it up, Theresa would cry. And so he learned. The emotions were still too raw. Pretend it hadn't happened. Shelter yourself in the shock of it all. Deal with it later.

"Beats me," said the big man, staring at the spot on the floor where he would wrestle with Tiger and wait for Joshie to pile on.

"You think the kids will make it through the night?" Theresa asked between the clinking of dishes.

"Prob'ly not. Stinky'll come climbin' into our bed about midnight, then Tiger'll holler 'bout nightmares a few hours later."

"You hungry?" She seemed desperate to talk about something—anything but Joshie.

"'Course not. Been doin' nothin' but eatin' and talkin' to visitors all day. Why does everybody in church think they've gotta bring food over, like we can't cook our own meals anymore?"

"I guess they just don't know what else to do." As she talked her voice quivered. Thomas could tell she was on the verge of tears again. He got up out of his seat and stepped into the kitchen. He leaned against the doorway and watched her for a moment. He saw the vacant stare in her puffy eyes and shared her bone-deep grief. Though she had never said as much, he sensed that Theresa blamed him. And why not? His lack of faith had surely caused this. It would be a burden that would haunt him the rest of his life.

Maybe he should walk over and rub her shoulders. Maybe he should just hold her and lie to her—tell her it would be all right. Truth was, he didn't really know what to do. Emotions were not his thing.

"You all right?"

"Yeah."

He nodded, then turned around to walk down the narrow hallway toward the bedroom. A firm but polite knock on the front door stopped him.

"Can you get that?" called Theresa from the kitchen.

"I reckon," he murmured to himself. "It's prob'ly another casserole."

When Thomas opened the door, the two men standing on the small wooden porch of the trailer were not smiling. They were dressed in the brown garb of the Virginia Beach Sheriff's Department. Their badges glistened in the light from the one bulb that had not yet burned out.

"Can I help you?" asked Thomas, standing in the doorway.

"Are you Mr. Hammond?"

He hesitated. "That's me."

"Well, Mr. Hammond, we don't enjoy doing this under any circumstances—but we've got a job to do and hope you'll understand." The officer thrust some official looking papers at Thomas.

"What in Sam Hill?"

"We're serving you with a summons for your arrest on charges of involuntary manslaughter and criminally negligent homicide," said the officer. "You are to appear tomorrow morning at 9:00 a.m. in Virginia Beach General District Court for your arraignment and bond hearing."

"Thomas...who is it?" Theresa called from the kitchen.

"Nobody you know, Theresa," Thomas replied. He stepped outside and closed the door behind him.

"Was that Mrs. Hammond?" asked the officer politely.

Thomas scowled. "Yes."

"We have a summons for her as well. Same charges. You can deliver it to her yourself if you want to."

Thomas reached out and took the papers without saying a word. The men did not leave.

"Is that it?" growled Thomas. They might just be doing their job, but he didn't have to make it easy. "Are you fixin' to take me to jail?"

"Not tonight," replied the officer evenly. "The commonwealth's attorney could have requested a warrant for your arrest tonight. Instead, this summons is basically saying that you're being trusted to show up on your own."

"Will I go to jail tomorrow?" Thomas pressed them. "Will I lose the kids?"

"You might go to jail. Depends on what the judge says about bond. As for the kids, well…the commonwealth is basically claiming that child neglect caused the death of your son. If you have other kids, there's a chance you could lose custody of them pending trial." As the officer spoke, he shuffled slowly back to the edge of the porch. Both officers eyed Thomas warily.

Thomas felt the warmth rise in his neck. His head started spinning and burning with anger. Who did these guys think they were? They come to his house the night after he buries his own son, they matter-of-factly accuse him of murder, and then they just stand there and calmly say they might take his other children from him as well. He looked down at his clenched fists and thought about how good it would feel to pop these guys.

"Leave," he sneered.

"Mr. Hammond, I know this is incredibly tough, but don't do anything drastic. Get yourself an attorney—"

"Leave," he said louder. *"Now!"*

"We're just doing our job, sir."

"Nobody takes my kids from me."

"What do you mean by that?" asked the officer who had not yet said a word, still hovering near the edge of the porch.

"You know exactly what I mean," replied Thomas, taking a step toward him. "Now, if you've finished your job, get out of here."

Both men backed down the steps without taking their eyes off Thomas. He stood on the small porch, arms folded across his chest, until the unmarked brown sedan backed out of the parking space next to his trailer and headed out of the trailer park.

Only then did he begin to read the official-looking papers that he held in his trembling hand. When he had finished, he punched the side of the trailer, and heard the pop of the siding as it yielded to the force of his blow.

"Over my dead body," he said. Then he braced himself to tell Theresa.

CHAPTER 10

Wednesday morning dawned hot and muggy. Virginia Beach in the early summer, the kind of weather that Nikki Moreno lived for. The tanning index registered a nine. Later she would catch some rays and work on her tan line. She would endure the late afternoon sun and the sand. It was tough work, but perfection had its price.

But first, unfortunately, there were matters of lesser importance requiring her attention. She would have to put in a few hours at her day job as a paralegal for Carson & Associates, a personal-injury firm that recently gained national attention on a high-profile civil rights case against the nation of Saudi Arabia. Nikki played a crucial role in that case, and for a few fleeting moments she had basked in the spotlight from the national media. She tried angling for an acting career, but the offers never came.

What did come was a whole boatload of new clients. Now Carson & Associates was busier than ever, incredibly short-handed, and stretched to the breaking point.

A second matter required Nikki's attention this morning as well. The courts called it their CASA program—Court Appointed Special Advocates. The program allowed nonattorneys like Nikki to serve the court system on a volunteer basis by looking out for the legal interests of innocent children caught up in custody disputes. Nikki would typically spend time reviewing reports from the Child Protective Services caseworkers and then recommend to the judge whether a child should receive foster care or not.

Nikki did not consider herself a do-gooder, the furthest thing from it really, and she had no desire to run around the courts protecting the best interests of children. But she had been required to serve one hundred hours of community service through CASA as part of a plea bargain she had entered into following the Saudi Arabia case. She considered herself a hero and believed her actions at the end of the case had been required by the circumstances. But the commonwealth's attorney had seen it differently. No matter. She would do it the same way again. And in a few more weeks, she would be done with this stupid program and the charges against her would be dropped.

After more than six months working the court system, Nikki was getting comfortable with the drill. Virginia Beach General District Court on Wednesday mornings. Review a few reports. Talk to a few kids. Interview some prospective foster parents. Then recommend to Judge Silverman whether the kids should be placed in a foster home. She was good at it, and though she had started off a little shaky with the judge, he now seemed to like her. She was one of the few special advocates who could maintain a sense of objectivity and remain detached from the kids. It made her judgment all the more valuable.

It was not exactly rocket science. But it was an extra obligation that she didn't need at the busiest time in her firm's history. And it kept her, one of the hottest single female professionals on the beach scene, from getting as much time in the sun as her dark tan required. But still, she wouldn't complain too much. It was better than picking up trash along the roadways with the guys in the orange jumpsuits.

With any luck she would be out of court this morning in forty-five minutes and at Carson & Associates by ten.

⋅—⋅≡◆≡—⋅⋅

Charles Arnold arrived early at the sprawling municipal complex in an area of Virginia Beach that was farmland a few decades ago. The courthouse building was a large four-story monolith that would have taken up an entire city block if it had been situated downtown. In its present location, it had replaced a good half-acre of cornfields.

Charles survived the madness of the parking lot derby, the metal detector lines, and the escalators that did not work. He eventually made his way to General District Courtroom No. 6, on the second floor, the Honorable Franklin Silverman Jr. presiding.

At 8:50 a.m., ten minutes before court, Charles Arnold sauntered down the middle aisle of the already packed courtroom, his confident glide and "don't mess with me" style masking the butterflies in his stomach. His charmed legal career had never landed him anywhere near General District Court, where traffic cases were heard, small-time criminals were prosecuted, small claims were resolved, and unimportant hearings on felony cases were conducted. General District Court was the Kmart of the legal world, rough-and-cheap justice for the masses, complete with blue-light specials when a liberal judge in a good mood on the right day might dismiss half the traffic tickets before him.

Charles had spent his career in loftier settings. High grades at Virginia Law School had earned him a coveted two-year clerkship at the Fourth Circuit Court of Appeals in Richmond, a federal appellate court just one step below the Supremes. Before heading to Richmond for this clerkship, he had married a fellow radical from his graduating class named Denita.

After his clerkship, he joined one of Richmond's largest and finest law firms, a four-hundred-lawyer sweatshop where billable hours were the currency of success. Denita had started working at a similar sweatshop across town while Charles clerked, and by the time he started as a private lawyer, she had made a name for herself defending corporate America against charges of sexual harassment. Meanwhile, Charles put in three long years as a litigation associate, pushing tons of paper, taking hours of depositions, and seldom seeing the inside of a courtroom. They were both too busy building careers to think about how thoroughly they had sold out—African American revolutionaries tamed by the white man's legal system.

And then, just four short years ago, Charles's radical conversion to Christianity changed everything. Charles came kicking and screaming to Christ, but when he came, he did so with every fiber of his being. He began preaching on the streets almost immediately. He pushed the gospel with equal fervor on his coworkers and his wife. He reminded Denita often that *his* faith was the faith embraced by Martin Luther King Jr. And he drove her further away.

She filed for divorce not long afterward. Charles needed to get out of town.

His chance came when Regent Law School, in an effort to further diversify its faculty, promised Charles a fresh start in Virginia Beach and the chance to become one of the youngest constitutional law professors in the country. He took a huge cut in pay to make it happen. But he still regarded it as one of the smartest moves he ever made. He loved the students, the academic challenge, and the fact that he had never even seen a time sheet, much less filled one out, since the day he left his firm.

But he still thought about Denita almost every day. And she would die if she knew her ex-husband, the African American legal scholar, the man who had clerked for the vaunted Fourth Circuit Court of Appeals, was now slumming in Virginia Beach General District Court, preparing to argue his own case for violation of a noise ordinance.

Oh, how the mighty have fallen.

He had dressed the part of a big-time lawyer and turned heads as he walked to the front of the courtroom. Buster would have been proud—Johnnie Cochran had nothing on Charles today. The man who taught law in jeans and a T-shirt was now sporting a dark gray custom suit with a suit coat that hung long on his body like a gunslinger's, a monogrammed shirt, and Gucci loafers that practically glowed.

He had a soft leather Tumi briefcase stuffed full of potential cases on the constitutionality of noise ordinances and the procedural rules for General District Court. He was ready for just about anything.

He strode confidently past the wooden railing that separated the lawyers and police officers from the litigants. There was a lot of chattering and bantering going on among the fraternity of regular General District Court lawyers, mostly older men with sport coats and cloth ties or younger women in pantsuits. There was not another African American lawyer among them. And they all ignored Charles.

"What's the drill here?" Charles asked a couple of seasoned-looking lawyers who were each holding dozens of manila folders.

"You a lawyer?" asked one, eying Charles suspiciously.

The man was round and had a meaty face. His white shirt didn't quite button at the neck, and his sport coat seemed two sizes too short in the sleeves. Then there was the guy's hair! Why couldn't these white guys just admit when they were going bald? He parted his hair just above the left ear, and with a liberal application of gel managed to paste a few long strands up over the top. He had plenty of hair on the nape of his neck and the inside of his ears, more fertile ground apparently, but to call the stuff on top "thin" would be stretching it.

"Yeah," Charles responded, "but this is my first time in General District Court."

"Sure," said the man, sounding disinterested. "Well, find out what line number your case is on"—he motioned to several pages of docket sheets sitting on the counsel table—"then wait for your case to be called."

"Hope you brought something to read," said another veteran.

"Plenty," said Charles. "What're the cameras here for?"

"Not sure," said the greasy-haired lawyer, as if television cameras and news reporters showed up in General District Court every day. "Must be an arraignment or bond hearing on some criminal case that will eventually be transferred to circuit court."

"Mind if I sit down?" asked Charles. He pointed to an empty seat next to the guy, the only empty seat in front of the bar on the lawyer's side of the courtroom.

"Actually, I was saving that for someone." The greasy-haired dude put a pained expression on his face. "She's a special advocate for the kids in one of my cases, and I've really got to talk to her before court starts."

"No problem," Charles responded. He made a mental note to keep an eye on the seat. Prejudice wore many faces.

He turned and walked to the other side of the courtroom where the police officers were sitting and chatting. He sat in one of the empty chairs without asking and pretended not to notice the stares. He began reading some cases that he had stuffed in his briefcase.

He had the look of bravado, but he felt very much alone.

—◦— ⹝◆⹝ —◦—

Twenty minutes later the judge was still nowhere to be found, and Charles had given up pretending to read. He started watching people and had the good fortune to be glancing at the back door when she burst through.

It was clear she had been running, but she broke stride and changed to a strut when she saw the judge was not yet on the bench. She carried a stack of files but didn't look much like a lawyer. She was all legs and accentuated them with three-inch platform heels and a short black miniskirt. She wore a sleeveless white blouse and rounded out her immodest outfit with large gold jewelry dangling from her neck and both wrists. If she had been a student and dressed that way for moot court, Charles would have flunked her.

She had a dangerous allure—the exotic looks of a Latin American woman, complete with tanned olive skin, long jet-black hair, and haunting brown eyes. She wore too much makeup for Charles's taste, and he immediately began disliking her, put off more by her arrogance than anything else.

He watched as the young woman became the center of gravity in the courtroom and greeted both police officers and lawyers with mutual warmth and a dazzling smile.

"Hey, Nikki, when are you gonna dump that bum Carson and come work for a real lawyer?" An older man flung the comment across the courtroom as Nikki talked to one of the cops.

"You couldn't handle me, Jack," she shot back over her shoulder.

The other lawyers moaned and guffawed.

Nikki finished her chat with the police officer and walked over to entertain the lawyers. The boys gathered around and yukked it up with Nikki, though the few female lawyers seemed unimpressed.

"All rise," announced the court clerk, who did not bother to rise herself. "General District Court for the City of Virginia Beach is now in session, the Honorable Franklin Silverman Jr. presiding."

Judge Silverman walked briskly to his spot on the bench and peered out through thick glasses. He looked older than Charles expected, a short and spindly man with a gaunt face. He had white hair, but bushy black eyebrows stuck out from his forehead and overhung his eyes. He placed both palms down on the bench in front of him and forced a thin smile.

"Be seated," he said softly.

Charles noticed that Nikki sat down in the reserved seat next to the lawyer with the bad hair. She crossed her legs, slouched in the chair, and immediately began whispering to the lawyers on each side of her. She ignored Judge Silverman as he called the court to order, and she also ignored the bailiff who stared at her with a stern look, apparently trying to get her attention so he could tell her to quiet down.

Charles found himself staring across the courtroom at the tattoo partially visible on Nikki's shoulder, and he was embarrassed when she noticed his gaze, looked straight at him, and flashed a brilliant white smile. He refocused his attention on Judge Silverman, who was preparing to hear the dozens of procrastinators who had just jumped in line to request a continuance.

He pretended that he had not noticed when Nikki winked.

CHAPTER 11

Ninety minutes later Nikki Moreno was still trying to catch his eye. *I've got to get a name and phone number.*

"Call the next case, please." Silverman had already been at it for an hour and a half, and the courtroom was thinning out. He had granted dozens of continuances and rejected dozens more. He had made sure that all indigent defendants filled out the proper forms to determine whether they qualified for court-appointed lawyers. And he had burned through more than fifteen traffic cases and three custody matters. Nikki's services as a special advocate had already been called on twice.

"Commonwealth versus Thomas and Theresa Hammond," said the clerk. "Case number 04-1489."

The sleepy courtroom came to life. Cameras started rolling. Nikki's head jerked up, and she nudged the grizzled old defense lawyer sitting next to her.

"This is your fifteen minutes of fame, Harry," she whispered to the lawyer with the stringy hair. "Don't screw it up."

"Watch and learn," Harry mumbled as he took his place at the defense table, joining Thomas and Theresa Hammond. Nikki would watch all right, with the same kind of morbid curiosity that compels you to watch *Fear Factor.* It would not be pretty.

Deputy Commonwealth's Attorney Rebecca Crawford took her place at the counsel table in front of the police officers and arranged her file. She had a no-nonsense look on her face, pretending not to notice the television cameras. But Nikki's critical eye saw Crawford sneak a quick glance at the camera and then adjust her chair just right, so the camera angle would be straight on as opposed to a profile.

I guess she thinks that helps, mused Nikki, not convinced that any angle could do the trick for Crawford.

"Mr. and Mrs. Hammond, you are charged with involuntary manslaughter and criminally negligent homicide in the death of Joshua Caleb Hammond. How plead you?"

Harry Pursifull rose to his feet and majestically buttoned his suit coat. The button strained but held.

"The defendants plead not guilty, Your Honor," he announced.

Crawford quickly rose to her feet. "The commonwealth requests bail in the amount of two hundred thousand for Mr. Hammond and fifty thousand for Mrs. Hammond," she said sternly, staring at the defendants. "This is the tragic death of a very young child who could have been saved if defendants had simply sought appropriate medical care—"

"Spare me your speeches," said the judge. "We'll try the case later. Are defendants a flight risk?"

"No, Your Honor," responded Harry. "On the contrary, they have lived in the community their whole lives. Mr. Hammond runs a lawncare business—"

"Whether he mows lawns or not is immaterial," snapped Crawford. "What is material is the fact that last night Mr. Hammond threatened the deputies who served him with the arrest warrant and told those same deputies that nobody was going to take his kids away. The commonwealth believes he is a substantial flight risk, Your Honor."

"What about Mrs. Hammond?" asked the judge, his hands tented in front of him as he eyed the defendants. "Does the commonwealth believe she poses a flight risk?"

"Not necessarily, Judge. That's why we've requested a lower bond for her. But we strongly urge that it be conditioned on foster care for the children pending trial. We can't run the risk that she'll neglect another child with similar consequences."

Nikki watched the Hammond woman tug on the suit coat of Harry and whisper in his ear. Nikki could see the urgency on her face but couldn't make out what she said.

"For these defendants," said Harry, "fifty thousand bucks is like a million. This case calls for a PR bond, Judge. And Mrs. Hammond is not willing to give up the children under any circumstances."

Crawford started to respond—she was always ready to respond—but Judge Silverman held up his hand and silenced both lawyers. He thought in silence, staring at the back wall for an interminable length of time, and then finally looked down at the deputy commonwealth's attorney.

"Is there any evidence of child abuse?" he asked.

"You mean besides the child neglect that caused the death of Joshua?" Crawford asked snidely.

"Alleged death," shot back Harry from the defense table.

"No, Harry, the death is not alleged, it's very real." Crawford turned on him. "If you want, we can go to the cemetery and I'll show you the body."

"*Counsel!*" Silverman barked, his frustration showing. "Address your comments to the court." He paused, changing his tone. "Is there any evidence of child abuse?"

"The commonwealth has a reasonable suspicion that such abuse has occurred. That's why we subpoenaed the other children to court today to testify. We would request leave of court to interview those children in the presence of a court reporter, defense counsel, and a court appointed special advocate, to determine if such abuse has in fact occurred."

"Are the children here?" The judge directed his comments toward Theresa Hammond. The woman's eyes went wide, and Nikki immediately felt sorry for her.

Theresa stood slowly and nervously. "Yes, Your Honor," she said, motioning to the back of the courtroom. "Right back there."

As she pointed at the kids, all eyes turned to stare at them. The girl raised her hand in a timid little wave and smiled nervously. Her little brother slid down in his seat and stared at the floor.

"Very well, then," said Silverman. "This case will be adjourned for half an hour while the children are interviewed. I will take the amount of bond under advisement pending the results of that interview... Ms. Moreno?"

Nikki rose to her full height and stared directly into the camera. *Crawford should be taking notes,* she thought.

"Yes, Your Honor."

"You will serve as the court's special advocate for the children during this process."

"Yes, Your Honor." She sucked in her slender stomach and squared her shoulders. She would have to make it home tonight in time to watch the eleven o'clock news on the NBC affiliate. If they were smart and cared about ratings, they would use the video of her as their B roll.

She looked again at the two kids sitting all by themselves in the spectator section. The little girl was cute and prissy. She had bright eyes and curly blonde hair. She wore a tattered light blue dress and scuffed-up black dress shoes.

Her brother looked scared or ornery, Nikki could not tell. His blue pants were so short that they hiked halfway up his cowboy boots. He wore a stained white shirt and a clip-on tie. He had the biggest blue eyes Nikki had ever seen. And she thought she could detect a glint of moisture as he blinked hard to hold the tears at bay.

Those poor kids, thought Nikki. They looked so innocent and naive. And they had no clue that they were about to be manipulated by the masterful cross-examination of a lady that defense lawyers called "the Barracuda."

Tiger felt small in the gigantic conference room with no windows and the stern looking adults. He climbed bravely into the high-backed leather chair where he had been told to sit. His feet dangled over the front edge, not touching the floor. He tucked his hands under his legs and stared down.

He determined not to look across the table at the woman who reminded him of a mean Sunday-school teacher he once had. He did sneak a glance at the pretty lady named Miss Nikki who was sitting next to him. His mommy told him that Miss Nikki was there to help him answer a few questions.

Miss Nikki shot him a quick smile, then reached over and rubbed his head. He hated it when people rubbed his head.

"What's your name, young man?" asked the lady sitting across the table.

I thought she already knew.

"John Paul," he said softly, with a slight hint of an attitude, still staring down. "My friends and family call me Tiger."

"Can I call you Tiger?" asked the Mean Lady sweetly.

Who does she think she is?

Without looking up, he shook his head no.

"Well then, John Paul, we will need to get some ground rules straight. Do you see that lady typing over there?" The Mean Lady pointed to a lady typing on a tiny little machine. Tiger snuck a quick glance. "She is writing down on paper everything you say. And it's very important that you tell us the truth. It will be very important for me. And it will be very important for your mommy and daddy."

The Mean Lady paused to let the weight of the responsibility settle in on him. She did not have to tell Tiger this was important; he could sense it. He was determined to pass this test, to get all the answers right. He knew that somehow his folks were depending on it.

"Now, do you know what it means to tell the truth?"

That's an easy one.

"Yep," Tiger said, pleased he was off to a good start.

"Do you know what happens if you don't tell the truth?"

"Yep," he nodded again, clearly on a roll. "I get a spanking."

"Who gives you a spanking, Tiger?"

The little guy was so focused on the questions that he didn't even notice she had used his nickname. These questions were easy, and he was anxious to answer.

"My daddy."

"Does your mommy give you spankings sometimes too?" asked the lady.

"Yes ma'am," said Tiger. "If I'm bad."

"And does your mommy hit you with her hand, or does she use a stick like some other mommies do?"

Tiger scrunched his face. *This is tricky.*

"Nope," he said.

"No, she doesn't use her hand? Or no, she doesn't use a stick?"

He was stumped again. This time he shrugged.

"Let's do it this way," said the sweet voice of the Mean Lady. "What does your mommy use to spank you with?"

"A wooden spoon," said Tiger.

"I see," said the lady, as she made some notes on her legal pad. "And how many times does she hit you with a spoon when she spanks you?"

These questions were getting harder. Tiger didn't know he was supposed to count.

"'Bout four or maybe six," he said, just to be safe.

"And your dad, what does he use to spank you?"

Should I tell her about the belt? Or will I somehow get my dad in trouble? He looked at Miss Nikki, who smiled without opening her mouth. No help there. He looked at the fat little man in the room, the guy they called "Harry." He had his head tilted sideways like he might be feeling sorry for Tiger. No help there either.

"Sometimes his hand," said the clever little guy.

"And other times?"

Tiger's eyes darted around the room from adult to adult, searching for allies. Finding none, he stared back at the floor.

"And other times?" repeated the Mean Lady, this time without sugar in her voice.

How does she know about the belt?

"Sometimes his belt," admitted Tiger. "But it doesn't hurt very bad," he added quickly.

"I'm sure it doesn't," said the lady, as she scribbled some more notes and frowned at her legal pad.

CHAPTER 12

You've been sworn in, Officer Thrasher. Why don't you just tell me what happened," suggested Judge Silverman, resting his chin on his hand.

It was nearly noon, and Thrasher had just taken the stand to testify against Charles. Judge Silverman had first required that Charles sign a document waiving his right to counsel, on the basis that Charles would act as his own lawyer.

"You know what they say about lawyers who represent themselves?" asked Silverman.

"That they've got a fool for a client," Charles replied. "But at least in this case, he's an innocent fool."

"We'll see," said Silverman.

Charles felt his palms go moist as he sat at the defense counsel table, his right leg bouncing nervously up and down. Crawford and her entourage had just returned to the courtroom and were waiting for the chance to resume the Hammonds' hearing. Charles noticed Crawford squirming in her seat, signaling her anxiousness to return to center stage.

First, thought Charles, *I've got some fireworks of my own.*

He rose behind the defense counsel table just as Thrasher turned toward the judge to start his narration. "Before he does that, Your Honor, the defense would like to challenge the constitutionality of this statute." His voice sounded louder than he had intended. It boomed through the courtroom and echoed back at him.

All eyes turned to Charles. Silverman raised a bushy eyebrow.

"You want to challenge the constitutionality of the Virginia Beach noise ordinance?" asked a skeptical Silverman. His chin still rested on his hand, and he added an eye roll at the request. It was getting late.

"Yes, I do, Your Honor." Charles was nervous, but he was also getting a little irked. It was the court's job to consider legal challenges, even for misdemeanors. He saw no reason for the judge to act so put out by the notion.

"On what basis?" mumbled the judge.

"Excuse me, Your Honor?"

"I said, On what basis?" This time Silverman took his chin out of his hand and spoke up. There was a slight edge to his voice.

I thought you'd never ask.

"The ordinance as written violates the free speech clause of the First Amendment, and as applied in this case, it violates the equal protection clause of the Fourteenth Amendment." Charles pulled copies of cases out of his briefcase and dropped them on his counsel table. He noticed Judge Silverman eye the papers suspiciously.

"The ordinance requires that anybody using amplification equipment on the streets, sidewalks, or parks must first obtain a permit," Charles continued, unfazed by the whispers and snickers behind him. "There are no objective guidelines for when the permit should be issued, leaving it in the total discretion of the city manager's office. This creates an unconstitutionally broad prior restraint on free speech."

Charles paused to let the concept sink in. Silverman obviously didn't spend much time deciding constitutional issues, and Charles didn't want to see the judge's eyes glaze over. Better to lead him through it one step at a time, let him become part of the process.

"You want me to declare the noise ordinance in Virginia Beach unconstitutional so that anybody can then use loudspeakers and amps anytime they want?" asked Silverman. He raised both eyebrows this time.

"Only until the city rewrites the ordinance to include some objective standards for when to issue permits," Charles responded. He wanted to say more, but instead he just picked up one of the cases he had placed on the table. From his years in judicial clerking, Charles knew that judges hated it when they thought a lawyer might know something they didn't.

"Do you have any authority to support this rather bold claim?" asked Silverman, mesmerized by the papers in Charles's hand.

Glad you asked.

"Yes, Your Honor. Several years ago the U.S. Supreme Court considered a very similar case. In Kunz versus New York, 340 U.S. at page 290, the

Court addressed a New York ordinance that prohibited public worship on the streets without first obtaining a permit from the police commissioner. This man Kunz, a Baptist preacher, applied for a permit and was denied one because he had supposedly ridiculed and denounced other religious beliefs in his meetings, which, by the way, I never do.

"Anyway, the Court held that the statute was unconstitutional because"—and here Charles looked down at his highlighted pages, carefully reading the words and giving them greater emphasis—"it gives an administrative official discretionary power to control in advance the rights of citizens to speak on religious matters on the streets of New York."

Charles looked up at Silverman in time to see the judge frown. "Let me see that case, Counselor."

Charles walked up to the judge and handed him the file. He noticed that Officer Thrasher no longer looked so smug. Charles smiled at the officer and headed back to his counsel table. He waited patiently as the judge read every word of *Kunz v. New York*.

—◦—⊨◦⊨—◦—

It was not her responsibility to prosecute misdemeanors, but the Barracuda couldn't resist a good fight. Especially in front of the television cameras. The Hammond case was in the bag. The kids had given her everything she needed. She would nail down her bond request in a few minutes. But first, an unexpected chance to be a hero.

She had no love for Thrasher. He probably deserved this. But it never hurt to have the cops owe you a favor or two. And the thought of impromptu street performers on every corner of the boardwalk—unrestrained by a noise ordinance—was a nightmare. It was already bad enough when the teenagers drove around blasting their car stereos and boom boxes. This would be worse.

Who did this black man think he was anyway, waltzing into a Virginia Beach court—*her* court—and advocating chaos at the beach in the name of the Constitution? She had seen his sound equipment in the exhibit room. He might have a nifty little case from New York City, but this was Virginia Beach, and this guy was about to meet his match.

She rose from her seat in the front row of the courtroom, on the side where the police officers hung out—on the side of the law.

"Your Honor?" said the Barracuda.

"Counsel."

"If it please the court, the commonwealth's attorney would like to get involved in this matter, given the fact that the defendant is challenging an ordinance on constitutional grounds."

"By all means," said Silverman, taking off his thick glasses and rubbing his eyes. "The more, the merrier."

⊷ ⊨◈⊨ ⊶

Now it was getting complicated. A real lawyer on the other side. Charles loved a challenge, but not with his own criminal record at stake. He gave Crawford an irritated glance.

"Do you have a copy of the case for Ms. Crawford?" asked the judge.

"Sure—"

"Don't need one," said the Barracuda, interrupting. "Your Honor has already read the case. And, as Mr.—" She pointed at Charles, apparently unable to recall his name. "As the defendant here has already said, the plaintiff in the *Kunz* case actually applied for a permit and was denied one. To my knowledge, this defendant"—and again she pointed at Charles, annoying him to no end—"never even applied for a permit. How can he now challenge an ordinance as an unconstitutional prior restraint on his speech if he never even bothered to apply for a permit?"

Thrasher smiled. Silverman nodded. All heads turned toward Charles.

"Judge," he began, palms spread, "the ordinance is unconstitutional on its face. It's the procedure itself I'm complaining about. I shouldn't be forced to use a flawed procedure in order to challenge it."

"Oh, come on," said the Barracuda, "since when do we let citizens just waltz in off the street and challenge the constitutionality of ordinances for sport when they never even try to comply with them? This court's got better things to do. Criminals to try. Bonds to set—"

"Okay, okay," interrupted Silverman. "Here's what we're going to do. Courts don't rule on the constitutionality of statutes except as a last resort. I don't even know the facts of this case yet. Let me hear the testimony first, then if it's necessary to rule on the constitutionality of the statute, I'll do so at that time."

Silverman glanced at his watch and stifled a yawn. "Is that acceptable to everybody?"

"Yes, Your Honor," said the Barracuda.

"Not exactly," said Charles.

Silverman sighed and ran his hands through his hair. "What do you mean, *not exactly?*"

"Judge, I've also got a selective enforcement argument," Charles talked quickly, trying to get it all in before he was cut off. "They singled me out. Everybody else gets to use sound equipment and make as much noise as they want. But even a constitutional statute, if it's applied with"—Charles picked up another case and began reading, speaking even faster—"'an evil eye and an unequal hand, so as to make unjust discrimination between persons in similar circumstances,' then it cannot be enforced." He put the paper down and looked up.

"And I suppose you've got another case?" asked Silverman.

"Yes, Your Honor. The Chinese laundry owner's case, Yick Wo versus Hopkins, where the city of San Francisco would not give permits to Chinese applicants to operate laundries."

Crawford snorted so loud she sounded like a horse. "Of course," she said sarcastically, "the old Chinese laundry case. This man is desperate, Judge. Last I knew, he had no desire to run a Chinese laundry…"

The cops all smiled.

"I cite it for the proposition of law it contains," responded Charles, turning and staring at the deputy commonwealth's attorney. "Every lawyer knows that."

She walked to his table. "I wouldn't want to miss reading this one," she sniped as she snatched the copy from Charles's hand.

"Counsel, address any comments to the court, not each other," demanded Silverman. "Mr. Arnold?"

"Yes, Your Honor."

"We'll deal with that case after we hear the evidence as well."

Charles nodded.

"Now, if you don't have any more cases in that bag of tricks of yours, let's hear some evidence."

— ⟩⟨⟩⟨⟩ —

The Barracuda flipped the case on her counsel table and turned to Officer Thrasher. She and the officer had danced the witness dance before. She led. He followed. He had not always been so accommodating. After their first case together, she had dressed him down in front of his buddies in the hall-way. A vicious shouting match that nobody won. But now he would follow her lead. Nothing fancy. He would just answer her questions.

After all, it was only a noise ordinance. How bad could it get?

After the preliminaries, she got right to the point.

"Had you ever met the defendant before the night of his arrest, Officer Thrasher?" She walked the entire well of the courtroom as she questioned the witness, her head held high. She used no notes, relying instead on her instincts and her formidable memory.

"No ma'am."

"Would you have any reason whatsoever to discriminate against him, or selectively enforce a law against him?" *Other than the color of his skin,* she thought to herself. Thrasher was not one of the most enlightened officers at the beach.

"Oh no, ma'am."

"And have you, in fact, enforced this very same ordinance against others?"

"Many times." Thrasher talked in short clips. No nonsense. Just the facts. He had learned his lesson well.

The Barracuda walked back to her counsel table. Thrasher's partner, a bodybuilder named Alex Stone, stood up and whispered in her ear. He then headed down the aisle of the courtroom and stood by the back door.

The Barracuda turned to the witness. "Please tell the court, *briefly,* about the arrest."

"At approximately 9:05 p.m., on Friday, June 3, my partner and I were patrolling the Virginia Beach oceanfront. We saw the suspect at the intersection of Atlantic and Virginia Beach Boulevard. He had set up an extensive sound system and could be heard at least a block away. He was verbally assaulting tourists and others walking down the sidewalk, trying to proselytize them as they walked by."

A sigh of disbelief floated up from the defendant—a sure sign she was scoring points.

"So what did you do?" she asked simply, clinically.

"We pulled over and asked him not to use the sound amplification equipment without a permit because it violated the Virginia Beach noise ordinance."

"What was his response?"

"The suspect started...I guess you could say...ranting and raving at us. He accused us of discrimination. He ridiculed us and called us names...5-0... pigs...that type of thing. He threatened us with a lawsuit, said he was a law professor and knew his civil rights. He basically tried to get the whole crowd riled up against us."

"Was he using his sound equipment while he insulted you?"

"The whole time."

Now for the fun part. The Barracuda turned and nodded to Officer Stone in the back of the courtroom.

She turned back to the witness: "Did you impound the equipment for evidence, Officer Thrasher?"

"Sure did."

As if on cue, Stone marched up front with the karaoke boom box and one of the speakers. He hooked up the first speaker and then brought in the second speaker and plugged it in as well. He plugged the boom box into an outlet and returned to his seat.

"Is this the sound system the defendant was using?" The Barracuda couldn't resist a small smirk. The speakers were huge.

"Yes ma'am. Except he had it hooked up to a car battery instead of plugging it into an outlet."

"Your Honor," announced the Barracuda, unable to suppress a smile, "I'd like to introduce this whole contraption as Commonwealth's Exhibit 1."

Silverman made a face. "The whole thing?"

"The whole thing," she said firmly.

"Any objections?" Silverman turned to the defendant. The Barracuda watched the defendant's face—*what was that guy's name anyway?*—for signs of panic, but she saw none.

"May I inspect it?" asked the defendant.

"Knock yourself out," said the Barracuda curtly. Then she leaned back against her counsel table and watched in bemusement as the lawyer carefully looked over every square inch of his equipment.

"No objection," he announced at last, "as long as I get it back when the case is over."

"All right, then," said Silverman. "Let the record reflect that this sound system has been introduced as Commonwealth's Exhibit 1."

"What volume level was it set on?" asked the Barracuda.

"I believe it was on seven," responded Thrasher. The Barracuda recognized the code language. An "I believe" answer meant that Thrasher had no idea.

She walked over to the boom box and put the volume knob at seven. She handed the mike to Officer Thrasher.

"Was the defendant talking or singing into the mike?" she asked.

"He was talking," said Thrasher.

"Thank goodness," said the Barracuda. "Otherwise, I would have had to ask you to sing." She waited for the chuckles to subside. "But if you wouldn't mind, say a few words into that mike."

"Testing one…two…three…testing one…two…three…" said Thrasher. His voice boomed through the courtroom and echoed off the walls. The mike squealed, and a few folks grimaced at the noise.

"That's enough," insisted Silverman. "The court gets the point."

Thrasher handed the mike back to the Barracuda. She turned off the machine and returned to counsel table.

She was exceedingly proud of her little show. She had kept Thrasher and his big mouth out of trouble. Short and sweet. Just the facts. No way that he could be trapped on cross-examination now.

The maximum fine for violating the noise ordinance was one thousand bucks. She would ask for the maximum and probably get half. She had teed it up beautifully. She hoped the young upstart lawyer at the defense table was taking notes. He would learn a good lesson. It would also be an expensive one.

"No further questions," said the Barracuda to Thrasher. "Please answer any questions that Mr.…um…the defendant…might have."

She sat down, turned around, and mugged for her friends in press row.

CHAPTER 13

He stood for a long time behind his counsel table, looking down at his notes, as if in a trance.

"Mr. Arnold," said the judge, "it's your turn."

"Oh...sorry, Your Honor." He looked at the witness.

"You sure you're remembering this right?" asked Charles softly, his brow furrowed.

"I'm sure," said Thrasher coldly.

"Isn't it true that there were others on Atlantic Avenue on the night in question who were using sound systems every bit as loud as mine?"

"That's *absolutely* not true," swore the witness.

"Have you ever seen a hip-hop band out there...with a boom box, amps, and speakers bigger than mine?"

"Never."

Charles smiled at the officer. Thrasher was good at this. Not the slightest hint of remorse.

"Isn't it true, Officer Thrasher, that I never called you and your partner 'pigs'?"

Confidently: "That's not true."

"Isn't it true, Officer Thrasher, that *you* were the one who threatened *me?* You told me to pack up and go home or I would be in a heap of trouble. Isn't that what you said?"

"Objection." The Barracuda jumped to her feet. "That's argumentative."

"I'll allow it," said Silverman.

The Barracuda shrugged and sat down.

"No, that's not true. It happened just like I said it did." Thrasher sounded bored, but Charles noticed a slight tightening of the lips, a slight narrowing of the eyes.

"In fact, sir, you arrested me because I was black and because I was preachin' the gospel, isn't that right?" Charles increased his volume but stayed behind his counsel table.

"Absolutely false, Mr. Arnold. We arrested you because you were violating the noise ordinance and because you tried to incite a riot."

The Barracuda shot her witness a hard look.

"Was I arrested for inciting a riot?" Charles had noticed the slip as well.

"No," said Thrasher. He didn't look at the Barracuda.

But Thrasher did fidget a little and seemed uncomfortable with the silence, so Charles let it linger. He pretended to be searching his notes.

"Mr. Arnold?" It was Silverman again, trying to keep things moving.

"Yes, Your Honor."

"Do you have any more questions?"

"Yes, Your Honor." Charles stared at the witness.

"You got something against blacks?" Charles asked, never breaking his gaze.

As soon as the words were out, the Barracuda jumped to her feet. "Judge, that's outrageous," she protested. "There's no foundation for that."

"Objection sustained," said Silverman curtly. "Watch yourself, Mr. Arnold."

"Sorry, Your Honor." A pause. "Isn't it true, Mr. Thrasher, that you called me a 'preacher boy' and ridiculed my 'nappy little head'?"

"That's ludicrous," responded Thrasher evenly. "I would never use phrases like that."

Out of the corner of his eye, Charles noticed the Barracuda shoot the officer another look.

"Never?"

"Never."

"And why not?" asked Charles.

"Because those words might be construed as showing prejudice. That's not who I am, and that's not the way I talk." Thrasher looked at the judge, his eyes asking how much longer he had to endure these ridiculous questions.

"How many more questions do you have for Officer Thrasher?" Silverman asked. "You'll get your own chance to testify when the officer is done."

Of course Charles knew that. And he hated being treated like a first-year law student. But he could take a hint. Silverman wanted this over. And Charles would oblige him. The trap had been set. Thrasher was in knee-deep.

"Just a few more questions, Your Honor," Charles promised. He walked out from behind his counsel table for the first time. "May I approach my equipment?"

"What?"

"May I approach my equipment?"

"Sure," said Silverman, scratching his head.

Charles walked over to his boom box and knelt down. He popped out a music CD and held it in his right hand.

"Is this the CD that was in there the night of my arrest?" he asked.

"The equipment wasn't touched or altered," said Thrasher. "I assume that CD was in there the night of your arrest."

"Good," said Charles, as he knelt down again. He punched another button and popped out a cassette. He held it in his hand and walked toward Thrasher.

"Then I'm assuming you haven't recorded over this cassette?" Charles asked.

A light popped on in the witness's eyes. He shot a "help me" glance at the Barracuda as the color left his face.

"Of course not," the witness managed.

Standing a few inches from the witness box, Charles turned to the judge. "Then I would like to introduce my CD, labeled WOW Gospel, as Defense Exhibit 1. And I would like to introduce my cassette, labeled Street Sermon, June 3, as Defense Exhibit 2."

Charles turned back to the ashen witness. "I take it, Officer Thrasher, that you were not aware that I record my sermons and the other sounds picked up by my microphone during my street preaching?"

Thrasher shook his head. He seemed to have lost his voice.

"Then if there's no objection from your lawyer, I'd like to play this cassette for the court, to see what was really said out there on the night in question." Charles spun around to see if Crawford had any objections.

It did not surprise him to see her sitting at the counsel table with her head in her hands.

"No objection," she muttered without looking up.

＋＋ ≡◆≡ ＋＋

Silverman announced a ten-minute break after dismissing the charges against Charles. In the hallway outside the courtroom, Charles became a mini-celebrity, especially to the other defendants.

"Have you got a card, man?" asked one. "I need a *good* lawyer."

"No, I didn't bring any cards."

"Will that Chinese laundry case work for a DUI? The cops let everyone else go but me? Just like that case you mentioned, pure and simple."

"I don't handle DUIs."

Charles looked past the other desperate defendants who had crowded around him for some free legal advice and spotted Deputy Commonwealth's Attorney Rebecca Crawford talking to some cops across the hallway. He pushed his way through the crowd and walked up to her, extending his hand.

"No hard feelings," he said.

She looked down at his hand and then back at his eyes. Her face was taut. She didn't extend her hand to shake.

"It doesn't really work that way," she said. Then she turned a cold shoulder and resumed her conversation with the officers.

CHAPTER 14

The best interest of the child.

It was her only guidance. Her only job as special advocate. Determine what is in the best interest of the child and make a recommendation to the court.

Easy in theory; hard in practice.

And it had never been harder for Nikki Moreno than right now, with the Hammond family and their complex mix of love and abuse, faith and neglect.

The parents needed counsel. She was clear on that. And turning these kids back over to an abusive father was not the answer.

In many ways Thomas Hammond was everything Nikki detested about the American male. A control freak. Domineering. Long on discipline, short on mercy. A simple view of life dominated by simple solutions. The kids get out of line, you whack them around a little bit. They'll learn. Nikki knew the type all too well. Add alcohol to the mix, and you would have her own birth father, dark memories from an early childhood.

But there was also something different about Thomas Hammond, something at war with the image of father as master. She saw it now as she watched him at the defense counsel table. He would reach under the table and gently touch his wife's hand. He would put his daughter on his lap and, with his enormous hand, wipe some blonde curls away from her eyes. He would reach back over the chair and tickle his little boy's ribs, then exchange ornery glances with the child.

He was not just father as master. He was also father as friend. And that image, mixed with thoughts of her own adopted father, the only man who had ever loved Nikki unconditionally, made this case incredibly difficult. She felt herself being drawn in on this one, losing that sense of emotional detachment that was so important. She somehow felt the warmth of her own adopted father's love wash over her every time that Thomas Hammond reached out for his kids.

She had lost him seven years ago, when she was nineteen, and she had been alone in the world ever since. He had been a single parent. And when his heart gave out, Nikki felt like she had lost both a father and a mother, the only real parent she had ever known. On days like today, when the memories came flooding back with such vivid force, she wondered if she would ever get over it.

There was good-natured banter going on all around Nikki, some of it directed at her. But she was not listening. In a few moments she would be asked to make her call. And the one person in the courtroom burdened with the responsibility of recommending what was in the best interest of the children had no earthly idea what she was going to say.

◦—◦ ≍◊≍ ◦—◦

"All rise," cried the clerk as Silverman shuffled out to the bench. "General District Court, City of Virginia Beach, is again in session. The Honorable Franklin Silverman Jr. presiding."

During the break the Barracuda had figured out exactly where to stand to generate the best camera angle—a head-on shot—and avoid a profile of her somewhat angular nose. She stood on that precise spot now, looking very grave and prosecutorial for the evening news. Lots of viewers, lots of votes.

"Judge, I request that we sequester the children for the next several minutes. I'll be discussing their testimony, and it would be in the best interest of the children if they're not present."

"Does the special advocate agree, Ms. Moreno?" asked Judge Silverman.

"Certainly, Your Honor."

"Very well then. Bailiff, please escort the children out into the hall."

The Barracuda glanced over and looked at Mr. Hammond. She saw him force a tight-lipped smile for the kids and nod. Then she watched as the children reluctantly followed the bailiff out of the courtroom. Tiger kept glancing over his shoulder and then glancing at the bailiff's gun holster, as if the little boy was trying to figure out whether to make a dash for it. In the end, he apparently decided to go along.

"What we learned this morning was shocking," the Barracuda claimed as soon as the doors had closed behind the kids. No preliminaries, no beating around the bush, straight for the jugular.

"Both parents are guilty of mental and physical abuse. During my questioning of the kids, I asked the court reporter to mark certain aspects of the transcript, and if there's any doubt about my summation of the testimony of the children, it can be read." The Barracuda paused and looked over at the defense counsel table. Harry Pursifull was sitting with his head propped on his left hand, elbow on the table. He had an empty legal pad in front of him, his clients sitting beside him, and Nikki Moreno sitting directly behind him.

Not exactly the dream team, thought Crawford.

"Both parents would humiliate and abuse these children based on the smallest offenses. Mrs. Hammond would inflict her punishment with a wooden spoon; Mr. Hammond would use his belt. If little John Paul didn't come in for dinner as soon as he was called, he'd get what he called a whuppin' from his dad. Talking back by either of the children would result in numerous blows from the spoon, the belt, or some other object. Their father would use his bare hand if nothing else was handy."

The Barracuda started pacing the courtroom, forgetting about camera angles, feeding her own anger at the abusive parents. Her voice took on a hard edge, her heels clicking on the hardwood floor as she lectured the court.

"The kids would endure humiliating lengths of time in solitary confinement, or time-out, as the parents called it. The kids would be forced to sit in a chair in the corner of the room, facing the wall for hours on end. And if they spoke, the punishment would escalate from time-out to a beating. They would be humiliated in public as well as private. And even today, when I talked with these children, I could sense the fear of their parents. They were absolutely terrified that they might do something wrong."

She watched Silverman as he took notes. He would not look her in the eye, which irritated her. She could not tell what he was thinking, if she was even getting through, having an impact. So she stopped, immediately in front of the bench, and paused. She waited for him to stop writing, then she lowered her voice melodramatically and continued.

"Judge, if we treated *animals* this way, the SPCA would be all over this court screaming 'cruelty to animals.' They would demand that the animals be removed from their masters. Are children entitled to less protection than our pets?

"These parents," she sneered, "who have themselves showed no mercy, now have the audacity to ask the commonwealth for mercy, the audacity to claim that the children will be harmed if we put them in foster care. Well, Your Honor, the commonwealth is not buying it. We don't believe that parents who abuse a child and neglect seeking medical care deserve a chance to put their other children at risk pending trial."

She paused and took a deep breath. She glared at Thomas and Theresa Hammond with the same look of contempt she visited on every defendant.

Theresa Hammond cried quietly, tears rolling down her cheeks, her eyes red and puffy. She slumped forward, staring down at the table—the look of humiliation and shame. *And,* thought Crawford, *the look of guilt.*

Her husband stared stoically ahead, the color of hot anger rising in his ears and on the back of his neck. He held his wife's hand tightly under the table.

The Barracuda felt no sympathy for either of them. They were killers. Sympathy and mercy were out of the question. Joshua called for justice.

"The commonwealth *emphatically* requests that bail for Mr. Hammond be set at two hundred thousand and bail for Mrs. Hammond be set at fifty thousand. And we also *strongly* request that, even if the defendants can post bond, the court condition their release on a protective order that would place the children in foster care and prohibit the parents from contacting them pending trial."

She turned to take her seat, her heels clicking loudly, her movements precise and confident. Her job, for the moment, finished.

"Yer Honor," began Harry Pursifull, rising slowly to his feet. "This is a bond hearing, not a trial, and not a custody case. And we therefore, um, believe, that this court should focus on the issues relevant to risk of flight. The fact is that both parents are here today and brought their children as well, I might add, of their own volition. If they were going to flee with their children, they, uh, they would have already done so."

The Barracuda eyed Harry skeptically as he spoke. He was gaining momentum, hitting his stride. He would steer the court away from the abuse issues. That was Harry's style. Unusual for a trial lawyer, he would avoid confrontation whenever possible.

As he warmed to his task and got used to the television cameras, his voice returned from a higher pitch to its normal nasal tone. His breathing became less labored, and his phrases no longer came in bursts. "Ms. Crawford seems to conveniently forget that these parents *did* take their child to the hospital." He licked his dry lips. "They *did* seek medical care, and they would do so for the other children if necessary. Sure, some of their discipline might have been inappropriate—"

"Inappropriate!" the Barracuda interrupted, jumping to her feet. The outburst stopped Harry in his tracks as she knew it would. He was a familiar adversary with familiar weaknesses. He turned to her with his mouth open, speechless.

"Putting them on time-out for hours *might* be inappropriate. Humiliating them in public *might* be inappropriate." The Barracuda glared at Harry, as if he were the guilty one, lecturing him like an angry parent. "But *beating* your children with a belt for the tiniest offense is not *inappropriate*. It's abuse, Counsel. Let's at least call it what it is."

She sat down and crossed her arms before the judge could scold her.

Harry opened his palms to the court. "Judge, I didn't interrupt Ms. Crawford when she was speaking."

"I know," said Judge Silverman evenly. Then he turned to the Barracuda. "I'd appreciate it if you'd grant Mr. Pursifull the same latitude he granted you."

"Sure, Judge." She allowed her voice to register her disgust.

But Silverman ignored it. He was a grizzled old warhorse and had seen it all before. He turned back to Harry. "Now, Mr. Pursifull, were there any marks or bruises on these children that were discernable today?"

"No, Your Honor," said Harry proudly.

"But, Judge"—the Barracuda was on her feet again, a calculated risk—"nobody is saying these beatings didn't occur. And the little girl testified that sometimes, after the spankings, there would be marks left by the spoon, the belt, or the imprint of her father's hand."

"What did the little boy say?" asked Silverman.

"He gave his favorite answer," replied the Barracuda. "He said he didn't know."

"Thank you, Ms. Crawford," Silverman said with a tone of exaggerated patience. He leveled his gaze at her until she again took her seat.

"Ms. Moreno," the judge turned to Nikki, "does the special advocate have a recommendation for the court?"

All eyes turned to Nikki Moreno. She stood straight and poised—her television pose. *Disgusting,* thought Crawford.

Nikki furrowed her brow, shook her head slightly, and wrinkled her face. "It's a tough one, Judge," she said matter-of-factly. "I'm not usually one to hesitate on making a call, but this one's not easy."

The Barracuda rolled her eyes and propped her forehead on her palm. "Gimme a break," she mumbled loud enough for her friends in the press row to hear.

But Nikki ignored her, annoying her all the more.

"Ms. Crawford is dead right about the abuse suffered by these children and about the three days of neglect that preceded young Joshua's death," Nikki said. "But strangely enough, there also seems to be an enormous amount of love in this family. I would agree that Mr. and Mrs. Hammond need counseling on how to discipline, and I would be concerned about whether they are willing to seek medical help when it's needed, but let me tell the court what concerns me even more.

"These children are scared. Ms. Crawford is right about that. But I think their real fear is that they will be torn from their mom and dad at a very vulnerable emotional point in their young lives. And to make matters worse, they will probably think that their testimony is what caused it, that they said something wrong to send their parents to jail.

"I'm no psychologist, Judge, and this is certainly your call, but it seems to me that the emotional trauma would be intense. I would recommend that Mrs. Hammond be released on a PR bond and that the children be given back to her on two conditions. First, that she agrees to a restraining order preventing her from physically hitting the children. And second, that a caseworker from the Department of Child Protective Services perform a comprehensive evaluation of the home and recommend whether the children should stay or be removed pending trial."

"Thank you, Ms. Moreno," Silverman said. "The court is helped by your unbiased and straightforward evaluation."

Unbiased evaluation? What kind of crack is that?

The Barracuda stood without knowing what she would say. It was intuitive really, a sense that the emotional energy driving her case had suddenly been drained from the courtroom by Moreno. This hearing was headed south. It was time to inject some fire.

"Judge, that's a wonderful speech by Ms. Moreno. And she's been put in a difficult spot, having to make a recommendation about a matter involving complex family law issues, even though she is neither a parent nor a lawyer..." Out of the corner of her eye, she saw Nikki cross her arms and narrow her glare. *Good.*

"But let's not forget, Your Honor, we have a dead baby here. And we have two other children at risk for abuse and neglect." Crawford's voice rose, and she punctuated every word. They would make good sound bites. "Yes, in the short term it will be traumatic for these children. But in the long term, it may well save their lives. Unlike Ms. Moreno, the commonwealth is not willing to force children to tolerate abuse in the name of love—"

"What?" Nikki's head jerked toward the Barracuda. "That is, like, so unfair." She pointed, her eyes flashing. "What's *your* problem?"

"*My* problem?" the Barracuda shot back. "*My* problem? I'm not the one trying to justify abuse—"

"I can't believe—" Nikki started.

"*Ladies!*" shouted Silverman, banging his gavel. The two stopped in midsentence, glaring at each other with molten gazes, ready to strike, the claws out and sharpened. *I can't stand this woman,* thought Crawford.

"This is no way to conduct a hearing," huffed Silverman, leaning forward and looking from one combatant to the other.

"Ms. Moreno, I want a word with you in my chambers," he said, his voice no longer soft and even. "And Ms. Crawford…"

"Yes, Judge," she said wearily.

"I will not tolerate that type of outburst again," he said emphatically. "You're much too experienced and much too good a lawyer for that. I'm surprised you let your emotions get the better part of you, even for a moment."

"Yes, Your Honor," the Barracuda said without conviction. She glared at Nikki one last time—*Moreno's no better than these abusive parents, and now she's going back to coddle up to the judge*—and then the Barracuda sat down and started plotting her next move.

CHAPTER 15

What's going on?" Silverman asked as soon as Nikki took a seat in his chambers.

Nikki crossed her legs and slouched in the large leather chair in front of the judge's desk. *Think I'll try a little pouting.*

"Crawford's a jerk," she said derisively.

"She's just intense," said Silverman. He sounded more like a grandfather now than the same stern judge who had minutes before demanded that Nikki meet him in chambers. "You two will never get along. You're both too high strung."

Nikki just shrugged. As usual, she knew he was right.

"And by the way, consider this the tongue-lashing you so richly deserve," Silverman noted with a wry smile. "I don't want those lawyers out there thinking I'm soft."

"Don't worry, Judge," responded Nikki, the life coming back into her voice. "They'll think you're Attila the Hun by the time I get done telling stories.

"By the way," she added. "Congratulations."

She watched the look of surprise flash across his face. "How'd you know?"

"Can't answer that. But word has it that you're first in line for the circuit court slot. The street says the appointment should come down next month."

"I can neither confirm nor deny," Silverman replied with mock serious-ness. Then a smooth change of tone and subject. "You want anything to drink?" He walked over to a small round table that held a tray with iced tea, a pot of coffee, and cups adorned with the emblem from Washington and Lee, his beloved alma mater.

"Nothing you've got," replied Nikki. "Besides, you know I won't drink out of a cup from a school that kept women out for so long."

"The good old days."

"Yeah, and Thomas Hammond thinks we're still living in them."

A pause, then Silverman said, "That's why I called you back here." He settled on the edge of his enormous desk, iced tea nestled in both hands. "You really threw a monkey wrench into my thinking when you recommended that the children stay with their folks. After all the cases you've handled in my courtroom, I thought I had you figured out."

He looked at Nikki pensively. "Were you just trying to pull Crawford's chain or do you really feel that way? It's important that I know what you're thinking."

Nikki loved the man's honesty. A few months ago they had started off on the wrong foot. These same chambers had been the scene of some strong-willed words between a disrespectful special advocate and a stubborn judge. The uneasy truce that resulted eventually changed into a grudging respect and then a mutual admiration. Now they were allies. Partners with a common desire to protect the children.

"Jerking her chain was only a bonus." Nikki smiled at the thought. "But I really meant what I said."

"And?"

Nikki shrugged. "I watched those kids around their parents. Yeah, the parents aren't perfect. But they aren't the picture of narrow-mindedness and abuse that Crawford is painting, either. I think they can be helped. It's just a gut feeling."

"I know what you mean," said the judge as he walked over to his window, his back to Nikki. "But that's a little thin for me to base a decision on—the gut feeling of the special advocate."

"Yeah," admitted Nikki, "but there's one other thing. Something I couldn't mention in open court."

The judge turned and looked at her, his silence urging her to continue.

She thought hard about opening this can of worms. But he was honest with her, and she owed him the same.

"These foster homes, Judge. I've been there, seen them. They're not good. The families have more kids than they can handle. And some of those parents are almost as strict as the Hammonds—minus the physical abuse, of course.

"Judge, I know we can't take these cases personally. But those kids are so cute and so innocent. And right now…so vulnerable. Is it really in their best interest to take them from their parents and stick them in a foster home?"

He stared into space. And she let him. She had learned to respect these long moments of silence, his way of sorting it all out.

She noticed the deep wrinkles, the crow's feet around the eyes and the skin sagging under them. He took his job seriously, too seriously. She wondered how he would survive the added responsibilities of the circuit court.

"You like those kids, don't you, Nikki?"

"They're cute, as far as kids go. But you know me, I'd take a twenty-five-year-old bodybuilder anytime."

"Putting them in a foster home does have its drawbacks, and it also has a degree of permanency that I'm not comfortable with until we get more facts." He stopped and took a sip of iced tea.

"I'm going to set a high bail for the husband," he continued. "I've been watching his expressions. He looks desperate. I think Crawford's right, he might do something stupid—try to run with the kids."

"I can see that," said Nikki.

"I'm going to let the mother out on a low bond, something like ten thousand. I don't think she's a risk. But I'm not ready to give her the kids without further evaluation.

"I'll need a complete report on the family and home. Risk assessment, mother's psychiatric state, the whole works. That'll take a week. In the meantime, I've got to have somebody to take custody of the kids."

He looked directly at Nikki, his lips forming the thinnest line of a smile.

"Wait a minute, Judge," Nikki tilted her head back, not sure if she knew where this was headed.

"Who better than the special advocate?"

"Judge, you can't do that!" Nikki jumped up.

"I'll give you community service credit for every hour you have them."

She thought for maybe half a second. "No way!" she cried. "You can't be serious! That's, like…totally *bizarre*."

Silverman started walking across the room toward the door.

"I don't know the first thing about taking care of kids." She stepped in front of him, her face aghast, visions of rug rats clouding her thoughts.

He did a nifty side step and kept walking, setting his glass on the table as he passed. "Come on, Nikki, we've kept them waiting long enough."

She bolted in front of him again, blocking the door. "You can't do this, Judge. This is crazy."

Silverman stopped, and the remnants of a smile left his face. He hesitated, as if trying to decide whether he should raise this next subject. "I knew your father, Nikki," he said softly.

She felt the wind leave her lungs, her thoughts spinning wildly. "What's that got to do with this?" she heard herself ask.

"Everything, Nikki." He paused. "And you know it."

⊷ ⇌◆⇌ ⊶

In the hallway the Pretty Lady had said to Tiger that he would get to stay with her for a week or so. But he didn't want to. She said he would get to see his mommy some. But his daddy would have to go away for a little while. He could see his daddy, too. But not as often.

At least his sister, good old Stinky, would be staying with him.

The Pretty Lady said that Tiger had not done anything wrong. Which he doubted. If she only knew. But he was happy to let her think that. Especially if he had to stay with her for a while. He hoped she was nice. She seemed nice.

But now he was back in the courtroom, the stuffy room with the high ceilings and bright lights and all the people. His stomach hurt. Real bad. He was standing in front of his dad. There were mean men standing behind his dad. Waiting.

His mom was next to him, kneeling and hugging Stinky. His dad knelt down too, on both knees. He put big hands on Tiger's shoulders, then leaned forward and spoke in a serious whisper.

"You're the man of the family now, Tiger. At least for a little while. Daddy will be back before long. You take care of Stinky and your mom. And say your prayers every night. Okay?"

Tiger bit his lip and nodded quickly. He blinked hard to hold back the tears. His dad didn't tell him not to cry. He didn't have to. Tiger knew that the man of the house didn't cry. And so he stood there, nodding bravely and shaking.

"I love you, Son," his dad said softly. Then he gave Tiger a hard hug.

"I love you too, Daddy," Tiger whimpered. He squeezed his daddy's neck and reluctantly let go as the bad men pulled his daddy away.

In the next moment his mommy was hugging him and kissing on him and talking to him. But he couldn't hear or remember what she said; his huge new job drowned out all her words.

He would take care of his mom. She and Stinky didn't have to worry.

Then the Pretty Lady took him and Stinky by the hand and turned to leave the courtroom. He held his head high and squeezed her hand tight. There were people asking questions of the Pretty Lady and crowding all around. Everyone talked and hollered at once.

His lip quivered, but he still refused to cry. He was the man of the house now. He would have led the way; he felt responsible. But he could not see through the forest of legs…and the unwelcome water that had suddenly flooded his eyes.

CHAPTER 16

The house, as usual, was hollow, lifeless, and depressing. It was also huge. That was part of the problem. But successful doctors don't live in condos or one-story ranch houses. And so, to maintain the appearance of a happily married and successful emergency room doctor, Sean Armistead lived with his wife, Erica, in Woodard's Mill—the most exclusive upscale neighborhood in Chesapeake, Virginia.

Sean entered his enormous foyer and gazed up at the elegant chandelier and the vaulted ornamental ceiling. *How did we get to this point?* he wondered. He hoped she was not awake or, better yet, not home. It was easier not to see her, not to be forced to deal with the disease racking his wife's body, changing the woman he once loved, and causing him to feel so distant.

He allowed himself, just for a moment in his own cold foyer, to remember those heady days when he and Erica had discovered this place. It was springtime then, and the young couple loved the house almost as much as each other. Sean had marveled at the lush green, manicured lawn, a full acre, adorned with stately pines stretching to the heavens and brilliant white dogwoods lining the driveway. The house itself, an elegant red-brick monolith, had the luxurious feel of a twenty-first-century southern plantation.

They could not have afforded it on his salary, but Erica came from money, and her parents helped. And while the mortgage payments stretched their budget to its limit, the house fit their station in life.

Now it was just another possession. An extremely expensive one. To be sure, it was still beautiful and immaculately maintained, but the work was now done by hired hands. Erica didn't lift a finger.

He placed his briefcase in the study and headed for the kitchen. He was famished. He had worked another double—sixteen straight hours—then finished some dictation. In truth, he could have left work earlier. But he had no reason to come home.

He turned the hallway corner with his head down, glancing through yesterday's mail that he had picked up on the way in. He stopped abruptly, avoiding a head-on collision with his wife.

"How was work?" Erica looked at him with vacant eyes. She did not reach out to touch him. He stepped back.

He was surprised to see her up and dressed in a fashionable dark pantsuit this morning. Her makeup was done just right, her shoulder-length blonde hair teased and sprayed into place. She looked presentable but tired. Her eyes, once piercing and alive, were now expressionless and empty. The crow's-feet at the corners seemed to have grown, even since yesterday.

Sean stepped forward, bent over slightly, and kissed her on the forehead.

"Fine," he said, then he stepped around her and continued for the kitchen. "How are you feeling today?" he asked over his shoulder. The question was cold and clinical, doctor to patient, not husband to wife.

"About the same." She turned stiffly and followed him. "At least good enough to try going to this meeting at the club."

He didn't respond. He had entered the kitchen, and the nostalgia of better days quickly disappeared. Her unwashed dishes from last night's dinner and today's breakfast were on the counter in the middle of the kitchen. The newspaper, a book, and other pieces of paper were scattered around the other counters. Shoes in the middle of the floor. A brush, a bag of groceries, and unopened mail on the table. They had maids galore. Still, Erica managed to keep the house a mess.

"Did you call the guy for the pool yesterday afternoon?" asked Sean. He knew the answer.

"No, I forgot. I'll call him as soon as I get back." She started rinsing the dishes and loading the dishwasher, the twitching in her hands improving as she put them to use.

"Did you get the registrations done for the cars?"

"I'll stop on the way back." Her voice was softer.

Sean started a slow simmer. Erica worked quicker at the dishes, as if she were now anxious to escape.

"Is it too much to ask?" He posed the question pointedly without looking at her. He fixed himself a bowl of cereal. *Might it ever dawn on her that I would like a hot meal? Just once?* He was ready for a fight.

But he also knew her style. She fought only with silence, soft answers, and tears.

And this time, as usual, she didn't answer.

He attacked his cereal and poured a glass of milk. Erica finished the dishes and cleaned up the counters without speaking, the dishcloth trembling in her hand. She checked her watch. Time to go.

"I'm sorry," she said softly.

"I just don't think I'm asking too much," Sean replied, sitting at the table, staring out the window. "I work, I take care of all our finances. I just need a little help once in a while on some of the small things around the house."

"I'm sorry, honey, I really am." She came over and stood behind Sean and began massaging his shoulders. He felt the tremors in her hands, yet she persisted. He wanted to squirm, take her hands off him. Instead he just tensed up a little. "I'm just tired all the time," she continued. "Forgetful. Depressed. I didn't choose Parkinson's. I'm doing the best I can."

There it was. The trump card. Every argument, every fight, every request degenerated to this. Blame it on the Parkinson's.

"I know," he said. He stood and faced her, put his hands on her shoulders. "Now go and have a good time." He kissed her again, this time on the cheek.

Erica took the hint. She slipped slowly into her shoes, grabbed her car keys from the counter, and walked deliberately toward the front door. He watched her shuffle away, slightly bent at the waist, the stiffness in her joints evident in every step. She would be devastated if she could see herself from behind and witness the triumph of the disease. He watched her turn the hall corner and then heard her pause just before she reached the front door.

"I love you," she called.

"Love you too," said Sean, his voice flat. With a long sigh, he turned his attention back to his cereal.

An hour later Sean stared at the computer screen in his study. He felt better with a full stomach, but now he felt guilty about the way he had treated Erica. The relationship was not salvageable. Still, he didn't have to make it harder on her. He would make it up to her tomorrow.

It had all started five years ago. She was only thirty-three, but she suddenly felt tired and achy all the time. Her compulsive workouts disappeared overnight. She started sleeping round the clock. The lean and muscled body that Sean had married became a fixture lying in bed or slouching in an easy chair watching television. She would go days without leaving the house. Sean assumed it was a midlife crisis, maybe even depression from an inability to have kids.

He spent more time at work.

Then one day he noticed the tremors. It started with a little shaking in her right hand. A few days later, he caught her downing extra-strength Tylenol. She claimed she had a migraine. But she couldn't hide the stiffness in her joints, the sudden cramps, or even the changes in her handwriting. Finally, he confronted her. She broke down and cried as he ticked off the symptoms she had been trying to hide: tremors, stiffness, cramps, insomnia, depression, withdrawal. It was an early onset of Parkinson's, he told her. Only later did he learn that she already knew. She had been on medication for months.

Over time the symptoms worsened. The tremors increased and walking became more difficult. She shuffled now, and she would often run her hand along the wall for balance. Once vibrant eyes had surrendered to a faraway look, a facial expression that Sean secretly named her "Parkinson's mask." Her speech was softer now and more monotonous. Recently, she had lost some control of her bladder. She needed to go to the bathroom constantly and eventually succumbed to wearing extra protection to avoid leaking. It embarrassed her. She and Sean never talked about it.

They slept in separate rooms. It was easy to avoid your wife in a house this big.

Sean shook his head briskly and brought himself back to the present. He took a swig of scotch and double-clicked onto Quicken, his financial software package.

The computer demanded a password.

Sean typed in the code known only to himself. There were some advantages to having a tired and trusting wife, especially one who had no desire to get involved in how he spent the money.

B-A-R-R-A-C-U-D-A.

"Welcome to Quicken," the computer replied.

Sean entered the usual bills to be paid electronically, including a monthly payment in the amount of twenty-four thousand dollars earmarked for the Virginia Insurance Reciprocal. He typed the words "malpractice insurance" into the notation line on the check, then hit the send button.

A few more keystrokes and he was checking out the balances in his investment accounts. It had not been a good year in the market, but he was still worth nearly a million, thanks largely to gifts from Erica's parents. His in-laws had been generous during life, but the big payoff was yet to come. By even conservative estimates, his in-laws were worth at least fifteen million. They were getting old, and Erica was an only child. Unfortunately, both of Erica's parents appeared to be in pretty good health.

Sean closed the program and typed in an Internet address. He pulled up the site for the Tidewater Savings and Loan and then navigated to their electronic banking menu. A few more keystrokes, and one more use of the Barracuda password, and he was looking at the balance for account number 096-48133, an account belonging to the Virginia Insurance Reciprocal. Despite the steady stream of checks out of the account to another local bank each month, this single account had grown to nearly half a million dollars.

The CEO and treasurer of the Virginia Insurance Reciprocal took another swig of scotch, leaned back in his chair, and smiled.

CHAPTER 17

The young lady was waiting for Charles when he returned to his office from court. She worked for Senator Crafton, she explained, and needed to talk with Professor Arnold in private. Charles had no idea why an aide from the office of Virginia's senior senator would want to talk with him. He braced himself for the worst.

He studied her card—Catherine Godfrey—and offered her the one seat other than his own. He sat down behind his desk, wanting for all the world to grab the small Nerf basketball sitting on his credenza and take a couple of shots. It would help clear his mind. He had an ominous feeling that clear thinking was about to be required.

"Do you have any idea why I'm here?" Catherine asked. She had an air of importance, though she couldn't have been more than a year or two out of college.

"Not really."

"Good." She crossed her legs and folded her hands around her knee. "At least not every secret in Washington has leaked out." She flashed a coy smile, seemingly enjoying the suspense. "It has to do with your ex-wife."

Charles decided to play it stoic, show her no reaction. But she definitely had his attention. "Okay."

"What I'm about to tell you needs to stay in strictest confidence," Catherine continued in her self-important tone. Charles felt like he was being lectured by a woman the same age as his students. She waited, apparently desiring a response.

"Sure."

"Good." She shifted. "You've heard about the Sunnydale nomination?"

"Of course." Sunnydale was one of the president's selections for the D.C. Circuit Court of Appeals. He had been nominated nine months ago, but the Democrats wouldn't let him out of committee.

"Well, the players in Washington have reached a compromise. Sunnydale and seven other judges will be approved by the justice committee and put to a vote. The Dems, including my boss, will support these nominations on one condition." Charles furrowed his brow, trying to figure out what his ex-wife, a Democrat herself, had to do with this.

"This is where it gets interesting," continued Catherine. She lowered her voice to a conspiratorial level, as if the office of this lowly law school professor might somehow be bugged. "The Democrats are insisting that they get one of their own in exchange. Your wife has some friends in high places."

You're kidding. Denita—a federal court judge?

"Tight," said Charles, though for some reason he couldn't muster much enthusiasm. "She'd be a great judge."

Catherine seemed to relax just a little. "Well, that's why I'm here. You see, the president is nervous about appointing a Democrat. But frankly, well... he likes what he sees in your wife's file. The president thinks she'll be pro-business but at the same time she'll, um, look out for the, uh...interests of minorities...create a little diversity..."

"You mean she's a three-fer," Charles interjected. He watched Catherine turn a little red. "Black, female, pro-business—everything you need for a good political appointment."

"I didn't mean it like that," Catherine said weakly.

"I know." Charles smiled to put the young woman at ease. No sense taking it out on her. While Catherine launched into a detailed explanation of the politics at play, Charles wrestled with the unexpected disappointment that enveloped him.

Why didn't he feel more elated about this? Was it jealousy? Some deep-down desire for revenge? A feeling that maybe Denita would never turn to God as long as things kept going her way? Or was it that she would never turn back to him?

He'd have to sort it all out later, he realized, as Catherine had stopped talking and was apparently waiting on him for a response.

"I'm sorry. What is it you need?"

"Well, as I was saying, the president has raised some reservations about a couple of things. He knows your ex-wife is not exactly going to be an ultraconservative, especially on issues like affirmative action, civil rights, and whatnot. But he wants to make sure that there aren't any surprises on other issues that might embarrass him after he nominates her. The senator has assured the president that there's nothing in her background on issues like abortion, gun control, vouchers, and the like. Frankly, that's part of what makes her appealing. Still…we thought it might be wise to check around a little."

"So you come to the vengeful ex-husband just to make sure he's not going to throw any hand grenades?" Charles was starting to dislike this young senator's aide, though he knew she was only doing her job.

"Something like that."

"She'd make a great judge," said Charles firmly. Then he stood behind his desk, signaling that the interview was over.

Catherine stood as well, but she had obviously been around politics enough to realize he had just dodged her last question. "So you're not aware of anything in her past that might embarrass the White House or Senator Crafton?"

"She'd make a great judge," said Charles. Then he extended his hand.

Catherine shook it and looked him dead in the eye. "Sometimes, there are things that only a husband knows about," she said. "And if he's willing to keep them to himself, it's as if they never happened."

Charles felt his jaw drop as Catherine turned to let herself out. She stopped at the door, one hand on the knob. Her voice was barely audible, in part because she did not turn to look at him as she spoke. "If you ever decide to talk about it, to take it public, please, call me first."

CHAPTER 18

The inmates' dining hall had no frills. Cafeteria-style institutional food. Bolted-down gray metal tables and bolted-down, gray metal chairs. Plastic trays, utensils, and dishes. No knives. These were career criminals being fed with taxpayers' money. There was no reason to splurge.

Thomas Hammond fell in line behind the others. Feeling humiliated and lonely, he kept his eyes glued to the floor. He thought about why he was here, the fact that he would never hold Joshie again. He thought about Theresa and the kids—the looks on their faces as he was being hauled from the courtroom. Brave little Tiger being led away by a stranger. Sweet little Stinky with tears in her eyes. Theresa looking like her heart had been ripped out of her chest. And worst of all, he was powerless to stop it. The father and provider watching helplessly as the state tore his family apart.

He took his tray and pushed it down the metal slide while the jail workers heaped large portions of some unidentifiable gooey substance on his plate. They called it a casserole. Beans, corn, and a roll completed the menu. It didn't matter. He wasn't the least bit hungry.

He raised his eyes in search of an empty seat. The tables hosted a sea of angry men, devouring food and engaging in spirited conversation. Thomas didn't want to talk to anybody and wondered how long he could survive in this place. He spotted a table close to the back wall that had a few empty seats. He picked his way carefully around the men, placed his tray on the table, and sat down in an empty chair.

He bowed his head and thanked God for the food.

Thomas didn't notice that he was the only white man at the table. Not that it would have mattered to him. At the other end of the table, several African Americans were going at it, though he couldn't really understand much of what they said—their slang totally unfamiliar to him. Unfortunately, about the only words he could understand were the curse words. Everybody used them in prison, the same disgusting words, over and over, peppering every sentence. The words rained down from everywhere, battering your skull, defiling your thoughts, penetrating your brain. You couldn't escape them. They made Thomas feel dirty, like he constantly needed a shower.

He tried to shut out the vulgar language. He grabbed his fork and began picking at his food.

After a few bites of lukewarm casserole, Thomas had company. He glanced up as a large African American inmate, a buffed man with virtually no neck, a short, scruffy beard, and a gold tooth pulled out the chair across the table. During his first few hours in prison, Thomas had been warned about this guy, the shot-caller for the black inmates, a brute named Buster Jackson. "Whatever you do, stay away from him," Thomas's cellmate said. "Ain't nothin' Buster likes better than movin' on the new white fish."

Thomas noticed that Buster did not have a tray. The room suddenly became much quieter.

Thomas took a bite of the beans and gave Buster a friendly nod that didn't seem to register. Instead of acknowledging the gesture, Buster just furrowed his brow, stared, and placed his large forearms on the table. Thomas returned the stare for a moment, then went back to picking at his food.

"Hey, white boy," Buster said in a menacing growl. When Thomas looked up, Buster ran his palm across the top of the table. "This ain't your table." Then he mumbled a string of profanity, most of it directed at the stupidity of Thomas.

The dining hall quieted some more. Heads turned toward the pair of big men.

Thomas put down his fork and looked Buster in the eye—again.

"I'd appreciate if you'd watch your language," said Thomas evenly.

Buster let out a deep baritone laugh, a mocking chortle that stuck in his throat. Then he followed it with an even more vicious string of profanity, shook his head, repeated "watch your language" in disbelief. Finally he said, "Watch this, white boy," and let out a torrent of curse words and slang, some of which Thomas had never heard before.

When the language had no apparent effect, Buster narrowed his eyes and clenched his jaw. He lowered his voice, rage riding on every word. "Go eat with your people. This here table's for the brothers."

"Ain't got no people here," Thomas said slowly, never taking his eyes from the chiseled and brooding hulk sitting across from him.

Buster looked around, as if he were checking to make sure the brothers were watching. Then he leaned forward so he was half standing. "You got ten seconds," he said, "before I bust you upside your sorry head."

Thomas leaned back in his chair, crossed his arms, and studied his tormentor. The last thing Thomas wanted on his first day in the big house was a fight. He forced himself to put on a half-smile.

"Don't mean to cause no trouble," Thomas said, "but I ain't goin' nowhere. I just wanna eat my lunch in peace."

Buster spit out another derisive laugh and nodded his head, a look that said there was no further use for words, a look that showed nothing but contempt for this stubborn white country boy. Then the quick hands of Buster grabbed the edge of Thomas's tray and flipped it over into Thomas's lap—casserole, beans, corn, and milk spilling everywhere.

"Doggone it!" Thomas jumped up, covered in food and milk. Buster jumped up as well, fists at his side, ready to spring into action. Several other inmates stood and hooted, ready to enter the fray.

But Thomas just shook the food from his hands and arms, brushed it off his jumpsuit, then knelt down on the floor to pick up his tray. With his bare hands, he started scooping the food from the floor and onto the tray while Buster hovered over him. Thomas wiped the floor the best he could with his used napkin. He felt the stares of Buster and the other inmates burning into the back of his neck as he quietly cleaned up the mess.

Then he noticed the pant leg of a uniformed deputy standing next to him.

"Everything all right here?" the deputy asked.

Thomas looked up at the deputy and saw that Buster had slipped back to the other end of the table.

"Everything's fine," said Thomas. "I just had a little accident."

⊷ ⊨♦⊨ ⊶

Tiger dropped the top part of his Drumstick ice-cream cone in the sand. He frowned and looked over at the Pretty Lady. She was wearing a very small bathing suit and lying on her back on a beach towel, sunglasses on and eyes prob'ly closed. He had learned not to bother her, even about something this important. Stinky was knee-deep in the ocean and wouldn't be able to hear him even if he yelled. He was on his own and needed to take some action. Fast.

He reached down with his sandy little fingers, picked up the ice cream, and jammed it back on top of the cone. The cone portion cracked slightly but held up. Tiger glanced around to make sure nobody noticed. He had been told by his mom a hundred times that he should never eat anything that fell on the ground. He took a long lick. A little gritty but not too bad. After all, it was still ice cream.

He took another lick, then a bite. The grit was gone, so he took another big lick. Then another. And another. He grimaced and squeezed his eyes together as the pain shot through his head. *Brain freeze!* He suffered in silence, waiting for the pain to subside.

He really liked the Pretty Lady, although she needed to loosen up and live a little. She had not gone in the ocean all afternoon, and she had not helped Stinky bury Tiger up to his neck in sand nor had she helped Tiger and Stinky with their sandcastle. All she did was lie on that beach towel, put that greasy stuff on her body, and turn over once in a while.

But she was nice. After they left court earlier that day, she bought Tiger and Stinky new bathing suits, sand shovels and pails, and headed straight for the beach. She even let them get Drumsticks from the ice-cream man who wandered the beach. And she didn't make Tiger keep putting that yucky white stuff all over his body that his mom usually made him put on about every five minutes the few times that his mom actually took him to the beach. In fact, the Pretty Lady had made Tiger put that stuff on only once all day.

Tiger finished his Drumstick and got ready to rejoin Stinky in the ocean. His nose and shoulders hurt a little bit, a prickly and stinging sensation that would not go away. It was prob'ly just the heat from the scorching sun; he prob'ly just needed to cool off in the ocean again. But first, there was a small item of business that needed immediate attention.

He hated to do it, but he walked over on top of the Pretty Lady's towel and tapped on her shoulder, right next to that little picture of a ratty little girl that for some reason the Pretty Lady had drawn on her body. She leaned up on her elbows and lowered her sunglasses, looking at him.

"How was the ice cream, Tiger?"

"Good, ma'am."

"Why don't you and Hannah go build another sandcastle?" the Pretty Lady suggested as she carefully brushed the sand off her shoulder from where Tiger had touched her and off her arms and legs where Tiger had accidentally kicked up sand as he squeezed his legs together and shuffled his feet.

Tiger frowned. There was no easy way to say this.

"I've gotta go potty," he admitted after a few seconds of dancing around.

The Pretty Lady rolled her eyes. "Oh, for goodness sakes," she said. "Why didn't you go five minutes ago when we took Hannah up to the board-walk so she could go."

"I didn't have to go then," said Tiger. It sounded logical.

"Number one or number two?" asked the Pretty Lady.

Who taught her the code? Tiger wondered.

"Number one," he answered.

"That's easy," said the Pretty Lady. "Just go in the ocean."

Tiger looked down at the waves crashing against the beach and smiled. *Why hadn't he thought of that? There was a lot of water out there. And he wouldn't even have to flush.*

"Okay," said Tiger. He bent down and gave the Pretty Lady a hug. Some of the sand that had been covering his body now stuck to the Pretty Lady's oily skin. Then he sprinted toward the ocean, sand flying everywhere.

The Pretty Lady is really smart, he said to himself.

CHAPTER 19

Thomas Hammond squinted as he stepped out into the bright afternoon sun. Rec time for the inmates. The barren ground stretched before him, reflecting waves of heat like a giant uncovered oven, baking the dirt into cinders so parched and hard that it felt like concrete. Within seconds Thomas felt his jumpsuit sticking to his back, the small sweat stains under his arms fanning out and changing the color of his garment from orange to dark brown. The rec area, surrounded by a high chain-link fence topped off by twisted barbed wire, served as a stark reminder that he was now a criminal. Worms had more freedom.

The men spread out and formed their cliques. It seemed that everyone in jail belonged to some sort of gang, seeking protection in numbers, the most notorious one being led by Buster. They called themselves the Ebony Sopranos, or ES for short. One of the white fish told Thomas that the name had something to do with a television show about organized crime. Thomas didn't care. He had no desire to join any gang, especially since the whites were led by a skinhead shot-caller from the Aryan Nation.

Thomas could take care of himself.

The asphalt basketball court was the site of a game that resembled football in sneakers. There would be some dribbling, a lot of pushing, a pass or two, more shoving, then a shot, and elbows would fly. Fouls would be called and denied, loud arguments would ensue, and the game would grind to a halt.

Thomas was never much for basketball anyway.

Other inmates loitered in groups of four or five, smoking cigarettes and playing cards. No prospects there. Thomas resisted the urge to lecture them.

The only thing that remotely interested Thomas was the group of inmates working out with free weights on a slab of concrete in a far corner of the lot. Thomas checked to make sure the group was integrated—he had learned his lesson at lunch—and headed over to get some exercise. He was not used to being cooped up indoors, and didn't want to gain any more weight than necessary during his time in the big house. He already tipped the scales at nearly two-sixty, and clothes were hard to find. The last thing he needed was more girth.

The bench press was not in use, so he would start there. He hadn't lifted weights since his wrestling days in high school; he didn't need to with the exertion of his daily work. He decided to start light. He threw one forty-five-pound plate and one thirty-five-pound plate on each end of the bar. Add in the bar and you were looking at two-oh-five. He lay down on the bench and took a few deep breaths.

He found himself staring up at the glistening pecs and gleaming gold tooth of Buster Jackson. *Where did he come from?* Buster had unzipped his orange jumpsuit to the waist, and stripped it off his arms and back so it exposed the top half of his body, showcasing mountainous deltoids. His biceps and forearms were sculpted like granite and accentuated with bulging veins. His hands were on his hips.

"I was usin' that," he growled.

Without a word, Thomas sat up and looked at Buster. Thomas shook his head and rose from the bench, giving way to his tormentor.

"Need a spot?" asked Thomas.

Buster snorted. "For this?"

Then Buster reached down, slid off the thirty-fives and threw a forty-five- and a twenty-five-pound plate on each end. For good measure, he added two tens on each side, then slapped on the collars.

Three fifteen.

The big man lay down on the bench and started pumping out reps. Five...six...seven. His muscles swelled, his enormous chest heaving in and out, veins popping out on his arms, blood rushing to his head. His arms started to shake. Eight...nine...ten. He finished his last rep and slammed down the weights. He exploded up from the bench and began stretching and preening around, a combination of a peacock and Mr. Universe.

Thomas took advantage of the opening and slid under the weights. He checked his grip, took a deep breath, and pushed with all his might. To his surprise, the bar actually moved. Adrenaline stoked by anger got him through the first few reps. But his arms grew tired quickly and started trembling. The fourth rep was a strain; he felt like he would explode. Five...six... seven...eight...and then the bar stuck halfway up.

He had been arching his back, cheating a little, pushing with his eyes closed. When he opened them, still straining against the weight, he saw Buster, one hand on the bar, slowly pushing down on the doggone bar. Smiling.

The bar inched down toward Thomas's neck, Buster tipping the scales against him. It stopped momentarily, suspended there, Thomas straining with all his might, Buster leaning and smiling. Thomas felt his strength oozing out, his tired muscles losing to the combined force of gravity and steady pressure from Buster Jackson. Thomas eased up and the bar lowered until it was just inches from his throat.

Then Thomas exploded. Every ounce of strength mustered for one last desperate second. The burst of power surprised Buster, and Thomas managed to lift the bar a few inches away from his throat and chest and then quickly slid out from under it. He let the bar drop on the bench and Thomas jumped to his feet, facing Buster.

"Better get yourself a spotter next time," Buster said calmly. "Man could get himself killed."

The other weightlifters gathered around as the big men squared off. Thomas didn't speak, couldn't speak, as the anger burned away any semblance of control. He breathed heavily and stared at Buster, the air red with a growing hatred toward the man standing in front of him, mocking him.

"You got a problem, white boy?" asked Buster, playing to the crowd.

"Yeah," said Thomas. "You."

This time there would be no backing down. Both men raised their fists. Buster moved quickly on the balls of his feet, graceful movements for a big man. Thomas moved in for the kill, flat-footed.

He didn't even see it coming. The lightning quick left jab sent pain stabbing through Thomas's cheekbone, snapping his head back. Then a right caught Thomas in the ribs. He gasped and reeled backward, catching his footing.

Thomas shook his head and ignored the searing pain from his ribcage. He snorted and lurched forward, this time shielding his face with his forearms. Buster danced and smirked some more, and his quick hands found their mark again—a combination to the right eye and jaw of Thomas. The dull sound of knuckles on bone. Blood spurting from the cut above the eye. The taste of blood filling Thomas's mouth.

He lowered his head and charged again.

More blows from Buster, but this time they were deflected by Thomas's forearms. The inmates were cheering now, and the guards walked slowly toward the fight, letting the men have a little fun. Buster backpedaled, measuring, looking for another opening. He found one and landed another flurry of blows. Thomas shook them off, blood and sweat flying from his face.

And still he kept coming, moving forward while Buster shuffled back.

"Is that all you got?" mocked Thomas.

Then he lowered his shoulder and lunged, a textbook tackle driving Buster hard to the turf. Thomas's wrestling instincts took over. In a flash he had Buster in a headlock, his body wrenched at unnatural angles by the powerful legs of Thomas. A scissor hold—Thomas's best move. He pried Buster's left arm behind his back, nearly ripping it out of the socket, while Thomas's strong legs squeezed the air out of Buster's lungs.

But Buster somehow wiggled his right arm free, grabbed a ten-pound weight lying on the ground next to the men, and swung it hard toward Thomas's head.

The weight never landed. The guards, who had arrived seconds earlier, deflected the blow just before it cracked Thomas's skull. In the chaos that followed, it took three guards and four inmates to separate the two gladiators.

The two giants stood there facing each other, chests heaving, held back by the guards and fellow inmates stationed between them. Buster tried to break loose, but a few guards formed a human wall while the others grabbed his arms.

"Let go of me," demanded Buster, and for some reason even the guards holding him obeyed, though others still held their ground between Buster and Thomas.

"You gonna die," Buster sneered, bouncing on the balls of his feet, looking for a chance to charge through the peacemakers.

"You ain't so bad," replied Thomas, spitting blood to the side. "You ain't so bad."

⚬⚬ ▰◆▱ ⚬⚬

Rebecca Crawford made Officer Thrasher wait nearly ten minutes in the lobby of the commonwealth's attorney's office before she asked the receptionist to send him back. Thrasher had blown the case against the street preacher this morning—couldn't stop running his big mouth—and he had made everyone look bad. The least she could do was make him wait a little. She did the same thing with any defense lawyer who came to her office, reminding them who was in charge.

When Thrasher did swagger in and stand in front of her desk, she was disappointed not to see any signs of penance. Must have been a productive search at the Hammonds' trailer.

"What'd you find?" she asked. There would be no small talk with Thrasher; they had nothing in common.

"No drugs."

The Barracuda tried not to let the disappointment register on her face. Searching the trailer for prescription drugs had been her idea. How easy it would be to convict parents who may have gone to the doctor themselves but refused to take their child. "Not even birth-control pills or antibiotics or pain medication—"

"No drugs."

"Did you check for prescriptions?"

Thrasher gave her a nasty look that confirmed he didn't like his professionalism being questioned.

"Just making sure," the Barracuda said quickly.

"I did find a few things." He placed a small and worn color photo on the desk, the kind that fits inside a wallet. Crawford looked at the photo, then up at Thrasher. She picked it up and studied the pudgy little face. It was Joshua, she knew. He was all dressed up with shorts and suspenders, a white shirt, and a bowtie that had fallen half off. It looked like the kind of shot you might have done at a Kmart store. Joshua was grinning broadly, bunching his cheeks into puffy little balls, and causing his eyes to nearly dance off the page.

The Barracuda felt the familiar rage begin in the pit of her stomach. She felt sorry for this kid, but sorry wouldn't help her through this case. It was the anger that motivated her. The anger that would start as a bile in her gut and eventually consume her when she gave her closing argument. Juries responded to righteous indignation, not pity. And the parents deserved every ounce of the Barracuda's scorn. They had let Joshua die...sat right there and *watched* him die. But first, they had let this defenseless little boy suffer in excruciating pain.

"I didn't put that one on the inventory," said Thrasher, snapping the Barracuda out of her thoughts.

"Thanks." She placed the picture next to the black trial notebook that would eventually be its home.

"One other thing," said Thrasher, placing a small notebook with a soft leather cover on the desk in front of the Barracuda. "And we definitely inventoried this one."

Crawford gave him a quizzical look and watched his lips form a wicked little smirk.

She flipped open the well-worn notebook and started reading. It was easy to see why Thrasher was so proud of himself.

"Almost as good as finding drugs," said Thrasher.

"Almost," said the Barracuda, too engrossed in her reading to even look up.

⊷ ⊶

"Miss Nikki," Tiger yelled. "Miss Nikki!"

She grunted and rolled over in bed so she could see her digital clock. Midnight. Tiger was calling her for the third time from the guest room down the hall of her condo. She had finally dozed off in her queen-sized bed in the master bedroom.

"You're gonna drive me crazy," she said under her breath as she padded down the hall. She was trying to be patient with the little rascal. It had been an emotional night. Tiger and Hannah had gone home earlier that evening, and their mom had packed their clothes and sleeping bags for them. It was a tearful separation, with their mom waving good-bye on the front stoop of their trailer. So Nikki was trying to cut them a little slack.

But her patience was wearing thin.

"What is it *this* time?" she asked as she knelt down next to Tiger's sleeping bag on the floor.

"My back and arms hurt," whined Tiger. "Like somebody's pricking me with a bazillion needles."

Nikki put some more lotion on his sunburned little body and got him yet another drink of water. Before she left, Tiger had her check behind all the boxes stored in the room, just to make sure the bogeyman was not hiding out and biding his time. She surveyed every nook and cranny for the third time that night. There was no sign of him.

Just as she left the room, she heard it again.

"Miss Nikki," came the squeaky little voice.

"Give me a break," she whispered to nobody in particular. *"What?!"*

"Can I lay down in your room?"

It was not her idea of a restful night, but it had been a traumatic day for Tiger. And he would only be there a week.

"Oh, all right," said Nikki.

"Yippee," shrieked Tiger, bouncing up and shaking Hannah. "We're gonna get to sleep with Miss Nikki!"

The three decided that it would work best for Hannah to sleep in bed with Nikki and for Tiger to sleep on the floor in his sleeping bag. They also decided, by a vote of two-to-one, with Nikki dissenting, that they should leave the hallway light on and leave the bedroom door cracked open. Nikki felt like she was sleeping in a spotlight.

She did insist, however, that Tiger would have to save a few of his 553 questions until the morning. And so, at nearly twelve thirty, the kids stopped squirming around and settled in for the night.

Hannah cuddled closer every time she moved, and Nikki gave her a little more room each time, until Nikki was nearly falling out of her side of the bed. It was going to be a long night.

Silence, blessed silence, filled the room for all of about two minutes.

"Miss Nikki, what's that picture on your shoulder?" she heard from the squeaky little voice on the floor.

She sighed. "If I answer this last question, will you go to sleep?"

"Uh-huh."

"Okay. It's called a tattoo. And it's a picture of a little girl."

"Is it your picture?"

"No, Tiger. Now go to sleep."

Two minutes later: "Miss Nikki, have you ever been married?"

"Tiger!"

"Night, Miss Nikki," he said quickly.

"Good night, Tiger," said Nikki, a little more calmly. "And good night, Hannah."

Hannah cracked open an eye, closed it, and snuggled closer to Nikki.

"You can call me Stinky if you want to," she said.

CHAPTER 20

Theresa Hammond rose early and wandered around her trailer, feeling very much alone. She had not really slept the prior night. In fact, she could not remember the last time she had achieved deep sleep. She would doze off briefly and then jerk awake, hoping for a split second that it was all a bad dream. Then reality would rush in and more sleep would be impossible. She was on the verge of going to the pharmacy to get some sleeping pills, but she figured God was already mad enough at her as it was. Another sin would only make things worse.

She had cried herself out. She felt depleted and exhausted, a helpless spectator to the cruel events swirling around her. She wanted to take some action, do *something*. But there was nothing she could do. Just survive. One day at a time.

She wandered into the boys' room, and the memories came flooding back. She had left Joshie's stuff just like it was the day he died. The crib that had been used by all three kids when they were babies still made up in the corner of the room. Joshie's stuffed Pooh bear that was a present on his first birthday, rubbed down to a nub from loving, lay lifeless in the crib. LEGOs scattered on the floor. Joshie's favorite book of Bible stories, opened on the dresser. The dresser itself, badly in need of paint, still bulged with Joshie's hand-me-down clothes.

She reached in and grabbed the Pooh bear, hugged it close, and breathed deeply of Joshie. Without thinking, she sat down on Tiger's bed. Her heart ached as she missed her little guys. She closed her eyes, and for a moment, it seemed that she was hugging Joshie again, rocking gently back and forth on the bed, gently humming, "Jesus loves me, this I know…"

But then reality hit, and her body began to shake. There were no tears this time, just convulsions of grief and unavoidable questions. *Why are You punishing me, God? Why take Joshie? What did I do to deserve Your wrath?*

She mustered the strength to rise from the bed, preparing to leave the room. She had to get dressed and find work. With Thomas behind bars, the money from his lawncare business would stop. They had a little money in the bank, a few thousand dollars in a house fund. She could make that last a month, no more. She was determined to hire a good lawyer, a real lawyer, not the sorry court-appointed lawyer they had been assigned at the arraignment. She would work two jobs if that's what it took.

She had to get her kids back. The child protective services caseworker would be interviewing her today. She had to get her act together. *Think clearly,* she told herself, *and get this trailer cleaned.* But it was hard to do all that—it was hard to even move—when you missed the kids so much.

She missed cuddling with Joshie, and she missed the cheery disposition of Stinky. She even missed the orneriness of Tiger. She glanced at the clock on the wall of the boys' room, a baseball face with hour and minute hands. Right now Tiger was probably concocting a scheme to avoid going to school. At least she had prepared Nikki for that. Their small church school met every weekday until the second week of June. It was important that Tiger and Stinky not miss a day, even in the midst of this turmoil.

She hugged the bear tighter, and this time the tears began to flow.

＋－ ≖◆≕ －＋

"It jus' hurts really bad," claimed Tiger, clutching his stomach. He had learned through the years that tummy aches were the hardest to disprove. He was not real good at fake coughing yet, and if he claimed a fever, they would always drag out the thermometer and poke it under his tongue. Although he was not sure if the Pretty Lady even had a thermometer, he was taking no chances. There was no way to measure a tummy ache; it was his word against hers.

"Where does it hurt?" asked the Pretty Lady, as if she were a doctor.

"Right in my tummy, and I think I might frow up." Tiger knew that the prissy Pretty Lady would want no part of any throw-up action. She didn't even like sand in her stuff at the beach. He could run into the bathroom and fake it if he had to. She would never follow.

"Tiger has a lot of tummy aches on school days," announced Stinky, bouncing around and getting ready for school. "They usually get better by recess."

It was not exactly being a tattletale, but it was close enough to make Tiger mad.

"Ooh," he groaned. "It's a really bad one."

"Well, I'll tell you what," said the Pretty Lady, returning to the room with a big cooking basin. "Why don't you get up and get dressed and then see how you feel? If you have an urge to throw up in the meantime, use this basin."

Tiger glanced up at her. He had heard that line before. She was so much like his mom, it was scary. The cooking basins even looked the same. It made him wonder if maybe his mom and the Pretty Lady were sisters.

He thought he noticed the Pretty Lady wink at Stinky, and the two girls headed out of the bedroom and into the kitchen.

"I guess if you've got a bad tummy ache, you won't be wanting any breakfast," the Pretty Lady said over her shoulder.

"No ma'am," said Tiger gloomily.

He was hungry, but skipping breakfast was a small price to pay for missing school.

For the next few minutes, Tiger moaned around the bedroom, barely able to put on his clothes. He stopped a few times for effect, doubling over the basin, and faking the dry heaves. The plan seemed to be working.

But he was a little worried that the girls were ignoring him, clanging around in the kitchen and chatting up a storm.

And then it hit him. He caught his first whiff. It was almost too good to be true. Chocolate-chip pancakes! He couldn't believe his nose. He never got chocolate-chip pancakes on school mornings.

Darn the luck. The Pretty Lady *would* have to pick the one morning that he had a pretty good tummy ache routine going to cook chocolate-chip pancakes! He wondered if it was too late to fake a headache. Sometimes these pesky diseases would mysteriously float from one part of the body to another, without any warning.

Chocolate-chip pancakes. Missing school. He weighed his options. But even as he thought about it, the smell of the pancakes drifted from the kitchen and seemed to draw him down the hallway. He could always skip school tomorrow. But his tummy, in serious bad shape just a few seconds ago, was demanding that he eat breakfast—*now!*

Another miracle cure.

Just before he emerged from the hallway to announce the cure and feast on a whole pile of pancakes, he overheard Stinky reassuring the Pretty Lady in a low voice. "He'll be out in a minute. He's just a little stubborn. My mom says that he got it from my dad."

⋇⋇

Thomas Hammond carried his tray across the dining room and headed for the same table that had proven so inhospitable the day before. Buster was there, along with about ten other gang members from the Ebony Sopranos. Like yesterday, there were no whites.

This did not stop Thomas.

Thomas sat down across the table and two seats away from Buster. Thomas sat next to a thin young African American who was talking up a storm. Across from him was an older and serious-looking man who did not join in the conversation. The banter stopped momentarily as Thomas took a seat. He bowed his head and prayed.

When Thomas looked up, Buster stared in his direction, narrowed his eyes, sent his signal of disdain, then turned back to his food. The talk around Thomas resumed with a vengeance, and most of it focused on him.

"That fool is *psycho,*" said one of the brothers. "He'll get hisself whacked."

"Nobody axed him to sit here," mumbled another.

"What's your problem, man?" asked a third. "Your momma never tell you you're a white boy?"

"The boy be *lookin'* to get jacked up again," said the man sitting next to him, "and I don't want no part a that action." He picked up his tray, shook his head, and headed for the other end of the table.

One by one the section around Thomas cleared out until he was left utterly alone with his biscuits and gravy. He stared down at his food, picked up his fork, and began shoveling it in. His jaw ached from the fight, and a cracked tooth forced him to chew on one side. Buster had inflicted some damage—seven stitches just over Thomas's left eye among other things—but Thomas had not backed down. And he was not about to start backing down now. He ate his breakfast slowly and deliberately at a table reserved for African Americans, in a jail reserved for men he would never understand. Out of the corner of his eye he watched Buster and wondered what today's rec time would bring.

CHAPTER 21

The Barracuda kept him waiting for fifteen minutes. He was a scumbag. A repeat offender who had phoned from the jail this morning, anxious to snitch on his roommate. He said he wanted to meet the Barracuda without his lawyer present; he didn't trust public defenders.

She wouldn't have wasted her time, but he promised to deliver some critical evidence in a murder case against Antoine Everson, a man known on the street as A-town. It was a case where the Barracuda had some strong circumstantial evidence. She also had motive and opportunity. She knew in her gut A-town was guilty. But she still lacked two critical ingredients, and without at least one of them, she would never win this case. She needed a confession or she needed the body of the victim. This inmate promised both.

The sheriff's deputies made him cool his jets in the conference room, wearing handcuffs and leg irons. They said the dude was strong as an ox.

She entered with a tape recorder, a legal pad, and a cup of coffee. She sat down across from the big man in the orange jumpsuit scowling at her. Neither spoke. She took a sip of coffee without ever taking her eyes off him. She didn't offer him any.

She slapped the tape recorder in the middle of the table and turned it on.

"State your name," she demanded.

"Buster Jackson," he replied, contempt filling his deep voice. "What's that for? I didn't agree to no tape recorder."

Still eying Buster, the Barracuda took another sip of her coffee.

"All right," she said. "The interview between Deputy Commonwealth's Attorney Rebecca Crawford and inmate Buster Jackson terminated at 10:16." Then she reached to the middle of the table, turned off the recorder, and stood to leave.

"Wait," said Buster. "You can turn it on."

"I thought so," said the Barracuda, sitting back down and starting the tape.

"This is a meeting requested by inmate Buster Jackson," the Barracuda said while looking at the tape recorder. "He has requested that I meet him without his lawyer present. Is that right, Mr. Jackson?"

"Absolutely."

"And you waive your right to counsel at this meeting?"

"Absolutely."

"All right then, what can I do for you?"

"I want a deal," said Buster, looking over his shoulder at the guards and then lowering his voice. "I can give up Antoine Everson for waxin' that dude. I know where the body is buried. I tell you that, den you let me cop on a possession charge for time served. 'At's my deal. Take it or leave it." Buster looked proud of himself and leaned back in his chair. After a few beats he leaned forward again, remembering something. He lowered his deep voice even more to share an especially sensitive secret with the prosecutor. "I even got the lowdown on the dude's dental records." He smiled, his eyes beaming with pride. The gold tooth glittered.

"You've got to speak up for the recorder," insisted the Barracuda. "What do you mean when you say that you've got the lowdown on the dental records?"

"A-town stashed the body," said Buster, "then stole the dude's dental records and stashed them as well. Guess he figured that even if you found the body, you couldn't ID the man without no dental records."

"How clever," sneered the Barracuda. "And you want to just walk out of jail a free man so long as you tell me where the body and dental records are so I can convict Mr. Everson?"

"Yep," said Buster. "'At's my deal. Like I said, take it or leave it."

"Just like that?"

"Jus like 'at." Buster sounded tough, sure of himself, a man holding all the cards.

What a moron, thought Crawford. *This will be too easy.*

"How do I know you'd be telling the truth about the body?" the Barracuda asked, looking serious.

"He's my cellmate," replied Buster. "My homey. He trusts me."

"How sweet," said the queen of sarcasm. "Look, you've got a pair of priors, and you're looking at a pretty serious drug charge. I can't just overlook that."

She had to at least look like she was trying to cut a tough deal. Otherwise, he might get suspicious.

"Can if you wanna bust A-town for murder one," Buster said smugly.

The Barracuda thought for a very long time. She wrinkled her brow and contorted her face. She eyed Buster as he watched every nuance of her facial expressions. Then she tilted the legal pad toward her so that Buster could not see it and scribbled a note.

"When did he tell you?" a skeptical Barracuda asked at last.

"Last night."

"And he admitted to killing Reginald James and told you where the body was buried?"

"True."

"Told you point-blank that he wasted James over a drug deal and then just up and decided to tell you something he's kept secret for months—where he dumped the body?"

Buster nodded his head.

"Is that a yes?"

Buster sat up straight in his chair, indignant. "Yeah, it's a *yes!*" he insisted loudly. "Now, we got a deal or not?" He leaned forward, fire in his eyes. "I'm tired of being treated like a fool. Let's do this deal and get outta here."

The Barracuda stood up, dropping the legal pad. She leaned forward, palms on the table, and looked down at Buster. Buster tried to stand, but the deputies stepped forward, hands on his massive shoulders, forcing him back down.

"No deal," grinned the Barracuda. "You've already given me everything I need. A confession is as good as a body. Everson confessed to you, and I intend to call you as a material witness at his trial. If you refuse to testify, or if you back off on what you just told me, I'll add a perjury charge and an accomplice charge on top of your drug charge. You got that?"

She reached down and turned off the tape recorder. Buster's contemptuous smile disappeared.

"And we will stop treating you like a fool," she snarled, "when you stop acting like one."

Buster bolted up from his chair, his eyes blazing. The deputies grabbed him, one on each side, while the Barracuda returned his acid gaze. Then she reached down, picked up her tape recorder, and headed for the door. She stopped, remembering something, and turned to the deputies.

"Keep this man and Everson apart until I get a chance to talk to Everson and his lawyer," she instructed. "And find Mr. Jackson here a new cellmate."

She turned and walked through the door, leaving Buster staring at her back.

She left behind her yellow legal pad sitting on the table in plain view. On it she had scribbled: *Public defenders: Never leave home without one.*

＊＋ ≡◆≥ ＋＊

The Barracuda and the deputies took their same places in the same conference room an hour later—a few minutes before noon. But this time Buster had been replaced by A-town, and a public defender came along to level the playing field.

A-town tried to play the tough guy—slouching in his chair, chin in his hand, copping an attitude. He was a slender young black man, midtwenties, with a sinewy build and tightly coiled muscles that came from years on the street. He distinguished himself with tight cornrows in his hair, a thin wisp of a mustache over an enormous upper lip, a jutting jaw, and dark brooding eyes. He tried to intimidate the Barracuda—after all, he had some strong gang connections—but he had no success. She had seen more than her share of losers like this.

"You plead him guilty to murder one," offered the Barracuda, "and I'll agree to life with no possibility of parole. I'll drop the request for the chair."

"What kinda deal is that," scoffed A-town. His eyes became narrow slits, and his lip curled into a snarl of indignation. "I didn't kill nobody."

His public defender didn't say a word.

"No?" taunted the Barracuda. "Then you shouldn't be mouthing off to your cellmate about where the body is buried." She watched A-town closely, saw him flinch, then his jaw tightened. "Big Buster Jackson says you gave him a full confession last night, including the clever little way you stole the dental records."

The Barracuda paused, waiting for an answer that did not come. She decided to fill the silence herself.

"We've got a confession, and by tomorrow we'll have a body and matching dental records. The trifecta." She leaned forward on her elbows. "So you see, my offer's not such a bad deal, after all."

A-town cursed at her, and one of the deputies removed a stun gun from his holster. Just in case.

A smirk crossed the Barracuda's lips. "Does that mean we have a deal?" she asked the public defender. "Or do you want to try your luck on the chair?"

"I need a minute to talk with my client," he replied.

"No you don't," said A-town. Then he turned to the Barracuda. He tilted his head back so that he looked down at her, over his nose, his upper lip still curled—condescending to the end. "I'll see you in court."

"And I'll bring Buster Jackson," promised the Barracuda, "to tell the jury all about your little confession last night."

"Don't count on it," A-town snarled, his voice a hoarse whisper. "My man Buster will never rat out a brother."

CHAPTER 22

Nikki and the kids were ushered into a small booth in a prison interview room. They were separated from Thomas by bulletproof glass, and forced to speak through some small metal slits in the bottom of the glass window. Normally, family would be allowed to spend a few minutes daily with the prisoners in a supervised rec area, a deputy had explained on the way to the room, but Mr. Hammond was on restriction because of an altercation the day before. Nikki tried to pry loose the details, but the deputy didn't know much about it.

At first the kids seemed taken aback by the whole intimidating setting. The humorless deputies, the cold and forbidding rooms, the heavy metal doors. But once they both squeezed into the chair opposite their father in the booth, they began chattering excitedly, often at the same time. Nikki stood behind them, arms crossed, her lips forming a gentle smile as she took it all in.

"What happened to your face, Daddy?" asked Stinky.

Thomas rubbed his fingers gently along the stitches. "This?" he asked, as if he were surprised that anybody would notice. "It's nothin'. Just had a little accident lifting weights. It'll be all right."

Nikki gave Thomas a cynical look that he pretended not to notice. Stinky started in on a play-by-play of the beach, of Nikki's apartment, and of riding in a convertible. She endured numerous interruptions from Tiger, who explained how he slept on the floor in the Pretty Lady's bedroom just to keep the girls safe. Fifteen minutes of chatter flew by, and their time was up.

There was a brief pause, and then Tiger spoke in a subdued tone. "I want you to come home, Daddy. When are you comin' home?"

"Pretty soon," Thomas promised. "But in the meantime, Miss Nikki is in total charge. You do whatever she says. Okay?"

"Yes sir," responded Stinky enthusiastically.

Tiger didn't speak, apparently hoping that his sister's response had covered them both.

"Tiger?"

"Yes sir," he answered without enthusiasm.

"Now, let me ask y'all a question," Thomas said, looking straight at Tiger. "Did you both git ready for school this mornin' with no complainin' and no playin' hooky?"

"I did," said Stinky, her blonde curls bobbing as she nodded.

"Kinda," said Tiger.

Thomas pointed his index finger at Tiger, touching the glass with it.

"'Kinda' ain't good enough, young man. Is that understood?"

Tiger nodded vigorously. At this moment he probably wondered if the glass could really hold back his dad.

"I want you to be the first one ready tomorrow. Okay?"

"Yep."

"Yep?" repeated Thomas gruffly.

"Yes *sir*, I mean," Tiger said quickly.

Nikki glanced at her watch and cleared her throat. She hated to do this, but she had no choice.

"We gotta go, guys," she said softly.

It was painful to watch the look on Thomas's face—a father denied the most basic impulse—the ability to hug his own kids. He looked quietly at both his children, biting his bottom lip. Nikki could only see the back of Stinky's head now as she leaned forward, but she suspected the little girl was crying. And there was no telling what was going through Tiger's mind as he sat up straight, trying with all his might to look brave.

Thomas reached out with both hands and placed his massive palms on the glass. Without a word, Stinky placed her tiny hand in the same spot against the glass for one hand, and Tiger followed suit on the other. For a moment they were suspended there, pressing against the glass as if touching each other, Thomas loving on them with his eyes.

"I love you guys," said Thomas.

"I love you, Daddy," sniffed Stinky.

"I love you too," said Tiger bravely.

"C'mon guys," Nikki spoke softly but firmly from behind them. This wasn't getting any easier, and memories of her own adopted dad—their final good-bye—were not helping. Almost at once, both kids got up from the seat and buried their little heads in Nikki's embrace, one on each side.

Nikki hugged the kids, her eyes locked on Thomas.

"Thanks," he said simply. A man of few words.

"You're welcome," replied Nikki. Her attention was drawn to the stitches over his eye and the huge bruise spreading across his cheekbone. "Take care of yourself in there. It's every man for himself. Don't get in anybody else's business." She couldn't read his expression. *What had happened yesterday?* "Trust no one. I mean it."

"Don't worry about me," said Thomas.

Then Nikki took the kids by their hands and, as they glanced back over their shoulders, led them from the room.

— ≍ ✦ ≍ —

Later that day Thomas Hammond stepped into the outside rec area, determined to keep his distance from Buster and the weightlifters. It had rained earlier in the day, but now the sun was burning off the last remnants of moisture. Another hot and sticky afternoon. Another day when the jumpsuit would cling to his skin like a wet blanket.

The weightlifters were grunting and sweating on the far end of the fenced-in area, a full hundred yards away. Thomas kept to himself, hands in his pockets, hanging out and talking to no one. After a time he decided to saunter past the basketball courts and find a seat alone by the back fence.

The inmates were playing their usual game of brutal basketball, egged on by small groups hanging around the basketball court, taunting the players. As Thomas walked warily around the court, he approached a group of three young black men, huddled together, talking intensely to each other, ignoring the game. He recognized the man with his back toward Thomas as the cellmate of Buster. The cornrows, the wiry build, the animated intensity of the conversation—all characteristics of the man the inmates called A-town.

The men talking to A-town were other members of Buster's ES gang. One was short and muscular with huge arms, a v-build—thin waist, broad shoulders—and a flat, square face. According to the jailhouse talk, he was in for some drug offenses and conspiracy to commit murder. It was all somehow related to the same killing that had landed A-town behind bars.

The other man was taller and thinner, an intense and volcanic type, who was in for aggravated assault and battery, his third major offense in as many years. If convicted, he was looking at serious time. His stature among the inmates was enhanced by a huge scar running from his forehead down the length of his right cheek, the remnant of a knife fight in which the other man nearly died. The inmate claimed self-defense. Everybody in jail claimed self-defense.

Thomas veered wide of the group. He did not want any trouble, so he gave them at least fifteen feet as he walked by. Still, he heard some of the words being whispered loudly and intently by A-town. He pretended not to listen, he just kept lumbering along, but the words startled him. He felt his chest pounding, the pressure building in his head.

Something about a bench press. A-town had definitely said something about a "bench press." And "the throat." He had heard A-town say it and then saw him draw his hands toward his own throat. If that were all he heard, it would have been just another group of inmates poking fun at Thomas, retelling the events of yesterday. But there was more.

"Like yesterday." Thomas was almost sure he heard A-town repeat the phrase "like yesterday." He could make out a few other words, isolated and out of context: "snitch…just in case…stabbing." Then one of the men talking with A-town saw Thomas, shot his eyes toward A-town, and nodded his head toward Thomas. The conversation stopped.

Thoughts raced through Thomas's mind. *He was not a doggone snitch,* he reminded himself. He had the opportunity to rat out Buster on day one, and he had refused. But he had clearly alienated the African Americans. Buster hated him, and Thomas didn't know why. Now Buster's gang was plotting to do Thomas in. *How long could he last in a place like this?*

All three men turned and stared at Thomas, drilling through him with their eyes. He stared down at his feet and kept walking, no faster and no slower. He would *not* be intimidated, so he shuffled along toward the back fence. He was now more determined than ever to avoid the weightlifters.

He found a place of solitude at the far end of the rec area, then sat down and leaned against the fence, closing his eyes. He cracked them momentarily, and through the slits kept an eye on both Buster at the weight area as well as the gang of three that Thomas had caught in their little conspiracy. It did not surprise him to see, after a period of time, the three conspirators start walking slowly toward the weights. Thomas eyed them warily but felt relatively safe. The weightlifters and the threesome were more than a hundred feet away, separated from Thomas by an open field of dirt and worn-down crab grass.

Buster was holding court on the bench press. He had started at three-oh-five, done ten reps, then added weight. Nobody even thought about trying to use the bench while Buster rested before his second set. Then he pumped out three-twenty-five for eight reps and added more plates. Three-thirty-five went up five times, and Buster was glistening with sweat. He unzipped the jumpsuit and slid out of the top half, leaving it hanging around his waist. Every muscle in his chest and arms bulged and gleamed as he pumped out another three reps at three hundred forty-five pounds. By now A-town was spotting for him and talking trash. Buster strutted around, shook out his arms, added one more plate to each side, then took his place back on the bench.

Three hundred fifty-five pounds! Thomas had never seen a man bench-press that much.

A-town stood on one side of the bar. Another spotter, the man with the scar, stood on the other. The man with the v-build commenced his own trash-talking exhibition by the military press station. He had a contest going, with some money on the line, against another inmate who was equally buffed. The other weightlifters were gathered around, watching the military press contest—that is, all but Buster and his spotters who were busy on the bench.

Thomas watched unconcerned, somewhat amused by this childish display of testosterone and somewhat disappointed that he could not be among them. But he was relaxed, and the slits of light coming through his eyelids started fading to black. The intensity of the sun, and his lack of sleep in the cell, began taking their predictable toll.

He was fading in and out of fitful sleep, when nightmares of yesterday came racing back—the bench press bar on his neck, pressing down, the scowl of Buster, the laughter of A-town and the others. Thomas jerked awake and sat straight up.

It would be the perfect jailhouse killin', he realized. The big man shuddered, as the terrifying picture formed vividly in his mind. A man lying on the bench, straining against the weights, hundreds of pounds hovering just above his chest. With nobody else looking, a couple of spotters could suddenly press down on the bar and drive it into the bench presser's throat. It would snap the man's neck; kill him instantly. A knife would only be needed as backup, in case the plan went awry.

It suddenly became clear to him: Those men had been plotting Thomas's death. The big man just tried to lift too much weight, they would say. He did it without spotters, they would claim. We tried to help but got there too late.

Another accident. Another lowly inmate dead. Who would know? Who would tell? Who would care?

Thomas vowed that he would never bench-press again.

He watched as Buster grabbed the bar, testing his grip. Thomas imagined himself there, an innocent victim walking into the trap. He said a prayer of thanks that God had revealed the plans of his enemies and given him the good sense to avoid trouble. He closed his eyes again, watching through the slits.

Then he saw it! The sun reflected off its blade for just a fraction of a second. With his left hand, A-town had reached inside his jumpsuit, looked around, then removed a small black object. A flick of the wrist, a push of the button, and the blade appeared, glistening in the sun. *A switchblade!*

Lord God, have mercy. A-town had a knife! Thomas watched, still pretending to sleep, as A-town pressed it against his left leg, held it hidden in his hand, and stared down at Buster.

The words came back in a rush: *"Bench press...the throat...like yester-day...snitch...just in case...stabbing."* Thomas stood quickly and began jogging toward Buster just as the big man pressed up on the weights, his arms shaking under the load. The other weightlifters were ignoring Buster, transfixed by the military-press contest going on several feet away from the bench. A-town and the man with the scar were on each end of the bench press, their backs to Thomas, their eyes focused on their prey. Thomas could see the tragedy unfolding before his eyes. Buster lowered the bar. A-town squeezed the knife. Thomas ran faster, drew closer, then A-town and his cohort grabbed the ends of the bar and, with a sudden force, pushed hard toward Buster's neck.

Take care of yourself, Nikki had said.

Thomas sprinted; he was almost there.

Don't get involved.

All of Buster's incredible power was not enough. The weights on the bar, the fatigue of his muscles, and the sudden thrust by A-town and his ally had forced the bar down hard onto Buster's neck. The big man's scream was trapped in his throat. He still pushed with all his might, his broad back arched, but the bar pressed down tighter. Buster's face turned purple, the veins bulging and eyes popping out, his mouth open in a silent scream. Only his amazing strength in those fateful seconds kept the bar up just enough that it didn't instantly snap his neck.

Trust no one.

A few more steps. But A-town heard him coming, let go of the bar, switched the knife to his right hand, and thrust it hard toward Buster's heart.

CHAPTER 23

As A-town lunged with the knife, Thomas left his feet, landing his shoulder squarely against the middle of A-town's back. The blow nearly snapped A-town in half and drove him hard to the ground. Thomas landed on top. The jarring violence of the hit knocked the knife loose just inches before it sliced into Buster, sending it skidding across the hard turf. A dazed A-town reached out for it, but Thomas brought his elbow down with a brutal thud against the back of A-town's head, the sound of a dropped watermelon, and the smaller man was stilled.

Without thinking, Thomas reached over and grabbed the knife.

Buster, meanwhile, had managed to squirm out from under the weights. As A-town got tackled, the man with the scar had turned and momentarily released his downward pressure on the bench-press bar. That was all it took. With his last ounce of power, Buster pushed the weights off to the side, and slid himself off the bench and onto the ground.

He gasped for breath and coughed. He tried to stand and go after the man with the scar, but Buster's eyes went glassy, his legs wouldn't cooperate, and his knees buckled. He collapsed in a heap.

The crunch of Thomas's flying tackle drew attention to the bench-press area. The inmates and deputies came running over, and bedlam erupted. Everybody started arguing at once and assessing blame. The scar man accused Thomas of an unprovoked and malicious assault on A-town and Buster. Thomas had, after all, been caught red-handed with the knife.

A-town was unconscious but still breathing. The hospital would later confirm a small fracture of the skull and a closed head injury. Buster was also okay, though shaken, and it fell to him to describe what had happened.

"Who attacked you?" the guard asked.

The glassy eyes of Buster moved from Thomas to A-town to the man with the scar and then back to Thomas.

Trust no one, Nikki had said. *I mean it.*

Buster's eyes narrowed, a flash of venom returned, and he pointed a thick index finger straight at Thomas.

—— ≡✦≡ ——

Against her better judgment, Nikki was getting emotionally involved. How could she not? It was her own childhood all over again. Every day with Tiger and Stinky brought back memories of the sweet man who had adopted her and nurtured her through some of the best years of her life.

She knew Judge Silverman had set her up. He had stuck her with these kids like some warped attempt at social engineering, to somehow complete the circle—so she could give herself to them, at least temporarily, the way her adopted dad had given himself to her. She did it because she had no choice and, truth be told, out of some strange sense of duty. Payback time. She really did it for her father.

She didn't know that the kids would steal her heart. Sure, they were a pain. But they were also a lot of fun. They had only been with her two days, and already she was dreading the loneliness of the condo without them.

It was now late Thursday afternoon. The hearing next Wednesday would be crucial. Judge Silverman would read the report from the Child Protective Services caseworker, then make a ruling on custody. Either Theresa would win back custody of her kids pending trial, or they would be sent to a foster home. Nikki had already decided that a foster home was not an option. The kids had been through enough. If Silverman couldn't see his way clear to return these poor little rug rats to their mother, then they would stay with Nikki for the foreseeable future.

She hoped they liked Chinese takeout.

And that is why, though she was not officially part of the defense team, Nikki found herself standing at the desk of the clerk of court and looking at the Hammond file. Tiger and Stinky were running around in the hallway, probably riding the escalators. Nikki's experienced fingers leafed through the perfunctory legal pleadings and stopped with the good stuff.

She started with the probable cause affidavit. This document had undoubtedly been drafted by the Barracuda, signed by a police officer, and submitted to a magistrate. They used it to justify their search of the Hammonds' home. The magistrate had, in fact, authorized the search—they always do. But that's not what interested Nikki. She read the affidavit to get a glimpse of the commonwealth's case: the witnesses the prosecutors intended to rely on and the evidence they intended to submit.

According to the affidavit of the investigating officer, the medical examiner had determined that the cause of death was peritonitis and septic shock occasioned by an acute case of appendicitis. It was a condition that was seldom fatal in small children if properly treated. The affidavit also contained details of the officer's conversation with the treating physician: Dr. Sean Armistead. Nikki read the paragraphs describing the anticipated testimony of Dr. Armistead twice, then blew out a long breath. Pretty strong stuff. She put the file down and stared into space. "It all comes down to Armistead," she mumbled.

Then she carried the file over to one of the computer terminals in the clerk's office and ran a quick records check on the doctor. The computer turned up no criminal cases, but it did register two civil cases. They both appeared to be medical malpractice actions involving Armistead as a defendant as well as various other doctors. Both cases had been closed out more than three years ago.

Nikki hailed the clerk again and talked her into retrieving the two Armistead civil files. The first one contained little substance, a standard malpractice case that had been settled quickly. But the second file proved more fertile. Another malpractice case, but this one involved a young child who had presented with what appeared to be a simple ear infection—otitis media. Armistead checked the child, had her monitored by a physician's assistant for a little while, then discharged the girl with a prescription for antibiotics. But Armistead had apparently missed the diagnosis. The child was brought back to the emergency room two days later in acute distress. Armistead, who was again working the ER, first tried to treat her at Tidewater General and belatedly decided to transfer her to Norfolk Children's. The child died during transit. It turned out that the child had leukemia, and the plaintiff's attorney contended that Armistead had missed several indications of a blood disorder in the initial visit. Unlike the other case, this one had been extensively litigated.

The plaintiff's lawyer who filed the suit had taken the deposition of Dr. Armistead. The deposition itself was not in the court file, which did not surprise Nikki, since attorneys typically did not file depositions with the court. But the plaintiff's attorney would have a copy, and he happened to owe Nikki a few favors.

She was on her cell phone instantly.

"Law offices of Mr. Smith."

"Is Mr. Smith in?"

"No ma'am. He's in court. Can I take a message?"

"Is he really in court?" Nikki asked. She knew the runaround.

"Of course," said the snippy receptionist. "He's been in court all day."

"Well, then tell him that Nikki Moreno called with a promising new case I just picked up on my police scanner. Tell him I thought it looked every bit as promising as the Harris case that I hustled for him, but unfortunately, this victim needed a lawyer right away—"

"Can you hang on for a second?" the receptionist interrupted. "This might be him now."

There was a brief pause on the phone. Then, "He just walked in, Ms. Moreno," she said chirpily. "He'd be delighted to take your call."

"It must be my lucky day."

By the end of the conversation, attorney Smith had promised to send Nikki a copy of the Armistead deposition. Smith didn't remember much about the case, except that Armistead was arrogant and defensive at his deposition. It had not been a pleasant day.

"By the way," said Nikki, as she prepared to sign off, "how was your day in court?"

"About as fulfilling as that new case you promised my receptionist," said Smith.

They both laughed and ended the call.

There was one more item that Nikki needed to check before she returned the court files to the clerk and went looking for her little terrors in the hallway.

She thumbed through a few more documents and found what she was looking for—the inventory list from the search of the Hammonds' trailer. For some strange reason, she had a bad feeling about this.

She forced herself to look down at the page, read the single item on the list, and frowned. The police would never have seized it if it didn't contain damaging evidence.

It was not, of course, presently in the file. The Barracuda would have it locked up somewhere in an evidence closet. Nikki jotted a note reminding herself to visit the commonwealth's attorney's office and look at it. But she wouldn't really need the note. The single entry was already seared into her memory, causing her to speculate wildly.

The Prayer Journal of Theresa Hammond, it said.

Thomas Hammond couldn't believe his eyes. He had risked his life for Buster Jackson, and this was the thanks he received? If Thomas hadn't put himself in harm's way, if he hadn't tackled A-town and taken him out, Buster would be a dead man. And now the man who owed every breath he took to Thomas was standing there gasping for air, sucking in the precious oxygen, and pointing directly at Thomas in response to the question of who had caused the attack.

Thomas would have said something in protest, but he immediately realized that he had no defense. A-town, the instigator of this mess, was lying on the ground unconscious. Buster, the same man who had tried to choke Thomas yesterday, had just been nearly strangled to death with the bench-press bar. And the most likely man to be seeking revenge, Thomas himself, was standing there with a switchblade in his hand.

"That man," coughed Buster, as he pointed at Thomas and tried hard to catch his breath, "saved my life."

"And that man," he turned his accusatory stare and big index finger on the fallen A-town, "tried to kill me."

Thomas slowly exhaled and dropped the knife. "Thank You, Lord," was all he could think to say.

On the ride back to Nikki's apartment, the questions started flying.

"Why is my daddy in jail?" Tiger wanted to know.

Nikki hesitated for a beat. This was sensitive, and she wanted to choose her words wisely.

"Because some people are confused and think he did something wrong and ought to spend some time in jail for punishment."

"What did he do wrong?" Tiger pressed.

"It's kind of complicated," said Nikki, again speaking slowly and reassuringly. She didn't know how much to say, but sooner or later they would figure it out, so she might as well be the one to break it to them. "When we get a chance to tell the judge in the big courtroom what really happened, I think they'll let your daddy out of jail. But some people think it's his fault that Joshie died."

"That's not true!" exclaimed Tiger. "It wasn't my dad's fault that Joshie got sick. And besides, my daddy took him to the hopsicle."

"I know, Tiger. That's what we'll tell the judge."

They drove on in silence for a few minutes while Tiger and Stinky appeared to be deep in thought.

"I miss Joshie," Tiger said at last. His voice quivered.

Before Nikki could respond, Stinky's motherly instincts kicked in. "I miss him too, Tiger. But he's in heaven now, and we'll see him again someday," she said reassuringly. "Right, Miss Nikki?"

"Um, sure," Nikki said.

"Did the police take Daddy away?" asked the little boy in the backseat with a million questions.

"Yes, they did."

"Are the police good guys or bad guys?"

"They're good guys," said Nikki. *At least some are,* she thought.

"Then why did they take him away?"

To a woman with more scruples this would have been a tough question. But Nikki answered it without hesitation.

"They were just following orders, Tiger. Doing what they were told."

"Who gave the orders?" he asked, just like Nikki knew he would.

"That mean lawyer lady you met in court the other day," Nikki responded, glancing at Tiger in the rearview mirror.

He stuck out his lips, lowered his eyebrows, and wrinkled his forehead.

"I *knew* it," he said. "I just knew it."

* * *

Even the stubbornness of Thomas Hammond had its limits. Those limits were reached as he loaded up his tray for Thursday-night dinner and looked around the crowded mess hall. There were a few extra seats at Buster's table, generated by the absence of A-town and his boys from the general inmate population. But tonight Thomas would steer clear of that trouble. He had seen enough of Buster for one day. It was time to start taking Nikki's advice. *Every man for himself.*

Thomas headed to his left and took an empty chair at a table of white boys, on the opposite side of the dining hall from Buster. As usual, Thomas found a seat where nobody occupied the chairs next to him or across from him. Amid the din of the mess hall, he was looking forward to eating alone.

He bowed his head and whispered a prayer.

"Thank You, Lord, for this food and for protecting me during rec time today. Thank You that Buster was not kilt. And I just wanna pray for the young man with the knife, that You will heal him and not allow him to suffer long from the blow I gave him to the back of the head. Forgive me for my sins. Keep Theresa and the kids safe and give them Your strength. And, if it's Your will, please get me outta here as soon as possible. Amen."

When he looked up, the seat across from him was no longer empty.

"This seat taken?" asked Buster. He had already placed his tray down.

And he was not scowling.

"It is now," said Thomas.

Buster pulled out the chair and took a seat. "Thanks," he said.

Thomas nodded, then attacked his food. For the rest of dinner, the two huge men ate in silence.

CHAPTER 24

Charles couldn't believe how nervous he felt. He hadn't seen Denita in what, six months, maybe more? They hadn't been alone together in nearly two years. But still, he had lived with her for three years, fought with her for four. Why should meeting with her now make him so ill at ease?

He glanced at his watch for the third time in the last five minutes, knowing how conspicuous he looked in the Grate Steak restaurant sitting alone at a table for two on a Friday night. She had insisted on driving from Richmond to Norfolk for the meeting. *Probably so she wouldn't be seen by anybody she knew,* thought Charles.

Thirty-five minutes late. She had called ten minutes ago. "I'll be there in a few minutes," she said. "Sorry. Some things came up."

"No problem."

So here he sat. Ten minutes later and still no Denita. He would punish her with silence when she finally came.

"Sorry I'm late," said a sweet voice behind him. He recognized the potent mixture of White Diamonds perfume and Vidal Sassoon shampoo immediately, the smell alone bringing a rush of emotions. Before he could respond she kissed him lightly on the cheek. "Thanks for meeting with me."

How'd she do that? he wondered. He had been keeping one eye on the entrance the whole time and still she had managed to get behind him. Vintage Denita. One step ahead.

"Thanks for driving all this way," Charles said as he half stood and watched her slide gracefully into her seat. "You look great."

"You look good yourself."

Though she had put on a few pounds since the last time they met, Charles was immediately reminded of why he had fallen for her in the first place. She had a handsome face: a strong jaw line, long forehead, smoldering brown eyes, and long ebony hair. She had braided her hair tonight and pulled it away from her face, the way Charles used to tell her he liked it. A simple but stylish black skirt and white blouse gave her a dignified, professional look.

She had an athletic build and stood five-ten without heels. "You would make a great basketball player," Charles used to say, though she would just scoff at the notion. "I'm tall and I'm black, so I must like basketball and chicken," she'd reply. And after watching her shoot around once, resembling something like Bambi on roller skates, Charles learned to drop the subject of Denita and basketball. Still, for the three years of their marriage, he harbored secret thoughts of making great little basketball babies—a whole team of future LeBron James superstars.

All this and a hundred more thoughts and memories, some good, others dark, flashed through Charles's mind during the first few seconds of small talk and nervous gazing at the woman he had once loved more than anything in the world. After a few minutes of catching up, a waiter arrived and took their orders. Denita, always counting calories, went for the fresh salmon—at a steak place!—and Charles ordered a twelve-ounce T-bone. After the waiter disappeared Denita mustered the courage to talk about the one thing they had both been working so hard not to mention.

"Thanks for calling me after Catherine Godfrey's visit."

"It's the least I could do." Charles paused and tried to inject some enthusiasm into his voice. "Congratulations."

"Thanks." Denita took a sip of iced tea that Charles had ordered for her even before she arrived. She set the glass down carefully and fixed her gaze on the table, avoiding eye contact. Charles couldn't remember when he had seen her this nervous. "And thanks again for meeting with me," she added. "I didn't want to talk about this over the phone."

He nodded, though she still wasn't looking at him.

"Charles, I don't know how to start…how to say this. So I've got to ask you to just hear me out. Let me stumble around a little. Okay?"

She looked up at him with sad eyes. He had braced himself for a lot of emotions tonight—anger, frustration, even a rekindled emotional attraction. But he had not expected the sympathy he now felt. Denita had never been one to cast herself in the role of a victim.

"Sure."

She leaned forward, reached her hand out, and laid it partway across the table. Was it an invitation? a natural gesture? manipulation? Charles's instincts told him to reach out, hold her hand, lean forward, and smell the White Diamonds while the last four years melted away—but he willed himself to sit back. What he had to say would not be easy under the best of circumstances. No sense making it tougher.

"Maybe I didn't try hard enough, Charles. I don't know." A pause. A sigh. "But you changed so much...so fast. All that God talk and pressure about coming to Christ and everything. I guess I just freaked." Denita scratched lightly at the tablecloth with her long fingernails, then withdrew the hand. Another sip of tea. "I mean, it was like, 'Who's this religious freak and what did he do with my Charles?'"

Charles stared without emotion. He kept his voice low and even. "We've been through this, Denita. I can't change who I am."

"I know, and I'm not asking you to." She looked into the distance for a moment, collecting her thoughts. "Charles, it just seemed like all of a sudden you didn't care about anything but the church and...well, getting me saved."

"You're the one who filed, Denita." For divorce, he meant. The words came out colder than he intended.

"I know," she admitted quickly. Too quickly, in Charles's opinion. He knew she wanted something and would say whatever was necessary tonight, even if it meant eating a little crow. "I didn't come here to fight, Charles. And I know I can't undo what's happened."

"Then what do you want, Denita? Why *did* you come here?"

She sucked in a breath. "I want this appointment to the bench, Charles. More than I've ever wanted anything in my life. It's what we dreamed about in law school—making a difference, standing up for those who can't stand up for themselves. I've put in my time defending corporate America. It's time to get back to my roots, give back to my people."

As she talked, Charles swallowed his rising frustration. He wanted to laugh at the idealism flashing in her eyes, shake her by the shoulders. *Can't you see what you're saying? I sold out, Charles. But when I get the power I lusted for, I'll use it to defend those less fortunate. Forget the fact that I had to trample the less fortunate to get here.*

Denita had always been the master at insinuation. She could make her point without ever really saying it and then deny that's what she meant. But there could be no mistaking the point she was making now. She wanted to be a judge. And Charles was the one person who knew the one secret that could keep her from that dream.

Somehow, Denita had overlooked an obvious flaw in her theory.

"Catherine Godfrey knows, Denita. And I didn't tell her."

Charles expected to see Denita's face register shock, just as he had done when Godfrey had dropped the bomb on him. Instead, Denita just gave him that smug little smile that he had learned to detest years ago.

"All she knows, Charles, is what I told her. And all I told her is that there might be one skeleton in my closet…but it's a skeleton that only my ex-husband knows about. I didn't tell her what that secret was, and she didn't ask."

At this, Charles experienced a sense of momentary relief—*our dark secret is safe*—followed by the increased weight of a new burden. It was like he had traded in a small backpack for a boulder that someone had now strapped to his back. "And as long as I keep my mouth shut, you'll get your chance…is that it?"

She narrowed her eyes and studied him. "I'm asking you to honor the confidentiality that is part of being husband and wife. If the tables were turned, I'd do the same for you."

"You can't ask me to lie, Denita."

"You won't have to. There are some things that will never be asked."

She had this all figured out, he realized. An answer for almost everything. But not quite *everything*. She still needed her ex-husband to be an accomplice. She still needed him to promise his silence.

"Denita, you may find this hard to believe"—he lowered his voice until it was almost a whisper—"but I still care about you." Her eyes showed her skepticism, though he meant every word. "But there are principles at stake here. Important principles. Biblical principles. How can I stay silent and just deny everything I believe?"

Denita did not hesitate, did not even blink. She had probably rehearsed this answer the entire two-hour drive, Charles thought. She even managed a weak little smile. "That's my Charles," she said. "Never wrong. Never in doubt." Then she leaned forward, and her eyes drilled into him. Now she was all business. "People change, Charles. Even without getting all religious like you, people still change. What I did was wrong, but I've changed. You've got to trust me on this. Let me prove it to you."

For this moment he had steeled himself. In truth, he could have scripted this whole evening—the braids, the perfume, the soft apologies, the subtle attempts at flirtation followed by an appeal to sympathy and his duty as a husband—it was all part of a careful plan to persuade him. Denita Masterson—always the temptress, always the lawyer, always the potter who could mold Charles like wet clay.

But not tonight.

"I've got to think about it," he said.

Denita pulled back and shook her head. "You think I'm just trying to play you, don't you?"

He shrugged. Why deny it? She could see right through him.

She stood. "You don't understand me at all. Never did." Charles saw the anger rising in her face, the tight lines that had become so familiar a few years ago. "I've got nothing to bargain with. No weapons, Charles... This is your dream come true."

"Denita..." He stood and reached out to gently touch her arm, trying to calm her down.

She pulled the arm away, not roughly, but decisively. She kept her voice low. "I mean it, Charles. My whole future's in your hands. You can crush me if you want. It's totally up to you." She paused long enough to throw fire with her eyes. "Just make sure you can live with yourself afterward."

Then she turned and left the restaurant, even before the waiter returned with her salmon. He would now have two meals to deal with, and he was no longer hungry.

You can crush me if you want to. Just make sure you can live with yourself afterward.

CHAPTER 25

By 10:00 a.m. on Saturday morning Rebecca Crawford had already been at the office for two hours. Before coming in, she had worked out, rushed through some relaxation techniques a counselor once showed her, squeezed into a black pantsuit—the blasted pants kept getting smaller—then grabbed a granola bar and a cup of coffee at a convenience store.

She made two calls from her cell phone on the way. One went to a junior prosecutor and another to an investigator. Both could have waited, but she wanted to make a point. Her Saturday morning calls were legendary among those who wandered the halls of justice. The workaholic never rested, they said. She didn't want to let them down.

She had downed most of her third cup of coffee before the child psychiatrist joined her in the cramped conference room.

Dr. Isabell Byrd was a kind and spirited woman who had gone to bat for the Barracuda before. Juries liked Byrd. She was small and thin, spunky, and quirky enough to keep things interesting. She had married into the Byrd name, but it seemed to fit her perfectly—a little busybody hummingbird. Isabell had short gray hair and sharp little features with a pointy birdlike nose, half-moon glasses, and inquisitive eyes that darted everywhere. She had seen more than her share of abuse cases during her twenty-eight years of practice, and she was willing to say whatever needed to be said to put the bad guys away.

"Good morning, Isabell. Want some coffee?"

"No thanks. Already had my one cup. What have we got this morning?"

For the next half-hour the Barracuda explained her case, her suspicions, and her strategies. They would be interviewing the Hammond children today. Based on the interviews, Judge Silverman would soon decide whether to allow these kids to stay with their mother pending trial. It would, of course, be disastrous if that happened. The mom would undoubtedly try to sway their trial testimony, and the kids would be in danger of further abuse. It would be Byrd's job, explained the Barracuda, to write an independent report after she watched the interviews to explain why the kids should not be allowed to live with their mom pending trial.

Not surprisingly, the Barracuda had some ideas that might be helpful. She had dealt with a few of these religious fundamentalists in the past. She had been studying up on her Bible stories and had an idea that might at least get the little boy talking. Dr. Byrd would have to watch closely during this process for the telltale, sometimes hidden psychological signs of abuse. Dr. Byrd nodded grimly in agreement.

The Barracuda couldn't disguise the fact that she was brimming with anticipation and intensity. This was no ordinary case. She was counting on Dr. Byrd. "You're the best in the business at detecting abuse, Isabell. Even if kids can hide it from the other docs, they can't hide it from you."

Dr. Byrd assured the Barracuda she was up to the task.

And then she decided she might have another cup of coffee after all.

━┄ ▰◆▰ ┄━

Round two of Tiger versus the Barracuda got off to a rough start. It commenced with a shouting match between Nikki and the Barracuda about whether Nikki should be allowed to sit through the interview. Tiger was traumatized by all the yelling and more determined than ever to defend his mommy and daddy.

"I'm the special advocate for these kids, and I'm entitled to be part of these interviews!" Miss Nikki insisted. She was about two inches away from the Mean Lady's face and yelling at nearly full volume.

"This interview will form part of the report from the Department of Child Protective Services," the Mean Lady responded. She was not hollering quite as loud, but she was definitely holding her ground. "The department mandated that Dr. Byrd and I do the interview. Not you. We've got our procedures…"

"Let me tell you what you can do with your procedures," huffed Miss Nikki.

"Look here, lady," now the Mean Lady was poking a finger at Miss Nikki. Muscles were tensed, jaws jutting straight out. "If you don't want me to call the sheriff and have you thrown out, I suggest you take a seat…outside the conference room."

The women stood there, toe to toe, neither backing down. Tiger looked up at them, wide-eyed, his mouth gaping open.

There could be a fight, he thought, *and I bet Miss Nikki can take her.*

But much to Tiger's great disappointment, there would be no fight.

"You disgust me," said Miss Nikki. "You and your power trips." Then she snorted at the Mean Lady and knelt down next to Tiger and Stinky.

"You guys go on in there and answer any questions this lady might ask," Miss Nikki told them. "She won't hurt you. She's just got a few questions about your mom and dad."

"I'd like to talk to the little boy first," said the Mean Lady.

Figures, thought Tiger.

"Okay, Tiger," said Miss Nikki, still kneeling so she could look him in the eye. "You go ahead and take your turn first. Tell the truth. And don't worry, she's not that bad."

Yeah, right.

"Yes ma'am," he said.

⊷ ⊷⊰⊱ ⊶

After proper introductions, Tiger climbed into a big cushy seat at a long table with a glass top. There were three other people in the room, all adults. There was the Mean Lady, a smaller lady who looked like somebody's grandma—she said her name was Dr. Byrd—and then some strange man operating a video camera.

Tiger decided to show right off the bat that he wasn't scared. So he propped both elbows on the table, then plopped his chin in both hands. *I'm bored,* he was telling the adults. But if the truth were known, he *was* a little excited about being on camera.

The Mean Lady spoke first.

"We're just going to ask you a few questions about your mom and dad and Joshua," she said softly. "You just answer them the best you can. Okay?"

Tiger nodded his head, keeping it in his hands. Joe Cool.

"Before we start," continued the Mean Lady, "do you have any questions for me?"

Tiger always had a few questions.

"Is that thing on?" he asked, pointing to the camera.

"Not yet," said the Mean Lady. "After we get done practicing a few questions, then we'll turn it on so the camera can record everything you say. Because what you say is very important."

"Why is your hair two different colors?" asked Tiger. He assumed it was still open season for questions.

"We'll talk about that later," said the Mean Lady, her face darkening. "But first, let me ask *you* a few questions."

"Okay," said Tiger, shrugging.

"Your mommy and daddy, they're very religious. Aren't they, Tiger?"

Tiger scrunched up his face, thinking hard.

"I mean they're very strong Christians. Aren't they, Tiger? They have a lot of faith in God?"

"Oh, yes ma'am."

"Have you ever heard the story about Abraham and Isaac, Tiger?"

"Yes ma'am. My daddy tells it to me."

"Did you know that Abraham had so much faith in God that Abraham was willing to sacrifice, or kill, his own son, Isaac, if that was what God wanted?"

"Yes ma'am. But he didn't have to. God sent a goat instead."

"That's right," the Mean Lady smiled. "But Abraham was willing to do what God told him, even if it meant that his son might die. And it took several days of walking up the mountain, thinking that Isaac was going to die, before God sent the goat. Does that make sense?"

Tiger nodded.

"Just like for your mom and dad, they knew that according to what the church said, they were not supposed to take Joshie to a doctor. Is that right?"

"I guess so," said Tiger.

"And it would take a lot of faith if Joshie was really sick for your parents to stick by what they believe, just like Abraham did, and not take Joshie to the hospital for three or four days, even if it meant that Joshie might die. In fact, I'll bet your parents waited three or four days, just like Abraham waited three or four days. Didn't they, buddy?"

Tiger squirmed. He really couldn't remember. But he knew his daddy loved Abraham. And he was sure his own daddy wouldn't be outdone by a Bible character, even if it was a Bible hero like Abraham.

"I think it was five," said Tiger.

"Wow, your parents really are strong Christians," said the Mean Lady, looking pleased. "I think we're ready to start the camera now. John Paul, you're really doing good."

The red light on the camera came on. Tiger sat up straight in his seat, put on his best serious face, and started answering every one of the Mean Lady's serious questions.

In the first ten minutes, Tiger painted a heroic picture of his parents and their unshakeable faith, describing how they refused to take little Joshie to the "hopsicle" for five days, even though everyone knew he was dying. After racking his little brain, Tiger was quite sure that he could even remember his dad once saying that if Abraham could do it, he could do it too. With each answer, Tiger would talk a little faster and longer, making sure he occasionally smiled at the camera for all those folks out there in television land.

Eventually the Mean Lady moved off the issue of Joshie's death and started asking some other strange questions.

"Do you ever have any nightmares?" she asked.

"Sometimes," admitted Tiger. "But when I do, my daddy comes in and lays down wif me."

For the first time in the interview, the gray-haired lady sat up, eyeballed the Mean Lady, and started asking questions herself.

"Did you say your daddy would lie down in bed with you?" asked the gray-haired lady.

"Yes ma'am," Tiger said proudly, happy to brag on his daddy. "All the time."

"What would he be wearing, and what would you be wearing?"

That seemed like a really strange question to Tiger. And it also seemed like none of her business. But he decided to play along—after he gave her a dirty look.

"I was wearing my jammies; he was wearing his underwear."

This appeared to make the gray-haired lady even more concerned. She wrinkled her brow and shook her head slowly.

"I know this may be hard to talk about," she said very softly, like she was telling a big secret, "but did he ever take his underwear off?"

"Not in my bed," said Tiger, insulted.

The concern did not disappear from the troubled face of the gray-haired lady. One question led to another, and before long Tiger was hopelessly confused.

Then, to Tiger's way of thinking, an incredibly strange thing happened. The gray-haired lady wanted to play dolls! She pulled five dolls out of her little bag—funny-looking dolls with no clothes on, with their private parts showing. The lady suggested that each doll could represent a family member, one for Daddy, one for Mommy, one for Tiger, one for Stinky, and one for Joshie. Then she said that Tiger could show her what happened in their family by playing with the dolls.

Not in a gazillion years, thought Tiger. He folded his arms across his chest. He was done smiling for the camera. *This is stupid!*

"I don't play with dolls," he said firmly.

But the ladies insisted over and over, and it didn't look like he would ever get out of that room if he didn't humor them.

Finally, he picked up one of the dolls.

"That's it, honey," crooned the gray-haired lady. "You just picked up Tiger. What is Tiger thinking?"

"That he would like to put his clothes back on," said Tiger, without smiling.

"I see," said the lady.

Then it occurred to Tiger—a way out. He could pretend they were not dolls but Power Rangers. He could show these women a thing or two about playing. He would ignore the fact that the dolls didn't have any clothes on and pretend they were fully clothed Power Rangers, armed to the teeth and ready for combat.

It was time to cut loose. It was time for war.

"Bam," said Tiger. "This guy smashes this one."

CHAPTER 26

To shake off visions of his wife, Charles Arnold immersed himself in legal research. But he didn't like what he was finding. He had been researching for three straight hours, and his eyes kept coming back to the same case: *Whren v. United States*, decided in 1996 by the Supreme Court. The majority opinion was written by none other than Justice Antonin Scalia, no friend of criminal defendants. The *Whren* case would not make it easy to punch Buster Jackson's get-out-of-jail-free card.

There were copies of court cases and law review articles scattered all over Charles's desk in his small office at the law school. They joined two empty soda cans, a cold half-cup of coffee, and a fat constitutional law textbook opened and highlighted. On one wall hung framed certificates and diplomas, on the other a Nerf basketball hoop. Charles hadn't taken a shot in half an hour. The case staring at him from his computer monitor had drained his enthusiasm. He had a feeling that he would be hearing a lot about *Whren v. United States* at Buster's suppression hearing.

It seems that poor Mr. Whren had been driving in a "high drug area" of the District of Columbia in a Pathfinder truck with tinted windows and a temporary license plate. Whren was sitting at a stop sign for about twenty seconds when a police car, passing from the other direction, did a U-turn and pulled up behind him. That caused Whren, who was obviously not the sharpest tool in the shed, to gun the engine, turn suddenly to the right, and take off at an "unreasonable" speed.

The police officer pulled Whren over at the next traffic light and approached his car. As he did so he noticed two large plastic bags of crack cocaine in plain sight in Whren's greedy little paw. Whren was arrested and "large quantities of illegal drugs" were seized.

Whren's clever defense attorney claimed that the stop and arrest violated the Fourth Amendment guarantee against unreasonable search and seizure because the stop was motivated by racial profiling as opposed to any real traffic violations. Besides, said the lawyer, the use of automobiles was so heavily regulated that it was "nearly impossible" to comply with all motor-vehicle laws, thereby creating unlimited opportunities for the police to use traffic violations as nothing more than a pretext for stopping black males just because they were black.

Justice Scalia was having none of it. The great defender of law and order grudgingly conceded that the Constitution prohibited "selective enforcement of the law based on considerations such as race." *That's big of you,* thought Charles. But then Scalia promptly gutted that principle by declaring that a decision to stop a vehicle is justifiable when the police have reasonable cause to believe a traffic violation has occurred or reasonable suspicion to believe that some other crime has occurred. Most important, Scalia rejected the notion that the actual motives of the police officers themselves made any difference. "We flatly dismiss the idea that an ulterior motive might serve to strip the agents of their legal justification for making such a stop," he wrote.

In other words, even if Buster had been pulled over by Mark Fuhrman or by Hitler himself, if they had a reasonable suspicion for stopping Buster, it would not matter one iota how racist their motives were. Charles's work was thus cut out for him. He would have to demonstrate that there was no reasonable suspicion that Buster had committed a crime. He would have to prove that Buster's only offense was that he happened to be a black man cruising in a Cadillac Escalade SUV with tinted windows in a predominantly white area of Virginia Beach. Sure, Buster had given some young punks a brief ride around the block. Some young *black* punks. But that was no traffic offense, and that didn't make him a drug runner.

If what Buster said was true—and that was a big if—this was racial profiling, pure and simple. Buster had done one thing, and one thing only, that had resulted in his arrest. It was an action that could not constitutionally justify an arrest, because it was an action that Buster really couldn't do anything about. It was not the tinted windows. It was not the nice car he was driving. It was not even the fact that he had given a few kids a ride around the block. It was certainly not a traffic violation, for Buster had been driving like a nun.

Buster had been pulled over, searched, and eventually busted for one reason and one reason only. Buster had been *driving while black.*

Easy to say, but because of Scalia's Supreme Court opinion, it would be nearly impossible to prove. How could Charles show that the police had unfairly stopped Buster while white motorists with tinted windows were free to cruise to their heart's content? How could he show that if Buster had been white, he would have been able to pick up a couple of kids and give them a ride around the block without harassment? In other cases, judges talked about statistical proof. But it was hollow talk, because police officers didn't keep records of who they stopped or who they didn't stop based on race. They only kept records of who they charged. Thanks to the *Whren* case, proving racial profiling by statistics would be incredibly difficult and maybe impossible.

And even if he *could* prove it, did he really *want* to? A pang of guilt hit him, then another. He felt guilty for representing Buster, for trying to spring a man who was guilty as charged and ought to be spending the next decade making license plates. Then he felt guilty for feeling guilty. Defense lawyers don't think that way, he told himself. *He* couldn't think that way. He was not the judge; he was Buster's advocate. It was his job to make sure the state could prove its case and could do so without violating the Constitution. Still, the guilt lingered, getting a man like Buster off…

Then another thought hit him. Right there between pages 65 and 66 of Scalia's opinion, which he was now reading for the fifth time. It was the thought of a defense lawyer, something Johnnie Cochran himself would have been proud of. He could turn this into a class project. He could set up his own experiment. Atlantic Avenue could be his laboratory; his students could be the guinea pigs. He could test whether Buster had been pulled because of his race and whether Anglos would be pulled for doing the same thing. And he would do it without ever once trying to get into the motives of the individual officers involved.

He would create his own statistics. If this *was* racial profiling, if Buster had been pulled for simply *driving while black,* Charles would get to the bottom of it. Charles would prove it. He had just figured out how.

And not even Scalia could stand in his way.

CHAPTER 27

The Virginia Beach City Jail brought back lots of memories for Charles Arnold—all of them bad. The slamming of the heavy metal doors, the smell of body odor, the dour looks of the guards, the absence of sunlight, and the pervasive dingy yellow haze of the fluorescent lights as he went deeper into the bowels of the place. It all came rushing back, reminding him of why he never wanted to return.

They escorted him past the cells, ignoring the catcalls of the men who had nowhere to go and nobody to see on another Saturday night. They took him to a small rectangular room with block walls, no windows, and a few dozen plastic chairs. About half the chairs were already occupied by slumping prisoners with surly looks—men who were sending every signal that they would rather be somewhere else, anywhere else, than in a Bible study in a jail on a Saturday night.

Charles did a quick visual survey of the room. All blacks with the exception of one burly white man, middle-aged, clutching a well-worn Bible in his large paw. Charles recognized him from court. It was the guy whose son had died for lack of medical treatment. None of the other men had Bibles or anything to write with or on. There was no chatter going on when Charles entered the room, just a show-me attitude as all eyes turned toward him. His buddy Buster stood in the back, leaning against the wall with his arms folded, as if he were guarding this brooding bunch against defectors.

Charles knew what had happened. Buster had turned out his posse against their collective will and probably under threat of force, and none of them were happy about it. Truth be known, even Buster probably would rather be elsewhere, but he undoubtedly saw Charles as his ticket to freedom and knew better than to alienate his lawyer. The white guy, on the other hand, was presumably here of his own volition. The only voluntary member of the bunch.

"They're all yours," said the guard with as much disdain as possible. He opened the door to leave. "I'll be back in an hour."

Charles passed out Bibles and made some introductions. He showed the men how to find the book of Luke and had them turn to the story of the crucifixion of Christ. He turned to the white man, who said his name was Thomas, and asked him to read the story of the two thieves crucified with Christ.

"Why don't you start reading in chapter twenty-three, verses thirty-nine through forty-three. And the rest of you men follow along."

The big man grunted his approval and started in. His voice was slow and halting as he pounded out the words with great difficulty.

"And one of the malefactors which were hanged railed on him"—*railed* became *righ'-eld*, the King's English, mispronounced with a southern drawl—"saying, If thou be Christ, save thyself and us—"

"Yo...yo... Hold up, man," one of the other prisoners interrupted. "Where's that mess in my Bible?"

"Yeah, bro, you doggin' us? What Bible you readin' from?"

A few others murmured simultaneously. The railroad picked up steam, and all the brothers jumped on the white boy's case.

"All right, hold on," said Charles loudly. "Thomas is just readin' out of a different version. He's got the *King James Version*. That's an old English language version. And I gave the rest of you the *New International Version*."

Now Thomas's eyes went wide. "They ain't usin' the *King James?*"

"No," replied Charles. "I thought they'd understand the NIV better."

Thomas furrowed his brow and looked around the room at his errant brethren. "It ain't authorized," he announced to them. "Only one version's authorized." He held his well-worn Bible aloft. "The *King James.*"

"That's just a white man's book," said one of the brothers. "A cracker's Bible."

"You want *authorized*," another brother said the word mockingly, with a tilting of his head. Then he stood up and gave Thomas an obscene gesture. "Authorize *this.*"

The blacks all laughed.

"What do you know about the versions of the Bible?" asked Thomas. "The *King James* is the *only* version with no translation mistakes."

A collective groan went up from the others, all instant Bible critics. And thus was born the first theological debate of the Virginia Beach Jail Bible study: the *King James*–only debate. It blew hot and cold for about five minutes, with opinions running against the *King James Version* by a margin of about twelve to one. But the one was a stubborn one, and he had some information that was hard to dispute.

"So King James sent a couple hundred scribes back to their monasteries to work independently on a translation of the Bible into English. And guess what? They all came back with *exactly*—I said *exactly*—the same translation, word for word. Now, was God in that or what?"

"Translated it from what?" asked a brother.

Charles just smiled and let the debate play itself out. At least the men were engaged, no longer slouched down in a picture of apathy. After a while Charles suggested a compromise. Thomas would read each verse first from the *King James Version*, since that was the earliest translation. Then one of the others would read from the NIV. Then Buster would translate the verse into street slang. This seemed to satisfy everyone, and he had their attention as they turned back to the story of the crucified thieves.

Thomas performed his part with great gusto and authority, emphasizing every *thee* and *thou* in the King's English. After another literate inmate provided a stilted reading from the NIV, Buster relished his role as the street translator and drew more than his share of laughs and critics.

It seemed like a circus, but they all got the gist. Two thieves had been crucified, one on either side of Christ. One of the thieves blasphemed Christ, "dissed" him in the words of Buster, saying, according to the NIV, "Aren't you the Christ? Save yourself and us!" The other thief was repentant, asking Christ: "Jesus, remember me when you come into your kingdom." Jesus responded to him, in the translation used by Thomas: "Verily I say unto thee," which, as translated by Buster meant, "This is straight up from yo momma," and assured the thief that he would be with Christ in paradise, or His "crib," that very day.

Having survived the reading of Scripture, Charles took control to drive home some points. The boys had had their fun, now it was time to get serious. He paced and preached for twenty minutes without eliciting a single amen or even a grunt of approval. The inmates stared past him with cold and hooded eyes, slouched down in their chairs again like this was the most ridiculous stuff they'd ever heard. Occasionally, one of the men would challenge Charles.

"What if he didn't do it?" one man muttered, referring to the thief who cursed at Christ with his final breath.

"Yeah, maybe he got set up."

"Maybe," said Charles. "Just like maybe some of the men in this room didn't do anything wrong to get here. It's all your mama's fault for the way she raised you, or the hood you grew up in, or the drugs that made you crazy..." He stopped, paused, and looked from one inmate to the other. "Get real."

A few of the men grunted and slouched lower in their chairs. Their defiant stares betrayed the hatred that ran deep behind their eyes. Charles was defending the white man's system and making no friends. He decided to focus on the love of God that saved the repentant thief just minutes before he died.

"This thief shows that you can't work your way into heaven—that you don't *need* to work your way into heaven," Charles exhorted. "This thief confesses to Christ one minute, and a few minutes later he's with Christ in paradise. Now I guarantee that man didn't have much chance to climb down from the cross and do good works."

From the looks on their faces, his point was lost on these men. Not many of them were apparently planning on working their way to heaven anyway. The mercy of God, the good works of men, it was all one huge yawn to this gang. They were apparently present only because their shot-caller, for some reason unfathomable to them, made everybody come.

Charles glanced at his watch and decided to wrap it up.

"There is a concept in the law called a 'dying declaration.' It's a statement made just before you die, when you know that you're drawing your last breath. It works as a corollary to the hearsay rule. Any of you jailhouse lawyers know how this concept of a dying declaration works?"

He looked around the room at the blank and scowling faces. Some of these guys probably spent a lot of time in the law library, trying to figure out new angles for their cases. Some of them would know more about the law than the lawyers who would be charged to defend them. But not one of them claimed to know anything about a dying declaration.

"You know what hearsay is, right?"

A few inmates nodded; the rest stubbornly refused to acknowledge the question. Charles the professor had some teaching to do.

"A statement made by somebody else outside of court cannot be repeated by somebody in court, even if they heard the statement. In other words—no gossip. A witness on the stand has to testify about what he saw, not about what someone else told him. Does that make sense?"

The same few heads nodded.

"And hearsay is not admissible because the person who made the statement is not in court and cannot be cross-examined to test the reliability of the statement. But there is one type of hearsay that is always admissible—anybody care to guess what it is?"

"A dying declaration?" guessed Thomas.

"This man's a genius," responded the professor, trying to encourage a little more class participation. "A dying declaration is admissible into evidence—and here's why. People don't usually lie when they know they are going to die the next moment. They are getting ready to meet their Maker and generally have very little incentive to shade the truth. So if you hear somebody make a statement just before he dies, you can come into court and testify about what that person said even though technically it might be hearsay.

"Which brings us back to these two thieves," continued Charles. "These two thieves each made a dying declaration. One accepted Christ as Savior and Lord, and when God the Father judges this man in the courts of heaven, that dying declaration will save him. The other rejected Christ. And when the Father opens the books of judgment in heaven, that dying declaration will damn him to eternity separated from God."

Charles paused for dramatic effect, stopped pacing, and lowered his voice.

"Now," Charles asked, "which thief are you? Because we're all thieves, brothers. The only question is what type."

He let the accusation linger. Then, as if on cue, a guard came busting through the door. "It's time," he said gruffly.

"We're about done. Can we finish?" asked Charles. "You might want to stick around for this part yourself."

"I said *it's time,*" the guard responded with terse authority, staring at Charles with an air of cockiness that comes from never being challenged. "Something about that you don't understand?"

The eyes of the inmates, which just a few minutes earlier had been glued to the floor or some distant spot on the wall, were now focused on Charles. The boys hated the guards, and they longed for someone to put the guards in their place, someone who the guards could not retaliate against. Charles felt the dynamics, the men coming psychologically to his side, but he also knew that he needed to be a role model, to preserve his integrity.

"Oh, I understand it just fine," Charles said. "So I guess the men and I better close out in prayer."

"Just make it quick."

Charles immediately began a lengthy and solemn prayer. He knew the guard probably had his eyes open, as would most of the inmates, but this did not stop Charles from praying for the souls of the men in the room with great passion. He prayed for their salvation, he prayed for justice in their cases, and he prayed for changed lifestyles once they were released. In a part of the prayer that probably infuriated the guard but greatly pleased the inmates, he also prayed for the souls of the guards. He prayed that God would help them understand that they were sinners too, just like these inmates, that there was no difference in God's eyes and that they also needed to repent. He ended his prayer by praying that the guards would be merciful and just and that God would cause revival in the jail.

When Charles concluded his prayer, it was punctuated by more than a few amens from the prisoners. Despite the growing impatience of the guard, Charles went around the room and shook hands with each man before leaving. Many of them promised to be back next week or said a simple, "Thanks, Rev."

When he reached the back of the room where Buster stood, the big man put his arm around Charles's shoulder and turned his body so they were both facing the wall away from the other inmates. Charles felt Buster's enormous bicep and forearm resting across his neck, and the steel grip of Buster's fingers on the outside of his shoulder. He was glad this man was his friend.

"Straight up," Buster whispered. "How's it look?"

"We've got a motion to suppress hearing a week from Wednesday," Charles said in hushed tones. "I won't lie. It's gonna be a tough one."

"Okay, bro." Buster squeezed the shoulder. It hurt.

"Let's go," barked the guard. "Or this will be the last one of these things you have."

This set off a round of critiques from the brothers.

"Loosen up."

"Give the rev a break."

"Chill."

Charles locked on Buster's eyes. "See you next week?" Charles asked.

Buster stuck out his lips and gave a slight nod of approval. "Ain't goin' nowhere else," he said, "till a week from Wednesday." He patted Charles on the shoulder, hard enough to get his point across, then donned the dangerous smile of an organized crime boss.

Charles left with the uneasy feeling that he had just been delivered an ultimatum. It would be hard to forget the hooded eyes and the gold-toothed smile of the shot-caller for the Ebony Sopranos.

CHAPTER 28

Charles stopped at a restaurant on the way home from the Bible study. He was still trying to shake his vision of Buster. "Table for one?" asked the hostess.

"Yeah."

She led him to a table with two seats surrounded by tables occupied by families, couples, and friends. As far as Charles could tell, he was the only person eating alone.

The place smelled of day-old grease and too-strong coffee. The table was sticky, so he kept his elbows in his lap.

His concerns about Buster soon faded. After all, the man was safely behind bars. He would only be getting out if Charles sprang him, in which case Buster would be totally indebted to Charles. The more important thing was the spiritual state of those men he had left behind. Hopeless. Dangerous. Lost.

Nearly ten minutes passed before a waitress with a pierced tongue finally ventured by to take his order. He ordered a pile of strawberry French toast with a side of hash browns. A Mountain Dew to drink. Then he pulled out his CD player, donned his headphones, and waited for his meal.

Somewhere between Kirk Franklin's first and second song, just about the time Charles drained the last few drops of his first Dew, he totally lost his appetite. It wasn't the music—Denita would never listen to Christian songs. And it certainly wasn't the restaurant. To his knowledge, Denita had never set foot in this kind of restaurant. But suddenly her memory came back so powerfully that he didn't quite dare reach out his hand and see if she might be real.

It was as if Denita came and sat down across from him, just as she did four years ago, in a different restaurant, a month after the big fight, a month after he had left their home for good. He wondered now, as he wondered then, how she had ever found him.

Her mournful eyes, brimming with tears, still drew him in. Though she had wounded him so deeply he could never heal, she still held sway over him. She had him four years ago. She had him tonight.

"There's no easy way to say this," her words came out velvety soft, almost like a song. He didn't respond, just waited an eternity while she drew her next breath. "There's someone else, Charles." The air left his lungs again tonight, the same way it had four years ago. "He understands me. Loves me. We're going to spend our lives together. I'm filing for divorce."

Charles rubbed his face as Denita laid the papers on the table. He remembered four years ago how he had tried to talk her out of it. Though he had walked out on her the previous month, he still wasn't ready to give up on *them*. They just needed more time to think...counseling...anything. She had listened patiently, said she didn't want to hurt him, but this was the only way. He remembered vividly how painful it was to stare at her back as she walked out the door, the feeling of loneliness descending like a fog.

And even now, at unpredictable times, the fog would descend again, bringing a ghost of Denita back into his life and reopening painful wounds. But this night he would have no chance to talk Denita out of it. For when he blinked, she was gone, the fog slowly clearing again, and the beautiful face of his wife replaced by the chubby smile of the waitress with the pierced tongue.

"You want another Dew?' she asked.

"No. I'm fine," lied Charles. "I'll just drink water." Then he stared at the back of the waitress as she turned and walked away.

It was nearly eight o'clock on Saturday night, and Erica Armistead had been sleeping most of the day. She had planned on getting outside, planting a few flowers, and running to the grocery store. But the Parkinson's had not cooperated. The disease seemed to know when she had plans and would strike with unrelenting fury on those days.

She had gotten up early, but the disease put her back down. The tremors and stiffness had been particularly bad today, probably because she was so stressed out. On her good days she would try to walk off the stiffness. On her bad days she would shuffle from one prop to the next, leaning on furniture, against the wall, or sometimes on the arm of a friend. It had been that kind of day. She felt like she was shriveling up, like a super slow-motion replica of the witch in *The Wizard of Oz*—doused with water and shrinking into nothingness.

Sean had left for work today without saying good-bye. He had left her in the family room, dozing in and out while watching another movie on the Lifetime channel. The medication she took—levodopa—made her incredibly sleepy and would sometimes create a sudden freezing, a brief inability to move at all. She wondered if the side effects of the medication were worse than just letting the disease progress.

She was determined that the disease would not steal her entire day. She would carry through on the plans she had made for the evening. She had rested, watched television, and eaten this afternoon. Sean had called and said he would be working a "double"—a second shift immediately following his first one. The second shift would start at eleven, and Erica would surprise him. She would take him something to eat, nothing fancy or heavy, just something special to get him through the night. It would be a show of her appreciation, her love for the long hours he consistently put in for the two of them. It would be a statement that not even the disease, on one of its most horrific days, could keep her from thinking about him.

She was losing him; she knew that. But this would be a start. And it would be worth the effort. This marriage, no matter how imperfect, was all that she had left. There would be no kids and no career. There was only Sean, and tonight she would begin the long process of winning him back.

She made it through the shower by steadying herself against the tile wall. She even shaved her legs, though there was no earthly reason to do so. When she stepped out of the long, hot shower, she felt better. And she felt clean.

She would go casual, jeans and a pullover—the blue one that Sean said matched her eyes. A few minutes with the blow dryer to get the hair ready. Then the makeup. It had been awhile. A little foundation brought the color back. Blue eye shadow, blush, mascara, and a light gloss on the lips. The wrinkles and the crow's-feet near the eyes remained but were minimized. They showed character. She was a woman of character.

And she was ready. In fact, she had not felt this ready in weeks, maybe months. She would surprise Sean, and he would love it.

With trembling hands she grabbed the keys to her Lexus, picked up her car phone and purse, and shuffled out to the garage. On her way to the hospital she made two stops: one for a warm cinnamon roll at a late-night deli she and Sean had frequented before the disease, and a second at a Barnes & Noble for a specially flavored Colombian cappuccino that Sean absolutely loved. Thus prepared, and with near-perfect timing, Erica Armistead pulled into the hospital parking lot at precisely 11:00 p.m., just in time for the start of Dr. Sean Armistead's second shift. She held her hand out before getting out of the car and noticed with pride that it was barely trembling. Getting out like this—surprising Sean—had done her more good than a megadose of levodopa.

She climbed stiffly out of her car, imagining the look of surprise on her husband's face.

She had parked in the handicapped spot—the only good thing to come out of the disease—and was grabbing the coffee and roll when she happened to look over the hood of her car toward the emergency room. Sean, big as life, was walking through the automatic doors, talking to another person—a woman—and removing his white lab coat. Something stopped Erica from just calling out. Maybe it was the intensity of the conversation. Maybe it was just a sixth sense. But instead of calling to him, instead of taking her bounty to him, she slowly settled back into the front seat of her Lexus and watched him walk across the shadows of the parking lot.

Sean and the woman parted ways. *Good! What a relief! Then why is my heart still racing? Why am I feeling nauseous? Why don't I trust this man I've been married to for nearly eleven years? He probably found out he doesn't have to work a double after all. He probably didn't want to call and wake me. He's probably just heading home.*

She was sure Sean hadn't seen her. She was also sure that for some reason—she really didn't understand why—she needed to follow him. She had a bad feeling about this, a premonition that comes from living with someone all that time. Perhaps it was woman's intuition, perhaps it was just paranoia.

Whatever it was, when Dr. Sean Armistead pulled out of the Tidewater General Hospital parking lot at a few minutes after eleven, he was discreetly followed at a distance of about fifty yards by his own wife.

She hung back, two or three cars behind him, as he pulled onto Interstate 264 and headed toward the beach. Several miles later, the interstate ended at a T intersection with Atlantic Avenue. Still a few cars behind, Erica hung a left, following Sean as he merged into the throngs of vehicles cruising the beach. She had been delayed at the turn onto Atlantic, and several more vehicles had inserted themselves between husband and wife. She was now about seven cars back and having a tough time keeping him in sight. She was also exhausted. And mad.

He turned into a small parking lot on the side of a large ten-story beachfront condo building. On the bottom floor was a T-shirt shop, a taffy place, and a bar—The Beach Grill. Erica turned in as well, now cruising no more than fifty feet back in the same parking lot, looking for a spot like her husband. *Why do I feel so guilty? I'm not doing anything wrong. He's the one who's sneaking around.*

Maybe he's just meeting a few of his buddies for a drink before he comes home. Maybe I should just leave. Why can't I bring myself to trust him?

Sean found a spot, and Erica kept cruising. She pulled over at the end of one of the rows, far enough away so he wouldn't see her. She watched as he got out of his car and walked toward the bar. Her heart dropped. A quick look around by Sean—a guilty glance just to make sure no one was watching. She had married this man, lived with him eleven years, and knew his look of guilt. She had just seen it.

She waited for him to go inside and then found an empty parking spot. She walked along the shadows of the building as she headed for the front door. The stiffness in her legs intensified, making her slump forward a little more. But something inside propelled her toward the door. She had to know. She had to answer these unbearable doubts.

She walked inside the front door, feeling vulnerable as her eyes adjusted to the darkness. It was a typical beach bar thronged with people on a bustling Saturday night. A second-rate band played in the far corner. The side of the bar toward the ocean opened onto a patio area with an overhang, and patrons were spilling out toward the boardwalk. The place pulsated with people and the relentless beat of the music. They lined up two-deep at the bar, the first row on stools, the second standing behind them and ordering drinks. There were couples and groups of women gyrating on the dance floor. And at the booths lining the walls there were more couples—some trying to talk, others all over each other—oblivious to the masses around them.

She should be one of them, Erica thought. At her age, she should still be dancing and drinking and catching men's eyes even as she clung to the arm of her husband. Instead, she felt like a grandmother at a college frat party. She straightened her back as much as she could but kept her head low. Slow movements would keep her from limping. *Don't grimace,* she reminded herself.

Erica wove her way through the crowd, small and hesitant steps like a frail old lady, wondering what she would do if she saw him. She found a spot near one of the corners, shielded by the broad shoulders of a young male on the prowl. She steadied herself and glanced around the place, booth by booth, then the dance floor, then the outside tables near the boardwalk. She finally saw him, his back toward her, sitting at one of the patio tables, his chair pulled snugly next to a woman, his arm draped comfortably over her shoulder.

The two of them ignored the band and the people around them, talking comfortably, their legs propped up together on another chair at their table. She felt sick as she watched the woman take a sip of her drink, then rest her head comfortably on Sean's shoulder. They sat there, a picturesque couple staring out at the ocean, and Erica's stomach began to churn unmercifully.

Her shield—the broad-shouldered student—moved, exposing her to this couple if they should turn around. She didn't care. She just stood there for what seemed like forever—was it five minutes, ten, fifteen?—watching her husband share his heart with a woman she had never seen before. Erica was transfixed—hurt, sick, boiling, betrayed—all the passions of the heart engulfing her at once. She wanted to cry but was too stunned for tears. It was the openness of it, not just the betrayal itself, but the open flaunting of the wedding vows that hurt the most. When the feelings settled out, she was angry, pure and simple. And that anger gave her a sense of courage she had not known before. A courage to stay and face the truth.

Then, suddenly, the woman stood and stretched. She turned and glanced toward the band, then toward the bar. She had looked, just for a second, directly at Erica. *Or had she?* The seducer turned back around, leaned down and gave Sean a kiss. *A kiss! On the lips!* And then she headed right toward Erica.

Embarrassed, ashamed, angry, and scared, Erica turned and shuffled quickly toward the door. Her hands shook as she navigated her way from one object to the next. She bumped into a man, almost spilling his beer. As she approached the front door, she glanced over her shoulder just in time to see the woman turn for the ladies' room. But in that instant, the split second when the woman passed under one of the dim lights and headed down the hallway, Erica got a perfect look at her profile.

She looked to be midthirties, nice looking but not a knockout. She had short, layered blonde hair (probably bleached), a dark tan, narrow eyes, and full crimson-red lips. She had the serious look of a career woman on a mission.

It was a look and a face that Erica would never forget.

She felt her anger boiling over, her stomach catching fire. She lost her focus on the seductress and things went into a spin. She had to get out of this place and get some air. She had to get home.

She staggered to her car and sat there in silence, her eyes closed, while she waited for her head to clear. After a few minutes she knew it wasn't going to get much better. She could make it. She would have to. With trembling hands—the hands she had learned to hate—she dumped the cappuccino on the ground, put the cinnamon roll right behind the front tire, then started the car, put it in reverse, and backed out of her parking space.

A few minutes later, after she reached the interstate, the tears began to flow.

CHAPTER 29

In Nikki's humble but informed opinion, this hearing was not Harry Pursifull's finest hour. He had arrived fifteen minutes late, causing Judge Silverman to "drop the hearing down half an hour" while he tended to other matters.

When Harry did show up, he looked even more disheveled than usual. Due to a relentless breeze outside, Harry's greasy hair, which he parted just above the ear and then threw over the top of his balding pate, had come unglued from the top of his head and hung in greasy strands well below his left ear. To fix this, Harry would self-consciously reach up and smear the hair back into place. It fell back down a few minutes later. Adding to the effect, Harry's shirt was unbuttoned around the neck, and his plaid suit coat appeared to have shrunk even since the last time he wore it. His pants, as always, were too small at the waist and too short in the inseam. He had pulled his belt tight, too tight, and formed his round little body into the shape a balloon takes when someone squeezes his hands around it, causing parts of the balloon to bulge out in all directions.

Harry had a hard time finding the thin Hammond case file in his overstuffed briefcase, and he had not read the report from the Child Protective Services caseworker. Nikki tried to fill him in on the details before Judge Silverman called the case, but Harry was no quick study. "I'll just wing it," he told Nikki.

And wing it he did.

Once the hearing started, the Barracuda strutted and preened around the courtroom, making all manner of accusation against Thomas and Theresa Hammond, which Harry made no effort to rebut. Thomas himself took it all in stride, sitting stoically at the defense counsel table adorned in his standard-issue orange jumpsuit. Theresa sat next to him, much more emotionally involved in the proceedings, her body language revealing her deep distress at the accusations the Barracuda flung her way. She would lean over and whisper vigorously into Thomas's ear, and he would calm her down with a nod of understanding or a word of comfort.

Mercifully, the kids had stayed in school. Nikki knew it wouldn't help for them to witness this fiasco.

The Barracuda submitted the Child Protective Services report and carefully built her case through her examination of Dr. Isabell Byrd. Throughout Byrd's testimony, Harry employed his classic bump-on-the-log strategy, not making any objections despite repeated urgings from Nikki, who positioned herself directly behind him.

"That's ridiculous," Nikki would whisper, loud enough for Harry to hear. "Don't let her get away with that! *Object*, for goodness sake!"

But all of this running commentary was lost on Harry, who showed an amazing ability not to be motivated by his clients or Nikki or even angered by the Barracuda's cheap shots. Harry just sat there like a rock, immobile and uninspired.

"Dr. Byrd, were your opinions regarding the unfit nature of Mr. Hammond as a father reinforced by the events of these last several days in the Virginia Beach City Jail?" the Barracuda asked.

"Oh yes, they were," chirped the witness.

"In what way?"

"Well, according to information I obtained from my interviews with jail personnel, Mr. Hammond has been in at least two serious fights since being incarcerated just a few days ago." Dr. Byrd spoke rapidly, wringing her hands as she talked. "This is consistent with the opinions I formed from interviewing the children—that Mr. Hammond has difficulty controlling his temper and that he physically abused the children when his anger got out of control."

Nikki glanced from the rounded back of Harry—the man was barely breathing—to the back of Thomas Hammond. She saw the color rising in Thomas's neck; his ears seemed to be on fire. *I even warned him! How dumb is this man? "Don't get involved in anyone else's business," I told him. "Take care of yourself; trust no one." Instead, the big man apparently decides to turn the jail into his own private boxing ring. Maybe he deserves this.*

But the kids sure don't.

"And did your interviews with the children tell you anything further about the fitness of either parent to maintain custody pending trial?" asked the Barracuda.

"Yes, they did."

The Barracuda lifted her eyebrows and motioned with her hands, prompting the witness to continue.

"Well, Your Honor," said Dr. Byrd, turning her attention away from the defendants and looking directly at the judge. "There is some evidence that indicates possible sexual abuse."

A gasp went up from Theresa Hammond. Even Thomas seemed startled by this accusation.

"I'm not prepared at this point to say such abuse *has* occurred," clarified the doctor, "but I would not risk putting the children back in that type of environment."

"What's the basis for your suspicion?" asked Silverman. He leaned forward, deep ruts of concern lining his forehead.

"The little boy, John Paul, said that his father would frequently come into his bedroom in the middle of the night and lie down with him. This caused my initial concern. I could tell the young man was very nervous and intimidated when he tried to talk about this, so I gave him some anatomically correct dolls to play with. We then role-played with them, involving him, his sister, and his parents. Judge, he described the types of activities that I see time and time again described by children of abusive parents. The larger dolls, the parents, would fight with and harm the smaller dolls, and so on."

"Did he describe any sexual activity?" asked Silverman skeptically.

"Not at that time," said the witness. "But it is not unusual for children to suppress that type of information, even when using the dolls as proxies, until much later in the process. I first have to develop a higher level of trust with this child. That's why I said I'm concerned, but it's not conclusive."

Silverman leaned back in his chair and gazed toward the back wall. "Okay," he said at last. "Anything else?"

"One further question," responded the Barracuda. "Do you have an opinion, Doctor, as to whether leaving these kids in the custody of their mother might impact the ability of the commonwealth to get a fair trial in this case?"

"Oh yes, that's a major problem. You see, leaving the kids in the mother's custody pending trial is a bad solution for two reasons. First, it's my understanding that Theresa Hammond will have to work full-time to support the household so long as her husband is in prison. So putting the children in her custody really means putting them in the custody of a day-care center as soon as school is out for the summer.

"And second, I'm concerned about the effect this would have on their trial testimony. Theresa Hammond is only human. By living with her pending trial, the kids would be influenced by her recollection of the events surrounding Joshua's death and by her subtle influences concerning what their own recollections should be. It's inevitable. I'm not saying that Mrs. Hammond would do this intentionally, I'm just saying that it's bound to happen."

"Thank you, Dr. Byrd, that's all I have. Please answer any questions from Mr. Pursifull."

"Nothing at this point, Yer Honor," Harry said without standing. He leaned over to whisper in the ear of Thomas Hammond. Nikki slid forward so she could hear.

"Her testimony wasn't too bad," Harry bragged. "Sometimes when you cross-examine an expert as sharp as her, it just makes things worse."

Thomas Hammond didn't respond.

"Does defense counsel have any witnesses?" asked Silverman. It seemed more of a plea than a question.

Harry at least expended the energy to stand this time. "Not at this time, Yer Honor," he said confidently.

"All right then," sighed Silverman, "if we are done hearing evidence. I'll entertain arguments from both counsel. Ms. Crawford, why don't we start with you?"

For the next twenty minutes, the Barracuda laid out a powerful argument. Nikki fumed as she listened to the distortions, half-truths, and hyperbole that flowed so freely from the prosecutor's mouth. And somewhere in the midst of that compelling argument, with Harry Pursifull sitting silently by and her blood running hot with anger at the hypocrisy and manipulations of this woman with the mesmerizing lips, Nikki decided to take a *very* personal interest in this case. Nikki herself would look after these kids, these little monsters who had stolen her heart. Nikki would get a lawyer for the parents, a *real* lawyer, who would give the Barracuda more than she bargained for. She would love to see her own boss, Brad Carson, defend this case, but she knew he was busy with high-paying personal-injury clients and didn't have the time. But Nikki did have some other ideas. On her own time and free of charge, she would investigate this case and mastermind the defense.

After he heard the arguments of the lawyers, Judge Silverman ruled that the children would not be returned to their parents pending trial. He said he didn't have much choice based on the evidence presented. But Nikki was determined that the kids not be sent to a foster home, and so she surprised everyone, including herself, by volunteering to take care of them until the trial was over.

Silverman stared at her for a moment, as if caught off guard by this request, though Nikki was pretty sure he had actually anticipated it. Slowly his expression changed as he turned to the Barracuda.

"Ms. Crawford," he said, "do you mind if I recall Dr. Byrd to the stand for a few questions of my own?"

"No, Your Honor," the Barracuda said suspiciously. Her tone of voice and contorted facial expression turned it into more of a question than an answer.

Silverman pretended not to notice and focused on a somewhat nervous Dr. Byrd, who slowly climbed back into the witness chair.

"Is it fair to say that every time the caregiver for these children is changed, it represents major trauma in their lives?" asked the judge.

The witness fidgeted. "Yes sir."

"And that can be particularly damaging to the psyche of a child when the caregiver is changed in the middle of other traumatic circumstances in their lives, like having their father placed in jail?"

"Yes, that's also true."

"And based on your visits with the children, do you have any reason to believe that Ms. Moreno, their current guardian, is not providing quality care or will somehow bias their testimony in this case?"

The witness fidgeted again; it seemed she just couldn't get comfortable in her chair. She looked at the Barracuda for help. As if by instinct, the Barracuda stood to object, but then apparently remembered that these were the questions of a judge, not an adversary. As quickly as she rose, the Barracuda sat back down.

"I have not investigated Ms. Moreno. But I have no reason to believe that she wouldn't provide excellent care for these children pending trial. However, I would note, that if the parents are convicted, then the children would be forced to change caregivers once again, and that would be at a particularly tough time in their young lives."

Judge Silverman scowled at the witness after this little piece of volunteered information. "How about if we cross that bridge when we come to it and in the meantime give the parents the benefit of the presumption of innocence."

"Very well," said the chastised doctor.

"Then based on the testimony from the commonwealth's expert," announced Silverman, "I will order that the children remain in the guardianship of Ms. Nikki Moreno pending trial." Silverman turned to the witness. "Thank you, Doctor."

Dr. Byrd slinked off the witness stand and took a seat next to the Barracuda. The Barracuda ignored her.

"Now, Counsel, let's pick a date for a preliminary hearing and for a trial."

The Barracuda jumped to her feet again. She undoubtedly wanted to look ready to prosecute the case immediately, content in the knowledge that Harry would stall until well after the fall elections. "The commonwealth is ready to try this case on the first available date."

This time Harry left his seat like a rocket. "Not so fast," he exclaimed. "There are witnesses to prepare, investigations to conduct, all that kind of stuff. We'll need at least…" Harry pulled out his pocket Day-Timer. He studied it and made a few faces and guttural noises, like he was trying to decide which important cases could be bumped or delayed in favor of this one. "At least six months."

"*What!*" The word came from Harry's own client, the stoic Thomas Hammond, who had not said a word all morning. He articulated Nikki's thoughts exactly.

"You may want to confer with your client," suggested Silverman.

Nikki watched the heated and hushed discussion between lawyer and client with amusement. There was loud whispering, which grew louder, and a folding of arms by Thomas. Finally, reluctantly, Harry stood back up and announced their joint decision.

"We want the first date possible for the preliminary hearing," he said, "and the first date after that for trial."

Calendars came flying out and negotiations between the court, the commonwealth, and Harry Pursifull began in earnest. The Barracuda was not about to back down, especially with the press present, and Harry didn't have any choice, not with Thomas listening carefully to every word. So when Judge Silverman suggested a preliminary hearing the following Wednesday, with a trial to commence exactly three weeks later, neither of the lawyers objected.

This schedule will work havoc on my tan, thought Nikki, as she prepared to break the news to the children.

After the hearing, on the front steps of the courthouse, the Barracuda thrust her head back and looked self-assured for the cameras. She predicted victory in the form of a conviction for the two negligent parents. It was not, she told the press, the type of case she relished, but someone had to speak on behalf of the deceased child.

"Let's not forget," said the thick red lips of the Barracuda, "that an innocent young child is dead here. And worst of all, it was an avoidable death. Young Joshua didn't ask to be born to parents who would rather let him die of a burst appendix than seek medical treatment that would have surely cured him. Young Joshua didn't choose a faith that would deny him the right to live. Somebody needs to speak for young Joshua. There's so much focus on these parents and on their rights as parents. But my job is to be the advocate for Joshua, who wasn't given a chance, and for all the other Joshuas out there."

The Barracuda paused, reminding herself that good sound bites, not long speeches, made the evening news.

"What kind of parents can sit there and watch their child die slowly and painfully without even seeking medical attention? We have a word for that in this jurisdiction. We call it *murder.*"

She paused for a beat and stared at the camera for dramatic effect. Then she walked boldly down the steps and headed for the commonwealth's attorney's office on the other side of the complex. She swaggered as she walked, the strut of a gunslinging sheriff ready for a shootout. She hoped it was a slow news day and that some of the local stations wouldn't fade out until they had shown her walking off into the sunset.

It *was* a slow news day and another tough day of coping in the life of Erica Armistead. She had not yet found the courage to confront her husband with what she had seen on Saturday night. Until that night, it had been relatively easy to keep on living separate lives, to ignore the painful and obvious truth that their marriage had become a sham. But she could no longer live that lie.

Her anger had turned into bitter disappointment. She would confront him and hope for an apology. She was ready to forgive, ready to make any changes necessary to make it work, but first he must admit his failure. She just wanted her husband back. She just wanted to start over with their marriage.

But four days later she had yet to find the strength and the right time to bring it up. Perhaps it was her fear, a premonition even, that he wouldn't care. Perhaps it was a voice deep down telling her that it was already over, that the last thread holding her life together had already been severed. *What will I do if he just shrugs and walks away? How can I go on living, fighting this disease that's tearing me apart, without him?*

She had become more lethargic and listless than ever. The tremors had worsened and become more constant. She spent her days watching television and reading, losing herself in the sagas of others.

It was only a short story on the local news, buried fifteen minutes into the evening newscast. It had something to do with parents who didn't seek medical treatment for their child and a young boy who later died. But it wasn't the story that caught Erica's attention. It was the young lady expounding about the case on the steps of the courthouse. The same businesslike and arrogant face Erica had seen in the bar on Saturday night. The same hair. The same eyes. The same angular profile. The same full, red lips.

Then, as if the news producer had read Erica's mind, a caption flashed on the screen identifying the woman as Rebecca Crawford, deputy commonwealth's attorney. Erica immediately turned up the volume to better hear the last of the woman's comments about the case. Then she watched, mesmerized, as the news announcer explained scheduling details for the trial and the camera showed the woman marching confidently down the steps.

It was in that very moment that Erica found the courage that had evaded her the last four days. Her husband was at work—or so he said—but he was no longer the target of her wrath. She would confront her husband later, but she would not start with him. *What kind of ruthless woman lures away the husband of someone with Parkinson's? What kind of desperate woman can prey on my failure to meet my husband's needs?*

Tomorrow, Erica vowed, she would get some answers. She would dress up, march straight down to the commonwealth's attorney's office and confront this Rebecca Crawford. She would demand an explanation, and she would get one. Then she would demand that this seductress leave her husband alone, or she would blow the whole thing wide open—scandal in the commonwealth's attorney's office and in Chesapeake high society.

And Erica would do it, she promised herself, because she had nothing to lose. Hell hath no fury like a woman scorned. She would sleep well tonight. And she would strike tomorrow.

CHAPTER 30

For Nikki Moreno it had already been a busy morning, and it was not even ten. She had dropped the kids off at school, ignoring the usual protests from Tiger about the latest ailment that ravaged his body. By the time school let out for the day, Tiger would be cured and would register no further complaints until the next morning, when another sickness would suddenly overtake him.

Nikki had given up on the chocolate-chip pancakes routine after the first morning. It was too messy and too time-consuming. Now she just resorted to threats and commands: "You *will* go to school, Tiger," "I don't care if you don't feel well, Tiger," "You'll feel better once you get there, Tiger." She had never actually had to drag him out to the car—threats had done the trick—but she was prepared to physically carry him if that became necessary. The morning routine was getting old, but school would finish this week. She wondered if the same diseases would attack Tiger when it was time to start going to day care.

Chocolate-chip pancakes had been replaced by granola bars for Nikki and Pop-Tarts for the kids. Making beds and doing dishes were luxuries that time would not permit. Laundry was neglected altogether. The kids didn't seem to mind, or if they did, at least they didn't complain.

She wondered how her father had done it—raised her while working full time. She had never before appreciated the sheer exhaustion he must have wrestled with on a daily basis, the endless chores that never got done.

The kids had taken the news pretty well last night, but then again, Nikki had soft-pedaled it. "In three more weeks we'll get to tell the court what really happened," she promised. "In three more weeks we can get your daddy out of jail, and you can stay with your mommy and daddy again. In the meantime, you're stuck with me." Stinky and Tiger just took it all in, eyes wide, heads nodding. Nikki did notice that Stinky snuggled particularly close last night and that Tiger thrashed around more than usual on the floor. All in all, though, the kids seemed to be pretty resilient.

After dropping the kids at school, she stopped by attorney Smith's office and picked up the deposition of Dr. Armistead from the medical malpractice case. She took the deposition out to her car and read it cover to cover before leaving the parking lot. She wasn't disappointed.

Armistead had made a bad judgment call. A young child presented to the Tidewater ER with some classic signs of a possible blood disorder: fever and vomiting, a history of gum bleeding, and some dried blood in her nostrils. The little girl probably should have been referred to a hematologist at Norfolk Children's. Instead, Armistead, missing the diagnosis, prescribed antibiotics and released the child. Two days later, the mom brought the kid, fevered and lethargic, back to the ER, but it was too late. Despite the best efforts of Armistead and his colleagues at Tidewater General, the child died a few hours after admission while in the process of being transferred to Norfolk Children's. The autopsy revealed that the little girl died from an infection caused by acute lymphocytic leukemia, a condition that could have been diagnosed on the initial visit and, in all probability, successfully treated.

What intrigued Nikki even more than Armistead's lack of judgment was the strategy employed by Smith. Instead of being content to portray the facts as a simple case of physician negligence, Smith tried to paint them in a far more sinister light. He dug deeply into Armistead's background during the deposition. Smith learned that Armistead had applied twice—and been rejected twice—to the prestigious residency program at Norfolk Children's. In the view of Smith, that fact alone explained why Armistead had not referred this child to Norfolk Children's for further testing during the child's first ER visit. It also explained why Armistead didn't immediately transfer this child to Norfolk Children's when she presented in critical condition at her second ER visit. Armistead had nursed a grudge against Norfolk Children's all these years because they had snubbed him as a young doctor. And now this child, a pawn in his game, had paid with her life.

Nikki loved the approach. It gave some pizazz to an otherwise bland malpractice case. At the very least, it would allow them to attack the credibility of the main witness for the prosecution and, at the same time, inform the jury that Joshua Hammond was not the first child to die under this doctor's care.

It would be critical for the jury to have someone to blame other than the parents. As far as Nikki was concerned, she had found just the right person.

As she left the parking lot, the mastermind for the defense mulled over her newly minted theory. It *could* work, she decided. It just *might* create reasonable doubt. All she needed was a lawyer who could make it happen.

Since the defendant was a blue-collar redneck fundamentalist, he might appeal to the jurors who were farmers in the southern part of the city or blue-collar workers. But Thomas Hammond would also turn off all the liberals and minorities. To appeal to them, Nikki would need a lawyer with a little more color.

She would take care of that detail at her next stop.

Regent Law School was part of the elegant and sprawling campus of Regent University in the heart of Virginia Beach. The buildings were large brick structures constructed in the Colonial Williamsburg tradition and separated by acres of perfectly manicured lawns.

The law school's mission was to train Christian lawyers to impact the world. Because of its unique mission, the school still struggled to gain national recognition. But the academic reputation of the professors and the quality of the students could easily stack up against the more prestigious national institutions with ivy-covered walls.

Nikki had spent little time on the campus of Regent Law School. The school was too stuffy for her taste, and frankly, the place gave her the creeps. She was on the opposite end of the political and religious spectrum from these folks. They were fanatics in her eyes, although she had to admit she actually liked a few of the graduates she knew.

But she had been doing a lot of strange things lately, a lot of things out of character. And now, for the sake of Stinky and Tiger, she was walking down the halls of the beautiful and ornate law school building and posing as a prospective student (at least that's what she told the admissions officer) on her way to observe the constitutional law class of Professor Charles Arnold.

She found Room 104 and checked her watch. It was 11:05. She was only five minutes late, and she was pretty sure that no college or graduate school class actually started on time anymore. Especially in summer school. She grabbed the handle, flung the door open, and strolled into the classroom.

Thirty-five law student heads turned and stared in her direction. Unfortunately, the door she had just entered was at the front of the classroom, and the students were sitting in stadium-style elevated seats all looking down on her. Nikki felt herself begin to blush, then decided, as usual, to go on the offensive. She figured she knew more about the practice of law than the combined wisdom of these wet-behind-the-ear lawyer-wannabes anyway and quite possibly more than the man currently serving as their professor.

"Are you Professor Arnold?" she asked sweetly.

"Yes. And you are?" She could tell from the look in his eyes that he remembered her from court a few weeks ago. It didn't surprise her; people usually remembered the first time they met Nikki Moreno.

"I'm Nikki Moreno. I'm visiting the school. Thinking about becoming a lawyer." She walked over to Professor Arnold, extending her hand.

He shook it. "Nice to meet you. Have a seat. We actually started five minutes ago."

"Oh, sorry."

Nikki climbed the stairs to the back row and watched in satisfaction as she turned the heads of a few male students. She slouched into her seat, propped her chin on her hand with a half-smile, and gave the handsome Professor Arnold her most flirtatious look.

He was in lecture mode, looking debonair in a pair of stonewashed jeans and a golf shirt—a nice contrast to the expensive suit she remembered from court. He paced back and forth as he talked, never taking his eyes off the students.

"For your benefit, Ms. Moreno, we were just discussing a potential class project on a criminal case I have recently agreed to handle. A young African American named Buster Jackson was recently pulled over by the Virginia Beach Police and arrested for selling cocaine under circumstances that make me suspicious of racial profiling.

"Just before you, uh, entered the classroom, I was asking for volunteers to help with a sort of lab project. We've just been studying the Fourth Amendment prohibition against unreasonable searches and seizures. If Buster's stop was racial profiling, then it certainly violated the Fourth Amendment. As his lawyer, it's my job to suppress any evidence seized illegally. But I'll need statistical proof at a motion-to-suppress hearing. I had just asked for volunteers to help, reminding them that they will be jeopardizing their driving records and may have to testify at the hearing if they decide to sign up."

Nikki nodded her head, never taking her gaze off the professor. This level of commitment to even a scoundrel like Buster Jackson only confirmed that Charles Arnold was the right guy for the Hammond case.

"So if I could have a show of hands of those who might be interested. I'll send around a sign-up sheet but just wanted to get a feel…"

Hands darted up all over the classroom. Nikki noticed that all five of the African American students volunteered, as did a couple of Hispanics. The whites were about evenly divided. Nikki suspected there were some who secretly hoped their professor would lose.

"Thanks," said the professor. "We'll have plenty. Now let's turn to the case of State versus Cromwell, page 409 of your text."

While the pages shuffled, Nikki decided to make her play. Her hand shot up but appeared to go unnoticed. She cleared her throat a few times until some of the students turned around to give her disdainful looks. Professor Arnold tried to ignore her but finally gave in.

"Ms. Moreno?"

"Yes, um, I'm new at this constitutional law stuff. But I was just wondering, do you think that this guy Buster is guilty? I mean, do you think he really was selling drugs?"

Eyes began rolling up into foreheads all over the classroom. These were sophisticated law students aching to be aggressive lawyers. They could not afford the luxury of getting hung up on guilt or innocence.

"That's a good question that many of us have wrestled with at some point," explained the professor patiently. "But at the end of the day, it's not a question for us to answer as criminal defense lawyers. Our job is to vigorously represent the defendant. That's our only job. And part of that job is to ensure that the Constitution is followed.

"If you're going to be a criminal defense lawyer, Ms. Moreno, then you must believe in your heart of hearts that it is better for ten guilty men to go free than for one innocent man to go to jail. If you can't buy that notion, then maybe you should be a prosecutor."

He turned back to his book, signaling his intention to move on. This time Nikki didn't even bother to raise her hand. "So what you're saying then, Charles"—he shot her a look—"I'm sorry, I mean Professor Arnold, is that a good criminal defense lawyer has to be willing to take cases that are unpopular?"

"Exactly," said the professor.

"Even if you might dislike the defendant?"

"Yes, *particularly* if you dislike the defendant and *particularly* if there's an overriding constitutional principle at stake."

"Then let me pose you a hypothetical situation," said Nikki, ignoring the professor's sigh, "to make sure I understand this. Let's say there's a fundamentalist white redneck whom you don't like as a person, but you're pretty sure that he is being prosecuted for political reasons. Let's just say that a deputy commonwealth's attorney, who will probably run for the top prosecutor's job in November, decides to prosecute this man simply because he failed to take his son to the hospital for medical help when his son first got sick. And let's also suppose that the reason this man didn't take his son to the hospital is because he has strong religious convictions against receiving any kind of medical treatment, which means there is an important constitutional principle at stake, namely the principle of religious freedom. Now let's assume this hypothetical redneck asks you to be his lawyer." She paused for emphasis—the whole class had turned and was looking at her, some shaking their heads. "Would you take that case?"

Charles smirked and shook his head too. "That's quite an elaborate hypothetical, Ms. Moreno. And here's my hypothetical answer. Part of being a good lawyer is realizing that you can't personally handle every case, that you've got to trust the system to mete out justice in most situations. You can only pick and choose those cases where you would make the most difference. In this case, I would assume, hypothetically speaking of course, that our alleged criminal would have a public defender who could make the necessary arguments to ensure that justice was done. So you can therefore tell your hypothetical redneck friend, Ms. Moreno, that I would not be available to offer my assistance."

The professor took his penetrating brown eyes from Nikki and glanced down at his class roster. He ran his finger down the page while the classroom fell into a tense silence. "Mr. Bircham," he said, "could you please tell us the facts of State versus Cromwell?"

This time the hand raising and throat clearing didn't seem to work, so Nikki stood up at her desk and just projected her voice loud enough to drown out Bircham.

"But let's suppose, Professor, just for the sake of argument, that the public defender is totally incompetent and can hardly stay awake during the hearings. What then? Does the Constitution protect only people of color, like Buster Jackson, while white men have to rot in jail while a stranger raises their kids?"

Bircham stopped talking as Professor Arnold placed his heavy textbook on the podium, thrust his hands in his pockets, and took a few steps toward the students, staring at the ground. He stood there for a couple of seconds, allowing the silence to make a resounding point. The students stared at their books or computers.

Then, very deliberately, the professor lifted his eyes and locked on to Nikki, the taut lines on his face revealing a smoldering frustration. When at last he spoke, it was in a soft and steady tone, conversational but curt, as if it took every ounce of his self-control not to lash out at her.

"In my classroom, Ms. Moreno—and make no mistake, this is *my* class-room—we have certain customs. They're pretty simple, really. One of those customs is that the students raise their hands when they have a question or comment, and typically they even wait for me to recite their names before they speak. Now you may not have spent much time in classrooms in your day, or maybe where you went to school people were a little more rude. I don't know. But I do know this, right now you're in *my* classroom, wasting *my* class time, on the pretense of raising a hypothetical question. If you want to hire a lawyer, I suggest you go to the yellow pages. But if you want to learn about constitutional law, you've come to the right place. Now, if you'll excuse us, this is a law school class, and we've got work to do."

The students nodded their agreement. Nikki could see them out of the bottom of her peripheral vision, but she kept her unblinking focus on the intense brown eyes of Charles Arnold. She would not be intimidated. She would meet his most intense stare—a look that could melt steel—with one of her own. This might be his turf, but she would *not* back down.

"And if you don't mind," he said, even softer than before but with greater intensity and professorial authority, "please take your seat and raise your hand if you have any further questions."

He turned and walked back behind the podium, and Nikki, despite herself and against her every intention, sat down quietly in her seat. A few other students turned to stare at her, so she took advantage of the professor having his back turned momentarily to sneer at them. *"What are you staring at?"* she whispered menacingly.

Nikki behaved herself the rest of the hour, never once even raising her hand to join the discussion on the intricacies of Fourth Amendment search-and-seizure law. But when class was over, she hung around and waited for Professor Arnold to answer the questions of the other students so she could have a personal word with him.

When the last student left, she stepped forward. "Well," she said cheerily, "that seemed to go well."

The professor tilted his head and eyed her suspiciously for a second, then relaxed his gaze. "I've got to maintain a certain amount of decorum in my classroom."

"I'm sorry," said Nikki. "I didn't know how else to get your attention."

"Let's see, you could try the telephone, e-mail... I hear the post office still delivers."

"Will you take the case?" Nikki hated this; she didn't like begging. And the professor wasn't making it any easier. "Please." She tilted her own head and batted her eyes a little—men loved that approach.

"No."

Huh? Nikki quickly decided it was time to get more direct. The professor obviously didn't appreciate the subtle approach. "Why are you being so stubborn?"

"Ms. Moreno, I'm a law school professor, not a trial lawyer. There are tons of good criminal defense lawyers in the phone book." The professor packed up his stuff. Case closed. Desperate, Nikki quickly donned her best on-the-verge-of-crying look, took a deep breath, and dropped her gaze to the floor. He gave her a long sigh. "Give me one good reason I should take that case."

Nikki perked up immediately. "I'll give you two. First, your potential client, a man named Thomas Hammond, is convinced that this is God's will—his words, not mine. He said he saw you in action on the day he was arraigned, and then he met you again in a Bible study at the jail. This man is absolutely convinced that this is not coincidence, that you are the man God has appointed to represent him."

A light clicked on in the professor's eyes. "Mr. *King James* Only," he muttered.

"What?"

"Not important. What's the second reason?"

"This," said Nikki, thrusting an envelope at him. "But before you read it, let me just tell you it wasn't my idea. I'm just the messenger."

The professor took the envelope and raised an eyebrow.

"I really am sorry about being such a jerk in your class today. It's just that I'm emotionally involved in this case. The kids that were taken from Thomas Hammond and his wife are living with me pending trial."

This fact brought a smile to the professor's face. "You?"

"It's a long story, but I'm a special advocate appointed by the court. And these kids, well, they're special. Just read the letter. You'll understand."

"I'll think about it," he said, looking at his watch. "But no promises."

"Here's my card," said Nikki, flashing another pearly smile as she wrote her cell-phone number on the back. "You can call me anytime."

⧆

Charles returned to his office, opened the end of the envelope, shook it to slide the letter out, and retrieved a photo and handwritten letter. The photo showed an all-American family of five. A huge dad that he recognized as Mr. *King James* Only and a mom who looked haggard and tired but happy. On their laps were three of the cutest kids he had ever laid eyes on. A pudgy little baby dressed in blue. A precocious young blonde-haired girl with a big bubbly smile and a pretty Easter dress. Sitting next to her on her dad's lap was her younger brother, dressed in a white shirt, fake tie, and blue pants he had outgrown the year before. He was pouting for the photo, but the fire was still sparking in his "dare me and I'll do it" eyes.

The letter was penned in the large block letters of someone who had just learned to write, using the paper with the solid blue lines spaced far apart and separated by dashed blue lines to guide the tops of the small letters. The penmanship was careful and precise, the product of a slow and methodical job. The words were brief but to the point.

Dear Mr. Arnold:

Please help my daddy and my mommy in court. The mean lawyer said they kilt my brother. Joshua. But they did not. My dad telled me you are the best lawyer that can help. He said you are the answers to our prayers.

Will you help us?

I have given you a picture so you will know which ones we are. There are lots of people in court.

Love,
Hannah Hammond

P.S. My brother John Paul wants you to help too. We pray for you every night accept for Monday when we both felled asleep in the car on the way home from McDonald's and forgot to pray.

Charles folded the letter and stuffed it inside his constitutional law textbook. He didn't have time to add even one more thing to his plate, regardless of how meritorious the case might be, regardless of how many cute little kids might see their parents go to jail.

Then why did you go to law school? he asked himself. *To turn down the Hannah Hammonds of the world so you can help drug dealers like Buster Jackson—felons who actually threaten their own lawyer?*

He stared at the wall and thought about the earnest face of Nikki Moreno pleading from the back row of his con law class. Though he had already tried to banish the incident from his mind, the words of Moreno came echoing back.

Let's suppose, Professor, that the public defender is totally incompetent and can hardly stay awake at hearings... Does the Constitution protect only people of color while white men have to rot in jail while a stranger raises their kids?

Charles rubbed his forehead thoughtfully and looked again at the picture. His wife was becoming a federal court judge—campaigning so she could help "her people"—and just what was *his* contribution to justice? Buster Jackson? Another class of law students passing con law so they could go out and prosecute the downtrodden?

The test of true justice was whether it could reach out evenly—like the statue of the blindfolded lady holding the scales—and embrace the most unfortunate and unsympathetic among us on the same basis as the rich and privileged. *And what have I done recently to advance that cause?*

If you're saying your prayers every night, young lady, then you deserve better than a sleeping lawyer, he silently told Hannah Hammond.

Then Charles Arnold, law professor and street evangelist, reluctant defender of the just and the unjust, guardian of the Constitution, and answer to the prayers of an innocent young child, pulled out Nikki's card and gave her a call.

CHAPTER 31

Are you sure you don't just want me to have Ms. Crawford give you a call?" the receptionist asked for the fourth time.

Erica Armistead had been waiting for nearly two hours and was not about to leave now. It had taken half the morning to work up the nerve to come in the first place and another hour to get dressed and primped. She wasn't sure she could muster the nerve or the energy to do it again.

She looked up from her book and forced another smile. "No, it's pretty time sensitive. I'll just wait." She said it pleasantly enough but with an air of finality that did not invite comment.

The receptionist commented anyway. "Suit yourself," said the middle-aged woman. She checked her watch and went back to her magazine. "Sometimes she stays in court until late afternoon."

"It's okay. I'll wait." Then Erica crossed her legs and buried her head in her book again. She read the same sentence for the third time.

It was 12:45.

Three chapters, ninety minutes, and three more questions from the receptionist later, Rebecca Crawford came strolling through the outer door and into the reception area. She was dressed in a white blouse and gray suit—matching skirt and vest. She looked tanned and fit. Her recently bleached hair showed no erosion to brown at the roots, and her full, red lips were pressed tightly together. She was all business, in another world, and walked right by Erica.

She looks smaller up close, thought Erica. She put down her book and stood haltingly. She had to grab the arms of the chair to help push herself up, and her arms shook miserably as she did so.

"This woman's been waiting to see you," the receptionist told Crawford. "Says her name is Erica Armistead."

The information stopped Crawford in her tracks, causing her to wheel and lock a cold stare on Erica.

She's got beady little eyes, thought Erica. *Dark and darting eyes full of contempt.*

"Come on back," Crawford said. No "Nice to meet you," no "My name's Rebecca," not even a "What are you doing here?" Just a cold and gruff "Come on back," as if she were a junior-high principal getting ready to discipline a student.

"Thanks," mumbled Erica. She immediately hated herself for saying it, for being so malleable. She hated the sweat that had already formed on her palms and upper lip as well as the knot that twisted her stomach. Without another word, she followed Crawford through the inner reception-area door, down a narrow hallway lined with legal assistants and secretaries in cubicles, and into a corner office that boasted the name "Deputy Commonwealth's Attorney Rebecca Crawford" on the nameplate. She shuffled as quickly as she could, small quick steps, catching her balance a time or two. Still, she had fallen several steps behind by the time they hit Crawford's office.

"Have a seat," said Crawford, motioning to a low-backed client chair in front of her desk. "I'd offer you something to drink, but I've only got a few minutes."

Erica struggled into the seat and clasped her hands in her lap. She watched Crawford shut the door to her office and walk around her desk, stopping to straighten a diploma on the side wall. Her desk was neat to the point of looking barren, and her diplomas and plaques hung at precise angles along the full length of the wall. She sat down in her high-backed plush-leather desk chair directly across from Erica. Behind her were two large windows facing west and overlooking the municipal complex. Either by accident or design, the windows caused the hot sunlight to stream directly into Erica's eyes, making Erica squint and giving Crawford a halo.

Crawford tented her fingers on the desk and looked straight at Erica. She was obviously not planning on making this easy. She did not speak.

Erica collected her thoughts and cleared her throat. "I guess you, um, wonder why I'm here," she stuttered the words out softly, looking down.

"No. I know why you're here."

There was a long and uncomfortable silence.

"Do you love him?" Erica asked, immediately regretting the words. She came here to lecture this unscrupulous woman, to warn her to leave Sean alone. She had scripted this, practiced it—sarcastic tone of voice, the whole works. But now, in her moment of truth, she had forgotten all about the biting sarcasm, the condescending tone, and the direct accusations. Instead, she spoke from the heart. And her heart still cared about Sean and didn't want to see him hurt.

"I love him," Crawford said without expression, "and he loves me. And I'm sorry to have to say this, but right now he needs me."

"Stay away from him," Erica demanded.

"Or what?" asked Crawford, tilting her head back.

"Or you'll regret it, that's what. I'll let it be known all over Tidewater that the deputy commonwealth's attorney has seduced the vulnerable—and rich— husband of a sick woman. I'll file for divorce based on adultery. And the reporters will be banging your door down." Erica was talking faster now and leaning forward, squeezing her trembling hands together. She squinted through the sunlight at this monster before her.

Crawford just smirked.

"You don't get it, do you?" she asked. "You think we're trying to hide this to protect my career?"

The question lingered for a moment, then Crawford continued. "We meet in the hottest bars in Virginia Beach. We're seen all around town together. We'd make love on the beach in broad daylight if it wasn't illegal. And you think we're trying to hide this?"

She paused again, but Erica could think of nothing to say. Erica felt the tears burning in the back of her eyes and blinked hard to fight them back.

Crawford narrowed her gaze and continued. "Don't you see? The only reason that *he* hasn't divorced *you* already is that he feels sorry for you. He doesn't want to hurt you emotionally. But you stopped being his wife a long time ago."

At this—the cold, hard truth of it—Erica felt a single tear crawling down her cheek.

"And scandal?" mocked Crawford. "*Puh-lease!* Where have you been the last five years? Don't you remember how Clinton's approval ratings soared after his little tryst in the Oval Office? Go ahead and spread the rumor that I'm getting it on with a rich and handsome doctor. I won't have to worry about those other rumors that always follow single career women." Crawford leaned forward and spoke in a mock conspiratorial whisper, "I wonder when she's coming out of the closet."

Then Crawford leaned back in her chair and shook her head again. She gave Erica a look of pity and indignation. "Don't kid yourself," Crawford said. "He's saving you some embarrassment, that's all. Otherwise, he'd have been gone a long time ago."

Erica stared down and felt the tear fall from her face. She felt so inadequate and ashamed. She had come to back this woman down, to humiliate this woman with the fake blonde hair and the all-too-perfect tan. But somehow she was the one who felt humiliated; she was the one who had failed Sean.

She watched as Crawford stood up, stepped around the desk, and opened her office door. "I've got some appointments," she said. "I'm sorry it turned out this way." She paused as Erica rose slowly from her seat, no longer trying to mask the pain of moving. "I won't tell Sean you came by. It's the least I can do."

Erica stopped on the way out, inches from the Barracuda. She tensed her jaw and felt her entire face tremble. She spoke in a whisper. "Stay away from him. Give our marriage one more chance. He loved me once, and we can rekindle it if you leave him alone. *That's* the least you can do."

Satisfied that she had said what she came to say, Erica turned from the cold stare of the Barracuda and limped down the hall.

·→· ≡◆≡ ·←·

The Barracuda closed the door then hit a speed-dial button on her phone.

"Hello," said the brisk, business voice of Dr. Sean Armistead.

"Hey, it's me."

"Now's not a good time. Can you call back in about an hour?"

"This can't wait, Sean. We've got a problem. I tried to bluff my way out of it, but I don't think it worked. We'll have to deal with this right away."

CHAPTER 32

Charles Arnold couldn't believe he was doing *this*.

He had wanted to meet the kids and get their take on things. They would be the best sources for what had really happened. Plus he would have to determine what kind of witnesses they would make. It was always dangerous to put kids on the stand, especially when they would be subject to the cross-examination of someone as lethal as the Barracuda. It was imperative that Charles get a read on how well these kids would hold up, how prone they were to be tricked by leading questions.

He also wanted some time with Nikki. She was obnoxious but very bright. He needed to pick her brain for a while about the details of the case. He had a few investigative assignments for her as well and wanted to bounce a legal strategy off her. Bottom line—he needed several hours with Nikki and the kids before the preliminary hearing on Wednesday.

Nikki agreed and promised to give him all day Saturday on one condition: that Charles meet them at the Busch Gardens amusement park in Williamsburg. It will give you time with the kids on an informal basis, she had argued. It will help you build rapport. We'll be standing in lines all day, and you can pick my brain clean about every aspect of the case.

Charles was certain it wouldn't take all day to pick Nikki's brain clean. And he didn't relish the thought of spending a Saturday in the blazing sun waiting in line for rides designed to make you sick. But the offer from Nikki was nonnegotiable. Saturday at Busch Gardens or nothing. She was rewarding the kids for finishing the school year on Friday. She couldn't cancel this trip, she said. And so he had agreed. But he had his own condition. He would drive separately. That way he could leave whenever he gained the information he needed for the case.

Charles had been sworn to secrecy by Nikki. Under no circumstances could Thomas and Theresa Hammond know about this. After all, Busch Gardens was run by a beer company, and the Hammonds would certainly disapprove. They would find out later, because Stinky and Tiger would eventually let it slip. But Nikki had postponed telling the kids about their excellent adventure until after they had finished school and visited Thomas in jail on Friday afternoon. It was easier to ask forgiveness than permission, she said.

So now Charles Arnold waited outside the entrance to Busch Gardens at ten o'clock on Saturday morning, inhaling the pungent odor of the nearby brewery and listening to the bagpipe music blaring over the speakers designed to make you feel like you were stepping into medieval Europe. He watched the families roll in with grins on their faces and a spring in their steps—dads and moms as excited as the kids.

And then it came. The fog of memories rolling in: the face of Denita, her slurred and painful words on the night he first left her. She had been out late after work, not answering her cell phone. The dinner Charles had planned— just the two of them, badly needed time alone together—never materialized. And when she came home giddy, with booze on her breath and her blouse unbuttoned part way, it was more than he could take.

He had lashed out at her lifestyle, her "sinful" selfishness. She called him "judgmental" and a "hypocrite."

He could see the rage on her face even now, could smell the mix of stale vodka and perfume, could feel the fist clench around his heart. He followed her around the house and demanded to talk. He told her that he still loved *her,* but he hated the things she *did.* "Can't you see what you're doing to yourself? to our marriage?" he demanded. "Look at you," he sneered, "strutting your stuff. Who are trying to impress? What happened to the woman I married?"

"Me?!" she screamed. "What happened to *me?!* I don't even know you anymore." The tears started flowing, and Denita tried to stalk away, but Charles grabbed her arm. "Let go of me!" she demanded.

"Not until you listen to me," he said between clenched teeth. "You're still my wife. And I won't ever let you go." She struggled, but he squeezed the arm tighter until she stilled. She winced, and a wave of shame swept over him. He had hurt her. Maybe just a little, but still, in his anger he had hurt her. It was something he had promised himself he would never do. Things had spun out of control.

Charles took a deep breath and dropped her arm. "You can fight me all you want, Denita, but I'm not giving up on us. I want to grow old with you, raise a family with you…"

She laughed. Even as Charles recalled it now, it was the most painful sound he had ever heard. Just a short laugh, a mocking tone from deep in Denita's throat. Then her eyes narrowed, and she put the dagger in his heart.

"A family," she said, sneering at the thought. "Look at us ready to kill each other, and you want a family." She looked down as she said the next sentence, a certain sadness shadowing her eyes. She nearly whispered. "I aborted our family six months ago."

The rest of the night was still a blur to Charles. Disbelief. Condemnation. Demanding details. Eventually it all came out. Denita unleashed a bitter narrative that made Charles feel like he had caused it. Though the RU-486 pill had not yet been approved in the United States, Denita had used her connections with some corporate clients to obtain the drug. She couldn't bear the thought of a clinic, she said. And she certainly couldn't discuss it with Charles. "Look at you," she said. "Even now you're judging me for it, convicting me with your eyes."

The self-induced miscarriage had been painful, personal, and something she had to endure alone because she couldn't even talk with her husband about it. She described flushing the fetus as well as the feelings of guilt and then anger at a husband who would never understand. She talked about it matter-of-factly, without a single tear, as if every ounce of emotion had already been drained from her body. She did it for both of them. They weren't ready for kids. Not even close. And she knew he would never understand.

Charles remembered listening, questioning, and riding a roller coaster of emotion. An abortion! An illegal abortion! Of his child!

To this day he couldn't remember what he said. He remembered trying to control his rage and expressing his own disappointment. The blunt force of his words landed even harder when delivered with a detached monotone.

He remembered aching to hold her, but her body language said to leave her *alone*. Like everything else in life, she could handle it *alone*. Most vividly of all, he remembered the cold finality of her response: "You'll thank me one day," then she turned and headed up the stairs, shutting the door of their bedroom behind her.

He went to his study and wrestled with his emotions. He typed out a note on his computer. He read it twice, the monitor blurred by his tears. "I forgive you," he wrote, "but I'll never understand. We need some time apart."

He left the note on the kitchen counter then quietly entered his bedroom. Denita had fallen asleep with the television on, the light from the screen partially illuminating her face. Charles quietly packed a gym bag, then knelt beside Denita, brushed some hair away from her face, and kissed her on the forehead.

He said a prayer, a silent one, asking God for forgiveness for Denita, and begging God to draw Denita to Himself. As he stood to leave, a fresh wave of grief overwhelmed him. His lip started trembling, and he felt the tears pooling in his eyes as he mourned his shattered marriage and a precious child he would never know.

CHAPTER 33

Four years later the wound was still raw, and it still had the power to summon fresh tears. And so, as he saw Nikki and the kids hop off the tram and start running down the hill toward the gates, he found himself wiping at his eyes and putting on a forced smile.

Tiger led the way, wide-eyed—no, wild-eyed—with excitement. Stinky ran close behind, and Nikki called out for the kids to slow down. "You don't have to run, we don't even have our tickets yet."

Charles's small grin turned into a full-fledged smile. His own little family for the day.

Nikki had exposed as much of her skin to the sun as the occasion would allow, revealing the small tattoo on her ankle and the larger one on her shoulder. She wore a bright tie-dyed halter top, short khaki shorts, and sandals. She had pulled her thick black hair into a tight braid and shielded her eyes with a pair of sleek Ray-Bans. She surveyed the landscape and finally spotted Charles. Her whole face smiled behind the shades.

She could have been a movie star.

She called the kids over and introduced them to "Mr. Charles." Stinky politely shook his hand. "Nice to meet you," she said properly. Tiger shook his hand too but just stared up at Charles for a few long seconds, squinting and wrinkling up his little nose.

"Do you ever get sunburned?" he finally asked.

Nikki laughed out loud, throwing her head back as she chuckled. Charles suppressed his own grin.

"Not as bad as you crackers do," he replied.

The little boy sure was cute. And Nikki was going to keep things interesting. *Maybe I'll stay a little longer than I first thought.*

But still, Charles couldn't believe he was doing this.

— ⊰◈⊱ —

The Loch Ness Monster.

They hadn't been inside the park for ten minutes, and they were already standing in front of the biggest and baddest roller coaster in the world—at least as far as Tiger was concerned. It was huge and it was fast and it was noisy.

It seemed to Tiger that it stretched miles into the sky. So close to the sun that you would probably get burned. And it made this terrible rattling noise, so loud he could barely hear his own teeth chattering. It was a miracle the cars even stayed on; the thing sounded like it would fall apart any minute. And the screams! People screamed every time they came down that first huge hill. They screamed like they were dying, or at least being tortured. And then they almost hit the water in the pond below, went around this curve and through a big upside-down loop and disappeared into a dark tunnel where the Loch Ness Monster himself actually lived.

On the other side of the tunnel, *if* they came out alive, they would go up and down some more hills and—get this—through a second loop, where they would scream some more and actually go upside down again. No kidding. Completely upside down. Two times.

Tiger watched the ride without blinking while holding tight to Mr. Charles's hand. A full five minutes passed before he took another step toward the line. As far as he could tell, during those five minutes not one person had fallen out, not even on the loops. But it would be just his luck to be the first. He carefully studied every person who stepped off the ride and headed back out to the park. They all looked okay. Some were even smiling.

The Loch Ness Monster.

Tiger Hammond couldn't believe *he* was doing *this*.

But he had come this far, and there was no turning back now. Mr. Charles gently pulled on his hand, and they started walking slowly and cautiously toward the line. Stinky and Ms. Nikki followed a step behind. Tiger was still not convinced that he should do the Loch Ness Monster this early in the day. Maybe they should save it till last or at least after lunch. But he kept walking. Right up to the big covered building where the line snaked in and out, guided by chains strung from one post to another.

He got stopped by a guy wearing a funny-looking outfit and holding a long stick in his right hand. "We'll have to measure this one," the guy said.

He held the stick next to Tiger.

"Stand up straight," said Mr. Charles. "You've got to be as tall as this pole to ride the ride."

"It's too dangerous for anyone shorter," said the helpful guy with the stick.

Tiger stood up as straight as he could. He stretched his legs, his back, and his neck. He even stood on tippytoe, at which point Miss Nikki insisted he was close enough. The guy with the stick was shaking his head, and Tiger felt the tears forming in his eyes. This wasn't fair. Stinky would get to ride the Loch Ness, and he would have to settle for the merry-go-round.

But Miss Nikki wasn't through. She wiggled up to the guy, wedged herself between him and Tiger, and put a hand on her hip. She spoke in low tones, so low that Tiger couldn't hear. But she seemed really into it, her arms flying around as she talked. And then she inched even closer to the guy and gently reached out and touched the measuring guy's arm, leaving her hand there, and Tiger heard her say something about his daddy being in jail. After a few more seconds Miss Nikki apparently achieved a breakthrough and gave the guy a quick and vicious hug. "You're a lifesaver," she gushed, and Tiger could see the guy's face turn red. Then Charles grabbed Tiger's hand again, and they were off to wait in a long line to ride the Loch Ness Monster.

If you're too short, does that mean the seat belt things won't be able to hold you in? wondered Tiger. *It's too dangerous, the guy in the uniform had said. And if anyone should know, he should know.*

Tiger fretted for the next half-hour surrounded by the sweaty legs of hundreds of strangers, each one taller than he. Mr. Charles, Miss Nikki, and Stinky each tried valiantly to engage him in conversation, but to no avail. He would utter an occasional "yes ma'am" or "no sir" or even an "uh-huh" or "huh-uh" to Stinky, but he was not in the mood to talk. He just couldn't stop thinking about that huge first hill, the big monster in the cave, and the very real possibility that he would slip right out from under the shoulder restraints—given the fact that he was an illegally short rider who had snuck onto the ride against all the park rules.

"Don't bite your nails, Tiger."

"Yes ma'am."

As he approached the front of the line, he said a final prayer. He confessed every sin he could remember and asked for forgiveness one more time, just to make sure he had a clean slate if something happened to him on the ride. He was now ready for the Loch Ness, and to meet his Maker, if it came to that.

He sat next to Mr. Charles in one of the shiny green cars. Mr. Charles held his hand as the roller coaster took off and began climbing that first humongous hill. The rattling chain sounded even louder in the car than it did on the ground, the incredible noise drowning out Tiger's pleas to stop the ride so he could get off. Mr. Charles was yelling some kind of encouragement at him, but Tiger couldn't hear a word he was saying.

He stole a peek over the side of the car and almost puked. He was way up above the trees, above the buildings. Pretty soon they would be above the clouds. And the stupid ride just kept climbing and climbing. And climbing.

He wanted off, he missed his mommy and daddy, he hated this park, he was too young to die, he... *"Whoaaaa!"*

The thing must have come loose 'cause it was hurtling straight for the ground. A total free fall. Little Tiger's stomach was up in his throat, and his breakfast was right there with it.

"Aieeeee!" screamed the other riders. Tiger opened his mouth as well and screamed at the top of his lungs, but nothing came out. He was too scared. He couldn't breathe. He gripped the shoulder restraints in a death grip. The idiots in front of him had their hands in the air. They were surely goners.

Just when they were ready to crash into the pond, everyone together, the tracks lurched upward and headed for the first loop. *Yikes!* The whole world was upside down...and then it wasn't. Tiger closed his eyes and prayed the ride would end. Then he opened 'em, but it was still dark. Maybe he was dead! No, wait, he was in the cave, lights flashing on and off, the monster lunging out at them.

A bright light—the sun—another loop. He was upside down again and surely slipping out of his seat. He sat tall, hoping against hope that the shoulder restraints would somehow work, somehow keep his short, little, illegal body in the car for a few more seconds. More screams, a sudden stop, and they were back where they started.

Tiger gingerly touched his legs and face. Everything seemed to be in place. He took a deep breath and heard his heart pounding in his ears.

"How'd you like it?" asked Mr. Charles.

"Please exit to your left," boomed a voice from the roof of the building. "Thanks for riding the Loch Ness Monster and enjoy the rest of your day here at Busch Gardens—*the Old Country.*"

Tiger grabbed Mr. Charles's hand and stepped out of the car. His feet hit solid ground. His knees nearly buckled. He had done it. Against all odds, he had survived. He had conquered the Loch Ness Monster.

"Can we go again, *please?*" begged Tiger.

━━◄✦►━━

The Festhaus was a huge building in the back of the park designed to look like an old German beer hall. The outside of the wooden building was lavishly decorated with carvings, balconies, and columns in the German gothic style. The inside consisted of a spacious dance hall with a wooden floor, massive ceiling beams, and hundreds of long wooden picnic tables arranged in rows around the outside of the dance floor.

At the center of the building was a festive little white pavilion decorated with ribbons and flowers to commemorate the Oktoberfest celebration. Every hour, right on schedule, an orchestra paraded out of the back doors of the Festhaus, took their seats inside the pavilion, and then began playing German folk songs. The floor of the pavilion would magically rise and take the orchestra up to the top of the pavilion so the lush melodies could float down to the dance floor and echo throughout the dance hall.

The rising orchestra would be followed by a group of sixteen young blond-haired, blue-eyed performers, the Festhaus dancers, who would entertain the masses with the polka and other classic German dances for the next thirty minutes. The girls were all decked out in frilly light-blue-and-white hoop skirts and puffy white blouses. The guys wore matching outfits: white shirts, blue bow ties, light blue lederhosen, and tall white socks. They were a festive group, smiling all the time and getting the crowd to sing along to songs that nobody knew.

Charles didn't have to be here. He had debriefed Nikki and the kids hours ago, and it was now dinnertime. He was even missing his Saturday night Bible study at the jail. But somehow he couldn't leave this motley little bunch to fend for themselves in this massive park. Besides, who would ride the rides with Tiger?

Okay, he would admit it, if only to himself. He was actually having fun. The amazement he saw in the eyes of Tiger and Stinky at every new adventure, the looks their little "family" would draw from strangers—the "blond hair is a recessive gene" he would tell them—and the way he felt like a hero when he finally put the basketball through that tiny little rim on the fifth try, despite unmerciful heckling by Nikki. It all added up to a marvelous day at Busch Gardens.

And now, having endured eight hours of park madness, he was sitting at one of the front tables in the Festhaus, eating pizza, and watching the kids watch the German dancers.

"You need to eat something kids. Don't just watch the show," Nikki suggested.

Neither Tiger nor Stinky moved. They were both slumped on the picnic bench, mouths wide open, eyes half shut, following every synchronized move of the dance team. The kids were not even facing their plates. Charles noticed that each time Tiger blinked, the little guy's eyes seemed to open a little more slowly. He was running on empty.

A song finished, and the frisky German dancers started heading out toward the crowd. It was time for some audience involvement, time for the guests of the park to learn a little polka. One of the pairs looked at Tiger and Stinky and headed straight for their table. Tiger's eyes flew open as the girl grabbed his arm and asked if he wanted to dance. Tiger looked at Charles, pleading for a bailout.

"Go get 'em, Tiger," Charles urged. "It'll be fun."

By now one of the guys had also asked Stinky, and the shy little girl reluctantly followed him out to the dance floor.

Charles turned his attention away from the dancers and over his shoulder to Nikki.

"That's great," he chuckled. "They'll be talking about this for years."

Nikki just nodded and smiled. Her sunglasses were perched on top of her head, and she seemed to have that same mischievous look in her eyes that Charles noticed that day in his classroom. She also seemed to be looking over his shoulder.

He turned quickly, and there she was. A Festhaus dancer, with her hand gracefully extended, in a curtsy position, inviting Charles to dance.

What's she thinking?! he wondered. *Can't she tell I'm not exactly from German stock? I don't know a polka from a fox trot.*

Charles began shaking his head no.

"Go on," urged the loudmouthed Hispanic woman who had gotten him into this fine mess in the first place. "Like you told Tiger—it'll be fun."

Before Charles knew it, all four of them were out there, getting twirled this way and that by the German dancers. It didn't take him long to figure out the polka. Still, it wasn't exactly rap, and despite his natural sense of rhythm, he felt silly as he stumbled around the dance floor, especially when he noticed Nikki whirling this way and that, mastering the polka like she was born in a German tavern, and laughing all the time.

It had to be the longest polka in recorded history, and Charles was immensely relieved when the last note finally sounded. He thanked the dancer who had called him out, then located the kids and headed off the dance floor.

Unfortunately, the orchestra was not finished, and before he reached his seat, he heard the mellow notes of a sad folk ballad—"Edelweiss"—and he saw the dancers start going after more prey for a slow dance. He had almost safely reached his seat when he felt a tug at his elbow.

"C'mon, handsome. One more dance?" It was Nikki, and the tug became a persistent pull.

She turned to Tiger and Stinky. "If you guys finish your pizza during this next song, we can get some ice cream."

The kids let go of Charles's hands and sprinted toward their seats.

He turned to Nikki, took her hand gently in his, and extended his other hand to place it gently on her shoulder. There was a good twelve inches between them.

"I don't bite," she said. She snuggled up closer, placing her arm around his waist, and laying her head against his chest. Her hair nearly touched his face, and even after a full day in the park, it smelled great. She immediately fell into step as they joined the other dancers and patrons, slowly—and grace-fully—making their way around the dance floor.

"You're a good dancer," she said softly.

"So are you."

He relaxed just a little and started enjoying himself. It was just one silly dance. Nothing more. He noticed the tired and jealous faces of the dads at the picnic tables as they all seemed to be looking at him, wondering how he rated a dance with the prettiest girl in the joint. He pulled her closer, and she didn't seem to mind.

She made a good dance partner and would make an interesting friend. Life was good. And Charles Arnold couldn't believe, would never have imag-ined early this morning, that before the sun had set on this marvelous day, he'd be dancing with Nikki Moreno, spinning her gently around on the Fes-thaus floor in front of hundreds of witnesses.

He had started today by mourning for a family he never had. But some-where along the way he had discovered the joys of simple pleasures: a theme park through the eyes of a child, a friendship with a woman who made him smile. Tonight, he would say a prayer of thanks.

He couldn't believe his good fortune. He couldn't believe he was doing *this.*

CHAPTER 34

Unable to get the disappointed face of Buster out of his mind, Thomas knelt to pray on the cinder block floor of his jail cell. Earlier that evening Thomas, Buster, and the ES had gathered in the same windowless room where they held last week's Bible study. This time there was not as much grumbling about coming, though the men still ragged on Thomas about his *King James* Bible. Thomas didn't care. At least they were showing up.

They waited fifteen minutes for Charles. After ten minutes the complaining started in earnest. Thomas kept making excuses—"Maybe his car broke down"—pleading with the men to stay, but he could tell Buster was getting frustrated. The man was not used to being stood up. After fifteen minutes Buster thrust out his jaw. "Some preacher," he said. The men murmured their agreement. "Let's blow this rathole," said Buster, and they called for a guard to open the door.

Now, three hours later, Thomas knelt for his nightly prayer. He always came back to the cell early while the other men were still lounging in the common area, playing cards, or watching television. This was the only way to get some solitude. As he did every night, he started by asking for forgiveness for what he had done to Joshie. Then he prayed for his own family and asked God to forgive Charles for not showing up tonight. Next he turned his thoughts toward his cellmate.

"Show Buster how much You love him, God. Somehow, help him figure out what it means to be saved and all. You know I ain't real good at talkin' 'bout this stuff, so if there's any way that Charles can hook back up with Buster, I'd be eternally grateful…" Thomas paused, sensing he was not alone. He realized that he had been mumbling his prayers out loud, just like he did at home, and he felt a little embarrassed. This wasn't exactly the Lord's prayer—"Thy Kingdom come" and all that great sounding stuff. If somebody was listening, he probably wouldn't be too impressed. Better wrap it up quick and with a bit of a flourish.

"Forgive my trespasses, God, as I forgive those who trespass against me. Amen."

He rose from his knees and turned in time to see the back of Buster as the man disappeared around the corner.

<hr />

The Blue Ridge Parkway winds for miles through the scenic Blue Ridge Mountains in the western part of Virginia. It takes nearly three hours from Virginia Beach just to get there. But anybody who has traveled the parkway can tell you that the breathtaking scenery is worth every minute of the drive.

It was for this reason, and because of his love for mountains and all they symbolize, that Dr. Sean Armistead proposed to a young lady named Erica Wilson at one of the most beautiful lookout spots on the entire parkway more than twelve years ago. He was a third-year med student then; she was a gifted high-school teacher. Their future together was limitless.

Sean took her to Lookout Peak, one of the highest spots on the parkway, where on a clear day you could see almost forever. The rolling mountains and yawning valleys all merged on the horizon, endless miles of green in the summer or blazing colors in the fall.

The lookout itself was just a small rest area along the side of the road with a few coin-operated telescopes on metal stands and some sturdy wire guardrails to keep cars from plunging more than a hundred feet from the road into the wooded valley. It was nothing special as far as rest stops go; it didn't even have a bathroom facility. But for Sean and Erica, it was the spot where he had popped the question and the spot where she said yes, and so it was the single most important spot on the face of the earth. During the first few years of their marriage, they would make annual pilgrimages here to renew their vows and contemplate how lucky they were to have each other.

A few hours after Busch Gardens had shut down for the night and the Virginia Beach inmates were all locked down, just a few minutes before midnight, a white Lexus crashed through the guardrails at Lookout Peak, bounced off the rocky overhang, and plunged the hundred or so feet to the woods below. The car flipped and bounced several times on the way down, and eventually landed deep in the woods, nearly buried by the foliage and trees. There was a brief burst of fire, a literal explosion of flames, but the woods themselves never caught, and the flames eventually burned themselves out.

There were no tourists driving the parkway at this time of night. And had it not been for the broken guardrail and the suicide note printed on the victim's home printer and left on her dresser, the body and the Lexus might not have been discovered for weeks.

Erica Armistead had come full circle. Her life and her marriage had now ended in tragedy at the same spot where, just a dozen years before, she had become engaged to the only man she had ever loved.

CHAPTER 35

Brandon was a young buck no more than twenty-six or seven with long blond hair, a broad Roman nose, and straight white teeth. He was six-two, one hundred ninety-five pounds, with washboard abs and not an ounce of flab on his entire body. He was always smiling and exhorting, egging people on with intense steel-blue eyes and those straight white teeth. Right now, he was exhorting the Barracuda. And right now, the Barracuda hated his guts.

It was Sunday morning at the gym, and Brandon, the trainer for the who's who crowd at Virginia Beach, was working her over. They had been doing ab work for an eternity. Or rather *she* had been doing ab work while *he* prodded her on. Her stomach had caught fire about ten reps ago and begged for mercy. But Brandon, smiling all the while, seemed to be just getting started. And loving it.

"Come on," said the young hunk, "four more this set." Brandon was towering over the Barracuda as she lay on her back. She would lift her legs straight up to a ninety-degree angle from the floor, then he would push on her ankles and throw her legs back down. She would squeeze and tighten her stomach muscles so her legs didn't bounce off the floor, then use those same tired muscles to bring the legs back up in the air, where a grinning Brandon would push them back down again.

"Twenty-seven…twenty-eight…twenty-nine…thirty… You're looking great. Let's squeeze out ten more," said the smiling sadist.

Are you kidding?! I'm dying down here, you jerk. What's with you today? I can't believe I'm paying you for this.

"Thirty-five…thirty-six…thirty-seven"—the Barracuda grunted and groaned, sweating like a pig, swinging her legs back up as Brandon clicked off the numbers—"thirty-eight…thirty-nine…forty."

"Aaaaah," she moaned as she let her legs flop on the floor, then curled them to her chest in a fetal position, rolling side to side. "Are you trying to kill me today?"

"If it doesn't kill us, it only makes us stronger," Brandon said, stealing a sideways glance at himself in the wall of mirrors.

The Barracuda slowly rose to her feet, sucked in her gut, and checked out her own image. She wore spandex shorts and a sports bra that exposed her midriff. The muscles in her back, arms, and legs were coming along nicely. But despite the last half-hour of complete torture, there was still a tiny roll of cellulite peeking out over the top of her spandex shorts, mocking her plans to wear a bikini this summer. She glanced in envy at the woman on the leg curl machine, all arms and legs, skin and bones. *Who made the decision that anorexic is in? Why do you have to able to count your ribs—look like a skinny little boy—to make it as a model? And where are the women's libbers when these idiots on Madison Avenue dictate these impossible body prototypes?*

The Barracuda was convinced that the Greeks and Romans had it right. They preferred their women and their goddesses, whom they immortalized in sculpture, with a little extra meat on their bones.

But Brandon apparently felt differently. He had been staring at his stop-watch. "One more set of abs—this time we'll use the ball," he announced with a broad smile. "Got to feel the burn."

The Barracuda took a swig from her water bottle and looked at him defiantly. But she obediently grabbed one of the large red rubber balls and sat on it. Her iron will could always get her through one more set.

She started a new round of torture. Keeping her feet on the floor, she arched her back over the ball, then did a sit-up while balancing herself—isolating her tired ab muscles: *One…two…three…four…five…* The fire was back in her stomach, Brandon was grinning, and she hated him with a renewed and burning passion.

And then…relief! She heard the blessed first ring of her cell phone when she was on her fourteenth rep. It was too good to be true! She stopped immediately and grabbed the phone lying next to her, as if someone's life might be in danger if she didn't answer before the second ring. She punched a button and answered breathlessly, in a manner that feigned frustration at this interruption of her workout routine.

"What?" she huffed.

"Becca, you've got to come over right away," said the stressed voice of Sean Armistead. "The police are already here."

The Barracuda caught her breath and looked at a frowning Brandon. "Is it an emergency?" she asked for the sake of the eavesdropping slab of beef standing next to her.

The Barracuda already knew the answer.

⊷ ≛♦≛ ⊶

The Barracuda arrived at the Armistead estate in Woodard's Mill clad in jeans and an old button-down shirt she had thrown over top of her workout clothes. She parked right behind the two Chesapeake police cars in the driveway—one marked and one unmarked. She entered without knocking. From the front foyer she could see Sean in his study, slumped on the couch and zoned out, his puffy red eyes staring straight ahead. The Barracuda resisted the urge to go in and comfort him, take him in her arms and reassure him that it would be okay. She introduced herself to Inspector Giovanni, the Chesapeake cop who was very obviously in charge.

The Barracuda flashed her commonwealth's attorney credentials, explained that she was a friend of the Armisteads, and asked for a status report. The inspector glanced over his shoulder at Armistead, then took the Barracuda by the elbow down the hallway and into the kitchen. In hushed tones, he explained what they knew about the apparent suicide of Erica Armistead and summarized the statement he had taken from Sean Armistead.

"He's been very cooperative," said Giovanni. "He let us look around the house. Even let us check a few things on the computer."

"Is his story checking out?" asked the Barracuda with as much detachment as she could muster.

The inspector made a clucking sound and silently nodded his head for a few seconds. "Pretty much," he said. "Pretty much."

His hesitation was not lost on the Barracuda.

"Mind if I have a word with him?"

"Knock yourself out," he shrugged.

The Barracuda walked slowly back to the study and softly took a seat in a wing-backed chair next to the small couch where Armistead stared into space. Sean did not acknowledge her. As she glanced around and gathered her thoughts, she noticed how dark the study seemed, even on a morning when the sun was shining brightly. Sean had closed the plantation shutters to block the sunlight, and the dark mahogany bookshelves and maroon leather furniture seemed to absorb what little light filtered in from the foyer. There was one dim reading light illuminating a corner of the room, keeping the two occupants from being in total darkness.

She sat there silently for a few minutes, torn between reaching out and touching him or just plain slapping him for his stupidity. The emotions in the room were raw, just below the surface, waiting to explode. She could understand his sorrow, but this was no time for zoning out. They both had to be thinking sharp. Why in the world did he let the police look at a "few things" on his computer? The husband is always a suspect when the wife dies "accidentally," even in the best of marriages.

Before speaking, the Barracuda got up and closed the French doors separating the study from the foyer.

"How're you doing, Sean?"

He slowly shook his head. "Not so good," he replied without looking up. "I can't stop thinking about her."

The Barracuda nodded grimly and sat back down next to Sean. She leaned toward him, her elbows on her knees, getting as close as she could without actually touching him. She knew the cops could look through the windowpanes on the French doors at any minute, and she was not taking any chances.

"I know it's hard," she whispered, "but you've got to pull yourself together. I'm here for you." At this, she reached out and took both of Sean's hands in hers, squeezing them strongly before she let go and checked over her shoulder to make sure no one was looking in. No one was, so she also reached out and gently rubbed his back.

This show of affection drew no response from the doctor other than a slight increase in the stream of tears trickling down both cheeks. The Barracuda withdrew her hands and checked again for the police. No onlookers. She leaned forward again, her mouth inches from Sean's ear.

Enough solemnities. The Barracuda decided to get right down to business. "What did they look at on the computer?"

It was as if she hadn't spoken, as if she hadn't penetrated the trance.

She grabbed his knee and shook it, firmly but gently. "Sean," she insisted, "what did they look at on the computer?"

"Oh, they were just looking at the documents file to see if she had written anything with more details than the suicide note they found... They were just...um... I really don't know."

"Did you watch them the entire time they were on the computer?"

"Yeah, of course." He now turned to look at the Barracuda. His voice took on an edge. "I'm not an idiot."

The sharpness of the response and the gauntness of his eyes shocked the Barracuda. But she was enough of a pro not to show it. Without the least hint of flinching or wavering, she returned his gaze and sharpened her own tone.

"It's not a good idea to let them snoop around on that computer. You've got financial dealings to protect."

"They'll never figure that out," Sean said wearily. "I've got that protected in so many different ways—"

"*Sean...*" The Barracuda's interruption was intense, stopping his ramblings in midsentence. "Listen to me. You cannot, you *must* not, ever let them look on your computer again. And when they leave, I want you to get a hard drive, just like your current one, pay cash for it, and reload every program, every document, and every transaction that's on your present computer into your new one over the next few days *except*—" Sean's stare had returned to the floor. "Listen to me, Sean." He nodded. "*Except* for any transactions showing money going to me. I don't even want it on your hard drive, okay?"

Sean nodded, still looking down.

The Barracuda paused and took a deep breath. It was time to deliver the bombshell.

She softened her voice, speaking barely above a whisper, knowing that the words themselves would have enough sting without a blunt delivery increasing their impact.

"Sean, they know that you were having an affair, and they know that Erica discovered it just a few days before she died."

Sean's head jerked up and he rocked back in his seat, rubbing his face in disbelief. "How?"

"I don't know how," replied the Barracuda ever so quietly, "but they know. They told me about it. They obviously don't know your affair was with me."

"They didn't say anything to me," Sean replied.

"Shh," cautioned the Barracuda. She glanced back over her shoulder. "It's the oldest police trick in the book. They withhold some vital information to see if you 'fess up, see if you try to hide anything. If you don't come clean, they figure there are hidden motives."

Sean cursed bitterly. The Barracuda could see the sadness turning to fear.

"Here's what we do, Sean. I call the police back in here like I've just cajoled a confession out of you about this affair. You tell them that you were sleeping around with somebody. Make up a name that's as believable as possible, but make it somebody with a Virginia Beach address. I'll tell Inspector Giovanni that I'll check her out myself, or if he won't buy that, I'll get one of my detectives at the beach to check it out. Either way, we'll confirm the affair. Are you with me on this?"

Sean nodded.

"But, Sean, you've got to be so incredibly careful. Don't give them anymore than you absolutely have to. I'll sit in here with you during the interview. And Sean…"

Their eyes locked intently on each other.

"If my name ever, *ever* slips out in connection with this affair, then I can't help you with this mess and you're on your own. You understand that, don't you?"

Though Sean nodded his head, his blank stare revealed that he wasn't understanding much of anything. He was in shock, on autopilot, marching to the orders of the one person thinking clearly.

"I love you, Sean," said the Barracuda. Then she touched him gently on the shoulder and rose from her seat to retrieve the lieutenant.

She found Giovanni in the kitchen, leaning against the counter, talking in hushed tones to the uniformed cops.

"Thanks for giving me a few minutes alone," said the Barracuda. "I think it did some good. There are a few things Dr. Armistead neglected to tell you."

CHAPTER 36

Twenty-four hours later, as Sean Armistead made funeral arrangements, the Virginia Beach inmates were baking in waves of heat from the late morning sun as they picked up trash along Interstate 264. It was a thankless job and a humiliating one. If the orange jumpsuits weren't enough to put the whole world on notice that these men were convicts, the dregs of society, then certainly the guards with their rifles held loosely by their side would do the trick. At least the guards had the decency not to require the men to wear leg irons or to be chained together like slaves.

The men moved slowly and methodically, bending occasionally to pick up some trash only if the guards were looking, determined not to expend too much energy on such a meaningless task. Buster was one of the most lethargic and sullen. He took pride in the fact that he only bent to scoop up large items, like pieces of cardboard or empty boxes. It would sometimes take him nearly an hour to fill a single bag.

Thomas Hammond, on the other hand, was a workhorse. He would always bring up the rear of the work crew, picking up all the little pieces of trash that the other men missed. The first day out he constantly told the others to slow down and be more careful—they were missing a lot of junk. He eventually realized that this was the whole point of what they were doing, cherry-picking the easy stuff, leaving the small and nasty items—half eaten hamburgers, disposable diapers, used snot-rags—for suckers like Thomas. He didn't mind. And he still filled up nearly as many bags as two or three of the others put together.

Thomas had just tied a bag, topped off with a couple of beer cans and an apple core, when he saw Buster walking back toward him. It was not unusual for Buster to come back and hang out next to Thomas, griping and sulking while Thomas worked. Buster dragged his empty bag behind him while Thomas filled his own. Then, without breaking stride, the men would switch trash bags and continue on until Thomas filled the second bag as well.

"What up, Pops?" asked Buster.

"Nothin'. Gonna be a hot one."

"What're you smokin'? Already is."

An SUV stuffed with teenage boys drove by. They had their windows down and hooted at the inmates. A Hardee's bag flew from the vehicle and landed about fifty feet in front of Buster and Thomas.

Buster cursed the boys, causing Thomas to wince.

"Punks," snarled Buster. "I'll waste 'em when I get out of this joint."

"How you gonna find 'em?" asked Thomas, heading for the Hardee's bag.

"I'll find 'em," promised Buster.

The two men worked on in silence, Thomas waiting for the bellyaching to begin again in earnest. But for some reason Buster was strangely quiet this morning, and it worried Thomas a little.

"You all right?" asked Thomas.

"Been thinkin'," replied the big man.

"'Bout?"

"'Bout what the rev said. You really buy that stuff, Pops?" Buster, staring ahead at the shoulder of the road and the other inmates, didn't even look at Thomas as he asked the question.

Thomas stopped stuffing his bag so he could concentrate on his answer. He didn't want to push too hard, but this was the first time Buster had ever asked about spiritual things. Thomas didn't want to blow this opportunity, couldn't live with himself if he did, but he really didn't know quite how to respond. He had never been to seminary, didn't have any formal education at all, as a matter of fact. Where was Pastor Charles Arnold when you really needed him?

"'Course I believe it," Thomas said.

Buster walked a few steps and kicked a soda can. "If it's true, why'd God let your kid die?"

It felt like Buster had punched Thomas in the gut all over again. It was the same question that had haunted Thomas every second since Armistead pronounced Joshie dead. *Why'd God let your kid die?* He wouldn't blame it on

God. *Couldn't.* How could he serve a God like that? It had to be his own lack of faith, his own failure to believe. God wanted Joshua healed, and Thomas just harbored too much doubt. It *had* to be that way, didn't it?

How could he ever explain this to Buster?

"Can't say as I know why," said Thomas softly. He walked a few more steps and picked up a foil wrapper. He had blown it. He didn't have a clue what else to say.

Wisdom, he prayed. *Just give me wisdom!*

He scoured the ground and took a few more steps in silence before a new thought hit him. "Maybe," said Thomas haltingly, "one reason's so we could meet. So I could save your neck and tell you 'bout Christ."

Buster gave him a skeptical look, his hard face twisting into a frown. "Since you brought it up, Pops, I've been meaning to ax you, why *did* you keep me from gettin' shanked?" Buster's deep voice sounded a little thick with emotion. He had never uttered a word about the stabbing incident since the day he and Thomas had dinner together.

Thomas shrugged. "Don't reckon I really thought about it. Just did it."

Thomas waited for a response, but Buster just kept shuffling along, squinting off into the distance again.

What do I say now? "But don't focus on me," Thomas continued, "Pete's sake, I just *risked* my life. Focus on Jesus, that man actually *gave* His life— *died* so you could be forgiven."

This time Thomas decided to wait for a response even if it took all day.

Buster took his eyes from the horizon and glued them on the ground. "For *me*," he said, the sarcasm dripping from his words. "Then God must be dumber'n I thought. Must not know what I've done."

Thomas *was* ready for this. "What you've done don't matter," he insisted. "I risked my life for you when you was showin' me nothin' but hate. And the Bible says that Christ died for us while we were yet sinners. It don't matter what you've done."

"You don't know, Pops. This black man's done some things."

"It don't matter." Thomas dropped his trash bag on the ground and

turned toward Buster. He was getting animated now, forgetting about his insecurities. "Don't you remember what Pastor Charles told us about the thief on the cross? That man was prob'ly a murderer. Least you never kilt nobody."

The silence from Buster caused the coil of tension in Thomas's neck to tighten a few more turns. His cellmate—a killer. Could God really save Buster?

"Even if you had"—Thomas watched Buster's face for a reaction, saw nothing—"it just don't matter. God loves you, warts and all."

"Warts and all"—that was a dumb thing to say, thought Thomas. It always sounded good when his pastor said it from the pulpit, but Thomas was speaking to a murderer. Warts seemed a little tame for this guy.

The silence lingered for what seemed like an eternity. But what else was there to say? Thomas had done his duty and stuck up for his God even as his mind swirled with unanswered questions. He'd done the best he could, though he'd said a few stupid things. But what more could God possibly expect of him?

"What does matter?" asked Buster. He stopped walking and studied the ground between himself and Thomas.

The question made Thomas tingle with nervousness and excitement. He looked around, half expecting God to just send Pastor Charles driving down the highway to stop by and help Buster sort this out. But there was no pastor, no angel. It was all up to Thomas.

"Just kneel down and pray to God," Thomas said with a shaky voice. "Just admit you're a sinner, tell God you're sorry for your sins, accept Christ as your Savior, and ask Him into your heart. He'll change everything."

Just then a car buzzed by and swerved toward the shoulder. The driver blew his horn, and the passenger flipped off the prisoners. The guards, still fifty yards back, just laughed. Buster didn't seem to notice.

"That's easy for you, Pops. But I've never talked to the Big Man in my life."

Thomas took a step toward him. "Tell you what. If you're ready to do this. If you're ready to git saved right now and git things right with God, you just kneel down next to me right here, and I'll tell you what to pray."

For the first time Buster looked up at Thomas. His eyes were red and wet, and now they widened with the realization of what Thomas was asking. "We gotta *kneel?*"

"Yeah, why not?"

"Here?"

"Yeah."

Buster looked around and nodded at the guards behind him and the other inmates ahead. "What 'bout them?" He said it in a near whisper, though they were still fifty feet away. "What're *they* gonna think?"

"If that's all you care about, what others think, then you'll just go to hell," stated Thomas, authority and conviction deep in his voice. He surprised himself with this boldness.

Buster jerked his head back and gave Thomas an astonished look. The comment seemed to rattle him. In all their time together, Thomas had never uttered even one curse word.

"Says who?"

"Says the Bible, that's who. If you're ashamed of Christ before men, He'll be ashamed of you before the heavenly Father." Thomas paused to gather his thoughts. "It takes a real man to believe in Christ, Buster, no matter what others think."

Buster looked front and back, then at Thomas again. His eyes were still red. "God can change *me*—Buster Jackson—shot-caller for the ES?"

"Yep."

"Then let's do this thing."

Without another word, right there on the shoulder of the interstate, with cars buzzing by and the prison guards glaring at them from fifty feet away, the two huge men in their orange jumpsuits sank to their knees, folded their hands like little children, and got ready to pray.

"Make it quick," mumbled Buster.

CHAPTER 37

Charles thought about what to say and how he would say it the entire two-hour drive to Richmond. He could have called Denita but decided that something this important really needed to be done in person. He owed her that much.

He tried to judge his motivations and gain a clear picture of his turbulent heart. He had moved beyond resenting Denita for the opportunity she had. Some serious prayer time had helped. And while he didn't share her views on many legal issues, that was really none of his business. The senators would have to plumb those depths. His role, his only role, was to decide whether he should disclose the fact that his wife had an illegal abortion four years ago, using a drug that had not been approved in the United States at the time and was even now the object of great controversy.

To complicate matters, Denita had managed to keep her views on the volatile issue of abortion secret throughout her legal career. Charles suspected that was one of the reasons both sides had settled on her as a compromise candidate. Only Charles knew the truth. She not only favored abortion rights, she had a personal history that would make it impossible for her to remain objective.

Charles also knew that this fact, if it ever seeped out in the press, would disqualify her immediately. The president would never stand for it. Senator Crafton would desert her in a second, throwing his weight behind some other female African American lawyer. And so it all came down to Charles and his decision whether to betray his ex-wife or imperil the future of so many unborn children.

Denita claimed she had changed. But one thing had not changed, could never change. He would be reminded of it later this afternoon, after he talked with Denita, when he visited a small plot in a Richmond cemetery he had purchased a few days after he learned about the abortion. "Baby Arnold," the marker said. It had been a little over a year since he had been there. He tried to make a pilgrimage every year, on the anniversary of the date Denita said she had induced the abortion. But this year he was a couple of weeks late.

When he arrived at the law firm of Pope and Pollard, Denita's secretary told him that she was in Juvenile and Domestic Relations Court, putting in a few pro bono hours representing youthful offenders. *Her people,* thought Charles as he drove down to Richmond J&DR court. He wondered how long she had been doing this public service. *Probably started as soon as she learned about the possible nomination.*

He found her in Courtroom No. 4 in the massive Richmond Judicial Center and was surprised at how comfortable she looked seated at the defense counsel table and whispering to the brooding young man sitting next to her, challenging the prosecutor's claim of a parole violation. Charles watched her for about fifteen minutes before she turned and gazed in his direction. Her eyes popped wide, she raised an eyebrow, and then shrugged her shoulders— a "why are you here?" look.

A few minutes later Denita had talked the judge into a quick break. She watched the deputies haul the defendant away to lockup, then immediately made her way back to Charles.

"Quite a surprise," she said, placing a gentle hand on his arm. "What's the occasion?"

"Our conversation the other night."

"Okay," she said tentatively, removing her hand. She somehow sensed that a personal visit was not a good sign. "Can you stick around for lunch?"

Charles shook his head. He glanced around to make sure there were no eavesdroppers. "I've given this a lot of thought, Denita. Prayed about it." He paused. This was harder than he thought. "I think you need to tell the senator."

He heard the wind come out of her even as it brushed lightly across his face. Her strong frame suddenly looked so frail; the shoulders sagged for a moment but then straightened. She started nodding her head a little, as if she knew this was coming, then looked him in the eye.

Charles felt his throat constrict, his mouth go dry under her intense gaze. "If you tell him," Charles continued, "I won't say anything to anybody else. You and the senator will have my pledge of silence. He may not yank the nomination, but at least he'll know." Charles watched her expression carefully as she weighed this proposal. Her face grew tight, the lips forming a thin line of rejection. "I will have done my part," he said, "and I'll be able to sleep at night."

"It won't work," Denita told him without a moment's hesitation. "The senator would disown me in a heartbeat." She took a half-step closer, and her eyes drilled down deeper into his. "You can't pass this off on me, Charles. I'm not saying anything about it. I've already decided. If you can't live with that, then do what you have to do." She sighed as if she had been drawn into an argument she didn't want. "I've made my decision, Charles. It's none of the senator's business."

She glanced over her shoulder toward the front of the courtroom, raising a hand toward a prosecutor who was looking impatient. "Just a second," Denita called out. As the prosecutor nodded her assent, Denita turned back to Charles. "Thanks for coming all this way," she said tersely. "I'm sorry you can't accept the fact that I've changed."

"Denita—"

But before he could explain himself, she turned and walked away.

⊷ ⋈⋄⊟ ⊶

On the way home he stopped at the cemetery to clear his mind and to honor the memory of Baby Arnold. He felt guilty that he had missed the anniversary of the baby's death this year and that, if he weighed his feelings honestly, this had become more a pilgrimage of duty than something he wanted to do. In the first few years, he had felt a peace at this grave. His journeys here lessened the aching in his soul. But the last two years, kneeling to pray on the grave of his only child had just triggered more destructive emotions—resentment, frustration, a brooding questioning of God's plan for this child. Instead of mourning, he found himself arguing with God.

As he walked past the other familiar headstones that marked the graves of those who had lived long and full lives, he felt the sadness descend. It wasn't just that Baby Arnold had never experienced the joys of life; it pained him equally that nobody cared even now. Other graves would be dotted with freshly cut flowers or landscaped with small plants growing around the head-stone. Relatives would kneel at other headstones and say a silent prayer. But never at the forgotten grave of Baby Arnold. He would be the only visitor. Once a year. And this year he had come late and hadn't found time to even stop for flowers.

And so it shocked him, literally sucked his breath away, as he stared at the freshly mowed gravesite for his child. He couldn't believe what he saw, couldn't believe what it meant.

Wilted flowers. Geraniums and pansies leaning against the tiny little headstone, as if they had been left there a few weeks ago. A small rose bush planted in front.

People change, Denita had said. *I've changed. Let me prove it to you.*

Perhaps she really meant it.

CHAPTER 38

It was Wednesday morning, and Nikki was running late. The alarm had worked fine, but so had the snooze button. Five times. By the time she and Stinky finally rolled out of her bed and nudged Tiger in his sleeping bag on the floor, it was already 7:15. She had to have the kids at day care by 8:00 so she could stop by the office and make it to court by 9:00. And she would require a minimum thirty minutes of primping before she could walk out the door.

At least Tiger no longer contracted deadly diseases every morning. He seemed to like the day care a lot better than he did school. It was run by a community church of some type or another. Nikki figured that as long as the kids had to be in day care, their parents would want them in a religious one. The people taking care of the kids seemed nice enough, and the kids were making plenty of friends.

They stopped on their way for Chick-fil-A biscuits, coffee for Nikki, and chocolate milk for the kids. Nikki had no idea how the supermoms did it— work, children, household chores, and husbands to boot. It was wearing her out, putting a hurtin' on her efforts to stay in shape and burn a tan. She could do it for one more month if she had to, all the way through trial. But she really only planned to do it for one more day. After today's preliminary hearing, after Charles tore into Dr. Armistead on cross-examination, Thomas and Theresa Hammond should be free to go home with their children.

Sure, it was unusual for any judge, particularly one as careful as Silverman, to kick a case out at the preliminary hearing stage based on lack of probable cause. But it was not unheard of. And with everything they had against Armistead, the prosecution's main witness...well, today just might be the day.

The prosecution would have to establish probable cause on two elements of the crime. First, the Barracuda would have to prove that Thomas and Theresa knew or should have known that their delay in seeking medical care created an unreasonable risk to the life of Joshua. Second, the Barracuda would have to establish that the failure to get Joshua to the hospital earlier was the cause in fact of his death. Since the Hammonds could not be forced to testify against themselves, the Barracuda would have to prove her case by the testimony of others.

The Barracuda had not subpoenaed the children to testify at this hearing. She probably didn't want to take an unnecessary risk on what they might say. Nikki and Charles had debated whether they should call the children as witnesses themselves, but ultimately they decided that their testimony would hurt more than help. The children would sit this one out, playing at day care while their fate hung in the balance.

"Oops," said Tiger from the backseat of the Sebring.

"Oh man," muttered an exasperated Nikki. "What do you mean 'oops'?"

"I dus spilt my chocolate milk, dat's all."

"Did it get on the car?" Nikki fought back visions of her fine leather interior stained and smelling like sour milk. Tiger was a walking, talking disaster area.

"A little," Tiger admitted. "But most of it spilt on me."

"Thank goodness," muttered Nikki.

"Here's some extra napkins," said Stinky cheerily as she handed them over the back of the front seat. "No sense crying over spilt milk."

"I ain't crying," said Tiger. "But it looks like I tinkled in my pants."

———— ⚓ ————

Ten minutes later Miss Nikki dropped Tiger off, milk stain and all, at the Green Run Community Church day-care center. She kissed him and Stinky on the cheek, something she had just started doing in the last few days, and told them to have a great day. She even reminded them to say their prayers for their mommy and daddy.

Tiger untucked his shirt as soon as Miss Nikki turned her back to leave. It hung down almost far enough to cover the wet spot on his pants, but not quite. This could be a very, very long day.

Tiger liked day care pretty well. It wasn't like school—all work and no play. Here, you would have prayer time in the morning, then do what you wanted until lunch. After lunch there would be nap time, then story time—

Bible stories with worksheets—and sometimes arts and crafts. Then more free time until Miss Nikki would show up to take them home.

Tiger liked the teachers at day care, and he liked the other kids. All except Joey. Joey was Tiger's age, but you'd never know it from looking at him. He outweighed Tiger by thirty pounds, and he had a mean streak. He had beady little eyes that seemed out of place on his moon-shaped face. And Tiger was sure that if Joey ever took off his shirt, he would already be growing hair under his arms.

Tiger made fun of Joey when Tiger was alone with Stinky at Miss Nikki's house—"Doughy Joey" he would call him. But at day care Tiger avoided Joey like the plague. He had already seen Joey get into two or three fights with other kids half Joey's size, and Tiger was sure it was just a matter of time before the dough boy would turn on him. If it ever happened, Tiger's plan was to kick Joey hard with his cowboy boots, then run like mad. It was a plan he was hoping he would never have to test.

Today Tiger and Stinky had arrived a little late, so Miss Parsons was already fielding prayer requests from the boys and girls who sat around her in a circle. Tiger scooted into a spot on the floor a few feet away from Joey, out of reach and out of harm's way. Tiger spread his shirttail out over his stained shorts and settled in to listen to the usual emergency prayer needs.

They had just started, so the kids were still raising their hands to voice prayer requests for their pets, who all seemed to be struck with some type of disease or another. Tiger desperately wanted a pet too—preferably a dog, but he would settle for a hamster—so that he could keep the class informed about his dog's health and request prayer for real or imagined illnesses. Tiger was sure that all these pets couldn't possibly have all the sicknesses they prayed about on a daily basis, but it was a surefire way to get attention and let the rest of the kids know that you were lucky enough to have a pet in the first place.

"Yes, Heather," said Miss Parsons, calling on a sad looking red-haired girl about Stinky's age.

"Pray for Rascal, please," requested Heather. She seemed about to cry.

"How's Rascal doing?" Miss Parsons seemed very concerned too.

"Not too good. He can't see very well anymore, and he won't eat hardly anything. My dad says we might have to take him to the vet. I don't want them to put him to sleep…" Heather's voice trailed off melodramatically. Her bottom lip quivered. Tiger thought it was a bit much to put on such a show about the sleep habits of an old dog.

But Miss Parsons was reassuring. "Okay, we will." She turned to a normally quiet little girl sitting to her right, hand raised straight up. "Jenny?"

"My cat, Slinky, is almost ready to have kittens."

Several of the little girls oohed and aahed at this news. Tiger did not join them. He didn't like cats—in fact, he would always secretly open his eyes when Miss Parsons lifted up the cats in prayer. He didn't want any part of that. Cats were fat and lazy and basically good for nothing. And he certainly wasn't going to pray that old fat and lazy Slinky would be able to bring about a dozen more of her kind into this world. As far as Tiger was concerned, the world already had enough cats.

Hands continued to shoot up, and eventually the requests turned from pets to grandparents. Seemed like everybody's granny or papaw was at death's door or at least in the hopsicle for something. Tiger was tempted to pop their balloons and remind them of what little good the hopsicle had done for Joshie, but he decided against it. The sooner prayer time ended, the sooner they could get outside and play. There was no sense complicating matters.

"Hannah?" said Miss Parsons, calling on Tiger's sister and snapping Tiger out of his daydream. "How can we pray for you?"

Uh-oh, thought Tiger. He never liked it when Stinky would share private details about their troubled lives.

"My mommy and daddy are going to court today"—this was news to Tiger; where did Stinky get this information?—"and if everything goes good, my daddy might get out of jail."

For a moment, a fleeting moment, this pronouncement made Tiger's heart flutter with excitement.

"Why's your daddy in jail?" asked a concerned voice from behind Tiger. It was one of the kids but not a voice that Tiger recognized.

Stinky's face went red. Tiger felt his own cheeks burning.

"It's not important to know the reason why he's in jail," explained Miss Parsons. "Let's just pray that court goes well for him today. Okay?"

Heads nodded, and more hands went up. But out of the corner of his eye, Tiger saw Joey slide over a few feet until he was sitting right next to him.

"What did your dad do?" Joey whispered when Miss Parsons wasn't looking.

Tiger shrugged. "I can't say," he whispered back while looking straight ahead.

"Is he really in jail?" Joey pried.

Tiger nodded his head. His cheeks were still burning, and now his eyes were starting to water. *This is no time to cry,* he told himself.

Joey slid back away. It was almost time to pray, and it looked like Tiger had dodged this bullet—the dough boy had lost interest. They moved on to other requests, and Tiger breathed a sigh of relief.

The relief was short-lived, shattered by a remark that Joey made just loud enough for Tiger and the others sitting around him to hear.

"Tiger's dad is a jailbird," mocked Joey. "Tweet-tweet. Tweet-tweet."

"Tweet-tweet," echoed another voice, softly but within earshot of Tiger.

"Tweet-tweet."

"Tweet-tweet."

"Let's bow our heads and pray," said Miss Parsons.

CHAPTER 39

Next case is Commonwealth versus Jackson, possession with intent to distribute," said the court clerk, stifling a yawn. "The matter is before the court on defendant's motion to suppress."

Charles Arnold took his place at one counsel table, the Barracuda moved to the other. They had not said a word to each other in the ninety minutes they had been waiting for the case to be called. Judge Silverman had concluded two other hearings and had not yet returned from a ten-minute break.

"Bring in the defendant," said the clerk.

The deputies disappeared out a side door and came back with Buster Jackson in tow. He was wearing an orange jumpsuit, leg irons, and handcuffs. He was the perfect foil for Charles, who was all decked out in his favorite suit: a light beige job, custom athletic cut, with five buttons down the front.

Buster settled in at the defense counsel table without acknowledging Charles. His sunken eyes stared straight ahead, his goateed jaw jutting out.

"I heard you accepted Christ," whispered Charles, leaning toward the big man.

"True."

The big man didn't look too happy about it. "Congratulations," said Charles.

"Who told you?"

"Thomas."

"When'd you talk to him?"

"Yesterday."

The big man shifted in his seat but still looked straight ahead. "Why you callin' him and dissin' me?" Buster asked through clenched teeth. "You don't come by. You don't call. You don't do squat."

Charles bristled at this unexpected attack. Buster wasn't acting like a man who'd just turned to Christ. Charles had worked too hard for this guy and was putting his own reputation on the line. This was the thanks he got? Right now, he didn't really care how big Buster was. He'd had it up to here with his attitude.

"The brothers say the Moreno woman's hot," Buster continued. "Is 'at why you're crawlin' all over that case and treating me like a ho?"

Charles turned and faced Buster, placing one palm on the table and the other on the back of Buster's chair. He spoke in low tones, so only Buster could hear. "You want me in or out?"

Buster looked straight ahead, tightened his face, and breathed hard through his flared nostrils. No answer.

"In or out?" Charles insisted.

"*In.*"

"Then here's some advice: Shut your face and let me do the talking." Charles paused, daring Buster to spout off again. "And put on a happy little smile. The judge has enough reason to put you away as it is."

Charles hovered there for a moment, inches from Buster's face, then leaned back in his chair. He felt the tension creeping up his spine and sensed the anger seeping over from his client. This was no way to start a major hearing.

A few moments later Silverman entered through the back door, and the clerk called the court to order. "I believe this is your motion, Mr. Arnold. Why don't you call your first witness?"

"The defense calls Rodney Gage."

Officer Rodney Gage, who had been sitting immediately behind the Barracuda, stood ramrod straight and took the oath. He climbed into the witness box, sat erect, and stared straight through Charles. Gage was the arresting officer; the man Charles Arnold was accusing of racial profiling. His demeanor made it clear that he did not take these allegations lightly.

He's so young, thought Charles. Gage had a boyish face, a full head of blond hair, smooth white skin—*very white skin,* thought Charles—and the build of a young athlete whose muscles had not yet succumbed to the erosions of gravity and time. Charles was hoping for an older man, a harsher looking man, someone who didn't look quite so, well, quite so honest.

Charles breezed through some preliminary questions, making sure to station himself directly between the witness and the Barracuda. No sense letting the witness get some free coaching.

"Are you the officer who arrested Buster Jackson on June 3 for possession of cocaine with intent to distribute."

"Yes sir, I am."

"Now you didn't see any drugs on Mr. Jackson or in his vehicle *before* you pulled him over, correct?"

"Not before, that's right. After we pulled him over, there were two bags of cocaine in plain sight, sticking out from under the front seat."

"But I didn't ask you about *after*, did I, Officer?"

Gage frowned. The Barracuda jumped to her feet, anxious to pick a fight. "Objection, argumentative."

Silverman, who had been watching the proceedings with the slightest hint of a bemused smile, lifted his chin from his hand. "Sustained," he said pleasantly.

Charles started walking in an arc now, as if circling his prey. The questions came faster, staccato style.

"You understand, sir, that you've got to have a reasonable suspicion that my client was committing or had committed a crime in order to stop him, correct?"

"Yes."

"You can't just stop a law-abiding citizen for no reason."

"Correct."

"And one of the reasons for stopping a person cannot be the color of his skin. You understand that, don't you?"

"Sure."

"Then please tell the court, sir, your reason for pulling over my client on June 3? What caused you to be suspicious?"

Officer Gage drew a long breath and leaned back slightly. This answer would be well-rehearsed. "First and foremost, the actions of Mr. Jackson. He was cruising the oceanfront, Atlantic Avenue to be exact, and appeared to be looking for somebody. I saw him, with my own eyes, pick up two young males, take them for a ride around the block, then drop them off at the same spot. In my opinion, the length of time they were in the car was sufficiently long for a drug deal to have occurred.

"Second, the conduct of the men that Mr. Jackson picked up and dropped off. After they got out of the car, I noticed that they looked around suspiciously, saw our police vehicle, then hustled off and disappeared into the crowd."

Charles kept a poker face but felt the sting of that second factor. He had not anticipated that part of the answer. It would tend to distinguish the stop of Buster Jackson from the stops of the guinea-pig motorists that Charles had recruited from his class.

"Third," Gage continued, "was the type of vehicle. It was a brand-new Cadillac Escalade SUV with tinted windows. The owner certainly had some bucks, and the windows could help conceal any illegal activities.

"And fourth, the location of the transaction. We have a lot of drug activity at the oceanfront in the summer, particularly on Atlantic Avenue." Gage paused for a moment, pretending to search the ceiling for other information. "I think that about covers it."

"Thank you, Officer Gage." Charles walked back to his counsel table and, just before sitting, turned back to the witness for one final question. "By the way, have you been on duty the last few weeks, and if so, what was your schedule?"

Gage looked perplexed. "I work the swing shift—3:00 to 11:00 p.m.—Tuesday through Saturday. That's been my schedule for the last two weeks."

Charles took his seat. "Your witness," he said to the Barracuda.

She rose immediately to the challenge and walked out from behind her counsel table. She stood next to where Charles was seated, so the witness could eye them both at the same time.

"Let me ask you the one question that Mr. Charles here—"

"Arnold," Charles corrected her without rising. "The name is Charles *Arnold.*"

"Okay. Let me ask you the one question that Mr. Arnold here was apparently afraid to ask—"

"*Objection.*"

"Sustained," said Silverman immediately. "Ms. Crawford, let's keep it from getting personal, shall we?"

"Sure, Your Honor." The Barracuda walked to the front of her own counsel table and stared at the floor for a moment, apparently thinking about a way to ask the question without drawing another objection. Charles found himself hanging on her every word, then realized what she had done. She had the entire courtroom—Charles, the law students who had come to see their professor in action, the newspaper reporter who had deemed this hearing worthy of coverage, and most important, the judge—anxiously listening and waiting for her next few words. She was *good.*

"Officer Gage, was the race of the defendant a factor in deciding whether or not there was reasonable suspicion to stop him?"

"Absolutely not."

"Did the fact that his skin color happened to be black, as opposed to white, even enter into your analysis as to whether it was likely he had committed a crime?"

"No ma'am. No way."

"Would you have pulled over and investigated a white man who did the same things that you have described?"

"Yes."

"And have you, in the past, pulled over whites for the same type of conduct?"

"Sure. All the time."

"Now, Officer Gage, if the court rules against you, how would that hamstring your attempts to combat drug trafficking at the beach?"

Charles bolted from his seat. "Objection, Your Honor, that question is totally improper."

"Sustained."

Charles sat back down, knowing he had procured a hollow victory. The question was improper, but it had planted a seed of the thought in the judge's mind. The Barracuda really knew her stuff.

"Do you make decisions about who to pull over and who not to pull over alone?"

"No ma'am. My partner and I will usually make those decisions together. I would certainly never pull over someone if my partner objected. I will usually say something like, 'Let's pull this guy and take a look.' Then I'll wait for him to concur or, if he doesn't think it's a good idea, to say so."

"Is that the type of thing that happened with Mr. Jackson?"

"I don't remember specifically, so I can't say for sure. But I'm reasonably certain we would have said something like that."

The testimony seemed innocuous on the surface, this talk about a partner, but it hit Charles hard. His stomach tightened and churned. *Could it be? Why hadn't he asked Buster? Why hadn't Buster said anything?* Charles took a quick sideways glance at his tightly wound client. The man was still seething from their earlier confrontation. But Charles needed to know. He leaned over and asked something he should have asked that first night in the cell.

"Is this guy's partner black or white?" whispered Charles.

"No further questions," said the Barracuda to the witness. "I'd like to recall this witness later if necessary. But for now, Your Honor, I'm through."

"Why does *that* matter?" Buster whispered back to Charles. The lawyer's stomach, already in knots, now dropped to his feet.

"You may step down," said Silverman to an erect and unbowed Officer Gage.

CHAPTER 40

Just answer the question," Charles whispered to his client.

"Black," said Buster. He gave Charles a look of disdain. "Chocolate, bro. Dark chocolate."

Charles resented the comment. Is that what Buster's lingering hostility was all about? A lack of trust because Charles's skin color and pedigree were too light?

"Why didn't you tell me?"

"You didn't ask," the big man snarled. "'Sides, what difference does it make? *Gage* busted me, not his partner."

Charles just shook his head. "It changes *everything*," he whispered emphatically.

"Next witness," Silverman called out.

"The defense calls Dr. Frederick Ryder."

At hearing his name, an unimpressive-looking man in the second row rose and proceeded to the front of the courtroom to take the oath. He was a short man with an uneven gait and an enormous head balanced on a pencil-thin neck. His sport coat hung limply on his thin, pear-shaped body, and he seemed ill at ease as he took his place in the witness box. He settled in and pushed his thick glasses to the top of his hawklike nose, an annoying habit that would be repeated many times during pressure-filled situations. He placed his folder of charts on the rail in front of the witness box, crossed his legs, and glanced nervously from Charles to the judge and back to Charles again.

It was on this quirky little man, this pencil-pushing statistician from Old Dominion University, that Charles pinned all of his rapidly fading hopes for an early release of Buster Jackson. And even if Ryder performed like a champ, Charles would still need a minor miracle to blunt the impact of an African American partner being part of the decision to stop Buster.

In a soothing monotone, Ryder shuffled through his charts and, at Charles's prompting, explained his methodology. He had been asked to conduct a scientific sampling of investigative stops at the Virginia Beach oceanfront to determine if there was a pattern of racial profiling, he testified. Using the students in Charles's class as guinea pigs, they had recreated the scenario of Buster's stop, as closely as possible, a total of fifty-six times over the last fourteen nights.

Four times a night, said the statistician, a student would drive down Atlantic Avenue in front of a parked Virginia Beach police cruiser and pick up a couple of other students who had been loitering the sidewalk. The driver would then drive once around the block and drop these same students off again, within viewing distance of the beach police, at approximately the same location. The cars would of course change, depending on the students involved. But more important, the race of the students would vary as well. Black drivers would pick up black passengers, and white drivers would pick up white passengers.

Based on this study, Ryder concluded that racial profiling was indeed occurring at the beach, and he had the charts to prove it. Chart one, a colorful pie graph, showed the total number of times white students performed this routine (42) and the total number of white students who were pulled over as a result (11). A second chart, equally colorful, showed the total number of times black students did this (14) and the total number of times the blacks were pulled over (7). Chart three was the punch line: Whites had a 26 percent chance of being pulled over for this conduct; blacks had a 50 percent chance.

In other words, said Ryder, blacks were almost twice as likely to be pulled over and searched for suspicious conduct. This was "unequivocal evidence of systemic racial profiling" in the informed opinion of Dr. Ryder. He pushed his glasses up with an index finger, his eyes darting from Charles to the judge.

"Dr. Ryder, were you able to determine if any of these instances involved Officer Gage?"

"Um, yes, I was. The students would always check the badges and identify the officers who had pulled them over."

"How many of these instances involved Officer Gage?"

Ryder shuffled loudly through some papers, dropping a few on the floor. Bending over to retrieve them, he bumped the mike in front of him, causing it to squeal. "Sorry," said the Ph.D. He found his page and looked back up at Charles, tilting that massive head to the side.

"Four involved Officer Gage."

Charles stopped pacing, paused, then asked: "How many involved blacks and how many involved whites?"

Thankfully, that information was on the same sheet of paper. "Three stops were blacks, only one was the stop of a white student."

Charles knew there were still unanswered questions. *How many times did Gage see a white student do this and not stop him? How many times did he see a black student do this and not stop him?* And Charles knew that the Barracuda was chomping at the bit to ask these and other similar questions. In fact, Charles was counting on it. She might be surprised at the answers, so long as his quirky little witness could remember the script.

"Pass the witness," said Charles.

By late morning, Tiger had grown tired of the tweety birds chirping all around him. He stood outside in the play area, trying hard to ignore Joey and his chorus as they periodically filled the air with tweets. He also tried not to think about his dad, though he couldn't help but get his hopes up based on what Stinky had said that morning. While he would miss the Pretty Lady, it would be great to be back home with his mommy and daddy, wraslin' his dad on the living room floor. Time seemed to crawl as he dreamed his happy thoughts in the midst of the annoying birds chirping nonstop on the playground.

Since Tiger wanted to be left alone, he waited in line for a turn on one of the precious few swings. It seemed that the girl occupying this particular swing would never leave, and it only inspired her to swing longer when she saw Tiger waiting patiently. And just as she finally did get off, after swinging for what seemed like hours, trouble showed up in the person of Doughy Joey.

Though he hadn't even been waiting in line, or really anywhere near the swing as far as Tiger could tell, Joey suddenly pushed himself in front of Tiger and plopped his big bottom down in the leather swing that Tiger had been waiting for.

"Hey!" protested Tiger. "I was waitin' for that."

"Tweet-tweet," said Joey.

"Stop it," said Tiger, "and wait your turn."

"I ain't waitin' for nobody who's got a drug dealer for a dad," said Joey as he began to pump his legs to get the swing going.

This made Tiger furious. His dad might be in jail, thanks to the stupidity of that mean lawyer lady, but he sure wasn't no drug dealer. And Tiger wasn't about to let some fat dough boy say he was. Tiger was on the verge of tears, and he fought the urge to run away. But he also felt the anger well up inside him, overtake the fear, then dictate his next move.

"Take it back!" yelled Tiger. "Take it back!"

Joey might be bigger and stronger, but right now Tiger was a lot madder. And Tiger had seen enough fistfights to know that when five-year-olds fight, the meanest and maddest kid usually won.

Joey dragged his feet and stopped the swing. He got up and took a few steps toward Tiger, looking down his nose at his skinny little foe.

"Make me," sneered Joey.

And Tiger almost did just that. He was so mad. He almost punched the big kid's lights out right on the spot. But looking up at Joey, who seemed to have grown six inches in the few seconds since he had gotten off the swing, Tiger had a sudden change of heart.

"I'm tellin'," he said, and he turned to find Miss Parsons.

Before Tiger could even finish his turn and show his back to his plump foe, Joey shot both of his short, pudgy arms out and popped Tiger hard on the shoulders. This caught Tiger by surprise, and it caught him just as he was turning. Before Tiger knew what hit him, he was sprawled out on the ground.

Someone yelled "Fight!" as Tiger popped back up, fists raised, facing Joey who now seemed to have grown another few inches. Tiger's lower lip was thrust out, his bony knees were shaking, and his eyes were watering as Joey slowly advanced. Tiger resisted with all his might the urge to turn tail and run, instead choosing to back-pedal slowly, fists raised, looking as mean as possible despite the tears and shakiness of his limbs. Joey circled and stalked; Tiger retreated and cried.

After ten or fifteen seconds—the longest ten or fifteen seconds of young Tiger's pitiful life—he heard the angry and welcome voice of Miss Parsons cutting through the crowd. "Boys!" she cried. "Stop it right now!"

Tiger gladly put down his fists without ever having to use the deadly weapons. He was just thankful that Miss Parsons had intervened before somebody—namely him—got hurt. Miss Parsons grabbed both Tiger and Joey by the arm and started yanking them inside. By the time the smoke had cleared, both kids were facing some serious time-out, though Joey definitely got the worst part of the noisy lecture. Miss Parsons even made both boys apologize, Joey for his thoughtless remarks about Mr. Hammond, and Tiger for his generally unchristian conduct. Then Tiger and Joey were sent to separate rooms, all by themselves, and instructed to think about their sorry behavior.

Tiger thought about survival. He had finished crying for now, but he was still scared to death of Joey. Though Tiger was no great fan of time-out, at least he was safe while he served his time in solitary confinement. If he were put back into the general day-care population, Joey would surely be out for blood, and there would be no guarantee that the chirping would have died down from the others anyway. No sir, the best plan for survival would be to figure out a way to spend the rest of the day on time-out, unpleasant as that might be. By tomorrow his dad would be home, and he could put all this day-care stuff in his rearview mirror.

After about half an hour of supposedly pondering his sins, Tiger looked up to see Miss Parsons entering the room. He tried to look dejected.

"Have you learned your lesson, young man?" Miss Parsons asked.

"Have you learned your lesson, young man?" Tiger repeated in a mocking tone.

This seemed to pretty much stop the day-care teacher in her tracks. She looked at Tiger suspiciously. "Do you need some more time in time-out?"

"Do you need some more time in time-out?"

That did it. Miss Parsons regained her composure and unleashed another stern lecture. "I know you're going through some tough times right now," she scolded, "but that's no excuse for this kind of behavior." She promised Tiger that he would spend all day on time-out if he didn't change his attitude.

Tiger could hardly suppress a smile. The plan seemed to be coming together quite nicely.

⚜

Charles watched an angry Barracuda stalk forward, notepad in hand. This was not going to be pretty.

"Have you ever even met Officer Gage before today?" she asked Dr. Ryder in an accusatory tone.

"No."

"So you have no idea what was going through his head the night that he pulled Buster Jackson over, do you?"

"No."

"Did you hear his testimony earlier this morning, where he enumerated his reasons for stopping Buster Jackson?"

"Yes."

"Did you hear him say that race was not even a factor?"

"Yes."

"Are you calling him a liar?" With this question, the Barracuda pointed sideways at Officer Gage, causing Ryder to make eye contact with the officer. Ryder's finger nervously and instinctively went to the glasses, pushing them to the top of his nose.

"No, I'm not saying that."

Charles tried to catch his witness's eye so he could give him a reinforcing look. *Show a little backbone, Professor.*

"The fact is, Officer Gage happened to be right, didn't he? I mean, this man"—the Barracuda pointed at Jackson—"had a whole car full of drugs, didn't he?"

Charles shot to his feet. "Objection, calls for speculation. How could this witness possibly know?"

"My point exactly," shot back the Barracuda. "But since defense counsel concedes it, I'll withdraw the question."

Charles sat back down, feeling suckered.

The Barracuda walked over and picked up the charts that Ryder had used during his direct examination. "Now, with regard to the fifty-six reenactments, if I can call them that, shown on these charts, how many were done in front of Officer Gage?"

"That information we do not have," answered Ryder, looking down at his hands. "But we know that at least four of the *stops* were conducted by Officer Gage, and three of them were on black drivers. And we know that Officer Gage was working on the nights when most of these reenactments were done."

The Barracuda took a step closer to the witness and raised her voice a notch, as if to punish the statistician for giving her a lengthy answer. "You weren't personally there, were you Dr. Ryder? You weren't out on the street watching these reenactments, were you?"

"No," Ryder said softly.

"So as far as you know, Officer Gage might have only seen this happen four times—three times with a black driver and one time with a white driver. He might have pulled over the driver *every single time* he saw it happen as far as you know, right?"

At last, thought Charles. *She had stepped into the trap.* He could almost hear the metal snap shut. *Now let's hope the prof has enough guts to spring it.*

"No, that's not correct," said Ryder in his soft monotone. "Last Wednesday night, for example, he pulled over Isaiah Gervin, one of the African American students. Every student who was pulled over was told to look at the name badge of the police officer and make a mental note of who it was. Isaiah noticed that it was Officer Gage, so he immediately called one of the white students in the class, who drove down to the beach with some classmates and was there within the hour—"

"Just answer the question," interrupted the Barracuda. "We don't need your speeches."

"He *is* answering the question, or at least he was trying to before *he* was interrupted," Charles interjected.

Judge Silverman looked at the witness. "You may finish the answer, but try to be concise."

Ryder nodded, bobbing his big head on his thin neck, like a bobble-head doll, and pushing his glasses all at the same time. "As I was saying, while Isaiah Gervin watched from across the street, the white student did the same thing that Gervin had done an hour earlier—picked up a couple of passengers from the sidewalk and gave them a ride around the block. Like Gervin, this white student did this right in front of Officer Gage's patrol vehicle. But this time, there was no stop. The simple truth, Ms. Crawford, is that the black kids were stopped, but the white kids were not."

The answer was delivered with such soft-spoken bluntness that it seemed to double its force. Charles could see the muscles flinch then tighten on the Barracuda's neck, the color of anger rising in her face.

"You weren't there, were you?"

"I said I wasn't."

"So you don't know whether Officer Gage might have been distracted when the white driver pulled his little stunt, or might have seen the black driver look suspiciously around in a way that the white driver didn't, or might have realized that this was all a game being played by a bunch of law students, or might have had any one of a dozen other legitimate reasons for not pulling over the white driver. *You don't know, do you?*"

The heat of the question—she was practically shouting now—was absorbed by Ryder and defused with a single, soft, sincere answer. "No, I have to trust what the students told me. But they're right here in the courtroom." He pointed to the spectator section behind Charles. "Ask them."

"I'm asking you," the Barracuda snarled.

"Objection."

"Sustained."

The Barracuda walked back to her counsel table, crossed her arms, and lowered her voice. "Your training is in statistics, right, Dr. Ryder?"

"Yes, that's correct."

"Not in police work."

"Right."

"And is it fair to say that nothing in your education, training, or experience qualifies you to in any way second-guess the work of an experienced police officer like Officer Gage?"

"I wasn't trying to second-guess him."

"You could have fooled me," said the Barracuda, slapping her notepad down on the counsel table and plopping into her seat. "For a minute there I actually thought you were trying to prove that Officer Gage might have been involved in this nasty little business of racial profiling."

This brought Charles out of his seat before he could stop himself. "I object to the sarcasm, Your Honor," he said.

"Ms. Crawford, do you have any further questions?" asked Silverman.

"Not for this man," huffed the seated Barracuda.

The judge released the witness. After one more push on the glasses, Ryder stepped down from the stand and scurried out of the courtroom, no doubt relieved to be heading back to the comfortable confines of academia.

CHAPTER 41

As Ryder beat his hasty retreat, Charles's client leaned close enough so that his nasty breath had Charles holding his own. "Is that all we've got?" asked Buster.

"For now."

"Impressive."

Buster leaned back and gave Charles a menacing stare as Charles stood to announce that he had no more witnesses. The Barracuda then made good on her threat to recall Officer Gage.

"Now, Officer Gage, you earlier testified that the investigative stop of Buster Jackson was pretty much a joint decision made between you and your partner, is that right?"

"That's correct."

"And the other stops that Dr. Ryder testified to a few minutes ago, were they also joint decisions between you and your partner?"

"I'm sure they were. That's the way we work. We do it together."

"Did your partner ever suggest that you should *not* have made these stops?"

"No."

"And if your partner had objected, would you have made them?"

"Not if my partner objected. He's got much more experience than I do."

The Barracuda paused for effect, looked at the judge to make sure she had his attention, then looked back at the witness for her last few questions.

"What's your partner's name?"

"Lieutenant Gary Mitchell."

"How many years has he been on the force?"

"Twenty-four."

"Is Lieutenant Mitchell black or white?"

"He's African American."

"Thank you, Officer Gage. That's all I have."

The courtroom was unusually still as Charles rose to his full height, walked around to the front of counsel table, and stared at the witness for a beat.

"I guess from your dramatic little interchange here with Ms. Crawford that you think having a black man riding along and concurring in your decisions makes everything fine. Is that what you're saying?"

Gage managed a derisive snort. "That's not it at all. I'm saying that my partner, who happens to be African American, concurred in pulling over your client, who also happens to be African American, because my partner knew I was doing it for reasons unrelated to race."

Charles acted unimpressed, but his mind raced for answers. All that statistical information overwhelmed by one indisputable fact—one of the arresting officers was black. He glanced at the skeptical face of Silverman, the smug look of the Barracuda, the cocky posture of Officer Gage. Charles knew it was a gamble, but he also knew he would lose if he didn't try.

"Where is Lieutenant Mitchell today?" Charles asked. "Is he in this courtroom?"

Gage shot a wary glance at the Barracuda, then turned back to Charles. "No, he's testifying in traffic court this morning. He couldn't be in both places."

"Then I request a brief recess so we might locate Lieutenant Mitchell and bring him in to testify," said Charles. "With all the emphasis that Ms. Crawford has placed on his role in this stop, I think I might have a few questions for him."

"Any objection?" Silverman asked the Barracuda.

The Barracuda stood. Charles knew she couldn't object without looking like she was hiding something. "I guess not," she replied.

"Very well then," said Silverman. "This court stands in recess for fifteen minutes."

<hr />

The Barracuda took advantage of the break by finding Sean Armistead in the spectator section. He followed her into one of the conference rooms just off the main hallway. The Barracuda closed the door behind them.

"How're you doing?" she asked.

"I've been better."

So much for the small talk, thought the Barracuda. She reached into her briefcase and pulled out a manila envelope marked *Confidential.* She handed it to Armistead.

"There are wiring instructions in here for a bank in the Cayman Islands," she said. "Two hundred thousand by the close of business today; two hundred thousand next Monday."

Armistead nodded, refusing to look at her.

"Wire it straight from the Virginia Insurance Reciprocal account," continued the Barracuda, "Don't mingle it with your personal accounts first."

"I'm not stupid," said Armistead.

"I know, Sean. I'm sorry."

"Are we done?" he asked.

"Not until we go over your testimony one more time. I can't afford to have you blow it on the stand."

＋・＝◆＝・＋

Lieutenant Mitchell showed every one of his fifty-five years as he stepped up to the witness stand with painful deliberateness. He was hunched slightly at the waist, and he stared out at Charles with sad and droopy eyes outlined in deep wrinkles that fanned out to every corner of his face. To Charles he looked like a man agonizing over a choice between "his people" and his partner. If Charles's instincts were right, it was no accident that Mitchell had been in traffic court earlier.

Charles paced the well of the courtroom as he covered the preliminaries. Then he stopped in his tracks, strategically positioning himself to block the line of sight between the witness and Officer Gage. It was time to get down to the crux of the matter.

"You are aware, are you not, of a practice called racial profiling, Lieutenant Mitchell?"

"Yes sir."

"And you would agree that racial profiling—that is, stopping a black man just because he's black and therefore supposedly more likely to commit a crime—has absolutely no place in proper police work."

"Agreed."

"Further, it's demeaning to blacks because it stereotypes all blacks as being prone to commit crimes. True?"

"That's true."

Charles noticed a small bead of sweat forming in a wrinkle on the lieutenant's brow. No sense waiting any longer. Charles took a deep breath, looked straight into the witness's eyes—brother to brother—and fired away.

"Keeping that in mind, Lieutenant Mitchell, would you pull a black man over just because he happened to be driving a nice car with tinted windows and gave a couple of black kids a ride around the block? If that's all you had, even if those black kids glanced around and hustled off down the street, would you pull the guy in the car over?"

Charles held his breath and waited. One second. Two. Three. Finally, the man spoke.

"No. If that's all I had, I wouldn't pull him."

Charles softly blew out a breath and relaxed. *Quit while you're ahead,* he told himself. Every good lawyer knows how important that is.

"Nothing further," said Charles, turning for his seat.

Before he sat, the Barracuda was on her feet, popping questions.

"Do you believe that Officer Gage engaged in racial profiling on the night he pulled over Buster Jackson?"

"Oh no, ma'am."

"Did you in any way object to him pulling over Jackson?"

"No, I didn't."

"And as his partner, it was really a joint decision, right? In other words, if you thought there was any type of illegal racial profiling involved, you could have just said 'I don't think this is a good idea,' and he would not have pulled Jackson. Isn't that right?"

"That's correct."

"And, by the way, Officer Gage happened to be right, didn't he? I mean, the defendant did have a whole car full of drugs, right?"

"Objection, assumes facts not in evidence."

"Overruled," said Silverman. Turning to the witness, he said, "You may answer."

"Officer Gage was right. It was a good stop."

"One more thing, Lieutenant Mitchell. You've worked with Officer Gage for how long as partners?"

"Four years."

"In that time, have you *ever* known Officer Gage to say or do anything that revealed *any* prejudice against African Americans?"

At this question, Charles thought he detected the slightest flinch from the witness, and a quick blinking of the sad eyes. "Never," said the witness. And without another word, the Barracuda sat down, her self-satisfaction obvious to all.

It was Charles's turn again. His instincts told him to repeat the question. "Never?"

Another pause by the witness, but then a decision to honor the thin blue line.

"Never."

"Let me see if I can get this straight," said Charles. "On the night of Buster Jackson's arrest, you were in the squad car with Officer Gage, correct?"

"Yes."

"And if you had been driving, and it had been your call, you wouldn't have pulled Jackson over under the circumstances I enumerated earlier, right?"

"That's what I said."

"But it wasn't your call, it was Gage's call. And you didn't object, right?"

"That's right."

"So on this one, you were basically just along for the ride?"

Lieutenant Mitchell's shoulders straightened a little, he looked offended for the first time since taking the stand. "We were partners. I was more than just along for the ride."

Charles felt the witness turning hostile and knew he wouldn't get any further with this guy. "No further questions."

With the evidence complete, the lawyers were invited by Judge Silverman to give a brief closing argument. It was hard for Charles to read which way Silverman was leaning, but at least the equivocal testimony of Lieutenant

Mitchell had put Charles back in the game. A lot would be riding on the closings.

The Barracuda went first. "What will criminals and their clever lawyers think of next?" she asked. "As if the police don't have enough to worry about in their fight against crime, we're now going to send law students out to play elaborate games in front of the police and see how many of those law students get pulled over and investigated. And if the numbers work out right, maybe we can spring a few criminals based on alleged racial profiling."

It didn't take long for the Barracuda to get rolling, railing against criminals like Jackson and clever lawyers like Mr. Arnold. She derided the statistical analysis of Dr. Ryder as a game played by law students to justify a preordained result. The black law students probably acted more suspicious than the whites because they knew if they could just get the cops to pull more of them, then their professor could win his case. Law students must not be busy enough these days, opined the Barracuda. Back in her day, law students spent their time studying the law, not baiting police officers.

She highlighted the case of *Whren v. United States.* Charles lost count after she mentioned it five times. *Whren* this and *Whren* that; Justice Scalia said this and Justice Scalia said that. Charles had to hand it to her. She knew the lawyerly art of overkill. And the whole time, Buster Jackson was sitting next to Charles, squirming in his seat, throwing the Barracuda dastardly looks, and playing the part of a vindictive drug dealer to a T.

Charles leaned closed to Buster's ear. "Happy face," he whispered.

"Shut up," said Buster.

Give the police officers the discretion they need to do their job, the Barracuda said. None of us were out there except for Gage and Mitchell. These are split-second decisions made by those risking their lives to keep our streets safe. Let's not sit back and second-guess them in the luxury of the courtroom and further handcuff our officers in the fight against crime.

Twenty minutes after she started, the Barracuda completed her "brief" closing statement and sat down. Charles drew a deep breath, glanced fleetingly at his client, then stood to respond.

This case is not really about Officer Gage or Buster Jackson or even the ability of police officers to do their job, Charles said. It's about the Constitution. It's about the rights of all citizens, black and white, rich and poor, to be treated equally under the law. It's about making America a place where you could never be arrested for simply driving while black.

As he spoke about the land of equality, he noticed Buster sit a little straighter in his chair. Five minutes of railing against racial injustice, and his client was actually nodding in a place or two. Declare the days of Rosa Parks over, Charles urged. Let African Americans know that they can ride in the front of the bus or the front of their own car without the fear of being treated differently. If our Constitution means anything, he said, it means that a man like Buster Jackson is entitled to the same equal treatment, the same dignity under the law, as the mayor of Virginia Beach or even the president of the United States.

"'At's true," he heard Buster mumble.

Charles completed his argument in just under ten minutes, and he did it without one reference to the *Whren* case. When he sat down at counsel table, he felt the handcuffed hands of Buster reach over and pat him on the back.

"Not bad," whispered the big man. "Flashes of Cochran."

"He had more to work with," whispered Charles. "Like an innocent client." This brought a soft snort from Buster and the faint hint of a smile. It disappeared quickly, but a new layer of respect lingered. They had just been through a battle together—fellow members of the darker nation fighting a lingering prejudice—but Charles still didn't know if he could really trust the man.

"Both lawyers have presented excellent arguments," Silverman said after several moments of silence. "And this is not an easy case.

"There's a lot at stake here," he continued, his face masking all emotion, "not just for Mr. Jackson but for the Virginia Beach police force. This is not the kind of case one can decide quickly or lightly"—he paused and looked from Charles to the Barracuda—"so I've decided to take this matter under advisement. That will give me time to think about the arguments of counsel and do some research of my own. I expect to render an opinion some time within the next few weeks."

He banged his gavel. "We'll take a ten-minute recess and then start the preliminary hearing in the Hammond case."

"All rise," said the clerk.

Charles shrugged and stood to his feet. He felt, well, he felt nothing. Okay, maybe a little cheated. All that work and—for today—it was like a tie. Kissing your sister. Nothing special.

"What happened?" asked a bewildered Buster.

"Overtime," said Charles.

As the deputies grabbed Buster to lead him away, Buster shook an arm free and gave them a wicked glance. "I need a word with my attorney," he snarled.

The deputies looked at each other. "Ten seconds," the older one said. They took a couple of steps back.

Buster moved next to Charles, glancing over his shoulder to make sure the deputies weren't eavesdropping. "Pray for me," Buster said gruffly. "I'm one of you dudes now."

"I will," promised Charles. But even as the guards escorted Buster away, he wondered if it was really true.

CHAPTER 42

The four of them—Charles, Nikki, Thomas, and Theresa—huddled in a small windowless conference room adjacent to Silverman's main courtroom. Thomas and Theresa sat on one side of the table holding hands. Charles sat on the other, suit coat unbuttoned and feeling spent from the morning's proceedings. Nikki paced back and forth behind Charles, giving some last-minute instructions to the Hammonds and generally pumping up the troops.

Unlike Buster, Thomas did not wear leg irons, handcuffs, or an orange jumpsuit. Charles had petitioned the court to allow civilian clothes for his client—unusual for a preliminary hearing but not unheard of—on the theory that the press coverage might poison the prospective jury pool if video of Thomas in jail clothes was broadcast all over Virginia Beach. The court agreed, so Thomas wore an ill-fitting sports coat, a dingy white shirt frayed around the collar, and a tie that was both too short and too wide. Theresa was no fashion plate either, but at least her dark blue pleated dress fit fairly well and had recently been cleaned. They made quite a contrast to Charles and Nikki, flamboyant dressers who pushed the bounds of courtroom fashion.

"Please try not to get your hopes up," Nikki said, "because preliminary hearings are notoriously difficult to win. The judge only needs to find probable cause, and then the case is bound over for a jury trial. It's a rare case where the judge doesn't find probable cause."

"Rare is an understatement," Charles piped in. "It's nearly impossible to win a case like this at a preliminary hearing."

"But that doesn't mean we won't try," promised Nikki. "Because it *is* possible, especially with the stuff we've got for the cross-examination of Armistead." She stopped pacing for a second and smiled at Charles. "And you've got one of the best in the business representing you."

Charles managed his own self-conscious smile. He wanted to prepare the clients for the worst that could happen at today's hearing, and Nikki was not exactly helping.

"Have you got any questions before we go out there?" she asked.

Thomas and Theresa shook their heads. But Charles didn't like what he saw in their eyes. They had a look of expectancy, a false hope that today might be the day. They needed to be ready for the long road ahead of them and the very real probability that today was just the start.

"Like we said a few minutes ago, don't get your hopes up at this preliminary hearing," Charles warned. "I'm going to play it by ear. If I sense Silverman is going to find probable cause no matter what I do, I won't even bother to cross-examine Armistead. There's no sense in previewing our cross-examination now and giving them two weeks before trial to think of good answers. So if I ask no questions, you've just got to trust me and know that I'm taking the long-term view and doing what's best for the case." He looked at both Thomas and Theresa. "Okay?"

They nodded their heads.

"Oh, that's beautiful," mumbled Nikki, standing behind Charles. "The old deaf-mute defense again." Charles turned to see her leaning against the wall, arms crossed, scowling at him. He frowned back.

"What?!" she exclaimed. "Why do I get stuck with all the lawyers who excel at sticking their head"—she paused and lowered her tone just a notch—"in the sand?"

Charles decided to ignore her. He didn't have the energy for bickering with her right now. He turned back to his clients, showing Nikki the back of his head, and asked in the most pleasant voice possible if they were ready.

"Can we pray before we go out there?" asked Thomas.

"Sure." Charles resisted the urge to turn and see the look on Nikki's face.

"And before we do, I do have one favor I hate to even bring up but really feel I oughta," said Thomas.

"Okay," replied Charles tentatively.

Thomas stared down at his hands. "If'n we lose today, and I'm still in jail for Saturday night's Bible study, could you bring Buster a *King James* Bible? I'd have Theresa buy it, but…things are pretty tight right now. He promised me he'd read it. I mean…he's done started readin' mine. I mean, the man ain't perfect, but God's doin' a work in 'im."

Charles heard Nikki sigh behind him. "Sure," Charles said. "If you're still in Saturday night, I'll bring him his very own *King James*."

He saw the look of satisfaction in Thomas's eye, then had an idea. He turned to Nikki and flashed her a phony smile. "How about you leading us in prayer?" he said sweetly.

Her eyes narrowed for a flash before she recovered. "I'm really kind of a fan of silent prayer," she said, killing Charles with her eyes. "I think I read something once about women not praying out loud."

⊷ ⊫⬩⊨ ⊶

Nikki was in a foul mood by the time the preliminary hearing started. After trying to embarrass her in front of the clients, Charles had arranged the seating in the courtroom so that he had a buffer from her. Charles sat on the left end of the counsel table, closest to the podium. Next to him sat Thomas, then Theresa, then Nikki. She was too far away for Charles to hear her suggestions. She might as well have been in Siberia. She shoved her chair as far to the left as possible, practically in Theresa's lap.

The Barracuda first called the Hammonds' pastor—the Reverend Richard Beckham. The pastor was heavyset and severe-looking, about fifty-five years old with a full head of greased-down jet black hair. His flat face settled into a natural frown as he testified, eyes sparking occasionally with barely controlled anger. He was under subpoena and not happy about it. He apparently had no desire to testify against faithful tithers like the Hammond family.

After five minutes of preliminary questions, the Barracuda paused, signaling the start of her important questions.

"Did Thomas or Theresa Hammond ever call you and ask you to come and pray with them because they thought Joshua was going to die?"

"Object," whispered Nikki from her perch in Siberia.

Charles had already stood. "Objection, Your Honor. That's clearly covered by the priest-penitent privilege. The reverend can't be forced to testify about what one of his church members told him."

But the Barracuda had a ready answer. "He can if the privilege is waived." And the fight was on.

It seemed that at little Joshie's funeral, the reverend preached for a good five or ten minutes on the incredible faith displayed by Thomas and Theresa Hammond. As the reverend told it, little Joshie had been on death's door for several days, and his mom and dad had never requested human medical help but simply prayed in faith for his healing. The reverend had personally prayed with them and talked with them during this ordeal. Theirs was an incredible faith, he told the mourners at the funeral; most regular folk would have taken Joshie to the hospital when it first became apparent that his life was in danger.

The Barracuda argued that this sermon waived the priest-penitent privilege. The conversations between the Hammonds and their pastor could hardly be characterized as confidential when the pastor later broadcast them all over the church and the parents never objected to his doing so.

Charles scoffed at the argument, making Nikki momentarily forget the fact that she was supposed to be mad at him. He peppered the judge with questions. Is the deputy commonwealth's attorney serious? Does she really expect two parents, who had just lost their child, to stand up in the middle of a funeral service and object to what the pastor said? If this doesn't qualify as priest-penitent privilege, what would? If Reverend Beckham is required to testify, how could any church member ever feel safe confiding in their pastor again?

The fireworks lasted about ten minutes, starting off with a heated discussion of the issues, then degenerating into personal insults between lawyers. Nikki was delighted.

Silverman shattered her mood with his ruling. "The priest-penitent privilege is only designed to protect those conversations held in strictest confidence between a pastor and a church member. Here Reverend Beckham apparently used those conversations as a preaching point in a sermon. The Hammonds did not object at the time or at any time thereafter to the way Reverend Beckham shared this information with the entire congregation. It defies reason to say that the reverend could share this information with an entire room full of people at a funeral but not be required to share this same information in a court of law engaged in a search for the truth. Accordingly, I hold that the privilege has been waived, and the reverend must answer the questions."

Nikki groaned louder than she intended, and Silverman shot her a reproving glance. Charles also gave her a scolding look, then scribbled a note. He folded it and passed it to Thomas, who passed it to Theresa, who passed it to Nikki. Nikki picked it up, unfolded it, and read it even as Reverend Beckham was telling the court about every conversation he ever had with Thomas and Theresa Hammond in the days preceding Joshua's death.

Relax, the note said. *I think it's good the court let him testify. Now we have an issue to argue on appeal if we lose the case.*

This was a mentality that Nikki could never understand. *Why try the case thinking you were going to lose?* Nikki scribbled a reply note: *Great strategy, Charles. Why don't we just have our clients jump up and scream out that they did it, then we can argue insanity on appeal?*

After Charles read the note, he made a great show of wadding it up, and throwing it in his briefcase. He looked down at Nikki, mouthed, "Chill out," and returned his attention to the damaging testimony of Reverend Beckham.

Fifteen minutes later the Barracuda had finished mining the nuggets of gold from the reverend's testimony and returned to her seat. Nikki had a page of notes ready to pass to Charles for cross-examination. She was really hoping for a ten-minute break. That way she could give the reverend a piece of her mind in the hallway, shake him up a little, and still have a few minutes to discuss his cross-examination with Charles.

But a break would not be necessary. When the judge turned to Charles, the lawyer simply leaned back in his chair, legs crossed nonchalantly, and declared that he had no questions at this time. Nikki almost came out of her seat. She leaned forward on the counsel table, staring at Charles, trying to get his attention. But he would not even look at her, and within minutes the Barracuda was calling her next witness: Dr. Sean Armistead.

Nikki, now smoldering, got up and moved to a chair directly behind Charles. It was Harry Pursifull all over again. "Object," Nikki would whisper at various points. "Shh," Charles would reply. "How can you let him get away with that?" she would exclaim, partway between a whisper and shout. "I'll deal with it at trial," Charles would respond over his shoulder.

"Gimme a break," "That's ridiculous," "He's lying," and other running commentary from Nikki peppered Armistead's testimony. Charles just sat there, legs crossed and hands folded in his lap, as if he were watching a play or having afternoon tea.

"Aren't you going to at least take notes?" whispered Nikki.

"What do you think the court reporter is for?" responded Charles over his shoulder. "You think she's missing something that I could get down better writing it out longhand?"

On the witness stand the doctor explained how Theresa's delay in seeking treatment had cost young Joshua his life. What made it worse, said Armistead, is that Theresa initially lied about how long Joshua had been sick. In order to hide her own shortcomings, Theresa at first told Armistead that Joshua had only been running a fever for three days. After Joshua died, Theresa finally fessed up and admitted that it had been more like five days. Incidentally, said Armistead, this five-day time frame was consistent with what the children said when their statements were taken by Dr. Byrd. If Armistead had known earlier that Joshua had been sick for five days, it might have changed his course of treatment.

"That's not true," whispered Theresa to her husband and Charles. "I never told Armistead that Joshua had been sick five days. It had only been three."

"I know," said Thomas, placing a soothing hand on top of his wife's trembling one. "Charles will handle it."

"At trial," whispered Charles. "At trial."

"Gimme a break," Nikki said, this time louder than a whisper. "Why not now?"

Charles didn't answer, choosing instead to focus on the testimony of a doctor who, in the opinion of Nikki, seemed very anxious—too anxious—to help prove a case against his former patient's mother. Perhaps it was just frustration at a senseless loss of life. But it seemed to Nikki like something more, something hard to put a finger on.

"No further questions," said the Barracuda.

"Nothing from the defense at this time," said Charles without standing.

"Figures," said Nikki.

The Barracuda then picked up the prayer journal, looked over at Charles, and put it back down. "The prosecution rests," she said.

Charles stated that he would be calling no witnesses and, to nobody's surprise, Judge Silverman found probable cause. The lawyers and judge discussed a few scheduling matters, then Thomas was taken back into custody and court was adjourned. The Barracuda, without acknowledging Charles, quickly left the courtroom to go hold forth for the media on the courthouse steps. Theresa looked at Charles and Nikki with vacant eyes, gave them each a hug, promised not to say anything to the media, and left as well. This left Charles and Nikki, the last two persons in the courtroom, packing their briefcases in stony silence.

Nikki could no longer hold her tongue. "I don't see why you couldn't at least—"

"Don't start on me," Charles said, cutting her off with an intense stare and an icy tone. "I've heard enough for one day."

"Then don't treat me like a child."

"You never quit, do you, Nikki? You never let up until you get your way." Charles was biting off each word. "I don't need your sarcasm today. I don't need your wisecracks. And I don't need your help." He grabbed his briefcase and started walking past the bar and toward the door.

"You're right," yelled Nikki after him. "You won't be needing anybody's help on this case!" She stood on her toes, chin high, spewing the next words out: "You're fired!"

Charles stopped just shy of the door and turned around. "Spare me the dramatics," he said. "Thomas hired me, and until he fires me, this is my case. I'll call you if I need you."

She grunted, so exasperated that words failed her. Charles quickly turned around and slammed the door as he left. It closed a mere second before Nikki's briefcase came hurtling down the aisle, hitting the floor just a few inches from the door and skidding into it.

"Men," she said in frustration to nobody but herself.

CHAPTER 43

Tiger was glad to be in the backseat of the Sebring. He normally would sit right behind Stinky, but tonight he had chosen to sit on the left side, behind Miss Nikki. That way it would be hard for Miss Nikki to reach over the seat and swat him. He leaned hard toward the door, so she would not be able to constantly look in the rearview mirror and catch his eye as she chewed him out.

Miss Nikki was not happy, and she was giving Tiger an earful. Apparently Miss Parsons had sorta given Miss Nikki a blow-by-blow of the day, and it wasn't pretty. Talking back to Miss Parsons, spending the whole afternoon on time-out, that type of thing. Tiger, of course, had been given no chance to defend himself. Instead, he was just yanked into the car and forced to listen to what a no-good troublemaker he was. At least he had not been hit…yet. That didn't seem to be Miss Nikki's style.

"I know you're going through some tough times right now, but that's no excuse for behavior like this," Miss Nikki said.

Where have I heard that before? Everybody feels sorry for me, but nobody wants to cut me a break.

"Yes ma'am."

"Miss Parsons is a good teacher, and there's absolutely no excuse—*none*—for disrespecting her that way."

"Yes ma'am."

"I don't ever want to hear another report like this again. Is that clear?"

"Oh, yes ma'am."

"Yeah," said Stinky. "Momma says to turn the other cheek even if someone hits you first."

Oh great, thought Tiger, *the old double team. Now Goody Two Shoes has to get her two cents in. There ain't no way I'm going to say 'yes ma'am' to her.*

"So," said Tiger under his breath, hopefully just loud enough for Stinky to hear but not Miss Nikki. "That's not what Daddy would say."

"Wait a minute," said Miss Nikki, gunning the engine to make it through a yellow—nope, red—light. "Who said anything about a fight?"

Stinky put her hand over her mouth—her big mouth in Tiger's opinion. Tiger himself was not about to breathe a word.

"Who said anything about a fight?" demanded Miss Nikki, this time much louder.

She glanced sideways at Stinky, and Stinky crumbled under the pressure. "Tiger got into a fight on the playground. Didn't Miss Parsons tell you?"

"She only told me that he got into trouble on the playground, then acted out the rest of the day. She didn't tell me it was a fight."

Stinky glanced over her seat at Tiger, who was glaring back at her. *There's going to be another fight at home,* he was thinking.

"It wasn't Tiger's fault," said Stinky. "This big kid named Joey kept teasing Tiger, and so Tiger told him to stop. Then Joey pushed Tiger down, and Tiger got mad. Instead of turning the other cheek, Tiger put up his fists to fight."

"Did you hit him?" Nikki asked, craning her neck to look at Tiger in the mirror.

"No ma'am."

"Why not?"

Why not? What did she mean by that? Tiger sensed this next answer might get him in trouble. But it was the truth, and he had a hard time thinking up lies as fast as Miss Nikki asked questions.

"'Cause I didn't have time…and he was bigger."

"You shoulda just turned the other cheek," said Goody Two Shoes.

Miss Nikki drove on in silence for a few minutes. Tiger knew he should leave well enough alone, but there was something else he just had to know.

"Is my daddy coming home?" he asked at last.

Miss Nikki shot a look at Stinky, one of those "I told you not to say anything" looks. Stinky quickly turned and looked out the window.

"Not today, Tiger. It's probably going to be about two weeks, at the trial, when the judge will hear our case and let your daddy out of jail."

Of all the things that had happened to Tiger on this very bad, no-good, low-down, rotten day, this was the unkindest blow of all. It sucked the wind right out of him, the last ounce of resistance to the events that were trying to overwhelm him. Miss Nikki and Miss Parsons were mad at him. Joey was out to kill him. The other kids all thought his daddy was a drug dealer and a jail-bird. His sweet little brother had died. And now this crushing news. *Two more long weeks, on his own, with nobody around to even show him how to fight back against Joey.*

The tears began to spill out of his eyes, and Tiger made no effort to stop them. He brought his legs up to the seat and cuddled into a little ball, facing the door of the car. Soon his entire face was wet, covered with tears, and the arm of his shirt got soaked from where he tried to wipe away all the tears. Miss Nikki and Stinky in the front seat seemed so very far away. Tiger was alone, all alone, and there was no way out.

A few minutes later, Miss Nikki pulled the car into the parking lot of a 7-Eleven. "Tiger," she said, "I want you to get out with me. Stinky, I need you to stay in the car."

Oh boy, thought Tiger. *This is it. I've been through this with my dad.*

But in the parking lot, Miss Nikki just put her arm on Tiger's shoulder and took him to the side of the building. She squatted down and turned him so they were face-to-face.

"How was Joey teasing you?" she asked.

"He called my daddy a jailbird," said Tiger, wiping the tears away in time for new ones to fall. "He kept saying 'Tweet-tweet,' and he got the other kids to say it too."

"How much bigger is he?" asked Nikki.

"Lots. I call him Doughy Joey."

This actually made Miss Nikki smile.

"Well, Tiger, I know what your mom would say, but she's not taking care of you right now...I am. And we're going to teach old Doughy Joey a lesson, okay?"

This sounded good to Tiger. He started vigorously nodding his head.

"Now, do you know what karate is?"

Tiger shook his head no.

Miss Nikki furrowed her brow, then her eyes lit up. "You know the Ninja Turtles, right?"

"No ma'am."

"Yes, you know, superhero guys who fight bad guys with incredible powers?"

"You mean like the Power Rangers."

"Yeah, that's exactly what I mean. The Power Rangers. You know what makes them so good?"

"Sure, they—"

"I'll tell you exactly what makes them so good. They know a special way of fighting, using martial arts, called karate. With it, you can beat up guys twice your size. Now, would you like to learn karate?"

Nothing had ever sounded better to Tiger. His eyes lit up, and he straightened his shoulders. *Fighting like the Power Rangers?* "Sure," he said.

"Do you think you can stay out of Joey's way for a couple of weeks while you learn?"

"I guess so," said Tiger.

"Good, then we're gonna sign you up tomorrow. And after a couple of weeks, you won't have to worry about Doughy Joey."

A big smile crossed Tiger's wet little face.

Miss Nikki put her finger to her lips. "Just don't tell Stinky, okay? It'll be our secret."

"O-kay!"

CHAPTER 44

The next morning Tiger's tummy aches were back with a vengeance—according to Tiger. Nikki suspected it was more the prospect of facing Joey again on the playground that was making Tiger sick. Either way, she didn't have the heart to force Tiger to go to day care, at least not today. By next Monday he would have to go back and face the music. But for the next two days, he could hang out with Nikki.

They dropped off Stinky, then went searching for a place where Tiger could take karate lessons. By late morning they had him signed up for Body by Karate. His private classes would begin later that afternoon at the Ho Kwan Do Academy. Nikki endured the usual parent lecture: Karate does not teach a kid how to fight in a few days or even a few weeks, it's a long-term lifestyle that builds self-confidence, self-discipline, and self-defense. Nikki nodded in all the right places and assured them that Tiger was signing up for all the right reasons. Besides, Nikki's plan did not really require that Tiger *know* karate by next week, only that he *thought* he knew.

The pair then picked up a drive-thru lunch at McDonald's—Tiger's stomach seemed to have no trouble digesting his Happy Meal—then they headed out to Woodard's Mill. They parked just up the road from Dr. Sean Armistead's estate, out of sight from the house itself, but close enough to see who was coming and going. Yesterday in court Nikki had seen something that bothered her. Armistead was not just a witness—a reluctant doctor testifying against a former patient's mother—he was an advocate. On at least one point he was clearly lying.

Instincts told her that it was more than just trying to cover his own tracks for losing a patient. They also told her that it had something to do with Erica Armistead's suicide, which had been reported in the paper the previous weekend. How it was related, Nikki had no idea. But she was determined to find out.

It was a fair bet, since Armistead lived in Woodard's Mill and his wife reportedly had Parkinson's, that he would have a cleaning crew take care of his house. It was also a fair bet that the cleaning crew would have a key to the house and the password for the security system. Nikki would wait in front of his house, day and night, until she found out who cleaned it. Then she would join them and infiltrate the house. Once inside, she would unlock the key to Armistead's secrets.

"What're we doing here?" asked Tiger.

"We're playing spy," said Nikki.

"Cool," said the little guy, now whispering. "Who are we spying on?"

"The doctor who treated Joshie." Nikki whispered back.

Tiger's mouth dropped open. "Why?"

"Because he said some things in court yesterday that weren't true. We're gonna spy him out and prove that he lied. That will help get your daddy out of jail."

"Wow!" said Tiger. "What do we do now?"

"We wait," said Nikki. "Just wait."

Waiting got old fast. Spying sounded glamorous, but after two hours of watching, the junior secret agent on the team started getting antsy. He had exhausted coloring books, Power Rangers, and LEGOs. Tiger was tired. Tiger was bored. Tiger had to go potty. Nikki was counting down the minutes until she took Tiger to his first karate lesson. Maybe that would wear him out.

Thirty minutes before they had to leave, the mailman came. Ten minutes later she was surprised to see Armistead himself drive by and turn down the driveway. Still no sign of the cleaning crew. And then, just eight minutes before she had to leave and take Tiger to Body by Karate, she saw another car pass by her on the road and enter the driveway. She quickly started her own vehicle and drove slowly by the Armistead house, putting on her shades and pulling her visor over to the side window to partially shield her face.

She stole a quick glance left, then another. She almost ran off the road! Walking to the front porch, big as life, at 1:45 in the afternoon, was the Barracuda. Nikki couldn't believe it and cursed quietly at her nemesis.

"What?" asked Tiger, now kneeling up on the seat, looking down the driveway too. "What did you say?"

"Nothing," said Nikki.

"Yes, you did. *Hold on!*" he yelled. "It's the Mean Lady! You saw her too, didn't you? What did you say? What did you call her?"

"Sit down," said Nikki, speeding up to get past the house without being noticed. "Yeah, I did see her. I called her, um, a witch." It wasn't exactly true, but it was close enough for Tiger's ears.

"That's what I thought you said," exclaimed Tiger. "She *is* a witch."

Nikki kept on driving, a little faster, hoping she had not been noticed. She settled Tiger down, waited five minutes, then circled back. The Barracuda's car was still in the driveway. Nikki's mind reeled with the possibilities, and she found herself sputtering, "What in the world is going on here? You don't go to the house of a witness in the middle of the afternoon to prepare them for trial. And especially not the day after a preliminary hearing, with the trial still weeks away…"

Hanging around longer would probably be fruitless. Tiger needed to get to class. And Nikki couldn't afford to be noticed. She drove away, suspicions raging, mulling the possibilities in her mind.

When she returned, after nearly an hour, both cars were gone. She parked in the same spot in the road and watched some more. Her patience was rewarded forty-five minutes later when a van bearing an emblem for Eagle Cleaners pulled into the driveway. Nikki pulled forward to get a better view. A heavyset woman in blue jeans and a white blouse with an eagle logo over the pocket got out of the van and entered the house.

Nikki copied down the number on the side of the van. Eagle Cleaners. She wondered if they were hiring.

——— ⧲◆⧳ ———

The next day, Friday afternoon, while Tiger was at Body by Karate, Nikki learned that Eagle Cleaners was indeed hiring. She filled out the necessary paperwork and talked to the manager for the Chesapeake region.

They would do a criminal background check on Jacquelyn Ferreira, Nikki's assumed name for purposes of this application. She had used this fake ID, including the "borrowed" social security number, on a few prior occasions. A few years ago, she had purchased the whole package from an underground company that specialized in creating new identities—no questions asked. The employees for Eagle Cleaners had to be bonded, and any past criminal convictions, even misdemeanors, would disqualify an employee. If they found no criminal convictions, and Nikki was pretty sure they wouldn't since she had paid a premium for a "clean" identity, then Nikki could begin training on Monday. Starting on Tuesday, she would be "on call" and filling in for anybody who called in sick. Nikki had a hunch that Armistead's maid would not be able to make it to work on Nikki's very first day.

It wouldn't exactly be breaking and entering, since she would be in Armistead's house with permission for legitimate business reasons. Well, okay, she was there under false pretenses, but that was probably a technicality that could be defeated in court. She had no intention of finding out. She would be very discreet as she looked around, and she would pray like mad that Armistead did not decide to come home in the middle of the day.

It had been two days since the preliminary hearing, two days since she had seen or spoken to Charles. Neither, of course, wanted to be the first to call. She could be as stubborn and strong-willed as necessary, but she had a feeling he could too. And that was a problem since there were only a few precious days to get ready for a trial that would determine the future of the Hammond family. The mutual sulking wasn't doing anybody any good.

But why should she be the first to move? He was totally unjustified in ignoring her at such a critical stage of the pretrial process. *The nerve.* She had hired *him.* He wouldn't even be in this case if it wasn't for *her.* He was the one who had performed gutlessly in court, not her. Sure, she had been hard on him, but his strategy was moronic. The more she thought about it, the madder she got. There was no good reason for her to make the first move toward patching things up.

Still, she had to admit, she missed him. There was chemistry there. He was good looking and quick-witted and, to be honest, one heck of a lawyer. She saw it in Buster's case. She had seen it weeks ago when he represented himself. All the more reason it made her so mad that he went into hiding on the Hammond case. She had to believe he really was saving it for trial. In a convoluted way, it made her respect him more. He believed in his strategy enough to stick with it even while she was giving him all that grief. Even if it was a dumb strategy.

Okay, she decided, maybe I owe him at least a *chance* to apologize. Maybe if he sees me, if I turn on the charm, he'll come to his senses and beg me to get back in the case. And if he doesn't, I'll do it anyway, for the good of the case, for the good of the kids. And because he's got too much potential to let him get away that easy.

She would drop the kids off for a few hours with their mom. They would be fine. As for Charles, she would give him his chance. She knew where to find him.

CHAPTER 45

Nikki planted herself in the back of the crowd, hiding behind a few brawny guys and her own Ray-Bans. She wanted to listen for a few minutes without being seen. *He really believes this stuff,* thought Nikki. *If only life were really this simple.*

His preaching is awesome, but I can't give him the satisfaction of knowing that. He owes me an apology. He's lucky I came.

She put on a scowl and stepped from behind the men. Her hand shot up in the air, the same way it had in his classroom.

"Are you open to questions here, or is this a monologue?" she wondered loud enough for Charles to hear.

He stopped in his tracks and looked at her, his own shades masking any hint of surprise. "I see the beautiful lady in the back has a question," said the preacher. All heads turned as Charles walked toward Nikki.

"Aren't you the lawyer I saw on TV defending that drug dealer the other day, trying to get him off on a technicality?"

Charles smiled broadly, catching on to the game. "I am a lawyer," he confessed. He heard a gasp or two from his crowd. "But I don't do technicalities. I think you must be referring to a case where I defended a man based on the United States Constitution. Hardly a technicality."

"I see," said Nikki, holding her chin high as she stared him down. "Well, let me ask you this: How does a man of the cloth, a religious man like yourself, justify trying to get a client off if you know he's guilty?"

"Great question," announced Charles. "You ought to be a lawyer yourself."

Spare me the sarcasm, thought Nikki. Then Charles repeated the question into the mike so everyone could hear it. She had to hand it to him, he didn't back away from controversy.

"I ask myself," said Charles, "what would Jesus do? And I think the answer is pretty clear from Scripture." Then the preacher started pacing, took a deep breath, and launched into his story.

"There was a woman during Christ's time who was caught in the act of adultery. I'm talkin' *in the act* here. No defense. No reasonable doubt. *In the very act.* The Pharisees, the religious leaders of the day, dragged her before Christ to make an example of her. They said that the law required her to be executed—capital punishment, death by stoning." Charles looked around. "Aren't some of you glad that's not the law today?" No response. "So the Pharisees asked Christ what He was going to do about it.

"So Christ, calmly, while they were accusing her, stooped down and wrote with his finger in the dirt." Charles knelt down, pretending to write on the sidewalk. Nikki and the others in the back strained to see. "And then Christ raised Himself up"—Charles stood as well, raising his voice—"and said, 'If any one of you is without sin, let him be the first to throw a stone at her.' Then Christ just stooped down again and kept writing on the ground. And one by one, the Pharisees were convicted by their own consciences and left." Charles lowered his voice to a soothing level, barely audible where Nikki stood. "Then Christ said to this woman, 'Neither do I condemn you. Go now and leave your life of sin.'"

Charles paused for a long time, looking from one audience member to another. "What in the world was Christ doing?" No response. "I'll tell you what He was doing. He was acting as this guilty woman's defense lawyer.

"You see, the Mosaic Law required that the first stone be thrown by someone who was faultless. And here Christ was using that critical procedural requirement, that technicality, if you will, to defend this woman. He was doing it as an example for those of us who tend to be judgmental..."

Nikki could have sworn he looked right at her as he said those words, but with those shades it was hard to tell.

"He was showing that we should have the spirit of mercy, not judgment. For Scripture says, 'Judgment without mercy will be shown to anyone who has not been merciful. Mercy triumphs over judgment!'"

Now he turned to Nikki and even took a few steps in her direction.

"And *that,* ladies and gentlemen, is why I defend those who our system says might be guilty. I'm not condoning what they've done, but I'm making sure they get judged fairly, and I'm making sure that mercy does not get overwhelmed by judgment."

A few murmured their agreement. Others looked down, thinking. Nikki maintained her stoic pose. She reminded herself she was angry with this man.

"Any more questions?" asked the preacher. "'Cause if not, it's time to get our praise on." He popped a CD into the boom box, pushing his sunglasses on top of his head while he chose the track for the song he wanted.

A little girl in the front blurted out a question before the music started. "What did He write in the dirt?"

Charles put the mike under her mouth. "Another excellent question," he said. "Could you please repeat it so everyone could hear."

The girl looked around, intimidated at all the big folks listening. "What did He write in the dirt?"

Charles smiled at the young girl, that broad smile of his—all teeth. "You've done it. You've stumped the preacher!" He held out his hand, and she gave him five. "'Cause nobody knows what Christ wrote in the dirt. But I, for one, intend to ask Him as soon as I get to heaven."

"Me too," said the girl.

Charles stood up again and looked around. "Some say He wrote the names of all the women these Pharisees had been having affairs with. Wouldn't that be cool?" This thought brought laughter from the crowd. "Some say He was just doodling in the dirt. But I've got to think He wrote something simple yet profound, something that turned judgment into forgiveness."

Then Nikki saw it—that telltale spark in Charles's eyes that signals inspiration has hit. She had seen it in court. She had seen it in his class. She had seen it with the kids at Busch Gardens. She had learned not to be surprised by what came next.

And so she watched with keen anticipation as Charles knelt down again, this time talking to the young girl's sister. He was looking at a clear plastic bag in her hand that contained a few items her mom had apparently just bought at one of the many stores lining the boardwalk.

"Is that sidewalk chalk?" he asked, still speaking into the mike.

"Yes sir," said the little girl. "I use it for playing foursquare."

"Can I buy a piece?" asked Charles. The crowd started pushing in a little closer, piqued with curiosity, blocking Nikki's view.

"What color?" she heard the little girl say.

"Let's try purple."

Then Charles put down the mike and changed the CDs again in his boom box. He gave the little girl some money—it must have been a lot because Nikki heard a squeal of delight—then he squatted down and started writing something on the boardwalk. As he wrote, the mellow sounds of Kenny G's saxophone filled the evening air, capturing the mood of the soft beach sunset.

The crowd of forty or so who had been listening to Charles moved tighter around him, anxious to see what he was writing. But Nikki, skeptical and tired of these preaching gimmicks, held back. If the truth were known, she was curious too, but she wasn't about to get sucked in with the rest of these gullible folks. She would see soon enough, after the crowd dispersed.

It was a moment she would never forget.

The crowd started moving gradually, then almost in unison. It was as if they split right down the middle and peeled away on both sides, leaving an aisle lined by human bodies between Nikki and a squatting Charles. He had his back to her, hunched over his work, sunglasses propped on top of his head. He was just putting the finishing flourish on it. He stood up and went to the other side of what he had written, and gingerly, tenderly, held out his hand with the piece of purple chalk resting in his open palm.

As Nikki read the message, at once juvenile and sweet, she couldn't stop a smile from invading her face. Right there on the boardwalk, for all to see, Charles the street preacher, Charles the law professor, *Charles the romantic*, had written a very personal note just to her:

Dear Nikki,

I am so sorry. Will you forgive me?

Please check one:

_____Yes _____No _____ Maybe

Love,

Charles

Maybe it was the Kenny G music, maybe it was the sunset, or maybe it was the pleading look on his face, but some kind of emotion overwhelmed Nikki, forcing her to step forward, hesitate for an instant, and then throw her arms around his neck.

"You're too cute for your own good," she whispered in his ear.

"I guess that means yes," someone shouted.

His congregation broke out in spontaneous applause.

CHAPTER 46

For Charles, the rest of the night flew by. They packed up his sound equipment, took it to his car, then headed back to the boardwalk. They stopped for ice cream at a sidewalk café. Then they took their shoes off and headed to the beach. The smell of the salty ocean air had always relaxed Charles, and the feel of wet sand under his feet invigorated him.

Nikki, of course, insisted on walking in the water, kicking some at Charles, running from the waves. She wore short shorts and a sleeveless T-shirt. Stray strands of hair fell from the bun on top of her head—the ocean breeze blowing it out of her eyes. Charles found himself looking too long at the sculpted lines of her face…and wondering about that tattoo on her shoulder.

"So what's up with the tattoo," he asked nonchalantly. "Is that you?"

"Nope." She bent down and picked up a shell, turned it over in her hand, then threw it into the surf.

Now she really had him curious. "And?"

"And what? You asked me if the tattoo is me. It's not." A large wave chased her up the beach. Then she came back to his side and started walking again.

"You want to tell me who it is?"

"Nope."

He paused, calculating how hard to push. "Your sister?"

"Okay," said Nikki, stopping and facing him. "You and I have a real communication problem here. I say 'no.' You hear 'yes.' Read my lips." She reached out and playfully grabbed his face, focusing it on her. "N-O. No. Nada. Huh-uh. No way. Forget about it."

Charles nodded his head as if he understood until Nikki let go. When they had both started walking again he looked out into the distance. "Your mother?"

She kicked water toward him, and he jumped back. "Must be your mother as a young girl," he said when they started walking again.

A few couples passed in the opposite direction on the dimly lit beach. Seemed to Charles that everyone was holding hands but them.

They walked on in silence, then Nikki quietly said, "Actually, it's got something to do with my father."

"My next guess," responded Charles, but Nikki didn't smile. He had hit a nerve, and he suddenly felt like a jerk. *Man,* Nikki kept him off balance. "I'm sorry. I'll drop it."

"You don't have to." Nikki turned toward the ocean, then took several steps back up the beach. She sat down on the dry sand and patted a spot next to her. He sat down and leaned back on his hands. She leaned forward and let the sand filter through her fingers as she talked.

"My mom died in a car accident when I was just four years old. Left me with an alcoholic father who hated my guts. He'd use me to get food stamps, social security checks, whatever. Then he'd leave me at some friend's house for a few days and go get drunk. When the money ran out, he'd come and get me, beat me around a little, get some more money, then drop me off somewhere else."

Nikki told the story with a soft detachment. Charles detected no bitterness in her voice, not even a trace of self-pity. Just the cold, hard facts of a tough childhood.

"I didn't realize it at the time, but the only reason he even kept me around was because he smelled some serious money. The guy who caused the car accident with my mom supposedly had big bucks, and my dad figured he could get more if a jury sympathized with him as a single father raising a young girl. Well, that backfired when the suit got thrown out before it ever went to court.

"When I was nine, one of the families he left me with turned him in to Child Protective Services. Next thing I know, I'm bouncing around some pretty bad foster homes and wishing I could go back with my dad. Like all foster kids, I prayed for an adoption. But nobody wants a gangly, sulking ten-year-old who hates the world." Nikki paused and looked out at the ocean as if her story were written there, being drawn in to her on the crests of the waves.

Charles had a hard time picturing her as gangly and sulking.

"Then one day, when I was about eleven, some widower about fifty years old takes me to live with him and his live-in housekeeper. Great guy—fun, kind, everything my real father wasn't. This was different than anything I'd experienced before, and I knew the guy must have pulled some strings to get me. His wife had died years before. Not exactly your typical foster-home scenario. I didn't realize it at the time, but he wasn't even in the system. At the same time, the guy had bucks and, you know, money talks…that type of thing."

Nikki suddenly turned to Charles, as if she had just come out of her trance. "I'm rambling… I don't usually talk about myself like this…" She started to rise, but Charles grabbed her arm and pulled her gently back down.

"No," he said. "Please…don't stop. I want to hear all about it."

Nikki shrugged.

"Really, I do."

"Okay, but can we walk again? Helps me think better."

They walked for about five minutes in silence, Charles sensing she would continue when she was ready. Sure enough, Nikki took a deep breath.

"This guy gives me everything I need, becomes my adopted father…and he basically raises me. I mean, he was a developer, so we went through our ups and downs. I didn't realize it at the time, but when I was fifteen, we almost went bankrupt. We moved to a smaller house, fired the housekeeper. He made me wait till I was eighteen to get my own car—that's the main thing I remember about the tough financial times. By the time I graduated from high school at nineteen"—Nikki smiled at the thought, seeming a little embarrassed—"I had such a good time, I took an extra year to finish school… Anyway, by then he was getting back on top. Celebrated my graduation by going to New York City."

"Sounds like a great guy, your dad," Charles said, sensing that Nikki needed some affirmation.

"Yeah…well, he takes me to Broadway. First time ever. And we see *Les Misérables*. Ever seen it?"

Broadway. It brought back memories of Denita. And sudden pangs of guilt at the way he felt right now toward Nikki. "Yeah. *Les Miz*. Victor Hugo.

When it ended last year it was the longest running Broadway play ever. Great story... Everybody dies."

Nikki chuckled. Then she took on a nostalgic look. "Just like real life sometimes."

Charles sensed how hard this was for Nikki to talk about. All the bluster that he had seen on prior occasions was gone now. She looked almost like that gangly little girl again, kicking the shallow water, head bent forward.

"It's really a morality play, you know," Nikki mused. "A play about redemption. Second chances. This convicted felon gets released from jail...ends up running a factory and then allows a woman that works for him to be fired without cause. That woman was supporting her little girl who lived with this horrible drunken innkeeper and his wife. Well, when the woman loses her job, she starts selling her body on the street so she can still send money to her little girl. She eventually dies. The reformed felon—the guy who fired her—finds out what he did and goes to this mom on her deathbed. He promises to take care of her child, Cosette. He eventually dies too, during the 1832 revolution, but not until after he has raised Cosette and loved her into adulthood. He also saved Cosette's future husband during the revolution...remember that part?"

Charles nodded. "Sure. Great play. Loved the music." Then it dawned on him. The tattoo on Nikki's shoulder—the picture of the dirty face of the little girl—he had almost forgotten about it. It was the trademark for the play *Les Miz*—a picture of the young Cosette that appeared on all the playbills, all the advertisements for the musical.

"You must have really liked the musical."

Nikki's lips formed a thin smile, her eyes lighting up just a little. Until that moment, Charles had not realized how somber the mood had become, how the lines of sadness had etched themselves on her face. The reflection of the moon on the water and the dim shadows from the lights on the boardwalk combined to give Nikki's face a captivating luminescence as her smile chased the lines away. He wondered how he had ever become so upset at this woman just a few short days ago.

"The day after the show, while my dad attended some business meetings in New York, I got the tattoo done. I thought he was going to kill me." She paused, her smile disappearing as quickly as it came. "That night, my dad told me something he had kept secret all those years." She lowered her voice until it was barely audible above the gentle roar of the ocean. "He was the man who killed my mother. He was the driver of the other vehicle."

Nikki stopped again and faced Charles straight on. Her face was now shrouded in darkness, his own shadow blocking the remnants of light from the boardwalk. "*Les Miz* was our story, Charles." A pause, and Charles thought he detected a slight catch in her voice. "I couldn't decide whether to love him or hate him." Nikki looked down and subconsciously drew a little line in the sand with her toe. A line between them? Was it symbolic? "Eighteen months later, he died from a heart attack."

He felt the wind leave his lungs. And then another feeling: a sense of sudden and complete sympathy for this woman. So different from the audacious woman in the courtroom, the bravado in the classroom, the Nikki Moreno who played the wild and carefree woman in her own Broadway play. He saw the child in her now, and he wanted to comfort her. He stepped sideways, just a half step, as he reached out and gently took her hand. She was no longer in his shadow, and the dim light seemed to mellow her even more.

"I'm sorry," he said.

She hesitated. When she spoke, the strength was back her in her voice. "You don't need to be," she said, her chin held high. "I survived it. And I knew the love of a father." She placed her other hand on his, just for a second, and then released it. Reading it as a signal, he let go too.

They stood there for a few more seconds in silence, then Nikki turned toward the direction they had come from and gave Charles a sideways glance. "See that lifeguard chair?"

Charles nodded.

"Bet you're pretty slow for a black guy." Before he knew it, Nikki was off and running, kicking up sand behind her.

He passed her less than halfway to the chair.

CHAPTER 47

Mondays used to be Nikki's least favorite day by a long shot. But since she started taking care of the kids, Mondays felt like a respite. In the old days, before Tiger and Stinky invaded her life, Nikki would party hard all weekend and dread Monday morning. But now, after taking care of the kids all day Saturday and Sunday, forty-eight straight hours with no school breaks or day-care breaks, Nikki couldn't wait for Mondays.

And this morning Tiger made the entire trip to Green Run Community Church day care without spilling a single thing in Nikki's car.

"We're so glad you're back!" gushed Miss Parsons to Tiger. She looked up at Nikki and winked, then back to Tiger. "We really missed you last week."

"Thank you, ma'am," said Tiger unenthusiastically. Nikki knew that Tiger was not terribly excited about being back. Seems he was fighting a nasty sore throat and headache this morning. But he was here. And that was a start.

Throughout the weekend Nikki convinced Tiger that his karate lessons had made him invincible. Tiger showed Nikki his aggressive karate stance—one arm out, the other cocked next to his chest, fists balled up, knees bent. He had mastered a mean war whoop. He had even learned a couple of elementary moves, like a kick move with a punch combination. His leg didn't get as high as it was supposed to on the kick move, and would pose no danger to anybody's face, but Nikki did notice that Tiger seemed to get his kick just high enough to do some real damage to a boy about his size.

Nikki allowed Tiger to knock her down a few times over the weekend and then pronounced Tiger ready. By now Stinky was also in on the gig. Nikki pulled Stinky aside and made her secretly promise that if Tiger got in a fight on Monday—if Stinky heard the telltale battle cry and saw Tiger coil into his karate position—she should immediately jump between the combatants and call for Miss Parsons.

To top off Tiger's newfound prowess, Nikki had allowed him to put a Power Rangers tattoo on his right bicep. It was a temporary tattoo, and Nikki chuckled to herself as the small tattoo wrapped nearly all the way around the toothpick-sized arm of Tiger. But it seemed to do the trick. Tiger said it was "cool" when she first applied it, and later she caught him flexing, staring at the tattoo, and smiling smugly.

Just before she left him, Nikki grabbed Tiger's arm around his skinny little bicep, her finger and thumb easily touching. Nobody was looking at them. "Give me a flex," she said.

The little guy squeezed his arm up tight, producing no discernible bulge of muscle, not even a tiny little wrinkle in the Power Ranger tattoo. "Awesome," whispered Nikki. "Nobody better mess with you." She leaned over and kissed him on the cheek.

As she turned to kiss Stinky good-bye, Nikki whispered in her ear to point out Doughy Joey. Stinky pointed at a corner of the room, in front of some wooden cubicles, where the kids placed their lunchboxes. At that moment Tiger's nemesis was the only one there.

Nikki walked up to Joey, grabbed him firmly by the bicep—his arms were twice the size of Tiger's—and leaned down so she could whisper to him.

"You're friends with Tiger, aren't you?" She squeezed the arm hard as she whispered, digging her fingers into the puffy flesh.

"Yeah," he said, trying to jerk his arm away. But Nikki squeezed harder, and Joey stood still.

"Good. I'm a lady from the court system that has custody of Tiger and Stinky right now," she whispered. With her free hand, she reached in her purse and pulled out a wallet, flashing an ID at Joey like they did on television. "Can I talk to you for minute about Tiger?"

"S-s-sure," stammered Joey, his eyes starting to water. "But can you let go of my arm first?"

Nikki dropped the arm, then lowered her voice even more. "Last week, some of the kids in day care were picking on Tiger about his dad being in jail, and I understand that Tiger almost got in a fight." Joey's head was nodding, a look of concern on his face.

"It's a good thing he didn't," confided Nikki, "or it might have turned out like the last day care. Did you hear about that?"

"No," Joey said in puzzlement.

"Mmm." Nikki studied Joey, looking suspicious. "I thought someone said you were his friend."

"I am," said Joey defensively.

"Well, I guess I shouldn't be surprised you don't know. Tiger doesn't like to talk about it."

"Talk about what?"

Nikki looked around. Nobody was listening. Still, she pulled Joey more to the side, and checked one more time, as if she were about to tell him something she had obtained directly from the head of the FBI.

"I'm going to tell you some top-secret stuff. It's supposed to be for court personnel only. You promise not to tell?"

Joey nodded.

"At the last day care, some kid goaded Tiger into a fight and, well, Tiger is a karate expert you know…" Joey's eyes went wide; he hadn't known this. "Anyway, the other kid ended up with some permanent injuries, closed head injuries, that type of thing. He still has trouble talking clearly today."

For emphasis, Nikki reached down and grabbed Joey's arm again, squeezing even harder than before. Another glance around, then, "If you ever see Tiger go into his karate stance, jump in between him and the kid he's going to hurt, scream for the teacher, do something…anything. But if you're truly his friend, don't let him hurt any more kids, okay?"

Joey nodded vigorously, he seemed to have gotten the point. Nikki rewarded him by releasing the arm.

"I don't want Tiger to end up like his daddy," she said in passing as she stood to go. "In jail for murder. They say even behind bars Tiger's daddy orders hits…murders on those who give his friends or family a hard time. We haven't been able to prove all of them, but we will. Just give us time."

Joey's jaw hung open, his eyes still wide. He closed his mouth and gulped. He was speechless, dumbstruck by these surprising revelations from this officer of the law. All he could do was nod.

"Have a nice day, kid," Nikki said, as she turned to leave the Green Run Community Church day care. She would not worry about Tiger today. The little karate expert would be just fine.

CHAPTER 48

There in the distance sat Denita in her judicial garb, high up on the bench—supersized, with a booming, echoing voice, laughing at him. "I've changed." Hideous laughter. "Trust me, I've changed."

Charles felt his stomach clench as he squeezed her hand tighter—her hand!—Nikki's hand! He turned to her and saw the tears in her eyes, the laughter of Denita raining down on them. He reached out and put his arm around Nikki's shoulder, drew her closer, felt her body sobbing.

Separating them from Denita were rows and rows of graves. All marked. All with wilted flowers. "Guilty!" Denita screamed. Then she stared at Charles and smiled. "Guilty!"

He knelt down with Nikki at the foot of the grave in front of him...saw the face of the little girl on the tombstone...Cosette's grave.

That's when the fog started rolling in.

Charles stood to object, leaving Nikki kneeling beside him, hardly visible in the fog, but the words stuck in his throat. He felt Nikki's future, the responsibility for all these graves, his own judgment hanging in the balance. But his tongue was thick, and before he could form the words, he heard Denita banging her gavel out there in the fog, once, twice... "Order in the court!"

Nikki continued sobbing.

He heard Denita's pronouncement—"Guilty"—over and over again. He objected, saw the officers of the court stepping out of the fog with handcuffs, then heard the music start to play...softly at first, then louder, then louder still...

He bolted straight up in bed, reached over, and silenced the radio alarm.

"Thank God," he mumbled. The dream was so vivid, so lifelike, that he knew if he closed his eyes he'd see it all again. The graveyard, Denita, Nikki, little Cosette's grave. He rubbed his face, searching for the meaning. He felt the sweat on his brow. He never did this, never had nightmares like this, never woke up in a cold sweat.

What did it mean?

Was God telling him something here? The graves. Were they the children who would die if Denita took the bench? And what of Nikki, holding his hand and crying? There was something strange about her, even for a dream. Her dress. That was it: her dress. Not the stock-in-trade Moreno miniskirt. It was a white dress, frilly, long...*a bride's dress.*

Slow down.

He reminded himself that it was just a dream. Perhaps a warning he was starting to fall for her? Too fast. Perhaps a warning that she was falling for him? And where would it lead? More broken hearts? The death of Nikki the little girl? The end of Nikki's happiness as Cosette?

It was all so confusing.

How could a relationship with Nikki end any differently than the one with Denita? The same underlying tensions—the incompatible religious beliefs—would be there. But Nikki wasn't Denita. There was something far more enchanting about Nikki, far more endearing. Wasn't that also the point of the dream?

What am I doing? he asked himself as he went about his morning routine. *This is just a dream! You're not some kind of soothsayer. If you want to know God's will, go to Scripture!*

With that thought in mind, Charles padded down to the kitchen table and opened his New Testament to the spot where he had left off yesterday, the gospel of John, chapter 11. The story of Christ raising Lazarus from the dead.

And since Charles didn't believe in coincidence, he immediately knew that God *was* trying to tell him *something.* It was a story he had read many times before. But it just so happened to be the same story that had caused such a ruckus on Saturday night during his Bible study time at the jail.

The night had started slowly, with only a few inmates attending. Buster was there, leaning against the back wall, arms crossed. But as a changed man, he no longer coerced the entire ES into attending. As a result, the group was down to six members, and Charles was beginning to wonder if it was really worth his time.

Charles used the occasion to present Buster with his very own *King James*

Bible, a brand-new, leather-bound version with gold trim around the outside edges of the pages. Though Buster did a good job disguising any emotion— "Thanks, Rev," he said without even a smile—Charles could tell it meant a lot. The big man held the Bible gingerly, as if it were the original manuscript. With a little help from Thomas, he proudly turned to the Scripture passage that Charles used as his text.

But ten minutes later, about halfway through the Bible study, the second grand theological debate of this jailhouse group erupted. It seemed that after Buster was converted, Thomas instructed him to begin reading through the gospel of John. So Buster, now a Bible scholar for all of four days, had read the story about Jesus raising Lazarus from the dead, found in John 11. And Buster was not buying it.

"Seriously, Rev," argued Buster, "if he did it for Lazarus, why didn't he do it for Dr. King? I mean, I ain't dissin' God's Word or nothin', but you know, dog, that can't be right."

Charles took him on immediately in front of all the other men.

"Do you believe God raised *Jesus* from the dead?"

"Aw, man, 'at's different," moaned Buster, "and you know it. You da one told me Christ is God's Son. 'At's different, man."

"That's my point," said Charles. "When we believe in Christ, we become God's sons. God will raise every one of us at the second coming of Christ. He just raised Lazarus as a sign to show what He can do."

"I dunno," mumbled Buster, shaking his head. "I mean, I hear what you're sayin', Rev, I jus' ain't buyin' it."

From the front of the room, Charles eyed this sullen convert, this stubborn doubter still leaning against the back wall. The men tried not to show it, but they were listening closely. Their eyes were all on Charles.

Without another word, Charles weaved among them and walked back to where Buster stood. He stopped a few feet away.

"Give me your Bible," said Charles, holding out his hand. Buster gave it to him with a scowl. "Mess with it, Rev, and I'll bust your skull."

Charles opened the Bible to John 11, the story of Lazarus, and handed it back to Buster. "Rip it out," he said.

"What you talking 'bout?" asked Buster, nodding his head indignantly, a snort in his voice.

"Rip it out," demanded Charles. "If you don't believe it, rip it out."

Thomas jumped to his feet. "Don't do it!" he said. "You do it, you'll flat out bring all the judgments in that book down on your head!"

Charles and Buster locked eyes, then Buster looked down at the beautiful Bible in his hand. "No way, Rev. Even if I wanted to, I couldn't. I'd rip out other stories with it; they're all on the same page."

"My point exactly," said Charles, looking around the room, and changing his Bible study topic on the spot. "This book"—he grabbed Buster's Bible and raised it up—"is God's Holy Word. You can't change it, cherry-pick it, or cannibalize it. You either accept the whole counsel of God or go follow some other religion. But don't claim to be a Christian if you're not willing to live and die by *this* book."

For the next fifteen minutes, Charles preached about Lazarus and the inerrancy of God's Word. That was then. And now here he was on Monday morning, not even two days later, confronted with this same passage of Scripture immediately after God had grabbed his attention with a horrific dream. It was no coincidence.

But after twenty minutes of prayer, Charles still couldn't quite figure out exactly what God was trying to tell him. What did Lazarus have to do with Nikki and Denita?

He was not good at waiting on the Lord for direction. He was a man of action. But sometimes, God gave him no choice.

CHAPTER 49

Waiting on God was one thing; waiting on Nikki was another. Charles paced his office, wondering what was keeping her this morning. She was supposed to meet him at 8:00. He checked his watch and took another shot at the Nerf basket. 8:30. Where was she? Should he call her on her cell phone or would that appear too anxious? Was she having trouble finding his office?

If she didn't hurry up, it would be too late. His next class started in half an hour. He and Nikki had to discuss the case and divide up the trial prep tasks. They had to talk strategy, witnesses, and evidence. And, most important, they had to discuss their relationship. Charles had to make sure they were not getting ahead of themselves. He had to talk to her about Denita. He had to explain that he could not be "unequally yoked."

He took another shot at the hoop and rehearsed his speech again, speaking softly to himself. *Friday night was great.* Was *great* the right word? Was it strong enough? Too strong? *Friday night was awesome.* No, that's way too much. *I had a great time Friday night.* There. Much better. *Thanks for sharing about your dad. Sounds like an amazing man. And he obviously did a good job as an only parent.* Nikki would love that line.

Next, Charles rehearsed his pause, a big sigh as if he were spontaneously struggling with these words. He would reach out and touch her gently on the shoulder… No, that would be hokey. He would just look deep into her eyes… No, that wouldn't work either. Those eyes could melt this next line away. Better to stare at the floor, stuff his hands in his pocket, and just say it: *Nikki, I feel like there's a lot of great chemistry between us, so much that's right…* Or what about *Nikki, I really love spending time with you.* Should he say "love"? No, that would be overkill; chemistry was the right touch. *And even though we've only been together a few times, I really value this friendship.* Friendship, that was the key. Use that word a lot. *But we've got to talk about a couple of things before this goes any further…* He knew he owed her that much.

"Hey," said Nikki, bursting through the door. "Sorry I'm late."

"No problem," said Charles, trying to gain his composure. His heart was already racing. "But I've got class in thirty minutes."

"Right, then let's get down to business," she said, plopping down in one of the chairs in front of his desk. "We've got so much ground to cover…now that we've kissed and made up."

She cracked a mischievous grin. Charles swallowed hard, his mouth dry. He smiled back nervously.

Nikki pulled a legal pad out of her briefcase and laid it on the desk. She began reading from a checklist.

"I'm going to take today and tomorrow to further investigate Armistead. Don't ask any questions about how. We can meet again on Tuesday night to discuss the results."

Charles leaned against the window, arms folded in front of him, trying to look cool. "Okay."

"If you get me a jury list, I'll start investigating potential jurors on Wednesday," continued Nikki. "In the meantime, you could work on the cross-examination of the witnesses and put together a draft of your opening…"

Charles watched Nikki as she spoke, all businesslike as she mapped out a trial preparation strategy. His mind began to wander. He thought about Friday night, about Busch Gardens, and about how exhilarating it was just to be around her.

In the four years since Denita had divorced him, he had never really felt this way toward another woman. So tongue-tied and alive in her presence. And this issue about dating only those who shared his religious fervor—or at least other Christians—something he had been so firm about just a few short days ago, suddenly seemed so murky. Why would God give him feelings for someone he wasn't supposed to be with? And wouldn't she more likely be attracted to Christ if he nurtured this relationship instead of cutting it off?

But those were rationalizations, and he knew it. He thought about Denita, and his undying hope that someday she might come to Christ and they might be reunited. And thoughts of Denita triggered feelings of disloyalty for being with Nikki at all. He knew that was stupid. And he knew that Denita herself had been with half a dozen different men since their divorce. But honestly, he still felt something for her. And he wasn't sure that he ever wanted those feelings to go away.

If his experience with Denita had taught him anything, it had taught him the importance of seeing eye-to-eye on matters of faith. He might feel differently right now, but a serious relationship with someone outside the faith would only result in heartache and disappointment later. The commands of Scripture were put there for his own good by a loving God. Charles knew that. But it didn't make it any easier. He knew what he had to do, and he steeled himself to do it. She had stopped talking. Now was the time.

But then he glanced at his watch. He was due in class in ten minutes. There really wasn't enough time to say what he needed to say. Tuesday night would be here soon enough.

"I missed that last part. Uh, you mind running through that one more time?" asked the professor.

She smiled. "Sure, but listen up this time, handsome. You can always stare at me later."

CHAPTER 50

By early afternoon Tiger was feeling his oats. Nobody had tweeted at him all day. And Joey seemed to be absolutely avoiding him. Maybe his reputation was getting around. Maybe they knew he was working on his yellow belt.

He prowled the playground looking for trouble. Sure, he started the day a little nervous, but as time wore on he started gaining some confidence. A couple of fun games of tag, a turn or two on the monkey bars, and now they were choosing up teams for soccer. Tiger usually didn't play. It was hard to get around in the cowboy boots, but he really felt pretty good about himself today. He decided to give it a shot.

The captains apparently hadn't yet heard about his new karate prowess, and they began choosing up sides while ignoring Tiger. He didn't expect to go in the first round; there were kids older and bigger and faster. But he hoped he wouldn't go last. It was always embarrassing to be the only kid left standing on the side, waiting to hear your name called. The last guy never really got picked. The captains never said, "Okay, we'll take Tiger," when you're the only one left. It's more like nobody would say anything. It was just understood that when the next-to-last guy was picked, and you were still left, you headed to the opposing team as fast as possible, so you didn't have to stand alone for long.

As it narrowed down to the final four undrafted players, Tiger glanced with relief at Anthony on his left. Anthony was a notorious sissy—twice as slow as Tiger even if Tiger wore his cowboy boots—and it was pretty much a given that Anthony would go last. Tiger hated that for Anthony but figured it was better Anthony than him.

Surprisingly, Tiger was chosen third to last, beating out both Anthony and Anthony's little sister, Amanda. This was no small feat. Even though Amanda was a year younger than Tiger and wore pigtails, she was generally regarded as one of the boys and unafraid of anyone even twice her size. Tiger considered it quite an honor to beat her out.

He took the field with his chest puffed out and his head held high. Life was good.

Tiger was back.

His exhilaration lasted exactly five minutes. That's how long it took Joey, whose team was losing, to start picking on Anthony, one of Tiger's teammates. In the old days, before his karate lessons, Tiger wouldn't have worried much about Anthony. After all, if Anthony wasn't being picked on, then Tiger himself would be a likely candidate. But with his newly developed powers, Tiger felt a certain responsibility to stick up for the underdogs of the world, guys like Anthony, guys who didn't know the first thing about karate.

Tiger tried to be patient. He let Anthony get knocked down once by Doughy Joey. A few minutes later it happened a second time. The third time, the ball was at the other end of the field, and Joey did it just for spite. And while Anthony lay on the ground, holding his shoulder and whining, Doughy Joey stood over him and called him a crybaby.

Tiger looked around and saw that Miss Parsons was a hundred feet away and talking to some other kids. Little Amanda, who was actually on Joey's team, came running over and turned on her teammate.

"You leave him alone," she yelled at big Joey.

"Make me," said the tough guy to the little girl in pigtails.

And that's when something inside Tiger snapped. As if driven by some outside force, some karate master from the past, he jumped into action. He ran in front of Joey, leaped into a picture-perfect karate stance—bent at the knees, one leg in front of the other, hands balled into tight fists, one arm stretched toward his foe—and wailed out a high-pitched karate yelp that pierced the entire playground.

"Aiiiiiyaaaaah!"

Joey tilted his head and gave Tiger a look of curiosity, as if Tiger had sprouted a third eye or something. But Tiger held his ground, and Joey took a step back, then two, carefully watching the intense looking little maniac standing before him. As Miss Parsons and Stinky came running toward them, Tiger unleashed another yelp and an accompanying kick move that whiffed through the air, causing Joey to nearly fall over backward as he scrambled to get out of the way.

There were no blows landed in those few seconds, but then again, there didn't need to be. Tiger had backed down the bully of the day care. David had defeated Goliath. The reign of terror was over.

For his part, Doughy Joey was smart enough to save face by telling his friends that he could have beat up Tiger, he just didn't want to get placed on time-out again. But he wasn't fooling anybody. The other kids had seen it with their own eyes. And they noticed that Joey pretty much steered clear of Tiger for the rest of the day. That one little incident—the humiliation of Doughy Joey—might not help Tiger get picked sooner in soccer. But as for fighting, he had established a reputation as a man not to be messed with.

Sure, Tiger endured a good chewing out from Miss Parsons. But he sauntered off the soccer field with his lethal weapons, those deceptively small and bony little hands, tucked safely in his pockets. He knew there would be no more tweeting. After all, you don't usually tweet at a legend.

CHAPTER 51

Nikki found the address for Latasha Sewell and immediately felt guilty. Latasha lived in a dingy apartment complex that undoubtedly qualified as public housing. The brick structure looked tired and worn, with knee-high weeds in the common areas and trash strewn around the dark parking lot. At three in the morning, the lot crawled with long shadows caused by the dim light of the few outside bulbs that had survived gang activity. Nikki found a remote parking spot, cut her lights, and stepped nervously from her car.

It was quiet except for the hum of some window air-conditioning units and the occasional car driving by the front of the complex. Nikki took a quick breath of the stale and musty air and decided to make this as quick as possible. She walked quietly through the parking area, occasionally flicking on her small penlight to check out a car or illuminate a license plate. She hated to think what would happen if she got caught.

It took about five minutes to find the beat up Chrysler New Yorker that had probably rolled off the assembly line during Reagan's presidency. The banged-in left rear fender, the missing back bumper, and the discolored paint were dead giveaways. Still, Nikki checked the license plate to make sure she had the right car, the same one she had watched Latasha get into after her shift at Eagle Cleaners the day before.

Nikki returned to her car and drove it up behind and perpendicular to Latasha's, between Latasha's car and the apartment complex. She slipped out of her car and left it running, glanced quickly around, and saw no movements in the shadows. She knelt down next to the back tires on Latasha's car, her body completely shielded from the apartment complex by her own vehicle. *Perfect.*

Nikki popped open a switchblade, took a deep breath, then went to work—first one rear tire, then the other. The air hissed out, and the old car hunkered down on the rear wheel rims. Then she quietly grabbed a brick from the front seat of her car and checked the envelope to make sure it was securely taped to the brick. Another look around, then she threw the brick through the back passenger-side window of the automobile. The shattering glass sounded like an explosion. Nikki knew she had to get out of there, but first she flashed her penlight in the broken window, her hands shaking a little now, to confirm that the brick had landed safely on the backseat. It had. In fact, it had landed squarely between the two infant car seats.

She flicked off the light, jumped in her car, and drove quickly out of the parking lot. She felt enormous relief as she put some distance between herself and the apartments, but none of the satisfaction that should have accompanied a job well done. Short of a miracle, Latasha would not be at work tomorrow. And her job of cleaning the Armistead house would fall to the new girl on the Eagle cleaning team. The eight, fifty-dollar bills that Nikki had left in the envelope would almost certainly pay for a couple of new tires and a new back-door window for Latasha's car. The tires were almost bald anyway.

But still, Nikki couldn't get the picture of those two dirty car seats out of her mind. Nor could she shake the despair that seemed to hover around that apartment complex, even at 3:00 a.m. What was it like raising a couple of kids as a single mom in a housing project? Did you worry constantly about the drugs, the drive-bys, the sex-for-cash that probably went down in that parking lot every night? What chance did those little kids really have? *How did Latasha deal with it?* Nikki wondered. Her own experience with Tiger and Stinky was proving nearly impossible. And they didn't have the odds stacked against them the way Latasha did.

At 4:00 a.m., after driving all the way back to her own condo and checking on her charges—they were sound asleep—Nikki headed back to Latasha Sewell's vandalized car with another envelope in hand. First, she stopped at an ATM, then stuffed the envelope with ten twenties. *New tires are expensive these days,* she told herself.

Four hours later, resplendent in her blue jeans, white blouse, and Eagle Cleaners logo, Nikki closed the front door of the Armistead estate behind her and gawked at all the marble in the cavernous front foyer. This place was worth a fortune.

There was, of course, nobody at home. Armistead was working, or so Nikki assumed. The house was empty and sterile. It was hard to believe that anyone actually lived here. She couldn't understand why Armistead hired someone to clean this place; it already seemed spotless.

She gave herself a quick tour of the downstairs. She walked through the huge formal sitting room to the left of the foyer. Antique furniture, Persian rugs, expensive paintings. Then she crossed the foyer and entered Armistead's study. The plantation shutters were drawn, and the maroon walls and mahogany wood seemed to absorb whatever sunshine bravely snuck through.

Across the back of the house was a massive family room with a catwalk above it and a wall full of windows looking out on the back deck and pool, complete with a waterfall splashing into the deep end. A large kitchen occupied the other side of the back and led to a beautiful formal dining room where the walls were lined with expensive china cabinets and floor-to-ceiling mirrors.

Nikki also glanced around the upstairs, memorizing the floor plan as much as possible. She paused for a moment in the spacious master bedroom, overwhelmed by its luxurious fireplace, vaulted ceiling, immense walk-in closet, and adjoining master bathroom. The master suite was larger than many starter homes she had seen.

She would have to run the vacuum cleaner in each of these rooms and do a few other small things to make it look like she had cleaned. She would make that token effort later, after she had fulfilled her mission. She decided to start in the study.

The computer would be a gold mine. But Armistead had shut it down, and she could not log on without a password. She checked some of Armistead's paper files, carefully leafing through the tax returns and bank statements, to see if she could get a clue about the password. She tried his birthday, Erica's birthday, social security numbers and address numbers. Nothing worked. Then she got creative and tried anything and everything she could think of.

E-R-D-O-C. Invalid. She noticed a picture on a bookshelf of the Armisteads in a motorboat. She typed in the name of the boat: F-A-S-T-A-N-D-E-A-S-Y. Invalid. Maybe it was obvious, something right under her nose. E-R-I-C-A. Invalid. D-R-S-E-A-N. Invalid.

Then a thought hit her. If he really had something going with the Barracuda, would he have the audacity to use her name as a password? R-E-B-E-C-C-A. Invalid. C-R-A-W-F-O-R-D. Invalid. B-E-C-C-A. Sorry, invalid password. B-A-R-R-A...

She stopped tapping the keyboard. A noise from the driveway, the distant and faint sound of an engine, wheels on cement. It quickly got louder and startled her, shook her to the bone. She jerked her head up and turned her ear toward the door. Someone had arrived. She heard the slamming of car doors outside.

She hit the power switch, shutting the computer down, and sprinted for her cleaning supplies in the foyer. Her heart pounded against her chest, the rush of adrenaline clouding her thoughts. *If it's Armistead, will he recognize me? Should I take my cleaning supplies and run upstairs or try to make a getaway out the back? Whose dumb idea was this, anyway?*

She grabbed her supplies and glanced through a French window on the side of the front door. She felt herself exhale and her muscles relax. She watched the lawn crew unload their mowers and Weed Eaters.

"You guys about gave me a heart attack," she muttered to the windows. Though she was relieved to see the lawn crew, she also realized that this would only make it harder, make it more imperative that she keep a close watch out the windows. The noise of any car coming down the driveway would now be masked by the noise of lawnmowers and other power tools.

Nikki immediately went back into the study, but she decided not to fool with the computer anymore. She was wasting valuable time. She would thumb through all the paper files first and see what she could learn.

The first half-hour proved fruitless, but the financial files contained pay dirt. She learned that Erica was the beneficiary of a trust set up by her parents with a corpus of more than one million dollars. She learned that Erica's will specified that all of her assets, including her rights under the trust, would vest in her husband upon her death. She noted that Erica's will had not yet been probated. Not unusual, given the short amount of time since her death. But when it was probated, Sean Armistead would benefit handsomely.

There was also a life insurance policy on Erica worth a quarter of a million. But Nikki assumed that if Erica's death was ruled a suicide, the policy would not apply. She didn't have time to read the fine print, but she thought that was the way most policies worked.

Nikki also rifled through the credit-card receipts, making furious notes of any restaurants or bars patronized by Armistead in the last six months. If she had to, she would go bartender by bartender to see if anybody could recall seeing the doctor and the Barracuda together. She was disappointed to find no local hotel bills on the credit cards. If there was something going on, then Armistead had been extremely careful to cover his tracks.

Nikki next wrote down the long-distance phone numbers from Armistead's telephone bill. She would call every one of them, no telling where that might lead.

But it was the bank records that produced the largest surprise. There were receipts for two large transfers of money that had each occurred within the last week. The first one, a two-hundred-thousand-dollar transfer from Armistead's investment account to another bank account, identified only by number, had taken place the day of the preliminary hearing in the Hammond case.

The second transfer, another two-hundred-thousand-dollar transfer, was a little more complex. It appeared that Armistead had applied for and received a line of credit secured by his expectancy interest in Erica's trust account. He had then exercised the line of credit to the tune of two hundred thousand dollars and transferred that sum to the same bank account as the first transfer. This second transfer had taken place just yesterday.

Although the face of the transfer receipts did not contain any identifying information about the owner of the recipient account, Armistead had scribbled a notation on both transfer receipts, indicating the payee as Virginia Insurance Reciprocal and indicating the purpose as "payment for malpractice settlement."

Both entries seemed suspicious to Nikki. She was no stranger to medical malpractice cases, and she had never heard of a company named Virginia Insurance Reciprocal. Further, she had researched all local cases pending against Armistead. To her knowledge, there were no unresolved cases, much less a recently settled case that would justify this kind of payout. Of course, Armistead might have settled out of court for a claim that was never officially filed, but why would he personally be paying that amount rather than his insurance company? Could his deductible be that high?

To Nikki's way of thinking, there were just too many implausible variables stacking up against Armistead. She would have to do some more digging, but she had plenty to think about as she climbed the stairs to clean the bathroom of a man she despised with a passion. She found his toothbrush in a pull-out drawer just under his bathroom sink. It would come in handy for cleaning the toilet.

CHAPTER 52

Charles seemed distracted late Tuesday afternoon as Nikki shared some of the details of her investigation. They were in one of the law school classrooms, giving them plenty of room to spread out.

She was still wearing her Eagle Cleaners' jeans but had changed into a button-down blouse. She had no plans to tell Charles that she now worked two jobs. Besides, she planned on giving her notice to Eagle Cleaners on Friday. She didn't really want to work for them that long, but she figured if she didn't stay at least a week, they would get suspicious. She would do plenty of complaining in the meantime, so they would be glad to get rid of her.

She gave Charles the bottom-line facts about Armistead with no details of how she learned them. The Barracuda had been at Armistead's house the day after the preliminary hearing. Armistead stood to inherit more than a million dollars from his wife's trust. And shortly after Erica's death, Armistead paid four hundred thousand dollars to a medical malpractice insurance company that she had never heard of.

The two racked their brains considering the possibilities. Nikki's theory was that the doctor and the Barracuda were having a torrid affair and Erica Armistead got in the way. Charles couldn't see it. Armistead was not the Barracuda's type, he argued. Besides, an affair wouldn't explain the four-hundred-thousand-dollar payout.

Charles tried everything to pry from Nikki the details of how she knew this stuff. It was critical to the case that he personally be able to weigh the credibility of the sources, he claimed. "Hogwash," replied Nikki. "You just want to know because your curiosity is killing you. They're reliable sources. That's all I can say."

After they exhausted the possibilities on Armistead, they started mapping out a game plan for picking a friendly jury. There were more than a hundred people on the prospective jury list, and it would be nearly impossible to investigate each of them. They would take what little information the court provided, put together an index card of information for each juror, and rank them against the list of desirable characteristics they wanted in a model juror. It wasn't perfect, and it sure wouldn't come close to what the Barracuda would do with her high-priced jury consultants, but it would have to work. It took money to hire consultants, and money was in short supply.

At a few minutes before five o'clock, Nikki announced she had to pick up the kids from day care. The place closed at five thirty, and she had a fifteen-minute drive. Stinky hated it when she and Tiger were the last ones to be picked up.

As Nikki started picking up the legal pleadings and index cards strewn around her, Charles sat down beside her on the floor. He placed a hand on hers as she was gathering her stuff, and his face turned serious, his eyes sad and downcast. It was a look Nikki had never seen on him before.

"Can you stop packing up for a second?" he asked. "I've got something I want to talk about. I don't really know how to say it, so I'm just going to blurt it out."

Nikki looked into his eyes. She decided to loosen him up, make it easier to say whatever was on his heart.

"You're not pregnant, are you?" she asked. "Having my baby?"

An unbidden smile creased his lips, though it died quickly, and the ominous look returned. "Nikki, I've got to be serious for a minute. Please hear me out on this."

He is serious, she thought. *And it's not good.*

She braced herself as Charles removed his hand from hers. He paused and took a deep breath before continuing.

—◆—

Charles said a quick prayer for courage and grace. He searched his heart for just the right words. He had already made a bigger deal out of this little speech than he intended. Now he couldn't remember a single line he had practiced so faithfully over the past few days.

"I want to talk about us, Nikki," Charles started. She tilted her head a little, like the notion of "us" had never crossed her mind.

"There's some great chemistry here…at least I think so…and, um, well, I want to make sure we don't move too fast—go beyond where we should." He saw confusion in her eyes and paused, searching again for those elusive words that would describe what he was feeling.

"For the past few days, I've been thinking a lot about you…about us," he continued. "You're my last thought at night and my first thought in the morning. I know that sounds corny, but it also happens to be true."

He thought he detected a little spark in her eye, the beginning of a smile playing on her lips. *Just wait.* He took another deep breath.

"But honestly, I don't think there could ever be more between us than this incredible friendship we're developing, and it's unfair to you if I don't say that up front. I mean, I guess I've never really gotten over Denita and"—he paused again and lowered his voice—"and though I don't expect you to understand this, I've made a promise to myself that I would never get serious with someone who's not a follower of Christ."

He saw Nikki's eyes go cold, her face expressionless. He instantly wanted to take the words back, but he was in too deep.

"I know you're not; we've talked about that. And I'm not trying to pressure you into saying otherwise. So…" his voice dropped off in midsentence. He felt like he had started babbling, just making things worse. He had already said what he needed to say.

The two sat there for a moment, frozen. Charles listened to the labored sound of his own breathing, each second of silence intensifying the pain of his second-guessing. Had he messed up completely? Misread Nikki's intentions? Had she even wanted to be more than just friends? Maybe it was just him; maybe she would laugh in his face.

He waited interminably long for the laughter, for the explosion.

Then he watched as Nikki resumed her packing, deliberately picking up the scattered papers and cards that represented that day's work. She placed them carefully in her briefcase—Charles had never seen her treat anything so neatly and carefully—then she stood to leave.

"First," she said, "your Dear John speech is incredibly arrogant. What makes you think I was dying for some type of deep and lasting relationship with you anyway? Sure, we had some fun Friday night. But that doesn't mean I'm making wedding plans."

Nikki talked calmly, deliberately. This was no explosion, and the calculated chill in her voice made it worse.

"Second, you've got a funny way of showing that you don't want to get serious, with your writing-on-the-sidewalk routine and all. If I didn't know any better, I might have actually assumed you had the hots for me. And while I'm on this subject, why would I want to convert to a religion that tries to tell me who I can and cannot date?"

She did not give Charles a chance to answer, and he knew she wasn't really interested in an answer. She just needed to vent. He stayed seated but glanced up as she turned to go. He saw sadness in her eyes, not the familiar flash of anger.

"And third," she continued, her back to him now. "Um, I don't even remember what else I was going to say, but it doesn't really matter." She walked to the door and put one hand on the knob.

"You want to be friends, you've got a friend—a professional colleague— at least until the end of the case. If that's the way you want to play it, that's fine with me. I'll report back in Thursday night, Mr. Arnold."

"Nikki…"

Charles stood up and headed toward the door, but Nikki left without answering him.

He knew it would do no good to chase her. He had nothing else to offer.

⊷ ⊷⊹⊱ ⊶⊶

The Sebring speedometer was now at eighty-two and climbing. Nikki was swerving through traffic on I-64, changing lanes with no turn signals, passing other cars like they were standing still. She was trying to outrun her emotions and put distance between her and the man who had just blown her off.

The radio blared some hard rock, no chance of running across a sappy love song on this station. She had secretly harbored some hope of a relationship with Charles. She didn't realize how much he mattered until he had dashed those hopes a few minutes ago. Sure, the two of them were very different, and they had only been together a few times, but he was the first man she had felt this way about in a while. Something about him was different than the others she had dated and dumped. She trusted him. Even opened up her past to him—something that she never did with men. The thing is, she could see herself with him long term. Until tonight, anyway.

She knew Charles really did care about her, but he was a fanatic about these religious matters. Over the last several days she had harbored her own doubts about their relationship. In fact, she had thought about giving *him* the Dear John speech. They were just so radically different, she was going to tell him. But the last thing she expected was to get the snub from him.

How dare he? Does he have any idea what he's giving up?

They would have to learn to peacefully coexist and work together on the case. There was too much at stake to let personal feelings interfere with business. They had only eight days to get ready for trial. First thing tomorrow morning she would really hunker down on the investigation.

But tonight she was heading for the Virginia Beach bar scene, if for no other reason than to prove that she had not lost her touch. It had been awhile since she had been out on the town. But after all, she *was* still the beautiful, fun-loving, and enchanting Nikki Moreno. She speed-dialed Bella, the secretary where Nikki worked, and talked her into picking up the kids from day care. Bella had met them at the office a couple of times when Nikki had them with her.

"They can stay all night if they need to," said Bella. "They're cute little rascals."

"I owe you," said Nikki as the Sebring accelerated. It had been a long day. Nikki Moreno was ready to party.

It took her less than three hours to prove that the Moreno charm had lost none of its magnetic force. Charles Arnold may have some religious hang-ups that blinded him to her beauty, but other men, millions of them, would walk across broken glass for a chance to wear Nikki on their arm. And one of those men, a dark-haired surfer named Dustin, was living that dream right now, leaving the Forty-Eighth Street Suds-n-Surf bar side by side with Nikki, trying to talk her into making a night of it. She had snagged him in classic Moreno style: Find a loser to dance with you, wiggle around the dance floor for a few hours casting eyes at other men—the "Moreno Shake and Awe," she called it—and walk away with the cutest dude in the joint.

Tonight that dude happened to be Dustin. Nikki was tired of the intellectual intensity of Charles. She needed a looker without much between the ears.

"I've got a condo on Rudee Inlet," Dustin was saying. He had already told Nikki how rich his parents were. "And when the sun comes up over the ocean"—he lit up with a smile so bright it belonged on a Crest Whitestrips billboard—"it's like totally awesome!"

Now that they were outside the bar, with no music blaring in her ears...now that Nikki could actually hear the guy talk...her first thought turned to how she could gracefully dump him. But she was finding it a challenge to think much at all. The toxic blend of Margaritas and Bloody Marys was catching up with her. As she walked next to Dustin, a parade of disjointed images marched through her head, most of them having to do with Charles. The thought of him made her conscious of how disappointed he would be if he could see her now.

"No thanks. Better head home," she said cheerily, as if her polite rebuff would easily settle the matter, then, "Oops," as she stumbled against Dustin. They both laughed.

"You're in no shape to drive," he said. He wrapped an arm around her shoulder and drew her next to him as they walked. "And I've got a hot tub."

Despite her cheery protests, Dustin guided Nikki toward his car. A few feet away she stopped abruptly.

"I really do need to go home," she said. The giddiness had left her voice, but the words slurred together, formed by a thicker-than-normal tongue.

"But dude, we're made for each other," Dustin argued. He grabbed her hand. "I can feel it. Let's give it a shot. See what happens."

Nikki pulled back. A thought hit her.

"Maybe you should come to my place instead," she said. "We can pick up my kids on the way."

Dustin twisted his head and looked Nikki up and down. "Kids," he asked. "With an *s*?"

Nikki nodded. "'Fraid so." She pulled out her cell phone and speed-dialed Bella while Dustin watched. Bella answered on the second ring.

"I should be there in about half an hour," said Nikki. "The kids sleeping?" Bella starting rambling on in response until Nikki cut her off. "Hang on a second," Nikki said. She held the phone toward Dustin, her arm swaying a little. "You want to talk to her?"

He stepped back and raised his palms, like he might get involved in some kind of paternity suit if he just touched it. "That's cool. I believe you. I mean…whatever."

Nikki chatted for a few minutes while Dustin waited. "Whoa," he said, after she hung up. "That just blows me away. I mean, you didn't seem like the type to have kids and everything."

She just stood there with a small grin plastered on her face, watching Dustin squirm in the uncomfortable silence, and wondering if he might still offer her a ride home.

She didn't have to wait long to find out. "You want me to call you a cab?" Prince Charming offered.

CHAPTER 53

The next day, as Charles sat alone in his office preparing his cross-examination of witnesses, a terrible truth hit him. It came as he sat jotting down questions for the Reverend Beckham, the pastor for Thomas and Theresa Hammond who refused to take even an ounce of responsibility for young Joshua's death. It was as if Beckham could preach something—don't ever seek the medical help of man—and then just ignore the consequences of what he was saying.

If you're going to talk the talk, Charles would say when he preached on the boardwalk, *then you better be ready to walk the walk.* And in this moment of clarity, in the quietness of his still office, the thought slammed him with the force of a head-on collision.

He was no different than Reverend Beckham.

The thought horrified Charles and made him lose focus on what he was doing. This man Beckham preached like a Pharisee, putting greater burdens on his congregation than he was willing to bear himself. This man turned his head while Joshua writhed in pain. How could he not see his own role in the child's death? Couldn't he see that by doing nothing he had condemned young Joshie to die?

And now Charles had to ask himself that same question.

How could he do nothing about the unborn babies that might be affected by his ex-wife's judicial decisions? Wasn't that the whole point of that awful cemetery dream? Denita had endured the trauma of an *illegal* abortion, of having to sneak around and keep it secret—she so feared the stigma of a public abortion. Denita would never get appointed by the current Republican administration if anyone knew of her secret bias. And even if Denita said she had changed, how could she ignore her own intense personal experience?

It had changed her. Charles had seen that with his own eyes. And it would *have to* affect her on issues like parental consent laws, informed consent, partial birth abortion, and other attempts to limit the procedure. If Charles helped hide her past, if he just remained conspiratorially silent, how was he any different than Beckham?

He wasn't, he realized.

He would have to write a letter to Senator Crafton, he decided. And he would let the chips fall.

He hunkered over his keyboard and started typing immediately, before he could second-guess himself again. He did his best to put his emotions aside as he typed. Writing this letter was painful—even now his stomach was in knots—but it was the only way he could live with himself, the only way he could sleep at night.

He prayed this whole mess would somehow bring Denita closer to God, not drive her further away. *People change, Charles. Even without getting all religious like you, people still change.*

But Charles didn't believe that was true. Apart from faith, people don't change. They can't. *The heart is deceitful above all things and beyond cure. Who can understand it?* Isn't that what Scripture said? Isn't that what Charles preached to his congregation of tourists and hangers-on every Friday night?

But still, even as he typed, he couldn't help but wonder about the wilted flowers on the grave of Baby Arnold.

Dear Senator Crafton,

I am the ex-husband of Denita Masterson, who I understand is being considered for nomination as a U.S. District Court Judge. Before that nomination is made, there is something that you need to know about Ms. Masterson, something very personal that may well affect the way she views cases regarding a woman's right to choose.

He swallowed hard and noticed that his fingers trembled a little. He tried to blot her picture from his mind.

During the course of our marriage, and without my knowledge, Denita obtained an abortion using the RU-486 pill. At the time she did so, the abortion pill was not legal in the United States.

Charles printed out the letter, signed his name, and felt a part of him die. *Why,* he wondered, *did something so right feel so very wrong?*

CHAPTER 54

Saturday night, July 2, five days from the start of the trial, and Thomas wondered what else could go wrong. First came the call from Charles—he couldn't make it for Bible study again, something about prior commitments for the holiday weekend. Buster reacted badly, cursing and throwing his Bible into the cell. Thomas picked up the Bible, smoothed out the pages, and laid it carefully on Buster's cot.

Buster was getting on his last nerve. The man just didn't take his Christian walk seriously enough. And Charles wasn't helping none with these last-minute cancellations.

Then there was the fight. Actually more of a beating, to be precise. Thomas didn't witness the events, but the inmates talked of little else. It all started when Buster was walking by a new white fish named Carl Stoner, a greasy biker dude with an attitude, long hair pulled back in a ponytail, and tattoos on every visible inch of his body from the neck down. During his first three days in jail, Stoner had been making quite a name for himself, picking fights with smaller inmates right and left. He was roughly the same size as Buster, though his bulk came more from fat than muscle. Buster claimed he heard Stoner mutter the *n* word to another Anglo, and Buster turned on him in a flash.

Stoner denied the comment, but a couple of other members of the ES gathered round and swore they'd heard Stoner use it on other occasions. Buster took a little spontaneous poll, asking the brothers whether they thought Stoner was innocent or guilty.

Twelve guilties; none for acquittal. The white boys who had gathered around were not given a vote.

That's when the shouting started, and Stoner removed all doubt by calling Buster the same name straight to his face. Buster responded with an explosive right to the midsection, cracking two of Stoner's ribs. With Stoner doubled over in pain, Buster grabbed the back of Stoner's head and slammed his knee into Stoner's face. Blood spurted from Stoner's mouth and nose as he crumbled to the ground in a heap.

The men scattered as the guards arrived. Turns out that nobody saw anything.

That night, in the dark quiet of the cell, Thomas knew that he had to confront Buster with the sinfulness of his conduct. It was the first fight Buster had picked since his conversion, and it was no way for a Christian to act.

"Heard about the fight tonight," said Thomas, keeping his voice down so that it couldn't be heard in other cells. "I can understand why you was mad—"

He heard Buster curse under his breath in the other cot. "No, you can't, Pops."

"Regardless," continued Thomas, "it don't justify what you done. Christians can't return hate for hate, Buster. Think how much God showed you love even when you hated Him."

Thomas waited for an answer. He was ready to work through this even if it took all night. You can't go around claiming the name of Christ and then start cracking people's ribs when they disrespect you. It was time for Buster to get serious about his faith. It was time for some good old-fashioned repentance.

But there would be nothing to work through. Buster answered only with silence. And a half-hour later with the sound of heavy snoring.

CHAPTER 55

For the next four days, Nikki and Charles prepared diligently for trial, like a couple of young professionals who had never had even a momentary longing for each other. Charles was thankful that Nikki had at least gone back to a first-name basis—no more of this "Mr. Arnold" stuff. But there was a distinct chill in the air when they were together and an unspoken rule that their past relationship would not be discussed.

Nikki sent every nonverbal message possible that she would never again give the relationship a second thought. She had always been a woman of casual but intimate touches, something that Charles loved. They would be talking together, and she would reach out and touch his arm, casually fling her arm over his shoulder, or playfully punch him. But now she was making an obvious effort to avoid any physical contact whatsoever. It was like he had an infectious disease, one she was determined not to catch, as she restrained her normally vivacious personality and ubiquitous sense of touch.

The investigation was proceeding no better, as Nikki reported running up against one roadblock after another. None of the bartenders or waiters at the restaurants patronized by Armistead could recall seeing Armistead and the Barracuda together. The long-distance phone calls listed on his bill were also a dead end. Nor could Nikki find out any information about a malpractice company called the Virginia Insurance Reciprocal or any recent settlement of an insurance claim by Armistead.

By the eve of trial, the two legal warriors were getting frustrated. They couldn't shake the feeling that they were close to a breakthrough on Armistead but couldn't quite make out the whole picture. After weeks of investigating and strategizing, the trial still seemed to hinge on the credibility of one witness—Dr. Sean Armistead—and they were missing the silver bullet for his cross-examination.

But that was something they could no longer control. The night before trial, they focused on things they could control: Nikki had completed her ratings of the potential jurors, Charles had completed his outlines for the examination of witnesses, and Charles had practiced his opening statement twice with Nikki playing the role of juror.

It was now nearly 11:00 p.m., and the two had their papers spread all over the classroom that Charles had coopted for use as an office in the days prior to the trial. Nikki used the floor; Charles's stuff covered several rows of seats.

She checked her watch. The kids were staying with their mom, and it was getting late. "I think we're ready," she announced, rubbing her eyes.

Charles looked up from the stack of papers in front of him. "Let me go over the last few minutes of my opening one more time. I've just written some new thoughts." He stood and started stretching his back.

"I'm sure it's fine," she said. "Really. I've gotta go and pick up the kids. I mean, technically, they're not even supposed to be with their mother if I'm not there."

But before she could stand, Charles was off, launching into a passionate appeal outlining the defendant's evidence and asking the jurors—no, *begging* the jurors—to keep an open mind until they heard the defendant's case. He was in his street preacher mode, pacing and cajoling, asking brazen rhetorical questions—all under the expressionless gaze of Nikki Moreno. His voice rose and fell in a mesmerizing rhythm. He was preaching the gospel of reasonable doubt, and the jurors were his congregation.

When he concluded fifteen spellbinding minutes later, there were beads of sweat glistening on his forehead. The room took on an uncomfortable silence. He stuck his hands in his pockets and looked down at his critic, who was still sitting cross-legged on the floor.

"How'd you like it?"

"It's fine," she said, shrugging her shoulders.

At this, Charles's shoulders slumped. He wiped his forehead with the sleeve of his T-shirt and sat down on the floor in front of Nikki, leaning back on his hands with his legs extended out in front of him.

"That's it? Fine?" he asked.

She shrugged again. "Nothing wrong with fine." She started stacking up some papers as Charles watched her every move. "It's late," Nikki continued, sounding defensive. "I've gotta go. It was fine."

Charles continued staring, unsatisfied with the answer. It wasn't that he was fishing for more praise, it's just that he expected some passion. Nikki wasn't being Nikki. He needed her unguarded feedback, not some polite answer from someone working hard to stay emotionally detached.

"Nikki, we've got to talk."

She rolled her eyes. "If I remember correctly, last time we 'talked'"—she made little quote marks with her fingers as she said the word—"it was more like you talked and I listened. And if I'm not mistaken, the gist of our little talk was that you were basically too good for me because you're a Christian and I'm not. So, needless to say, I'm not real excited about talking again." She stood to go.

Charles reached out and grabbed her wrist. "Sit down, Nikki."

She glared at him, pulling the wrist away.

"Please."

She narrowed her eyes and sat.

"Is that what you believe?" asked Charles. "That I somehow think I'm too good for you?"

Nikki shrugged again. She stared past him at the wall.

"Look, Nikki, nothing could be further from the truth. During the few times we spent together before the now infamous 'talk,' I had to pinch myself just to make sure it was real. I mean, I couldn't believe that someone as beautiful and charming as you would ever spend any time with me."

The expression on her face seemed to soften slightly. Charles studied her as he waited for a response. None came.

"When we talked," he continued, "I knew I didn't phrase things right. What I was trying to say is that our friendship really mattered to me, and I didn't want to hurt you by making you think I was looking for something more. Now we've got this trial to get ready for, and I'm just walking on eggshells wondering what you're going to think about this or what you're going to say about that."

Charles softened his voice and looked down at the floor as he continued. He bent his knees and leaned back on his hands. "I understand why you're mad at me, but I've got to get this off my chest before we head into trial. I've got to know that we're in this together, that we can talk openly, and that we'll guard each other's back. We've got enough people shooting at us, trying to put our clients away. I've just got to know that you're with me no matter what."

Charles decided to wait her out. He had to have an answer. He couldn't suffer through a two-day trial with this battle going on in his own ranks. *Why couldn't they at least be friends?*

This time Nikki sighed. A look of sympathy came over her face, lingering there for a moment only to be replaced by that mischievous smile. "You sure that's what you want?"

"I'm sure."

"Okay," she said. She reached out her hands and grabbed his. They pulled each other up. She let go of his hands, brushed off her jeans, and said matter-of-factly, "I'm with you as long as you'll promise me a few things."

"I'm listening."

"First, no more bump-on-the-log defense."

"Of course not."

"Second, don't try to embarrass me in front of the client by asking me to pray."

"Sorry. I never should have done that."

"Third, you've got to rewrite that sorry opening."

What? Is she serious? "Can't we go back to just being professional colleagues, Ms. Moreno?"

"No way," she said. "You asked for this." The spark in her eyes returned, and she broke into a wide Nikki Moreno smile.

He had forgotten how beautiful she was when she smiled.

CHAPTER 56

By midmorning they had picked the jury. In Virginia state court, the judge asked most of the questions and kept the lawyers on a tight leash. Silverman, as usual, had been efficient and fair, tolerating no nonsense from either the Barracuda or Charles.

Nikki leaned back in her chair, seated this time at the right hand of Charles, studying her handiwork. She had made the final calls on which jurors to strike and which to keep. They ended up with seven men and five women—only four mothers. Nikki thought the mothers would be brutal on Theresa and wanted to keep as many as possible off the jury. Four of the jurors were minorities: two African Americans, one Asian American, and one Hispanic. Under Nikki's theory, the minorities would be good, especially with her and Charles sitting at the defense counsel table. But the Hispanic and one of the African Americans were mothers, so they would be hard to predict.

To Nikki's great disappointment, there were no fundamentalists on the jury, but there were a few Baptists and one AME church member. Not the most religious jury she had ever seen. They would have to play the religion card carefully. But overall, it was a jury they could work with. Nikki began trying to make eye contact with the young male jurors, especially the unmarried ones. It might, she thought, be her most important contribution to the case.

The Barracuda seemed to be quite smug about the jury as well. She and her jury consultant had not stopped smiling since Judge Silverman had announced the final panel and seated them in the box.

Nikki hated the Barracuda's act—her phony friendliness in front of the jury. Nikki had never seen the Barracuda smile unless she was in front of a jury or television camera. At the first break, she determined that she would approach the Barracuda and try to make some small talk. She wanted to suggest a new hair-dye product the Barracuda might want to try, something that would help take care of those nasty dark roots. Nikki would also be sure to mention how much she hated these television cameras, based on the well-known fact that the cameras added ten pounds to your weight when you showed up on television.

"Does the commonwealth wish to give an opening statement?" asked Judge Silverman.

With all those cameras rolling, thought Nikki, *wild horses couldn't drag the Barracuda away from making an opening statement.*

The Barracuda stood, looking more slender than usual in her tailored black pinstripe suit. "Yes, Your Honor," she said and then strutted toward the jury box.

Her first five minutes contained a lecture in American civics. She explained all about the trial, who was who, why they were there—that type of thing. She thanked the jury at least three times, as if they had any choice in the matter. Then she began stroking the jurors' egos in earnest.

She told them that they were the most important part of the American legal system. She told them that they had all the tools necessary to decide this case: their own common sense and innate sense of justice. She told them that she would be pleased to trust the fate of the commonwealth's case, the "people's case" as she called it, into their capable hands. Nikki thought she noticed a few of the jurors sit up a little straighter. Nikki wanted to gag.

After an appropriate season of complimenting the jurors on what a great job they were going to do, the Barracuda got down to basics. She represented the interests of the people, she reminded them, and her only concern was to see justice done. And in this case, she carried a heavy responsibility not just to represent the people generally, but to also represent one little person in particular. He was a child who did not live to see his second birthday. A tiny boy named Joshua Hammond, with his whole life in front of him, who died a senseless death because his parents refused to get him medical help.

She stopped talking for a moment, swallowed hard, and then forced herself to continue. Right inside the front of her trial notebook, she told the jury in a whisper, was a picture of innocent little Joshie. It helped remind her what this case was all about. And when she looked at that picture, she couldn't help but wonder how any parents could allow such an innocent little boy to die needlessly.

In fact, said the Barracuda, turning and pointing at Thomas and Theresa Hammond, raising her voice, these parents allowed their baby to suffer in excruciating pain for five days. She shook her head like she couldn't possibly understand it. Five days, with an infected and ultimately ruptured appendix, before they even took him to the hospital. Five days of squirming in agony with a fever of more than 103 degrees before the parents went for help.

There were laws to protect innocent children like Joshua from uncaring or deluded parents. Sure, the Hammonds would claim that their faith required them not to go to the hospital, but that was no excuse under the law. Religious beliefs do not justify murder, said the Barracuda. So let's just call it what it is.

Having pointed and shouted and accused, the Barracuda then seemed to calm down and began discussing the evidence. She took the next thirty minutes to talk about appendicitis, how easy it was to cure, and how hard the good Dr. Armistead worked to save this child even at the last minute. But it was no use; the child had been doomed by the delay in treatment caused by his own parents. The jury would also hear about a statement given by young John Paul Hammond, who desperately tried to defend his parents, but had to admit that his mom and dad had waited a full five days before seeking medical help.

The Barracuda also promised that the jury would hear private thoughts from Theresa Hammond herself in the form of a prayer journal that covered some of the critical days in question. In addition, the jury would hear testimony from the minister of the Hammonds' church. Both the journal and the minister would confirm that Thomas and Theresa Hammond knew their son was dying but refused to seek treatment.

At the end of her opening, the Barracuda turned religious. Little Joshie was probably in heaven right now, she opined, and he was looking down on the trial, wondering whether justice would be done. He had been denied the opportunity to do so many things we all take for granted, denied the chance to realize the potential God had put in his little breast. Now the only question remaining, said the Barracuda, was whether he would also be denied justice. That decision, she said, was in the jury's hands.

And with that thought ringing in their ears, the Barracuda took her seat. She had been at it for fifty-five minutes.

Nikki was nauseated. Watching the Barracuda suddenly turn so religious was almost more than she could take.

◆◆◆

Charles had the daunting task of following this vintage performance. The jurors had already started squirming and shooting mean glances in the direction of Thomas and Theresa Hammond. Charles said a quick and silent prayer, then rose and buttoned his suit coat jacket.

"She's good," he said to the jury, ignoring the usual niceties and introductions. "She's *real* good."

He smiled at the jury, then stuck a hand in his pocket, striking a casual pose. With the other hand he leaned against the jury rail. He lowered his voice.

"That's why the judge told you to keep an open mind until you've heard both sides of the case. And that's why the judge reminded you that opening statements are not evidence. What she said was good. And it would make a good case. Only problem is: It happens *not* to be true."

Then slowly and quietly Charles began building his defense. Thomas and Theresa were loving parents but also parents of faith. They waited longer than most would have waited before they took Joshie to the hospital, but that doesn't mean they're murderers. After all, they violated the very tenets of their faith by taking Joshie to the hospital at all. It was not an easy decision. When they did take him—on the third day of fever, not the fifth—Joshie still had every chance in the world to survive. But mistakes made by Dr. Armistead, and the doctor's refusal to acknowledge that there was better care available at another hospital, cost young Joshie his life.

"Is it unreasonable to pray for a miracle, and wait a few days for that miracle, before you take your child to the hospital?" Charles asked. "And if Joshie was in such bad shape when he was admitted to the hospital, why did he have to wait twenty-six minutes—twenty-six long, painful minutes—before he even saw a doctor? And why, after the decision was made to spend time—

ninety minutes to be exact—trying to resuscitate him through an IV line and make him ready for surgery, why wasn't he transferred to Norfolk Children's Hospital while all this was happening?"

Charles promised the jury they would learn the answer to that question during the cross-examination of Dr. Armistead. He also promised them that when they did, they would be shocked.

He had only been talking for fifteen minutes, but he noticed some of the juror's eyes starting to glaze over. A juror in the back row yawned. It was hard keeping their attention when he was being purposefully low key about the whole thing—trying to keep emotions from driving their decision.

He walked over and stood behind his clients, Thomas and Theresa Hammond. He could not risk having them testify, so this would be the next best thing. He placed a hand on each of their shoulders and looked up again at the jury. As only a teacher could do, he waited until he had eye contact from each juror, then he spoke barely loud enough so they could hear.

"Reasonable doubt does not require perfect parenting. Reasonable doubt does not require that these two act exactly as you would have. Before this case is over, you will hear a lot about what the law requires. But the issue in this case is really very simple and straightforward. Are Thomas and Theresa two loving parents who made a simple mistake or are they really cold-blooded murderers who, by their own inaction, purposefully caused their youngest son to die?

"Ms. Crawford says that justice requires them to suffer more…to serve stiff prison sentences. I say they have suffered enough. They have lost their youngest son. What greater price should they have to pay?"

Charles gently squeezed their shoulders. It was a subtle gesture, but not one lost on the jury. Nor could they miss the steady stream of tears trickling down Theresa Hammond's face.

CHAPTER 57

The Barracuda took advantage of the lethargic time right after lunch to call the Reverend Beckham as her first witness. He looked more like a mortician to Charles than a man of the cloth, his black hair sprayed perfectly into place, his suit holding up without the slightest hint of a wrinkle. He wore a permanent scowl, and Charles could just imagine his typical Sunday morning sermon—a forty-five-minute diatribe against the evils of the world and the sins of the flesh. The reverend took his oath, emphatically repeated "so help me God," then climbed into the witness chair. He squared his chin, determined to tell the whole truth.

As she did at the preliminary hearing, the Barracuda had him destroy the case of his parishioners while appearing to praise them. Beckham spoke of the amazing faith of Thomas and Theresa Hammond and how they waited until things were beyond hope to take Joshua to the hospital. Beckham testified, in a loud and certain voice, of how he spoke with the Hammonds every day that Joshua was sick, though he couldn't remember exactly how many days that happened to be.

A few days before Joshua was taken to the hospital, the reverend actually went to the Hammonds' trailer to pray for Joshua's healing and to anoint him with oil. During that visit the reverend remembered Theresa saying that she believed Joshua was dying and that he needed medical help right away.

But after a few hours of tears and soul-searching, Thomas and Theresa pledged to hang tough and have faith in God, not man. They both realized, said the reverend, that their lack of faith could have been the one thing keeping their son from being healed.

Twenty minutes of the reverend went a long way, in the opinion of Charles, and the Barracuda kept him on the stand for thirty. She finally got to the end of her checklist, paused for effect, and asked the reverend her final two questions.

"Do you have any doubt whatsoever that Thomas and Theresa Hammond knew, on the night you visited them, that this was a life-and-death situation with Joshua?"

"I have no doubt they realized that."

"Yet they were still determined not to take him to the hospital?"

"That's correct. They were determined to rely on Jehovah-Raphah—the God who heals."

"Thank you," said the Barracuda, turning smartly and heading back to her seat. "That's all the questions I have. Mr. Arnold may have a few for you."

"Indeed I do," said Charles, rising quickly and moving toward the witness stand.

"Where do you suppose Thomas and Theresa Hammond got the idea they shouldn't take their son to the hospital? Where did that come from?"

"It comes from the Holy Scriptures and from the teachings of the church," said the reverend proudly.

"And would you agree that the Hammonds came under a lot of criticism for taking Joshua to the hospital at all?"

"There was some criticism. I wouldn't say a lot."

"Enough that you felt compelled to bring it up in your sermon at Joshua's funeral?"

"Yes."

"So regardless of what you taught them and what you told them on the night you prayed with them, and regardless of all the criticism they would face at church, they still had the courage to go against the flow and take Joshua to the hospital. Right?"

The reverend grudgingly nodded his head.

"The court reporter can't record a head nod," said Charles. "You need to answer verbally."

He scowled at Charles as if the lawyer were the devil himself. "Yes."

"Sometimes when church members violate your teachings, they are subjected to church discipline, including getting kicked out of the church. Is that right?"

"In serious cases, that is what Scripture teaches. And that is what we do."

The reverend tensed his jaw as he clipped off the words. He seemed unaccustomed to being questioned in such a fashion.

"The Hammonds risked church discipline and ostracism by the church when they took Joshua to the doctor—true?"

"Yes."

"But they did it anyway."

"I think it's obvious, Mr. Arnold, that they did it anyway."

Charles smiled. The reverend was getting feisty.

"Another church family, the Parsons family, was disciplined about eighteen months ago and made to apologize to the entire church body, were they not?" Charles positioned himself in his favorite spot between the witness and the Barracuda, crossed his arms, and waited for the answer.

The witness bristled. The Barracuda rose.

"What's that got to do with anything?" asked the reverend.

"My point exactly. I object," said the Barracuda.

Judge Silverman looked at Charles.

"Because it shows the psychological pressure my clients were under to follow the reverend's teachings. And it makes it all the more remarkable that they went to the hospital at all."

"I'll allow it," ruled Silverman.

"What's the question again?" asked the reverend.

"Was the Parsons family disciplined by the church?"

"Yes."

"And were they told to apologize to the entire church or risk having all fellowship cut off by the church body?"

"Yes."

"Why were they disciplined? What horrible sin caused the church to come down on them so hard?"

The reverend did not hesitate. "They were being disciplined for failing to obey the Scriptural command to tithe."

"Tithing. That's giving 10 percent of your income to the church. Is that right?"

"Yes."

"And how would you know whether or not somebody is giving 10 percent of their income to the church?"

This time the reverend did pause, giving the Barracuda plenty of time to object. When she said nothing, he answered, though his voice was lower this time. "We require church members to show us their tax records...and we know how much they give."

Now Charles paused, allowing the jury to digest this nugget. "And how much of that tithe income ends up in your salary?"

"Objection." The Barracuda jumped to her feet. "That's totally irrelevant."

"More than a hundred thousand?" persisted Charles.

"Objection!"

"Ms. Crawford, the court can hear you just fine. Now sit down," Judge Silverman answered.

The Barracuda shot the judge a killer look, then threw herself back in her seat.

"Mr. Arnold, what is the possible relevance of that question?"

"I just thought," said Charles with his palms spread out, "that since the reverend takes a look at all the tax returns of his congregation, he wouldn't mind telling the folks on the jury what he makes."

Out of the corner of his eye, Charles saw the jurors lean slightly forward. They were probably wondering if this man of the cloth was really hauling down a six-figure income.

"Objection sustained," said the judge.

Charles feigned a little frustration but knew the point had hit home.

"You don't know exactly how long Joshua was sick, do you?"

"Not exactly."

"You don't even remember the length of time between the day you visited the Hammonds' trailer to pray and the day they took Joshua to the hospital, do you?"

"Like I said—not exactly."

"It could have been the very next day?"

"Doubtful."

"But possible?"

"I suppose."

"So if the prosecution were trying to prove that Joshua was sick for five days instead of three before he was taken to the hospital, you wouldn't be able to back that up, would you?"

Reverend Beckham leaned forward in the witness chair, lowered his bushy eyebrows, and narrowed his eyes at Charles. "As I've said three times now, I can't say if they took him to the hospital the next day or waited five days. I just know that when I saw him, Joshua was extremely sick."

"And at that point, did you suggest that the Hammonds take Joshua to the hospital?"

"No, of course not."

Charles walked over to his counsel table and started to sit. Then, in the style of Columbo, as if he had just remembered something, Charles put his hand to his chin and turned back toward the witness.

"Oh, I do have one more question," said Charles. He waited a few seconds to make sure the jury was listening. "Do you accept any responsibility for young Joshua's death?"

This question lit a fire under the Barracuda. "That's ridiculous," she growled.

"Is that an objection?" asked Silverman.

"Yes."

"Objection sustained," said the judge.

Charles Arnold shrugged his shoulders and took his seat, his unanswered question ringing in the ears of twelve jurors.

"The commonwealth calls Dr. Sean Armistead," announced the Barracuda.

Charles turned to see the doctor walking down the aisle, his beady gray eyes already darting about.

"He looks nervous," Nikki whispered to Charles.

"Yeah," said Charles, his own palms moist with sweat. "Imagine that."

CHAPTER 58

Armistead had dressed casually but professionally for the occasion—just like a doctor—a blue blazer, khaki pants, white shirt, red tie. His posture was ramrod straight, but the dark circles under his eyes revealed the toll of recent events. He somehow looked markedly older than he had just two weeks ago at the preliminary hearing. And he spoke with a sense of grim determination, like a man duty bound to perform an unpleasant task. He avoided eye contact with Charles and focused intently on the Barracuda.

First, they covered his credentials. Med school, board certifications, years of experience in the emergency room; it was all very impressive stuff. Armistead's answers were precise and matter of fact. The receding blond hair, the wire-rimmed glasses, and the prominent jaw all lent an air of credibility to the witness, and the jury seemed to like him.

After going through his résumé, the Barracuda proffered Armistead as an expert witness, thereby qualifying him to give opinion testimony.

"Any objection, Mr. Arnold?" asked Judge Silverman.

"No objection."

The Barracuda next launched her witness into a medical lecture about the appendix. As far as medical science knew, the appendix was basically a useless organ attached to the end of the small intestine. But when it got infected and inflamed, it could present some major medical problems that should be treated immediately.

An inflamed appendix is excruciatingly painful but not life-threatening if treated promptly. For little Joshie, the first few days of his inflamed appendix would have produced unbearable pain, like a thousand knives stabbing his abdomen. If untreated, an inflamed appendix presents a danger of rupturing, which in turn presents a critical and life-threatening situation. A ruptured appendix spews fecal material directly into the abdomen, creating a poison in the system of the patient. The immune system will quickly be overwhelmed by this bacterial infection, eventually leading to peritonitis and the onset of sepsis.

This is precisely what happened to Joshua Hammond. In fact, said Armistead, his appendicitis had been untreated for so long, he was in an advanced state of septic shock when he presented to the emergency room. The sepsis had begun affecting his circulatory system and central nervous system. An immediate operation was nearly impossible because the child was in no shape to survive surgery. Armistead first had to resuscitate Joshua using IV fluids to restore his strength before the doctor could remove the appendix and clean out the fecal material.

It was, according to Armistead, a race against time he was destined to lose. Despite his best efforts and the involvement of nearly every specialist at Tidewater General, Joshua never had a chance. The official cause of death was multiple organ failure precipitated by septic shock.

As he discussed Joshua's death, Armistead's gray eyes became downcast, and his voice softened. He confessed that he had lost very few patients in the course of his practice. It was something you never get used to. And it was particularly heartbreaking to know that this death could have been prevented if the child's parents had just sought medical care during the first few days of the child's illness. Instead, they sat idly by for five days while Joshua was tortured to death by his own appendix.

The Barracuda, expressing just the right amount of righteous indignation, strutted around the courtroom. When Armistead mentioned the five-day time frame, she gave him a puzzled look and asked how he could possibly know that information.

An interesting question, said the witness, and one of crucial importance. When the ER nurse first asked Theresa Hammond how long her son had been sick, Mrs. Hammond said it had been three days. This was an important fact that Armistead relied on in his treatment of Joshua. Later, said Armistead, Theresa Hammond admitted that it had actually been more like five or six days.

Charles glanced down the defense table at Theresa. Her eyes were wet with tears, and her bottom lip quivered. *She looks guilty,* thought Charles. And he knew the jurors were thinking the same thing.

"What did you do when Theresa Hammond admitted that she had lied to you about how long her own son had been sick?" asked the Barracuda.

"I was shocked," said Armistead. "And I called you."

"And did you later become aware of any additional information supporting the opinions you just gave us about how long Joshua had been sick and what kind of shape he was in when he arrived at the hospital?"

"Yes, I did. You later showed me a videotaped interview of Joshua's older brother, John Paul Hammond."

The Barracuda then asked the court's permission to show the jury a segment of the videotape of Tiger. Charles objected, and the judge called the lawyers forward for a sidebar.

"It's hearsay," whispered Charles.

"Dr. Armistead's an expert witness," the Barracuda shot back. "He's entitled to rely on hearsay in forming his opinions. I just want the jury to see some of the factual statements he relied upon."

Silverman let the lawyers argue for a while and then placed his hand over the mike in front of him. "I agree with Ms. Crawford, and I'll instruct the jury accordingly." Charles felt the wind leave him, knowing that he would now have to bring Tiger into the courtroom to testify. *As if he hasn't been through enough.*

When the lawyers returned to their seats, the judge told the jury that they would be watching segments of the videotaped testimony of John Paul Hammond. "What he says is not being admitted for the truth of the matters he asserts," instructed the judge, "but to demonstrate part of the basis for Dr. Armistead's opinions. Is that clear?"

As they were expected to do, the jurors all lied, nodding their heads like robots.

"You may proceed," said Silverman, and the Barracuda rolled the tape.

The camera was focused on Tiger. The sweet voice of the Barracuda in the background asked him whether or not his parents waited three or four days before they took Joshua to the hospital.

"I think it was five," said Tiger.

The Barracuda turned off the tape and looked again at Armistead. "What did you think when you first viewed this videotape?" she asked.

Dr. Armistead took out a pocket handkerchief and cleaned his glasses. He shook his head and looked down at his hands, then back up at the Barracuda.

"It confirmed what Mrs. Hammond had already told me," said Armistead at last, "though I still found it hard to believe that any mother would allow her son to suffer for five or six days from this painful illness and then, just to make herself look better, lie to the nurses and doctors about how long her son had been sick."

"Object!" Nikki whispered to Charles. "How can he testify about *why* she lied, even assuming that she did lie?"

"If I object," Charles whispered back, "I might just as well put a neon sign over that answer so the jury can remember it."

"You won't need to," said Nikki. "They're all taking notes."

"Your witness," announced the Barracuda.

CHAPTER 59

Hᴏᴡ many times have you paid money to settle a malpractice claim?" Charles demanded, rising to his feet.

"Objection, relevance."

"What's the relevance, Mr. Arnold?" asked Silverman.

"I intend to prove that Joshua would have survived if he had received proper medical treatment. The skill and judgment of this doctor is therefore very much at issue."

"I'll allow it," said Silverman.

"How many times?" Charles asked again. He watched as Armistead glanced briefly at the Barracuda. He could sense the wheels turning in Armistead's head, but Charles already knew what the answer would be.

"Two," said Armistead.

"Are you sure it's just two?" asked Charles, raising his eyebrows.

He noticed some of the color drain from the doctor's face.

"Of course, I'm sure," said Armistead. "You don't forget something like that. And the way lawyers are suing everyone in sight these days, I'm fortunate that it's just been twice."

Charles heard one of the jurors snicker. That's okay, let the doctor have a little fun.

"I'll tell you what," said Charles. "We'll come back to that answer. Okay?"

"Suit yourself."

Charles then moved out from behind his counsel table, holding a copy of Joshua's medical chart in his hand. "When Joshua Hammond first presented to the emergency room, is it your testimony that he was *in extremis* and that time was of the essence?"

"Yes."

"With a burst appendix, delays in treatment of a few days count, don't they?"

"Absolutely."

"In fact, hours count. Yes?"

"Of course."

"Minutes count too, don't they, Doctor?"

"Every delay matters, especially if a mother waits six days to bring a child in to see us."

Now it's six days, Charles noticed. He handed the hospital chart to the doctor.

"Is this a true and accurate copy of the medical records from Tidewater General Hospital pertaining to the care of Joshua Hammond?"

Armistead leafed through the pages. "Appears to be."

"I'd like to introduce this as Defense Exhibit 1," said Charles.

Since the Barracuda had no objection, the thick package of papers was marked by the court reporter and handed back to Charles.

"Now tell me," said Charles, "how much time elapsed from the minute that Joshua Hammond presented to the emergency room to the minute he was first seen by a doctor of any kind?"

Armistead frowned and looked through the chart. "Twenty-six minutes. But remember, he'd been seen by a physician's assistant during this time."

"Can a physician's assistant prescribe medicine?"

"No."

"Can a physician's assistant diagnose an illness?"

"Not officially, no."

"Can a physician's assistant send someone to surgery?"

"No."

Charles paused, sure the jury had gotten the point. "So tell me again, Doctor. How long was it before Joshua Hammond was seen by any kind of doctor?"

"Twenty-six minutes," Armistead said, his voice heavy with disgust.

"And how long before he was actually taken in for surgery?"

"About ninety minutes," replied the doctor. "But during most of that time, we were trying to resuscitate him, to get him ready for surgery."

"In other words, you were feeding him and providing nutrition through some IV tubes, is that right?"

"Essentially, that's correct. We were monitoring him, providing nutrition and hyperalimentation."

"And all of those things could have been done in an ambulance, correct?"

The Barracuda apparently saw where this was heading and stood. "Objection, Judge. This is a lot of hypothetical talk about what could have been done. I think Mr. Arnold ought to stick to the facts."

"Give me a minute," said Charles. "I think it will soon be clear why this is relevant."

"All right," said Silverman, "but let's link it up quickly."

"How long does it take to transfer a patient to Norfolk Children's Hospital?"

"About thirty minutes."

"And would you agree that Norfolk Children's Hospital has highly trained specialists in pediatric medicine, including a specialized pediatric intensive care unit?"

Charles watched Armistead's eyes dart back and forth. He hoped Armistead would try and dispute the superiority of Norfolk Children's. Nikki had lined up two specialists to testify if he tried that tactic.

"Most believe," said Armistead, choosing his words carefully, "that Norfolk Children's Hospital has a level of care not available at less-specialized hospitals like Tidewater General. But, Mr. Arnold, I did not have the luxury of sitting back and nitpicking this decision. I had to use my best medical judgment on the spur of the moment, and that judgment told me that Joshua would not survive a transfer."

"He didn't survive staying at Tidewater General, either, did he?"

"*Objection!*" shouted the Barracuda. "That's argumentative."

"I'll withdraw the question," shrugged Charles. "I think it's rather obvious anyway."

Charles walked back to his counsel table and selected some more documents. The pause in the action served to refocus the jury.

"One of those two malpractice cases that you settled involved the death of another small child from a blood disorder, correct?" Charles began pacing in front of the witness box.

"Yes. When the child first presented, she had symptoms of otitis media and was discharged with appropriate follow-up instructions."

"No blood tests were done on the first visit; there was no referral to a hematology specialist at Norfolk Children's Hospital and no immediate transfer to Norfolk Children's when the child came back four days later in acute septic shock, correct?" Charles had been ticking the points off on his fingers. He watched the muscles tighten in Armistead's face.

"Another case of lawyers second-guessing doctors," Armistead replied, his mouth taut. "It was cheaper to settle than defend it."

"Have you got something against sending children to Norfolk Children's Hospital for specialized help? Is there some grudge you're holding against that place?"

Armistead looked at the Barracuda, probably wondering why she wasn't objecting. "No," he said. "That's ridiculous."

"My mistake," said Charles. "I thought Norfolk Children's was the hospital that turned you down, I mean, flat said no to your application for a residency position. In fact, I heard they turned you down twice."

Armistead dropped the chart in his hand. It fell against the handrail in front of him. "What is this? Am I on trial here?"

"No," Charles replied quickly, even as the Barracuda came out of her seat, "but maybe you should be."

"Objection! Move that Mr. Arnold's remarks be struck from the record!" The Barracuda's face was dark red.

Silverman banged his gavel. "Order!" He stared out at Charles from under his huge gray eyebrows. "Mr. Arnold, I will not tolerate those types of satirical comments from counsel." He then turned to the jury. "Please disregard that last comment by Mr. Arnold. It is not evidence and has no relevance in this case."

"Thank you, Your Honor," said the Barracuda as she returned to her seat.

Armistead glared at Charles. He leaned back in his chair, arms crossed, a scowl on his face. Charles pretended not to notice and started shuffling through some papers, letting the silence linger until Armistead could stand it no longer.

"Those two malpractice cases have nothing to do with this case, and they're both more than two years old," Armistead insisted. "I can't believe you're even bringing them up."

Charles looked up from his papers and smiled. "I'm sorry," he said. "Did I ask a question about how old those cases were?"

"Objection. He's badgering the witness."

Charles just spread his palms and looked at Silverman.

"Let's get back to the examination," suggested the judge.

"You never answered the question I did ask," insisted Charles. "Were you or were you not twice rejected by Norfolk Children's Hospital for a spot in their residency program?"

For a full five seconds, Armistead just glared at Charles, his jaw clenched, breathing hard through his nose. A searing silence engulfed the courtroom, and some jurors shifted nervously in their seats.

"Yes, I was."

Charles walked deliberately across the well of the courtroom and leaned against the rail in front of the jury box. The eyes of Armistead followed him warily. Charles didn't usually put his back to the jury, but for these questions, it was critical that the jury see the look in Armistead's eyes.

"Look through those medical records," suggested Charles, "and show me where it says that Theresa Hammond waited six days, as opposed to three days, to get medical treatment."

Armistead didn't even glance at the documents. "It's not in there. As I already testified, your client lied to us at first and told us it had been three days. That information got into the medical records. Later, she confessed to me personally that it had actually been five or six days. Because Joshua was already dead, there was no reason to put that fact in the records."

"So it's just your word against hers? There's no proof in the records?"

"Are you calling me a liar?" Armistead asked.

"I'm not just calling you a liar," said Charles. "I'm getting ready to prove it."

"Objection."

"Sustained."

"What," asked Charles gruffly, "is the Virginia Insurance Reciprocal Company?"

He watched Armistead swallow, the doctor's Adam's apple bobbing up and down. He knew the jury saw it too. There was a long pause.

"I believe it's a medical malpractice insurance company," said Armistead.

"You believe?" repeated Charles. "You *believe?*"

Charles walked all the way over to his counsel table and picked up two sheets of paper from Nikki. The pages were just copies of some old class notes, but Charles treated them like they contained enormous secrets. He asked the next question while looking at the documents, as if he were reading them.

"Now, keeping in mind our ability to subpoena bank documents and documents from your home study if we need to, I want to ask you a very important question. Is it true, Dr. Armistead, that as recently as two weeks ago, you paid the Virginia Insurance Reciprocal a total of four hundred thousand dollars for a purpose that you described in a handwritten notation on the transfer receipts as settlement of a medical malpractice case?"

Armistead stared at the Barracuda while his Adam's apple bobbed some more. Charles didn't believe the money was actually used to pay off a malpractice claim, but he also knew that Armistead had gone to great pains to make it look like it had. Now Armistead was stuck with his own lie, which was aired out in court for everyone to see.

"It was a confidential settlement of a malpractice case," Armistead said slowly.

"Who was the person making the claim?" asked Charles.

"I'm not at liberty to say," replied Armistead. "That's why I didn't mention it earlier."

"That's interesting," said Charles. "I thought all of your malpractice cases were settled confidentially."

Charles looked at the Barracuda, who was now vigorously taking notes, unable to look at Armistead or the jury. She shook her head back and forth—tsk, tsk, tsk—as if signaling to the jury that this information was news to her as well.

"Would you care to restate your testimony and tell the jury the truth about how many malpractice cases you've settled?" asked Charles.

"Three," said Armistead.

"Including or excluding the malpractice you committed on Joshua Hammond?"

This got the Barracuda's attention. *"Objection!"* she barked, as all of her pent-up frustrations came to the surface in one word.

"Withdrawn," said Charles. "I think I'm done with this witness."

Charles sat down, and Nikki patted him on the leg.

"Not bad for a street preacher," she said.

CHAPTER 60

After the break, the Barracuda decided to end the day's testimony with the one piece of evidence that could not be cross-examined by Charles Arnold.

"Both sides have stipulated that this prayer journal of Theresa Hammond is authentic and admissible," announced the Barracuda. "I'd like to introduce it into evidence and read excerpts from the two entries critical to this case."

"Any objection?" Silverman looked at Charles.

"No, Your Honor," Charles replied, trying to look uninterested.

"Okay," said the Barracuda. She walked to the front of the jury box. "The journal does not contain entries for every day. But there are two entries that fall into the time frame of Joshua's illness. The first is dated June 1, two days before Joshua died."

There was stillness in the jury box as they anticipated the thoughts and prayers of a mother who had watched her baby die. The Barracuda must have sensed it too and took her time finding the page.

"Here's the entry: 'I have never seen Joshie so sick. God, why are You punishing him? I have prayed, Thomas has prayed, and Tiger and Stinky have offered the innocent prayers of children. Why won't You heal him, God? Why does the temperature just increase, his pain just get worse? What could he possibly have done to deserve this? What have I done? God, I can't hold out much longer. Please heal him and don't let him die. I will dedicate him to Your service forever.'"

The Barracuda looked at the quizzical faces of the jurors. The entry seemed to hurt the prosecution's case. It seemed to present Theresa in a sympathetic light—the suffering mother. But the Barracuda was not done.

"The next day, June 2, the day before Joshua was taken to the hospital, the entry reads as follows: 'Josh was burning up all night and so sick this morning that he became almost lifeless. God, I fear that if I don't get him immediate help, he will die. But I have spent hours in prayer, by myself and with Thomas and Reverend Beckham. I will trust You, God, and You alone, for healing. I will not trust man or seek man's medical help. Though You slay him God, I will trust You. Today You have given me the spiritual strength to see this through to the end, whatever that might be.'"

As the Barracuda finished reading the journal, Thomas Hammond stared stoically ahead with his hands folded on the table in front of him, just as Nikki had told him to do. Next to him, Theresa stared at the Barracuda, tears rolling silently down her cheeks.

The Barracuda closed the journal and cleared her throat. "That entry was made at 10:00 a.m. on the fifth. For more than thirty-six hours, Mrs. Hammond refused to seek medical help for her deathly sick son—"

"Objection," said Charles. "I stipulated she could read the diary, not give a speech."

"Sustained," said Silverman.

The Barracuda looked each of the jurors in the eye, then tucked the beloved journal under her arm and returned to her seat. "I'd like to introduce this as our next exhibit," she said.

"No objection," said Charles. He appeared unconcerned. Yet he couldn't help but notice a few of the mothers on the jury glaring at Theresa Hammond.

CHAPTER 61

After the first day of testimony, Charles, Nikki, Thomas, and Theresa huddled in the same small, windowless conference room that they had used for the preliminary hearing. The deputy sheriffs had given Thomas an extra half-hour before he would be returned to the general inmate population. Charles noticed that Theresa had not said a word in the last five minutes. Her hollow eyes stared lifelessly ahead, reflecting a wound that might never heal. Nikki was busy giving the team a pep talk and singing Charles's praises, much to his great embarrassment.

Thomas seemed to be only half listening to Nikki and took advantage of the first pregnant pause in her speech to ask Charles a question.

"Give me a straight answer—no fluff—how'd we do today?"

"We had a great day," continued Nikki, pacing the room. "The opening statement was perfect, and the cross-examination of Armistead was a home run. It doesn't get any better than this."

"Do you agree?" Thomas looked at Charles, putting the question straight to him.

"We had a good day," Charles said in measured tones. "Armistead came across as duplicitous"—Thomas gave Charles a quizzical look—"as someone who wasn't telling the whole truth. But to find for us, the jury will have to believe that Joshua would have survived if he had been transferred to Norfolk Children's. On that count, our evidence is pretty speculative."

Thomas nodded his head, taking it all in. He seemed to appreciate the bluntness of Charles's assessment.

Nikki's face turned serious, and she took a seat next to Charles, across from Thomas. "The prayer journal really hurt us," Nikki said somberly. "The reverend was immaterial. No great shakes for either side. But with that journal, the jury now has sufficient evidence to find Theresa guilty of knowing that Joshua was dying, though they don't have the same level of evidence with respect to you."

"That's insane!" said Thomas, his first visible reaction since the trial started. "I was the one telling Theres that we *couldn't* go to the doctor. She wanted to go on day one."

Thomas placed his hand on top of Theresa's. She blinked slowly and looked down at the table while Thomas stared at—through—Charles. "I've got to testify. I won't allow anyone to place this blame on Theres."

"Nobody's placing this blame on Theresa," said Charles firmly. "And you're not testifying. Calling you to the stand and subjecting you to cross-examination would be suicide."

The big man sighed a disgruntled sigh and shifted in his chair. The look on his face worried Charles.

"Listen, Thomas, if anybody had told me a few weeks ago that after the first day of trial we would have the prosecution's main witness, their *only* witness really, admitting on the stand that he was a liar, I would've said that's too good to be true. But that's what happened. We're in the driver's seat. Let's not do anything rash to mess that up."

"I just don't want Theres taking the fall," said Thomas. "I want you to put me on the stand if that's gonna happen."

"She not taking the fall," said Nikki. "There won't be any fall to take."

Thomas turned to Charles. "You agree?"

Charles hesitated, there were no guarantees in jury trials. "Having you take the stand is not the answer."

There was a knock on the door from the deputy sheriff. "Just a minute," called Charles. He turned to Thomas and Theresa, blowing out a deep breath while he rubbed his forehead. "We've got to call Tiger as a witness tomorrow. He's going to have to recant his videotaped statement about Joshua being sick for five or six days."

"We can't put him through that." Theresa sounded desperate. "There's got to be another way."

"I wish there were," Charles answered calmly. "But there isn't."

Another knock on the door. "It's time," called the deputy.

"We're coming!" yelled Nikki. "Give us a break."

Thomas stood and stared down at Charles. "I need to talk to Tiger for a few minutes before court," he said. "Can you arrange for us to meet him here a few minutes early?"

"I'll try," said Charles.

Thomas then glanced nervously at Nikki and Theresa, before turning back to Charles. "Can I ask you somethin' alone?"

Charles looked at Nikki. "Can you buy us a minute with the guard?"

Nikki let out a quick puff of air, as if insulted that Charles would even ask such an obvious question. "He's a man, isn't he?"

Another knock, this one louder than before.

After Thomas and Theresa hugged, the women left the conference room. Nikki started in on the deputy even before she had closed the door behind her. When the men were alone, Thomas sat down heavily and stared at folded hands.

"My faith kilt him, didn't it Rev? Or maybe I should say my lack of faith."

Charles thought for a moment about the question—had been thinking about it dozens of times since taking this case. "No," he said, shaking his head slowly. "I think you had plenty of faith, Thomas." Charles hesitated, wondering whether the big man could handle what Charles really thought. "This isn't about faith, Thomas. It's about love. Scripture says that when all the smoke has cleared, three things will remain—faith, hope, and love. But the greatest of these is love."

At this, the eyes of Thomas rose slowly until they locked on Charles. They were deep pools of sadness, reflecting a bitter loss compounded by Thomas's unyielding guilt. An overwhelming sense of sympathy almost prevented Charles from saying these next words. But sometimes, Charles knew, the most necessary truths were also the most painful ones.

"I'm no expert," said Charles quietly, "because I've got no kids of my own. But it seems to me that being a dad is not as much about faith as it is about love. Next time, let your heart tell you what to do."

Thomas nodded, but before he could respond, the deputy knocked on the door and entered without waiting for a response. Nikki was right on his heels, complaining loudly.

"No more favors for you guys," the deputy said. "I give you an inch and you take a mile."

On the way back to the office, Charles stopped at a FedEx place and removed the letter to Senator Crafton from his briefcase. He knew time was running short.

He was so emotionally sapped from the long day in court that he didn't have the energy to even think about what he had to do. Besides, he had prayed about it and thought about it practically nonstop for the last seven days. He had carried the letter with him everywhere he went. He had to get this behind him.

He could convince himself one way before he went to bed at night and change his mind the next morning. He had never felt so torn.

He hand-scribbled a note on the bottom of the letter: "This is the only copy of this information I have sent. Call me." He wrote out his cell phone number just to be sure. He addressed the overnight package, paid the cashier, and tried to put it out of his mind.

Charles prayed he had done the right thing.

He drove away from the FedEx office feeling despondent. The images from the dream still haunted him—rows and rows of graves, Denita's loud and mocking laugh so vivid he could still hear it ringing in his ears. He needed to stop thinking about it and get back to the case. There was so much to do. And the fates of the Hammond family, including little Tiger and Stinky, hung in the balance. He needed to get Denita out of his mind for now, process these emotions later—but how could he?

He picked up his cell phone and dialed Nikki.

"What time can you make it to the war room?"

"I've got to pick up the kids and take them to Theresa's. It'll probably be at least eight."

"Plan on staying late. We've got jury instructions to get ready…a closing argument to prepare."

"I'll just let the kids stay with Theresa tonight," said Nikki. "That way we can work as late as we need to. One night won't matter."

Charles had a bad feeling about leaving the kids with their mother, but didn't want to say anything that might disrupt the tenuous relationship he had established with his volatile partner. "See you at eight."

"See you at eight, handsome."

The phone went dead, and Charles grinned. He loved it when she called him that.

＊　＊　＊

At precisely eight, the Barracuda's office phone rang. She had already been to the gym and worked off her frustrations with Brandon. Armistead had bombed today, and she would never forgive him.

She let it ring three times. She had a lot to do. She thought about just letting it go. They could always leave a message.

Curiosity won out. "Hello."

"Ms. Crawford?"

"Yes."

"This is Frank Morris, deputy sheriff at the jail. Sorry to call so late."

"I'm pretty busy here. What's up?"

"You're the prosecutor trying that case against the parents who let their kid die, aren't you?"

"Yes." He now had her attention.

"Then I've got somebody you need to talk to, and you need to talk to him right away."

"Go on."

"His name is Buster Jackson, the cellmate of the kid's father, Thomas Hammond. Jackson says he's got some information that'll help you. He wants to make a deal. Wants to talk to you without his attorney present."

"Interesting," said the Barracuda. "Buster Jackson. I think I know this guy. Can you bring him over right away...without Hammond knowing what's happening?"

"Sure," said the deputy sheriff. "I'll see you in twenty minutes."

CHAPTER 62

Nikki was wearing out the rug in the small windowless conference room on Thursday morning. Thomas, Theresa, and Tiger watched her pace. They were all waiting on Charles.

Nikki looked at her watch. Court would start in ten minutes.

"How much longer?" asked Thomas.

"I'm not sure," said Nikki. "These sessions in the judge's chambers can sometimes run right up until court starts. When I left, Charles was still arguing his motion."

"What motion?" asked Thomas.

"That the Barracuda not be allowed to question Tiger about what type of parents you've been."

"Why not?" Thomas looked dumbfounded.

"Because she'll imply that you've abused your children and that's got nothing to do with whether you took Joshua to the hospital in time for treatment. She just wants to use some statements that Tiger made to a child psychiatrist to raise the suspicion of abuse and fire up the jury."

"Did I do something wrong?" asked Tiger.

"No, sweetie," said Theresa. She reached out her hand and started rubbing his hair.

"C'mere, buddy," said Thomas. Tiger hustled to the other side of the table and climbed into his daddy's lap.

"Look at me." Thomas said. Tiger lifted his chin and looked squarely in his daddy's eyes. "Now, I want you to listen real carefully to what I'm about to say. Okay, Tiger?"

Tiger nodded. "Yes sir."

"Daddy's done a lot of things wrong in his life, Tiger, and I'm just plain sorry about them." Tiger started to object, to defend his daddy against these self-inflicted charges, but Thomas put his finger on the boy's lips. "Shh, just listen."

Nikki stopped pacing. There was something special going on here, and she didn't want to miss it.

"I've had a lot of time to think while I've been in prison, Tiger. And I been doin' a lot of prayin' and readin' my Bible." Thomas swallowed hard, a glimmer of moisture coming to his eyes. "I realize I been way too hard on you and Stinky, way too strict. There's been too many spankings and not enough love…" Thomas's voice began to crack, but he swallowed again and continued.

"If'n I ever get out of here, things are gonna change. I'm gonna change. We'll need help from others, people who can make me be a better dad. But I want you to know one thing, Tiger. Regardless of what happens today, I'm proud of you and"—Thomas looked down as he completed his sentence, unable to look at Tiger as he said it—"I love you, Son, no matter what."

Tiger instinctively hugged his daddy's neck. Thomas hugged him back, practically squeezing the air right out of him. "Just plain tell the truth today on the witness stand," Thomas whispered. "Don't you worry 'bout what I'm gonna think or what anybody else is gonna think. Just tell the truth, and everything'll be all right."

Tears began welling in Thomas's eyes.

Nikki, who had been watching in silence, her hands pressed together with her fingers gently touching her lips, suddenly realized that it was the first time in this entire ordeal she had ever seen Thomas cry.

⚓

After his dad's pep talk, Tiger approached round three of Tiger versus the Barracuda more confident than ever. After all, he was now a certified karate expert, making great progress on his yellow belt. His job was easy: Just tell the truth. Okay, maybe his daddy was acting a little strange, but Tiger wouldn't worry about that right now. He had a very important job to do. He was now the man of the house, and today he would prove his worth.

He had left the small conference room and sat on the hard wooden bench in the hallway of the courthouse, his cowboy boots dangling over the edge, waiting for his name to be called. He hated wearing his clip-on tie, but

Miss Nikki had assured him that even cowboys had to dress up when they went to court.

He had practiced all kinds of questions and answers with Miss Nikki early this morning and seemed to get them all right. He was ready to do his part in springing his dad from jail. He would set this jury straight. He was a lean, mean, truth-telling machine.

And he was ready.

Suddenly the big courtroom doors opened, and a man with a gun and uniform called out his name.

"John Paul Hammond."

With a quizzical look, Tiger pointed toward his chest, as if to say, "You mean me?"

"Are you John Paul?" asked the huge man.

"Uh-huh," said Tiger.

"Then come on in." The big man held the door open and pointed down the aisle.

Tiger peeked inside and froze in his tracks. It seemed like there were a thousand people inside, all turned to stare at him. The aisle looked as long as a football field, and the judge sat at the other end of it way up high, looking stern.

Tiger told his legs to move, to start heading down the aisle. They didn't seem to hear. So instead, he just stood there with his mouth hanging open, waiting for Miss Nikki to come down the aisle from the front and lead him in by the hand.

They made him raise his right hand and swear to tell the truth. He was planning on doing that anyway. Then he climbed up in the witness chair and watched in petrified silence as Mr. Charles lowered the mike so that it came down to eye level.

Mr. Charles walked a few steps away and smiled.

"Good morning, John Paul."

"Yes sir," said Tiger. Somehow his voice came out in a squeak. He hardly recognized it.

"Could you please tell the ladies and gentlemen of the jury your name and how old you are?"

"Um...sure." Tiger looked down at his shaking hands and decided to tuck them under his legs. "John Paul Hammond. Five and a half."

"Do you have a nickname, buddy?"

"Yep... I mean, yes sir."

"And what is it?"

"Tiger."

"Now, Tiger, are you the son of Thomas and Theresa Hammond?"

"Yes sir, that's me."

Tiger had practiced these questions and answers many times. He started to loosen up a little and look around.

"And were you living with your mom and dad and Joshua when little Joshie got sick?"

"And Stinky," Tiger corrected Mr. Charles.

"And Stinky," repeated Mr. Charles.

"Yes, I was."

"Did your mom and dad at some point take Joshie to the hospital?"

"Yes sir."

"Now this is a very important question, Tiger. Do you remember how many days Joshie was sick before your mom and dad took him to the hospital?"

Tiger knew the answer: two days. He had practiced it many times early this morning and it also happened to be the truth. But Tiger decided to add a little drama to his answer—after all, the cameras were rolling. So he scrunched up his forehead and looked hard at the ceiling, as if he were searching for the answer. After a few seconds, when he was sure he had everyone's attention, he went ahead and said it.

"I'm pretty sure he was sick for dus two days. We took him to the hopsicle on the third day."

"Are you sure about that, Tiger?"

"Um...yes sir."

It seemed to Tiger that Mr. Charles let out a big puff of breath, as if he had just come up from a long underwater swim.

"Now Tiger, did that lady sitting there at counsel table"—Mr. Charles turned and pointed at the Mean Lady—"did she ask you a few questions on videotape about Joshie?"

Tiger narrowed his gaze and shot the Mean Lady a nasty look. He didn't like what he was about to do, and it was all her fault.

"Yes sir."

"And did you tell her the truth when you answered all those questions?"

Tiger shrugged his shoulders. "Not really," he said. He happened to look past Mr. Charles and directly at his dad, who gave him a stern look as soon as he heard the answer. "I mean…no, I didn't." His dad nodded.

"In what respect did you not tell the truth?" Mr. Charles asked.

"I told her," Tiger nodded his head toward the Mean Lady, "that Joshie had been sick for five days."

"Was that true?" asked Mr. Charles.

How many times have I got to say this? wondered Tiger. *And whose side are you on anyway?*

"No," Tiger said softly.

"Then why did you tell her that?"

At this, Tiger looked right at the Mean Lady, just as Miss Nikki had told him to do. "'Cause afore she turned the camera on, she told me it might help my daddy get out of jail if he waited a long time afore he took Joshie to the hopsicle. The lady"—Tiger had thought about calling her Mean Lady, just for emphasis, but decided not to—"told me the story of Abe-ham and Isaac and what a great man Abe-ham was cause he waited three days on the mountain and was ready to kill his son afore God sent a goat. So I dus said if Abe-ham waited three days, my daddy prob'ly waited five."

"But did your dad really wait five days before taking Josh to the hospital?"

"No sir. I made it up."

"Thank you, Tiger, that's all I have. Please answer any questions that Ms. Crawford might have."

"Okay," said Tiger with as much enthusiasm as he could muster. The Mean Lady did not look happy.

CHAPTER 63

Nikki couldn't resist a smile as she watched her cute little protégé on the stand. He was dwarfed by the massive courtroom and the judge's bench that towered over the witness box. Tiger had hammed it up a little on direct examination, but that was to be expected. All in all, the little bugger had followed the script and done a masterful job.

Now came the hard part.

The Barracuda strode forward and positioned herself directly between Nikki and the witness stand. Nikki could no longer see Tiger as he talked, her view blocked by the unflattering backside of the Barracuda. Nikki wished a few of the shots for Court TV would use this angle. She scooted over slightly to the right but still couldn't get Tiger in her line of sight.

"So you lied before to help your daddy?"

"Yes ma'am. I guess so."

"Even though you knew it was wrong?"

"Yes ma'am."

"But this morning, you just happened to remember that Joshie was sick for three days instead of five days, and you want everyone to believe that's the truth?" The Barracuda spoke softly, but her words were like daggers hurled at the little guy. Nikki did not envy the Barracuda on this cross. She had to cast some doubt on Tiger's testimony without seeming like she was picking on him.

"Um…y-y-yes ma'am."

"Was it your idea to come into this courtroom and change your story or did somebody else"—the Barracuda now turned and pointed to Charles and Nikki—"like Mr. Charles Arnold or Miss Nikki Moreno tell you that you should do this?"

When the Barracuda moved, Nikki could see the fright in Tiger's eyes as he contemplated the question. His eyes grew as he stared at Nikki, as if afraid to implicate her, yet mindful of his unbending obligation to tell the truth.

"Yes," he said at last. "It was Miss Nikki's idea."

"Let the record reflect," said the Barracuda forcefully, "that the witness is pointing at Nikki Moreno, who is working for the defendants and has served as the court appointed special advocate for the children pending trial."

The Barracuda turned back toward Tiger and took a few steps closer. She was blocking Nikki's view again. Nikki could stand it no longer and moved to an empty seat at the far end of counsel table.

"And did you and Ms. Moreno practice questions and answers that you might be asked today?"

Tiger nodded.

Nikki felt her pulse quicken, the blood rising in her neck. The Barracuda was leading this poor kid, one step at a time, like a lamb to the slaughter. Nikki glanced toward Charles. *Do something!*

"Let the record reflect the witness nodded his head, answering in the affirmative," said the Barracuda to the court reporter. Then she turned back to Tiger and lowered her voice, "And did she help you decide what to say for your answers?"

More nodding from Tiger. "Yes ma'am."

"That's what I thought," said the Barracuda who was actually smiling at Tiger. She then took a few steps back to her own counsel table and picked up a piece of paper.

⋅⋆⋅≡⋅≡⋅⋆⋅

It was the opening Tiger had been waiting for. He could sense that things were not exactly going his way. The look on his dad's face. Miss Nikki's, too, for that matter. This Mean Lady was a bigger bully than Doughy Joey.

But Tiger had a secret weapon.

The other night he had watched carefully as Miss Nikki applied the Power Ranger tattoo to his upper arm. Just wet the little piece of paper and rub it on—no big deal. The lucky thing was that more than one tattoo was on that same piece of paper. Miss Nikki had thrown the others in the trash, but Tiger had scooped them out and saved them.

So now, as the Mean Lady stepped back to her table, Tiger quickly unbuttoned the cuff of his ragged white shirt and started rolling up the sleeve. He thought he remembered putting it on his right forearm… Yep, there it was, a little messy, the colors running together.

He flexed his little arm and put his elbow on the rail in front of him, resting his chin on his fist. It wasn't exactly a natural pose, but it got the job done. When the Mean Lady turned around, she would sure be surprised…and probably a little scared. It would serve her right.

She would be staring right at his newest Power Ranger tattoo.

———— ⚔ ————

"Oh my goodness," Nikki heard Theresa Hammond whisper. Nikki felt the eyes of Thomas Hammond boring into her, no doubt remembering Nikki's own tattoo on her left shoulder.

"Where did he get that?" wondered Theresa. Thomas nodded his head in Nikki's direction.

The Barracuda turned toward the judge, not yet noticing her beaming little witness. "I would like to introduce into evidence, as our next exhibit, this court order regarding custody, which forbids the Hammond children from having any unchaperoned contact with their parents." Nikki could hear one or two of the jurors snicker. Silverman had his own hand nonchalantly over his mouth, probably suppressing a grin. "I would like to draw particular attention to paragraph 3, which mentions that one of the reasons for this stipulation is the possible prejudice that would result in the testimony of the children if such contact were allowed."

The Barracuda finally seemed to realize that she was the only one in the courtroom missing something. She glanced at Tiger, snickered without thinking, and shook her head.

The courtroom burst into laughter. Tiger looked stunned.

"That's really nice," the Barracuda said.

"Thanks."

Then she lowered her tone, a signal that the fun and games were over. "Now, are you ready to roll your sleeve back down and answer some more questions?"

Tiger shot a puzzled look toward his dad and then scrunched up his worried little brow. Nikki didn't dare look at the expression on Thomas's face, but she knew it promised Tiger a heap of trouble later. "Sorry," Tiger said quickly, "it's dus a tattoo."

"I know," said the Barracuda, "but let's get back to the questions."

Tiger quickly rolled down his sleeve, and Nikki surveyed the jury. Most were smiling. One of the moms had her head tilted to the side, the softest look of sympathy on her face.

The Barracuda stiffened. "Now, John Paul, have you had any contact with your mom or dad when Ms. Moreno was not present between the time of your original videotaped statement and your testimony in court today?"

Tiger looked thoroughly confused and just shrugged his shoulders.

"Okay, let me ask it this way." The Barracuda moved over in front of the jury box. "Before today, when is the last time you saw your mom?"

"Last night," said Tiger helpfully.

"What time?"

"The whole night. Me and Stinky stayed overnight there."

"Stinky is a nickname for your sister, right?"

"Oops," said Tiger, smiling an embarrassed smile. "Her name is really Hannah."

"Was Ms. Moreno there with you and Hannah the whole night?"

"No ma'am. She dropped us off."

Nikki noticed, out of the corner of her eye, Silverman glaring at her. Nikki decided to keep her gaze fixed on the witness.

"So regardless of what the court order says, Ms. Moreno dropped you off at your mom's house for the entire night last night. Then the next day—today—you come in here and change your testimony?"

"Objection," Charles interjected as he stood. "Argumentative."

"I guess so," said Tiger.

Charles turned up his palms and sat down.

"In addition to telling you what to say as a witness and violating a court order by dropping you off at your mom's house, did Ms. Moreno ever say anything bad about the police or myself?" asked the Barracuda.

This brought Charles to his feet again. "Objection. Ms. Moreno is not on trial here."

"Goes to bias, Your Honor," said the Barracuda. "And to witness tampering."

"That's ridiculous," shot back Nikki, now also standing.

"*Sit down,*" snarled Silverman. He gave Nikki an icy stare as she took her seat. Then he turned to Charles. "Your objection is overruled, Mr. Arnold. I think it does go to the issue of bias."

All eyes turned back to Tiger, who had that deer-in-the-headlights look.

"Do you remember the question?" asked the Barracuda.

Tiger vigorously shook his head from side to side.

"Did Nikki Moreno ever say anything bad about the police officers or about myself?"

"Yes ma'am." It was barely a whisper. Tiger looked down, embarrassed, his hands tucked under his thighs.

"What did she say?" asked the Barracuda. "And when did she say it?"

Tiger hesitated for the longest time, perhaps racking his brain for a loophole in his obligation to tell the whole truth. Apparently he could find none. "She called you a witch," said Tiger firmly. A few of the jurors snickered.

"A *witch,*" said the Barracuda emphatically. "Imagine that. Are you sure *witch* was the word she used as opposed to something that sounds like witch?"

"Oh yes, ma'am," said Tiger, "'cause I asked her to say it again dus to make sure."

"And when was this?" the Barracuda asked condescendingly.

"Well," said Tiger, pursing his lips and wrinkling his forehead as he thought. "One day we were playing secret agents, spying on that doctor guy's house in the middle of the day"—Nikki slouched down in her seat, wishing she could become invisible—"and then, all a sudden, we saw you! And Miss Nikki said, 'She's a witch,' and then we saw you go inside—"

"That's not what I asked," interrupted the Barracuda sharply. "I only asked what she called me and when this was." The Barracuda's face suddenly flushed. "Judge, I ask that his remarks be stricken from the record."

Charles was on his feet once again. "Judge," he cried, "the witness is entitled to finish his answer."

Tiger's eyes darted back and forth from Charles to the Barracuda and then quickly to Nikki. Then suddenly, in the split second while everyone waited for a ruling from Judge Silverman, Tiger decided to take his right hand out from under his leg and raise it straight up in the air, as if he were the smart kid who sits in the front row of the classroom and knows all the answers.

"Son, you may put your hand down," said Silverman kindly. Tiger looked confused but obeyed the judge's instruction. "However, I will not strike his answer from the record. Ms. Crawford, you asked the question. Just because you don't like the answer does not mean that it's irrelevant."

The Barracuda crossed her arms and stared at Silverman.

"Thank you, Your Honor," said Charles.

For the next few seconds, the Barracuda made an elaborate display of going back to her counsel table and checking through some notes. Tiger's eyes followed her every step of the way. Finally, she looked at the judge and said simply, "No further questions," then took her seat.

Charles rose immediately. "A brief rebuttal, Your Honor?"

"Keep it short," said Silverman.

Charles buttoned his suit coat and approached the witness stand. "I couldn't help but notice that you had your hand up a few minutes ago when you were trying to answer one of Ms. Crawford's questions. Was there something else you wanted to say?"

Tiger's eyes brightened. "Yes sir. She asked me when this happened, and I 'membered what happened as she was talking to…" He pointed to Silverman.

"The judge," said Charles.

Tiger, grateful for the chance to explain, spit the words out as quickly as his little tongue could go. "Yes sir, the judge. But what I 'membered is that it happened the exact day after my daddy went to court the last time. 'Cause I got into a little fight at day care the last time my daddy went to court with Doughy Joey, but it wasn't my fault, and we're good friends now. So I was with Miss Nikki instead of being in day care, and she called the Mean Lady a witch, and then I said, 'She really is a witch,' and then Miss Nikki said how strange it was that the Mean—uh, the lady over there—would be at the doctor's house instead of meeting at the office in the middle of the day on the very next day after everybody had gone to court. And Miss Nikki said there must be somethin' strange goin' on between them cause there's dus no reason for that 'cept—"

"Objection, Judge," the Barracuda shouted. "This is nothing but pure hearsay."

"Sustained," said Silverman. "Mr. Arnold, I think you'd better change your line of questioning."

"I'm sorry for calling her a witch," said Tiger sincerely, looking up at the judge with puppy-dog eyes. Then Tiger quickly looked back down at his lap.

Nikki just wanted to run up and hug him. Then she saw a thin, sweet smile cross the lips of Silverman and a sympathetic smile form on the face of practically every juror in the box.

"It's okay," said Silverman. "We've all been called a lot worse."

Then Tiger himself grinned, the big toothy smile of a boy who has just gotten all his permanent front teeth but not yet grown into them.

"No further questions," said Charles, also smiling.

"That's my boy," said Thomas softly.

CHAPTER 64

The defense rests," said Charles proudly. Tiger had returned to his seat in the spectator section, showing off his tattoo for some curious reporters. Stinky, who had been at day care that morning, would come to court during the lunch break. Charles knew it would be important to have both kids there for closing arguments.

"Rebuttal witnesses?" Silverman raised an eyebrow at the Barracuda.

She stood and looked at Charles. "The commonwealth calls Buster Jackson. He's in lockup, so it may take a few minutes to get him here."

Charles had the sinking feeling of a case headed south—the same type of feeling he experienced when he found out that one of the officers who arrested Buster was black. Buster Jackson! Whatever it was that Buster had to say, it wouldn't be good. Charles thought about trying to exclude Buster from testifying based on the fact that he wasn't on the Barracuda's witness list. But Charles knew that the court would generally allow an attorney to call a rebuttal witness who wasn't on the list, especially if the testimony was unavailable or unanticipated when the trial started.

"What's *this* all about?" Charles whispered to Nikki. She passed the message along to Thomas, who seemed to have no idea.

⊶ ⊰◈⊱ ⊷

Charles stared at Buster as he took the stand but couldn't get the big man's attention. This was going to be bad. His own client appearing as a witness for the other side and avoiding eye contact.

The Barracuda had dressed Buster up, but he still looked like a thug. The suit coat could not hide his massive pecs and lats. And the dress shirt seemed to strain around his neck—what there was of a neck—and barely hold together. The huge forehead that shadowed his dark eyes, the close-cropped hair, the scruffy Fu Manchu, and the occasional gleam from the gold tooth all gave Buster the look of a professional prizefighter. He wore the clothes of a preacher on the body of a brawler.

The Barracuda walked him through the preliminaries. Like any good lawyer, she decided to air out the dirty laundry on direct so it would not come up for the first time on cross. This forced Buster to confess his two prior drug convictions and his pending charge for possession with intent to distribute cocaine.

"Has the commonwealth promised you anything in exchange for your testimony today?" the Barracuda asked.

Charles tensed, holding his breath. He had already concluded that he would have to withdraw from Buster's case as soon as the Barracuda was done with her direct examination. He knew Buster must have cut some kind of deal. And now he was about to find out, in open court, about an apparent immunity deal where his own client would stab another of his clients in the back. *This was bizarre.*

"Yeah. In exchange for ratting out Pops *and* coppin' a plea this morning," corrected Buster.

"I stand corrected," said the Barracuda. "Has the commonwealth promised you anything in exchange for your testimony in this case *and* your guilty plea on the pending charge of possession with intent to distribute?"

"Yeah," said Buster gruffly. "You spring me on time served. Which ain't so hot 'cause me and my lawyer had a motion to dismiss pending anyway based on racial profilin' by your boys—"

"Who is your lawyer?" interrupted the Barracuda.

Buster narrowed his eyes and gave the Barracuda a reproving glare for the interruption. "Plus... Can I finish here?" A beat of silence followed, accentuating the animosity between lawyer and witness. "Plus, that guilty plea will be on my rap sheet, and I've got three years probation. If I get busted again, I'm toast."

"Are you done?" asked the Barracuda.

Buster stuck out his lips in defiance and nodded.

"Then please tell us who your attorney is on the possession-with-intent-to-distribute charge."

Charles jumped up. In his law school classes, he had always taught his students that the most important thing any lawyer brings to the courtroom is his or her own credibility. Once you lose that, you lose everything. And Buster Jackson was about to paint Charles as the type of lawyer who would represent anybody, claim anything, just to see the guilty walk.

"Objection," said Charles. "May we approach?"

But before Silverman could answer, Buster extended his muscled arm and pointed his thick finger straight at Charles. "That man," he said.

Charles felt like he had been shot. He slumped back into his chair.

"The witness will wait to answer the question until *after* I have ruled on the objection," scolded Silverman. "Is that clear?"

"Yeah, sure," said a surly Buster. But the damage had already been done. And to make matters worse, Charles knew the jury would think he was trying to hide it with his objection.

"Are you presently an inmate in the Virginia Beach City Jail?" asked the Barracuda.

"Yeah."

"And who is your cellmate?"

"That man," Buster pointed. "Thomas Hammond...Pops."

"Did Mr. Hammond discuss this case with you last night?"

"Yeah."

"Please tell the ladies and gentlemen of the jury, to the very best of your memory, precisely what he said."

"Well, last night Pops was mopin' around the cell...and I'm like bustin' on him tryin' to get him to chill a little. Ain't nothing workin'. So, I'm like, 'Pops, what's doggin' you, man? I heard your lawyer broke bad in court today, but you're actin' like you're goin' down.'" As he spoke, Buster, who had been looking at the Barracuda, now shifted and faced the jury.

"So, Pops says, best I remember, 'We had a good day in court, but I still need to testify and my lawyer says I can't.' Pops says, 'If I don't testify, the jury will wonder why. If I do testify, it all comes out. How can a jury let me skate if'n they hear—Pops is always sayin' if'n—if'n they hear that I knew my boy was gonna die, but I wouldn't take the kid to the hospital? What else can a jury do to someone who demanded—I mean flat-out demanded—that his woman not take the kid for three solid days—all the time knowin' the kid is dying?'"

The Barracuda waited for several seconds to let this testimony sink in. Then she took a few sideways steps and asked another question, obviously designed to have the witness repeat the same damaging information.

"Is that what Thomas Hammond said to the best of your memory, that he knew Joshua was dying but refused to take him to the hospital for three days?"

"'At's what he said. He talked like it was him, his decision, nobody else's." Buster flipped up his palms. "'At's what I know."

"And what did you say to him after he confessed these things?" asked the Barracuda.

"I jus' told him, 'A man's got to do what a man's got to do.'"

"Meaning what?"

"Meaning Pops had to decide if he was gonna' take the stand or roll the dice on the Fifth."

"And then what did you do?"

"I called you."

"No further questions. Please answer any questions that Mr. Arnold might have." And with that, the Barracuda sat down and rested her case on the broad shoulders of Buster Jackson.

Charles wasted no time in going on the offensive. "First, Your Honor, I'd like to make it clear that I am withdrawing as counsel of record in the case of Commonwealth versus Buster Jackson. It would be unethical to continue representing someone I'm about to prove a liar."

"Objection, Your Honor," called out the Barracuda. "I don't mind if Mr. Arnold wants to withdraw in Mr. Jackson's case, especially since that case is basically over. But his gratuitous comment is prejudicial, unprofessional, and uncalled—"

"Unprofessional?" snarled Charles. "You're calling *me* unprofessional?"

"Counsel," snapped Silverman, his face flushing. "Mr. Arnold, you keep your editorial comments to yourself. Ms. Crawford, you stop baiting him."

"Yes, Your Honor," said Charles.

"Yes, Your Honor," echoed the Barracuda.

"Your motion is granted," Silverman said.

Charles quickly turned to the witness. "Now, let's talk rap sheet," said Charles. "1999. Possession with intent to distribute marijuana. Right?"

"That's right, Rev."

"Don't call me Rev," demanded Charles.

"Hey," replied Buster with a smirk, "you're the one always comin' to jail and preachin' at us."

"2001. Possession with intent to distribute cocaine and possession of an illegal firearm, right?" continued Charles.

"Yeah."

"2004. Possession with intent to distribute cocaine again. Have I got that right?"

"Already discussed that charge with the prosecution lady."

"And those are just the felony convictions, aren't they?"

"If you say so."

"They don't include your misdemeanors, do they?"

"Prob'ly not."

"They also don't include juvenile offenses, right? I mean, you're only twenty-three, so you've just been working on this rap sheet for five years."

"Didn't say I was perfect."

"That's for sure," scoffed Charles. He took a few steps closer to the massive witness and noticed a few beads of sweat forming on the big man's forehead. Charles felt his own shirt sticking to his skin, his own heart pumping overtime. He would have to make Buster mad, provoke this mammoth man who would be discharged from jail today. He didn't have much time to consider the irony: intentionally baiting the same man who had terrified Charles that first night in the Virginia Beach jail. What other choice did he have?

"You're aware of Virginia's 'three strikes and you're out' rule, aren't you?"

Buster nodded.

"Your third felony conviction means you serve some serious time, right?"

"That's right, Rev. But I wasn't planning on doin' much time, 'cause you were gonna get me off on that racial profilin' defense, remember?"

Charles felt the muscles tighten in his own face. He forced himself to control the frustration so he could think clearly.

"A judge hadn't decided on that yet, had he, Mr. Jackson?"

"True."

"And you were worried enough about it to try everything possible to deal your way out, weren't you?"

"Nah, not really."

"Well, Mr. Jackson, was this the first deal you tried to cut with the prosecution while you've been sitting in prison waiting for trial?"

This stopped Buster in his tracks. He narrowed his eyes at Charles but didn't answer.

"I can wait all day if I need to," mocked Charles.

"No," said Buster grudgingly.

"Truth is, you tried to rat out another inmate, a man accused of murder, in exchange for your freedom, didn't you?"

"I talked to that lady"—Buster pointed at the Barracuda—"'bout somethin' I heard this dude named A-town say. But there was no deal."

"But you tried to cut a deal"—Charles's voice had a razor edge—"didn't you, Mr. Jackson? You tried to cut a deal, and she said no."

"I mighta been lookin' for one."

"And when this guy named A-town, as you call him, heard about you snitchin' on him, he tried to kill you, didn't he?" Charles paused. He got no answer as Buster stared straight ahead. "Didn't he?" insisted Charles.

"Maybe," growled Buster.

Charles paced in front of Buster and stopped directly in front of the jury box. "And tell me, Mr. Jackson, who saved your life when A-town tried to ambush you and stab you while you were in the rec area? Why don't you tell the ladies and gentlemen on this jury who it was that risked his own life to save you from being stabbed to death by A-town?"

Buster's eyes went from Charles to the jury members, then back to Charles.

"Well?" asked Charles.

"Pops," said Buster softly.

"Who?"

"Pops," this time much louder, defiant.

"And afterward, you and 'Pops' became cellmates, right?"

"You got it."

"So now you want the ladies and gentlemen of this jury to believe that my client, who knows you already tried to snitch on another inmate, who saved your very life, just happened to come up to you last night and bare his soul to you—the jailhouse snitch?"

"That's basically it," sneered Buster.

"And this is how you reward someone for saving your life? By coming in here and lying about some alleged confession last night?"

"I ain't lyin' Rev. It's the truth, and 'the truth shall set you free.'"

Charles shook his head. "No, Mr. Jackson, I'm afraid it's not the truth that's setting you free. It's an overzealous prosecutor who's willing to let a three-time drug dealer walk so she can try to convict a father of two—"

"Objection," the Barracuda shouted. "I *strenuously* object."

"—and further her own career."

Silverman banged his gavel and demanded order. While Charles seethed, Judge Silverman delivered a strong tongue-lashing in front of the jury. After the judge finished, he asked Charles if he had any further questions.

"Just one," said Charles. He glared at the witness. "You did say three days, didn't you? You did say that Pops said he had waited three days, not five days. Right?"

"Three days," said Buster.

Charles nodded and headed back toward his counsel table.

"Anything else?" asked Silverman.

"For this guy?" asked Charles. "Why bother?"

"In that case," Silverman said to Buster Jackson, "you are free to go."

CHAPTER 65

"Closing arguments," Charles would tell his students, "are like preaching to the choir. Every good sermon and every good closing needs to have a memorable theme. You also need passion. But don't kid yourself into believing that you will 'convert' many jury members during the closing. Most jurors have already made up their mind. Your job," Charles would explain, "is to give ammunition to the converts that they can then use during deliberations to convince the others. Your job is to give the converts a reason to fight hard for you once they get behind closed doors. Your job is to establish eye contact with those who believe in your case, to send them the message that they are *your* champions.

"Your job is to preach to the choir."

The Barracuda began her sermon immediately after the lunch break. She stood behind a wooden podium that she had moved just in front of the jury box during the lunch hour. She had notes in front of her but didn't need them. She had placed the small and worn picture of Joshua Hammond on the podium. *This one's for you.*

"The critical facts of the case are undisputed," she began. "Young Joshua Hammond had acute appendicitis, not a life-threatening condition if treated promptly, but fatal if left untreated. For several days—some say three, some say five or six—his parents refused to seek medical help. For days both parents watched Joshua suffer in excruciating pain, knowing that his very life hung in the balance.

"By the time they finally took him to the hospital, after days of fever and pain, his appendix had burst and had poured poison into little Joshie's system to such an extent that he was in septic shock. He was barely alive. His cardio-vascular and circulatory systems were in such poor shape that he couldn't be transferred or operated on immediately. And despite the best efforts—the heroic efforts—of Dr. Armistead and others, little Joshua passed away later that night.

"Those, ladies and gentlemen, are the facts of this case. And they are undisputed."

The Barracuda played this first part of her closing softly, captivating the jurors with her smooth presentation and mesmerizing lips. She now moved out from behind the podium to begin strutting back and forth in front of them, alternating between looking down at the floor and then into their eyes. The stillness of the jurors indicated she had their rapt attention.

"Now, the defense has put on quite a magic show these past few days in an effort to obscure and confuse these facts. Smoke and mirrors, misdirection, hocus-pocus, now you see it, now you don't. If it weren't such a serious matter, it would have been fun to watch. But ladies and gentlemen, *facts are stubborn things,* and all the magic tricks in the world cannot change them.

"The defense tried to saw Dr. Armistead's testimony in half. Here was a good and decent man, unbiased in this case, relentlessly attacked because he has had two medical malpractice judgments against him in his career. The defense even provided a little cloak-and-dagger with Dr. Armistead. 'Oh my gosh,' they said, 'we saw the commonwealth's attorney at his house during the plain light of day'—as if that is some type of crime. Did it ever occur to them that he may have simply left some medical records in court the prior day or that he might also be a witness in another case—"

"Objection," called out Charles. "She's arguing facts not in the record."

Silverman's head jerked up as if Charles had awoken him. He gave a memorized spiel to the jury that the Barracuda had heard before. "What the lawyers say in closing arguments is not evidence. You are the sole judges of the evidence and should rely on your own memory as to what was or was not said about that incident." Then he looked at the Barracuda: "Let's stick to the facts introduced from the witness stand, Counsel."

"Yes, Your Honor," said the Barracuda sweetly.

She then turned back to the jury. "When Buster Jackson took the stand, the defendant's magic act continued. They tried to make Mr. Jackson's testimony simply disappear based on the fact that he's had prior felony convictions, based on the fact that he cut a deal. Well, I've got news for defense counsel: The prosecution doesn't get to choose its witnesses in a case like this, and boy scouts aren't generally the ones serving time in prison. It should not be surprising to you, ladies and gentlemen, that Thomas Hammond chose to talk about the most important thing in his life last night, chose to unburden his guilty conscience to the man he's been living with for the last several weeks. Nor should it surprise you one iota that when he did that, his cellmate happened to be a man who has had two priors and one pending felony conviction.

"Did I cut a deal with Jackson? Yes. Did I like doing it? No. Then why did I do it? Because as Buster Jackson mentioned on the stand, his conviction was no sure thing. The same type of hocus-pocus you're seeing in this case was used by Mr. Arnold in Jackson's case. In that case, he claimed racial profiling, and the court has been considering for the past few weeks whether to throw the whole case out. I decided it was better to get a guilty plea from Jackson, and at the same time get at the truth in this case, than to watch both men walk free when we all know they committed the crimes they are accused of.

"Now the defense takes John Paul Hammond's testimony, puts it under a handkerchief and...*voilà!*...it changes right before our eyes. In his unprompted videotaped statement, the boy says his mom and dad watched Joshua suffer for five days—five full days—before ever taking him to the doctor. Then he spends some unchaperoned time with his mom—contrary to a court order I might add—and comes back saying it was only three days. Was he lying before, or is he lying now? And does it really matter?

"And then there's the prayer journal. I guess the defense figures if they ignore it, it'll just go away. But ladies and gentlemen of the jury, it's not going away. In those pages, with her own words, Theresa Hammond writes about her dying son and how she has made a conscious decision not to get him medical help even though she knows his very life is in danger."

The Barracuda stopped pacing and returned to her spot behind the podium. She rearranged some papers, glanced at the photo, then looked directly at the jurors.

"At the end of the show, after the oohs and aahs are over, we are left with these facts. And they are stubborn things. A young child died. His death could have been prevented. His parents, knowing he was dying, chose not to get him proper medical help. In our society, we call that criminally negligent homicide. It is a conclusion that Houdini himself could not escape. The facts are in. And they compel a verdict of guilty as charged."

The Barracuda paused for a moment, her lips pursed solemnly together as she eyeballed her jury champions one last time.

"Thank you," she said and returned to her seat.

CHAPTER 66

It was, Charles knew, a strong closing. He could feel it in the air as he rose to address the jury, the future of the Hammond family in his hands.

His mouth was dry, and his heart pounded in his throat. He hadn't thought he would even be nervous, but the pressure snuck up on him, engulfed him through the stares of jury, judge, and television camera. This was his moment. He had trained his whole life for this. The street preaching, the lecturing, the constant analysis and dissecting of other trials—it all came down to this. Twelve strangers daring Charles to persuade them.

As he walked toward the jury box, he glanced quickly around the courtroom and froze in his tracks. There, in the second to last row, looking somber and professional—chin held high, her hair in beautiful ebony braids—sat Denita. She gave him a thin smile, very subtle, hardly noticeable to anyone else who might have been looking. But you don't live with someone for years and mistake their body language. It was a look of pride, a subtle encouragement: *I'm here for you.* Charles nodded almost imperceptibly, his spirit buoyed as he approached the jury box.

He spent some of his built-up adrenaline moving the podium away from the box so he could have the freedom to roam in front of the jurors without any barriers. He approached the rail of the jury box without notes. He would speak from the heart. Nikki had insisted it was the only way to go.

He smiled and tugged his suit coat sleeves partway up his forearm. "Nothing up my sleeves," he said. They did not smile back. He straightened his sleeves back out.

How many times have I told my class that the closing argument is no time for humor?

"Contrary to what the prosecution seems to think, I am no magician," he confided. "But I have been to a few magic shows in my childhood as a spectator, and I always came away with a 'how did they do that?' feeling. It's the same feeling I have right now.

"How did she"—Charles turned to point at the expressionless Barracuda—"just now make a case that totally fell apart at every turn sound so good? How did she do that?"

He started walking back and forth, hitting his rhythm. "How did she make it seem like an act of patriotic duty to turn a drug dealer back on the street in order to entice him to testify against a loving mother and father? How did she do that?

"And how, I am wondering to myself, did she turn a doctor who came into this courtroom and lied through his teeth, who put his own pride and reputation above the well-being of his patient, into someone who sounds like Marcus Welby, M.D.? How *did* she do that?

"And finally, ladies and gentlemen, how is it that she can stand there with a straight face and argue that Thomas and Theresa Hammond didn't take Joshua to the hospital for six full days when innocent young Tiger and even her own corrupted drug dealer of a witness, Buster Jackson, both testified that it was only three days? How in the world does she do *that?*"

Charles shook his head and smiled. This time one or two jurors seemed to let their eyes reflect the hint of a grin. "I've seen rabbits get pulled out of hats before, and I've seen elephants disappear. But I've never seen anything quite as befuddling as the prosecution's case the last few days.

"And now, listening to her closing argument, I'm left to wonder just one thing: Were we even at the same trial?

"Where was the commonwealth's attorney when Dr. Armistead admitted that he had lied about how many malpractice cases he had settled? Didn't we hear him, with our own ears, admit that he settled a very similar case where he should have transferred a child in acute distress to Norfolk Children's? But he chose not to transfer in that case, and he chose not to transfer Joshua. Was it because he had to operate on Joshua right away? Not according to the medical records. It took Dr. Armistead twenty-six minutes just to see young Joshua, then another ninety minutes of resuscitation before the patient was rolled into surgery. By then, Joshua could have been transferred to Norfolk Children's and back at least three times.

"Why does it matter? you ask. It matters because the commonwealth cannot prove this case unless it shows, beyond a reasonable doubt, that the actions of the *parents* caused the death of Joshua. If it was Dr. Armistead's malpractice that caused Joshua's death, you must find Thomas and Theresa Hammond not guilty.

"And why does it matter whether it was three days or six before Thomas and Theresa sought medical help? Because the commonwealth's attorney knows that reasonable parents often wait a few days before taking their child to the hospital. Oh, I know that when that first precious baby has a slight fever and a cough, we rush him to the hospital right away. But by the time we have our third one, and especially if our pastor is beating us over the head saying we should *never* take him to the hospital, well, folks, the truth is, most of us wait a few days. But that does not make us murderers."

Charles abruptly stopped pacing. He needed to wrap it up, he could tell by the looks in their eyes. He had so much more to say. He needed to pound on Buster, he wanted to talk about the bravery of Tiger, and he wanted to show minute by minute where Armistead had failed. But the jury had heard enough, they were anxious to start deliberating, and they were fading fast.

It was not time for details; it was time for motivation.

Charles reached back into his memory, filled with words and stories from the master trial lawyers, searching for just the right anecdote to summarize his entire case. As he did so, he glanced around the courtroom, and his eyes locked once more on the supportive eyes of Denita. A thought flashed through his mind: *My future is in your hands,* she had said. *You can crush me if you want, it's totally up to you.* The thought triggered another thought, a story he had heard on Court TV used by the masterful Gerry Spence in a closing statement. It seemed to fit.

"Ladies and gentlemen, this case reminds me of a story I heard several years ago about a wise old man who lived in the forest. And this wise old man loved all living things: the animals, the birds, the insects and snakes. But most of all he loved families. He loved the way dads wrestled with their kids. He loved the way moms hugged them."

Charles turned and looked at his own counsel table where Thomas and

Theresa sat. Behind them, in the first row, sitting up straight and paying unblinking attention, were Tiger and Stinky. The jury turned with Charles and looked into the faces of those they would soon judge.

"One day, my friends," continued Charles, looking back at the jury, "a young know-it-all came to the forest and said to himself, 'I'll show this old man. We'll see if he is so wise.' So the young man caught a tiny bird and cupped it in his hands. And the little bird was there in his hands, trembling and frightened."

Charles now stood before the jury, his own hands clasped, looking from face to face, searching for champions.

"And the know-it-all young man with the bird cupped in his hands went to the wise old man and said, 'Old man, old man, if you are so wise, you tell me. I have a bird in my hands. Is it dead or alive?' And the know-it-all young man thought he would win in any case. If the old man said, 'It is dead,' then the young man would open his hands, and the bird would fly away."

Charles opened his hands and smiled. Then he cupped them again. "And if the old man said, 'It is alive,' then the young know-it-all would squeeze his hands together"—again Charles demonstrated, grinding his palms to-gether—"and drop the bird dead at his feet. The young man thought he was brilliant, he thought he couldn't lose."

Then Charles walked over to his clients, filling the courtroom with a tense silence. He stood behind Thomas and Theresa, placing his hands on their shoulders, the same posture he had adopted in the opening, and turned back to the jury.

"But the old man shook his head sadly and said, 'Oh my son, oh my son…the bird is neither alive nor dead. For the life of the bird is in your hands.'"

Charles paused, then, "Ladies and gentlemen of the jury, the life of this family, the future of these kids, the freedom of these parents, are all in your hands. They have suffered enough. Give them back their future. Let them fly. Choose life."

He looked straight at two jurors seated side by side in the second row.

They had given him good vibes throughout the case, and he had pegged them as champions for his cause. One was nodding his head ever so slowly; the other was blinking a tear from her eye.

Charles waited long enough for the silence to add an exclamation point, then took his seat next to his clients. He waited another beat, then turned discreetly toward the back of the courtroom to nod his thanks toward Denita. He wanted her to know how much her presence meant to him—driving two hours or more just to hear his closing. He wanted to see the look on her face as she digested the significance of his closing parable: the story of the young know-it-all and the little bird. He wanted to see her face one more time and draw on the reservoir of strength he seemed to find there.

But when he turned and searched for her, scanning back and forth on the row of seats where she had been a few minutes earlier, she was gone! Disappeared. He wondered if she had been there at all. Was he just imagining things? The pressure of the case constructing ghosts before his very eyes?

No! She had been there. He had seen her with his own eyes, felt the magic of her presence the way he had felt it years ago. He quickly surveyed the entire courtroom, but there was no sign of her. He shook his head, turned back to the judge, and tried to put her out of his mind.

CHAPTER 67

Waiting.

It was driving Charles crazy.

For three hours on Thursday afternoon the jury deliberated while Charles and Nikki fretted. Thomas quietly prayed, and Theresa busied herself amusing the children. At six o'clock Thursday evening the jury announced they were not even close to a verdict. They would like to reconvene Friday morning, they said. After dire warnings about listening to news coverage or talking to others, Judge Silverman dismissed them for the night, promising that a good night's sleep would help their deliberations.

There would be no sleep for Charles, only late, late shows on television, second-guessing every decision made during the trial, and counting sheep. On Friday morning the vigil continued. By Friday afternoon the speculation swirled as to why the jury was taking so long.

It could only be good for the defense, surmised Nikki. How could anybody say there was no reasonable doubt when it took the jury two full days just to reach a verdict? Charles was more pessimistic, fretting about a possible compromise verdict or hung jury.

"But I wouldn't do anything different if I had to try the case again," he said, mostly to himself. It was about the tenth time he had said that since the jury started its deliberations.

"It went as good as it possibly could have gone," replied Nikki.

And the longer they waited, the more they reminded themselves that they had tried a great case. There was no way the jury could come back with guilty verdicts. *Could they?*

By four o'clock on Friday afternoon, the combatants had to seriously consider the possibility that the jury might not reach a verdict before the weekend. State law required a unanimous verdict for either guilt or innocence, otherwise the jury would be declared "hung," and the case would be tried again at a later date. Nobody wanted that.

The lawyers and court personnel could hear muffled shouting from the jury room, but it was impossible to make out what the jurors were saying. Despair descended on both camps by late Friday afternoon as the very real possibility of a hung jury loomed large.

At 4:17, the jury rang the buzzer for the third time that day asking for the bailiff. The first buzzer had resulted in a question to the judge. The second buzzer had been a request for a lunch break. This time they handed the bailiff a note.

"We have a verdict," the bailiff announced to the courtroom. Then he disappeared out the back door to get Judge Silverman.

———— ❈ ————

Charles leaned over and reminded his clients that it was traditional for the defendants to stand for the reading of the verdict. As Silverman scrutinized the jury form, just to be sure everything was filled out correctly, the others followed Charles's cue and solemnly rose to their feet. Thomas stood next to Charles. On the other side of Thomas was Theresa, then Nikki. When Charles felt the big man reach over and grab his hand, he glanced to his right and saw the others holding hands as well. Over his shoulder, in the front row, he saw Tiger and Stinky, also standing, squeezing each other's hands so tight that their knuckles had turned white. He felt an incredible surge of pride for representing these folks…good folks…innocent folks.

"Has the jury reached a verdict?" asked Judge Silverman.

"We have," said the jury forewoman, standing. She was one of the mothers. Not a good sign.

"What say you?" asked Silverman.

"In the case of Commonwealth versus Theresa Hammond, on the sole charge of negligent homicide, we find the defendant"—the forewoman paused and looked at Theresa, an unmistakable sign—"not guilty."

"Praise God," whispered Charles.

"Yes!" exclaimed Nikki.

Theresa Hammond began to quietly sob. "Awright!" said a squeaky little voice behind Charles.

Silverman banged his gavel. "Order in the court."

All eyes turned back to the forewoman. "In the case of Commonwealth versus Thomas Hammond, on the sole charge of negligent homicide, we find the defendant"—she did not look up, did not even pause as she read—"*guilty as charged.*"

The words sucked the wind out of Charles. His knees felt weak. He went into a fog, things becoming dreamlike, nightmarish.

"No!" cried Theresa, her face in her hands. "Lord, please no!"

Nikki stood speechless.

Thomas stared straight ahead, showing no emotion, barely blinking as the words sunk in. Then he turned toward Theresa and sheltered her face in his chest, holding on to her and staring into the space over her head. Tiger and Stinky scampered forward and threw their arms around their daddy's waist.

"I'm sorry," said Charles, looking into the blank stare of the big man.

"Please be seated," Silverman requested, banging his gavel.

Slowly Thomas freed himself from the clutches of his family and slumped back into his seat. Charles felt nothing…almost like he was floating in space, not really there at all. He was just so…stunned. He thought he was prepared for the worst, but this?! *What was the jury thinking?*

Judge Silverman thanked the jury and discharged them. They walked silently from the jury box, none even looking in the direction of a sobbing Theresa and a stoic Thomas.

"The defendant will be remanded to the custody of the Virginia Beach City Jail," said Silverman. "Sentencing will proceed at 10:00 a.m. Monday morning."

"All rise," said the clerk. "This honorable court is adjourned until 10:00 a.m. on Monday morning."

Charles stood, his legs somehow miraculously working, and leaned across to the big man. But the words caught in his throat for a precious few seconds, and then the deputies were there, handcuffing Thomas. Charles watched in horror and helplessness as Tiger lurched forward, broke through the deputies, and flung himself around his father's waist.

"You can't go!" screamed Tiger. "I won't let them take you."

Tiger hugged his daddy with all his might and wrapped his little legs around his daddy's immense left calf. But Tiger was no match for the deputies. They pried his bony fingers and skinny legs away from his dad. In the chaos, Thomas just kept repeating, "It'll be all right, buddy. It'll be all right." A sobbing Theresa reached out and drew Tiger to herself, trying to comfort her son through her own tears. Stinky joined them, the water flowing from her big blue innocent eyes, as she watched the deputies escort her daddy from the courtroom.

"We'll appeal," Nikki whispered insistently to the family. "We'll move for a new trial. We'll get him out." But her words of comfort were drowned in the wave of grief flooding Theresa and the kids.

Charles just stood there watching this tragic scene unfold before him, as if he were detached from it. He had never felt so helpless, so utterly useless, in his whole life. The horrid images seared into his mind. A slump-shouldered Thomas led from the courtroom. An inconsolable Theresa. The courage of Tiger, wanting to fight back, but not knowing how. And the innocence of Stinky. The pure little bird. Crushed in the hands of the young know-it-all from the forest. Her innocence and faith in the system shattered by the ambitions of the Barracuda.

There was a tap on Charles's shoulder.

"You tried a good case," said the Barracuda, extending her hand.

"Is this your idea of justice?" demanded Charles.

The Barracuda withdrew her hand. "No, this isn't justice." She sneered. "Justice would have meant I nailed them both."

Then she turned on her heel and walked down the aisle of the courtroom, answering questions from the press along the way.

Charles turned and grabbed Nikki by both arms. "Meet me in the war room in an hour," he said.

"I'll be there," she said.

There was fire in her eyes.

CHAPTER 68

Charles had his back to the door when she entered. He was poring over some legal cases, trying to find some basis for a new trial. Something—anything—that Silverman had done wrong. A bad evidentiary ruling, a flawed jury instruction, an objection that should have gone the other way. The more he dug, the more discouraged he got. Unfortunately for Thomas Hammond, Silverman had made few mistakes.

The room was a mess, but Charles knew that Nikki wouldn't mind. There were papers scattered all over the floor as if they had been thrown into the air before falling randomly. Charles still had his dress slacks on, his monogrammed shirt unbuttoned at the neck, and his incandescent tie loosened so the knot hung low on his chest.

She was already fifteen minutes late, so he didn't bother turning around when he first heard the door to the war room close. He lifted his head and rubbed his eyes. "Why'd we have to get Silverman?" he asked, turning toward her. "Not much to appeal unless…"

He blinked…and stood slowly, not taking his eyes from her. She just stood there, staring back.

"Denita?"

"I'm sorry," she said, moving slowly toward him. "I heard about the verdict…tried to reach you on your cell phone…"

Charles glanced around the disheveled room, "Left it in the car, I guess. How'd you find me here?"

"The custodian," she said sheepishly. The softness of her voice surprised Charles. It was so unlike Denita. She fidgeted a little as she stood in front of him, fumbling with the envelope in her hands.

She was dressed in jeans, a white button blouse, and sandals. Very casual. Her hair was pulled back away from her face and gathered with a couple of hair clips. How often had he brushed her hair away from her face before kissing her? How strange that he wanted to reach out and touch that hair again and pull her close right now. *I must be on the ragged edge emotionally.* They had been through a lot, but she still held this sway over him—the ability to infuriate him one minute and mesmerize him the next.

"You okay?" she asked.

"I don't know." Charles shrugged, surprising himself with the honesty of his answer.

"I was there for your closing," she said, still fidgeting.

"I saw you."

"You did great. I thought you had them."

Charles sighed. "Me too."

She took a deep breath and a small step closer, looking deep into Charles's eyes. "Thanks for this," she said, glancing down at the FedEx envelope. "Is this really the only copy you sent?"

Charles looked at it and nodded. "I couldn't bring myself to send it to the senator, so I just sent it to you. Figured you would have shredded it by now." He looked up and met her eyes. "You'll make a good judge, Denita."

For the first time in as long as he could remember, he saw that quick and natural smile he had fallen in love with so many years ago. "I've been trying to tell you that," she said. "What changed your mind?"

Charles waited a few seconds to answer. He wasn't really sure. "Flowers on our baby's grave," he eventually replied, his voice suddenly hoarse. He swallowed hard, felt his throat constricting with emotion. "Ones that I didn't put there."

Without hesitation, she stepped forward and embraced him. "I'm sorry," she whispered. "For a lot of things."

He hugged her back, didn't even have to think about it, really. It just felt so natural. The scent of her, her shampoo and familiar perfume, brought back so many memories. For Charles, the four years of separation began melting away. Had she really changed that much? She pulled back slowly, but they somehow still held hands, her left hand resting comfortably in his right. Her other hand was still holding the envelope.

And then he felt it.

A ring! A diamond! Without thinking he stared down at it. No wedding band, but definitely an engagement ring.

He felt like he had just been sucker-punched for the second time that day. His hope of reconciliation, so improbable yet so powerful just a few short seconds ago, now crashing around him. His emotions instantly locked down—an unbidden defense mechanism—leaving him flat and empty, momentarily devoid of feeling. He absorbed this blow without blinking. He had already taken such a beating at the hands of others today. Now his ex-wife had piled on.

She must have sensed his thoughts—it seemed like she had always been able to read his mind—and withdrew her hand. She looked down at it herself, then up at him.

"Congratulations," he managed.

"You'd like him, Charles," Denita said blushing. "Reminds me a lot of you during our first few years."

He knew that she meant it as a compliment, but it devastated him nonetheless. The message was clear. If he had never changed, never been converted, he would have never lost her. An inconsolable sadness pierced his defenses. It was over this time, really over. He could feel the awful finality of it. No hope of reconciliation; no prospect of Denita accepting Christ and renewing their vows. He felt as crushed as he did the night she first told him about another man in her life; the night she told him she wanted a divorce.

What did I expect? That somehow this letter—this decision to protect our secret—would make everything right? Bring us back together? Why can't I get over this woman? Why do I still care so much?

He took a deep breath, the air suddenly heavy and stale in the room. He needed to be alone so he could process this.

Just then Nikki, never one for subtle timing, came bursting through the door. "Sorry I'm late," she called out, then pulled up short when she noticed Denita.

Nikki had changed into a pair of cotton shorts that hung low on her hips with the waistband rolled down and a cropped cotton shirt that exposed her midriff and pierced navel. In her right hand she carried a pair of sandals, which she promptly tossed on the floor. In her left hand she had the two remaining bottles from a six-pack of Corona.

Charles gathered himself and introduced the women, watching Nikki's eyes go dark when they shook hands. "Thanks for joining us," Nikki mumbled.

"I was just leaving," Denita replied. She was suddenly all business. "Just wanted to stop by and talk to Charles about a few things."

Though Charles politely protested, Denita insisted on going. He walked her out to the hallway, where they stood facing each other for a long time. Denita tilted her head toward the war room. "Doesn't seem like your type."

"She's not," he said, though he wasn't sure he meant it. He really wasn't sure of anything right now.

"You're a good man, Charles." Denita spoke the words tenderly. Then she took his arm, leaned forward, and kissed him on the cheek. "I'm sorry it wasn't meant to be."

Before he could answer, before he could admit how much he regretted that too, she let go of his arm and turned away. And then, like so many times before, Charles found himself watching her go, staring at her back, his heart throbbing with the familiar pain of what might have been.

He stood there for a few minutes, scenes of their time together racing through his mind like a home video on fast forward. He felt the corresponding rush of emotion, as if reliving everything he had ever felt toward Denita in those same few moments. It left him totally spent. He needed time alone, just to crash, just to sort things out. Get over her one more time…somehow release these emotions he had been keeping inside for so long.

His mind flashed to the dream he had just a few short days ago: an arrogant Denita sitting high on her lofty bench, overlooking a graveyard of children, laughing at him. He thought about how different the real Denita was from the one he had imagined in his dream. God had humbled her somehow. He felt a little ashamed for even thinking about writing a letter to Crafton, for putting so much stock in a stupid dream. After all, wasn't that the same dream that had him marrying Nikki?

Right.

Nikki. His bride-to-be. Waiting for him in the war room, three sheets to the wind, plotting legal strategies that would never work. He suddenly didn't have the strength to go back in there and deal with *that*.

But he knew that he owed it to Thomas to try.

He placed his head in his hands, slouched down against the wall, and began to pray.

┅ ≡◈≡ ┅

Nikki was sprawled out on the floor when Charles made it back into the war room. She was reading a document and drinking her Corona. "Want one?" she asked holding the bottle toward Charles.

"Huh?"

"Want a beer?"

Charles looked at her and lowered his eyebrows. "You can't have beer in here. This is a *Christian* law school."

"Okay," said Nikki. Then she took a long gulp. "Sure you don't want one?"

"Yeah."

"Your loss."

Charles joined her on the floor, and they sat there in silence for a while, Nikki gulping down her beer, Charles leaning back on his palms, staring straight ahead. He hoped Nikki would ask a question about Denita. He would take that as a cue to open up about it. But she didn't and so he tried to chase thoughts of Denita from his mind by focusing on the case. Neither subject brought him any joy.

"It was Buster," he finally said. "They must have believed Buster."

Nikki burped. "Yep. I can't believe they bought his act. He's such a moron."

"But a free moron," complained Charles. Suddenly, the events of Buster's testimony and the case seemed so far away, so insignificant.

"But a free moron," repeated Nikki. For some reason that must have seemed funny to her, and she started giggling. She looked at Charles who totally missed the humor. "Sorry," she said.

She took another swig, then spoke in the exaggerated manner of someone having a little difficulty with her tongue. "So, Charles, since you're the magician, how you gonna pull a new trial outta your hat this time?" Her voice went up an octave at the end of the sentence to emphasize her question.

He sighed. It wasn't the question he had been hoping for, but he tried to focus on the case. "I've been doing nothing but research since I got back here more than ninety minutes ago," said Charles. The mild rebuke about time was lost on Nikki. "We've basically got two grounds for requesting a new trial, both of them long shots."

Charles watched Nikki peel the label from her bottle.

"First, I'll argue that Silverman should not have allowed Reverend Beckham to testify because his testimony breached the priest-penitent privilege. Second, I'll argue that no reasonable jury could convict Thomas but not Theresa. I mean, they were both totally in this together. There was no evidence to make his conduct different from hers—"

"Except Buster," interrupted Nikki.

"Yeah, except Buster," agreed Charles.

More silence followed as they pondered the treachery of Buster Jackson.

"A jailhouse conversion," muttered Charles. "I had my doubts all along, but I never saw this coming. He owed his life to Thomas."

"And now his freedom," said Nikki.

Charles nodded his head. "This morning, which seems like forever ago now, we were in the catbird seat. Armistead imploded on the witness stand yesterday, and then Tiger ate the Barracuda for lunch. I just couldn't believe we could lose. And after Theresa's diary was read on the first day, I figured if anybody was in danger of getting convicted, it was her, not him. I should have spent more time attacking Buster in my closing. I just didn't think anybody would believe him—"

"Wait," Nikki said, holding her palm straight out. "Rewind it. What'd you say?"

"I should have spent more time on Buster in closing, I just—"

"No. Before that."

"Um, I thought if anybody might get convicted, it'd be Theresa, not Thomas?"

"*Stop!*" said Nikki. "*That's it!*" She placed her bottle, nearly empty, on the floor. She started to stand but tripped and fell back to her hands and knees. She crawled a few feet toward Charles, then stopped. She was on all fours, her dark eyes dancing with excitement.

"Don't you see it?" she exclaimed. "We got set up."

"Nikki, let's just get you home. We'll talk about this in the morning."

She crawled closer, and then sat up on her knees facing Charles. She placed her open palms against both sides of Charles face. "Look at me," she pleaded, "and listen to me. We...got...set...up."

"And?" said Charles.

"And I intend to do something about it," said Nikki. Then she let go of Charles's face and quickly stood. She took a little sideways step to catch her balance. "Just as soon as I get back from the bathroom."

CHAPTER 69

Twenty-four hours later, Nikki sat across from Thomas Hammond in the Virginia Beach City Jail interviewing room. Her raging headache had receded a little. She had spent the entire day searching for Buster Jackson to no avail. She was hot, tired, and in no mood for Thomas's sullenness. She had been with him for fifteen minutes, and he had barely spoken.

"Where's Buster Jackson?" she asked for the third time.

Thomas shrugged.

"Look," Nikki said, exasperated, "I'm just trying to help you here. But I can't help unless you let me."

"You've done everything you can," said Thomas. "It's over."

"It's *not* over," said Nikki, slapping the table. "Why are you so determined to be a martyr?"

Thomas did not answer. Nikki stared at him and waited more than a minute.

"Where's Charles?" asked Thomas.

"He's working on a motion and brief for a new trial to free *you*. He's working on the evidence for the sentencing hearing to keep *your* jail time to a minimum. I've been all over Tidewater, Virginia, today trying to find Buster Jackson so I can spring *you,* and you're the only one who doesn't seem to care how much time you serve."

"That's not true," said Thomas.

"Then tell me where Buster Jackson is!" shouted Nikki.

"I can't," said Thomas.

"Come on!" Nikki stood and loomed over the table. "What is wrong with you?" Thomas shrugged again.

"You want to know what I think?" she asked. There was no visible response. "Okay, I'll tell you what I think. And you can just sit there like a miserable self-inflicted martyr and wallow in your own pity. But here's what I think.

"I think you put Buster up to it. I think you heard us say, in the conference room after the first night of trial, that everything had gone great on the first day *except* the introduction of Theresa's prayer journal into evidence, which we didn't have an answer for. You said you wanted to testify. You said it wasn't right for Theresa to take the fall. I said there wasn't going to be any fall, but you didn't believe me. You couldn't be sure."

Nikki watched Thomas's face as she talked. It was a blank mask.

"Then you went back and talked to Buster in your cell that night. You asked him to be your snitch, to take Theresa off the hook, to guarantee your conviction and her acquittal, didn't you?" Thomas just stared ahead, as if he hadn't heard a word.

"I thought it was strange the next morning, after such a great first day in trial, that you got so emotional—so melancholy, really—with Tiger. It's the first and only time I've seen you cry. It's as if you knew something bad was going to happen.

"Then, when Buster testified, he was very careful in what he said. I checked my notes first thing this morning. Then I called the court reporter—had her read that testimony to me over the phone."

Nikki pulled a piece of paper out of the pocket of her jeans and read her scribbled notes: "Here's what Buster said you said: 'If I don't testify, the jury will wonder why. If I do testify, it all comes out. How can a jury let me skate if'n they hear—Pops is always sayin' if'n—if'n they hear that I knew my boy was gonna die, but I wouldn't take the kid to the hospital? What else can a jury do to someone who demanded—I mean flat-out demanded—that his woman not take the kid for three solid days—all the time knowin' the kid is dying?'"

Nikki folded up the paper and stuffed it back in her pocket. "There are a lot of 'ifs' and 'if'ns' in that statement, Thomas. And you know what I think?"

She leaned forward across the table. "I think you made this confession up just to protect Theresa," she whispered. "I think it's incredibly noble of you to do that, but also incredibly stupid. We would have gotten both of you off if Buster hadn't testified. But if you tell me where Buster is now, we can at least get him to court on Monday and try to get you a new trial. And

Thomas, it won't take away from Theresa's innocent verdict. Nothing can touch that now."

"I can't," Thomas said simply. "I promised."

Nikki sighed and leaned back in her seat. "Thomas, Thomas...so noble, but so misguided."

She stood to leave but decided to give it one more try. "If you can't tell me where he is, then at least get a message to him to meet me. Tomorrow night. The McDonald's on Battlefield Boulevard in Chesapeake. Across the street from the hospital. Nine o'clock."

Thomas did not speak, but Nikki thought she noticed a slight nod of his head.

"Thanks," she said, as if he had guaranteed that Buster would appear. Then she called for the guard quickly, before Thomas would have a chance to think this through and change his mind.

CHAPTER 70

By Sunday night the words on Charles's monitor were growing bleary. He had been holed up in his office all weekend reading case after case. He had gotten so desperate that he called Denita on Saturday, just to pick her brain about possible issues for appeal. By midafternoon she had e-mailed some research results. She had hit the same stone wall he did.

Time was running out, and he was getting nowhere. He reached for his Nerf basketball and stood to stretch. He took a few shots. He took stock.

Even if Nikki was right about Thomas and Buster, and he suspected she was, it would make no difference. Technically, Buster had told the truth on the witness stand. He had simply repeated what Thomas had told him in the cell the previous night. And what Thomas had told him was also technically true, since it was so wrapped up in hypothetical statements. "If a jury heard this, then they would do that." It was frustrating that Thomas tried to take justice into his own hands, but it was hardly the basis for a new trial.

Charles could just see himself trying to convince Judge Silverman to give him a new trial based on Buster's testimony. "Well, you see, Judge, my client's alleged jailhouse confession wasn't really a confession. He was just making this whole thing up so the jury could come to a compromise verdict and find him guilty and his wife innocent." He could just hear Silverman's response: "Now, that's original, Mr. Arnold, claiming that a confession wasn't really a confession. That's exactly what the last five defendants said." No, Nikki's theory might be interesting, but it wouldn't do them any good.

He reread Denita's long e-mail and the cases she had sent. While he appreciated her efforts, his ex-wife had done no better than he had. The most promising avenue was the discrepancy between the verdict in favor of Theresa and against Thomas. But in reality, that argument was pretty thin. Juries rendered split verdicts against coconspirators all the time. It hardly made the verdicts suspect, especially in this case since Buster's testimony provided a basis for a verdict against one but not the other. And the priest-penitent privilege issue was not working out either. Silverman had been right in ruling that the privilege was waived, at least based on the cases Charles and Denita had turned up.

Charles threw up another shot. It bounced off the rim and out. At this stage, he admitted to himself, it was time to focus on getting Thomas the lightest sentence possible. Silverman would have a wide range of options to consider: twelve to thirty years. There were plenty of mitigating circumstances Charles could bring out on Monday. Silverman seemed like a reasonable man. If Charles could get Thomas the minimum, and if Thomas were a model prisoner, he could be out in five. Not perfect, but the best he could hope for under the circumstances.

Another rim shot. Another miss. It was time to work on an argument for mercy. If Silverman decided to get tough and make an example of Thomas, the kids would grow up without a father. Charles sat back down at his terminal and rubbed his eyes. He fired up his Westlaw search engine and resumed his quest for the perfect case.

＊＊＊

At 9:15, Nikki started getting restless. For once in her life she had been on time, even five minutes early. She had been sitting at this same booth inside McDonald's for twenty minutes now, watching every car that pulled into the parking lot, searching for Buster Jackson. She had drained two Diet Cokes and made one quick run to the bathroom. She was losing heart.

She decided that she would wait until 9:30, no longer. She could do this tonight without Buster, but it would be a lot easier with him. One thing was sure, if she waited much past 9:30, the opportunity would be lost.

She wore a pair of black stonewashed jeans and a black T-shirt. Her long dark hair was pulled back in a ponytail and tucked under a Nike hat—also black. In her right front pocket was a pair of black latex gloves. In her other front pocket she carried a pen and a few of her business cards, in case she needed to jot some notes on the back. She carried a penlight in her left rear pocket and a small switchblade in her right rear pocket. She wore no makeup and no jewelry.

She had seen enough spy movies to know precisely how to do this.

But she was hoping for a supporting actor.

For fifteen more minutes, she continued to watch every car, van, and SUV that pulled into the parking lot, waiting for Buster to step out. There was precious little traffic, and certainly nobody who looked remotely like Buster. At 9:30, she talked herself into five more minutes, then ten. It was now dark, had been dark for forty-five minutes, and time was short. She would have to do this on her own.

She walked slowly to her Sebring, straining her neck to look up and down the highway, sure that Buster would pull into the parking lot just as soon as she left. But she couldn't wait any longer. Armistead worked the three-to-eleven shift and would be home no later than 11:30. She was already cutting it too close for comfort.

She sighed, softly cursing Buster under her breath. She climbed into the Sebring and gunned it, took one last look at the McDonald's in her rearview mirror, and headed for Woodard's Mill.

CHAPTER 71

Nikki left the Sebring about a quarter-mile from Armistead's estate. She parked on a side road a few streets over in the neighborhood, then cut through some backyards until she was on Armistead's street. She walked briskly to the driveway, checked carefully for cars in all directions, then started jogging toward the house. She saw no cars in the driveway and only a few lights on inside. Armistead had left the front porch light on as well as a light in the family room in the back.

She walked quickly up the steps to the front door, looked over her shoulder, and rang the bell. She held her breath and waited. Nothing. She wasn't really sure what she would have said if Armistead himself had answered the door. "Oh, I'm just here with Eagle Cleaners ready to clean your bathrooms. Can I borrow your toothbrush?" Fortunately, she didn't have to worry about that. She took out her key and opened the door.

She stepped inside, closed the door behind her, and punched the security code into the alarm panel on her left. It would be just like Armistead, with his compulsive personality, to change the code every week. She waited a few seconds. No sound. She supposed it could be one of those silent alarms that only goes off at a police station somewhere, but that was a chance she would have to take.

She had done it now. Breaking and entering. No excuses, no defense. She pushed the tiny light on her watch and checked the time: 9:59. She had one hour. She would need to hustle.

She started in the study. She had a few more thoughts about passwords. She tried the name of his college and the name of his med school. No luck. On the back of one of her business cards, she had written down every combination of the dates of his birthday. No luck. Social security number. Nothing. Mother's maiden name. Wrong. She tried the old standby: 1-2-3-4-5. No luck. For fifteen minutes she tried various logical password combinations. None worked.

Using her small penlight, she started afresh through the financial files. She had given this a lot of thought. An unusual liaison between the Barracuda and Armistead, the perjured testimony of Armistead in the Hammond case, and the payment of four hundred thousand dollars to somebody shortly after Erica Armistead's death. All these factors led to only one conclusion: Armistead and the Barracuda were having an affair. Erica must have found out and threatened to divorce Sean, threatening his interest in her million-dollar trust account. Sean must have paid someone to take out his wife, freeing him to carry on with the Barracuda and making him a very wealthy man.

The Barracuda had been a broker for the hit—a go-between for murder.

But Nikki needed proof. She thumbed furiously through the financial files, looking for something she had missed before. The cell phone bill held some promise. Armistead was apparently on one of those plans that limited his minutes, and the bill listed every number he had called together with how long the call lasted. Last time she had copied down every long-distance number; this time she would focus on local calls. There was one number in particular that Sean Armistead had called more than any other. Nikki was willing to bet it was the Barracuda's cell phone. She would call it on her own cell phone as soon as she got back to her car. She folded up the phone bills for the last three months and stuffed them in her pockets.

It was now 10:28. Nikki's heart seemed to pound faster with each passing minute. She had illegally broken into Armistead's house, now she had committed petty larceny by taking the phone bills.

Another twenty minutes in the financial files revealed nothing new. Time to check some other hiding places. She would avoid the family room in the back because it was too well lit. Though you would have to be in Armistead's back lawn to see in, Nikki wasn't taking any chances. She climbed the front steps, walking as lightly as possible, and headed straight for the master bedroom.

Using only the small beam from her penlight, she searched quickly through sock and underwear drawers, between mattresses, and in every nook and cranny of the dresser. She closed a drawer and accidentally knocked something off the dresser. As she bent to pick it up, she heard another noise. *Was it the sound of tires on asphalt?* She turned the penlight off and went to the window that overlooked the front driveway. She slowly twisted the rod that opened the plantation shutters.

She stood stone still, breathlessly waiting. No car. No further sounds. 10:58. *Settle down, girl, you're making yourself crazy.* She stepped into the master closet—a huge walk-in room filled with clothes, shoes, and storage items. She looked around and realized that none of Sean's stuff was in there. They must have been sleeping in separate rooms. Erica's stuff was jammed everywhere. She was a little surprised that Sean had not yet cleaned it out, given his compulsive personality, but then again it had just been a few weeks. She knew that it typically took months before a spouse would remove the personal effects of a spouse who had passed away. And in this case, Sean would probably not feel right about sleeping in the bedroom that had belonged to Erica. Nikki would not be surprised to see the house on the market in a few months.

As she surveyed the closet, she spotted a dozen purses, some stuffed with junk. She immediately grabbed them and started searching through the contents.

One was a plain beige cloth purse jammed with brushes, papers, photos, hygiene products, and a wallet. The wallet overflowed with credit cards, receipts, and other valuables. Nikki began shuffling through the papers, awkwardly holding the small penlight under her chin. *"Yes!"* she whispered. It was a small scrap of paper with the name and address for Rebecca Crawford. It looked like a woman's handwriting. With a handwriting expert, it could be strong proof that Erica had found out about the affair.

Nikki jammed the paper into her pocket and replaced the purse. She still wanted to check a few places downstairs and the glove compartments of the cars in the garage. She checked her watch again. 11:10. She was pushing it. At most she would have another five or ten minutes.

Another noise. *Relax!* She took a deep breath. The silence seemed to pulsate through her temples, throb against her brain.

She walked slowly and quietly out of the closet and into the master bedroom. She glanced around, saw nothing else of value to her investigation, and prepared to leave the bedroom. Another noise rumbled in the distance, no mistaking it this time, and it was followed immediately by a flash of light, high beams shooting through the shutters of the second-story window. A car in the driveway! Nikki instinctively jumped back away from the window, then flattened herself against the wall and started inching toward the window to peer out.

She moved her head slowly around the frame of the window and glanced through the shutters. The car stopped, and the driver killed the engine. The headlights remained on momentarily, probably operating under some type of delay. She waited for the car to beep, the sign the driver had hit the remote lock, but she heard nothing. She stared without blinking into the night and gasped. There, walking up the steps to the house, was the shadowy figure of Sean Armistead, still wearing his white lab coat.

Nikki's heart pounded so loud in her ears she couldn't think straight. She checked her watch again. *How could this be?* He was home earlier than she had planned! She was trapped in the master bedroom!

To avoid being seen through the window, Nikki got down on her hands and knees and crawled across the room toward the phone on the bed stand. She gently removed the receiver from the cradle just as she heard Armistead insert his key in the front door. It sounded like he locked the door then unlocked it again. He stepped into the foyer, flipped on a light, and took a few steps, probably toward the alarm panel. She knew the green light would tell him the alarm had already been disarmed.

She would be busted. It was just a matter of time.

"What the...? Hey! Is anybody in here?" Armistead yelled. His words echoed through the house.

Nikki tried to think about an escape. She would wait for Armistead to start up the front steps, giving her a split second to start running down the back steps and into the family room. But that room was lit up, and she was sure the back door was locked from the inside. By the time she got it unlocked, Armistead would be on the catwalk overlooking the family room, and he might get a good glimpse of her.

She heard Armistead open a closet just off the foyer, and then she heard the tumblers of a lock combination. A few more noises—indecipherable—and then the unmistakable twin clicks of a safety lock being released and a gun hammer cocking into place.

Armistead was armed.

Nikki walked quietly toward the door of the bedroom, preparing to make her mad dash. She heard Armistead walk back toward the kitchen, a move that would put him between her and her escape path. He flicked on a few more lights, also bad news, then picked up the phone. Nikki heard him curse, click the receiver a few times, then curse some more. Then he made the one move Nikki was hoping against. He started climbing the *back* steps—she could actually see his shadow now—gun in hand, swinging and pointing it in all directions. She stood, frozen, just inside the master bedroom door, a mere six feet from the top of the steps.

Her head pounded until she thought it might explode. She could barely breathe. She willed herself to retreat—quietly, on the balls of her feet—farther inside the room. She headed back toward the master closet, hoping that she could—what?—she suddenly realized she had absolutely no plan. She was cornered.

She slipped inside the closet. The bedroom light popped on. Armistead entered. She retreated a step or two and tried to hide herself among the clothes.

How long before Armistead would notice the bedroom phone off the hook, replace it, and call the police? How long before he would search the closet, find her, and shoot her in "self-defense"?

Think!

Just then the master bedroom went totally dark. For some strange reason Armistead had turned the light off! But then she heard him curse, and it chilled her blood.

So much for that theory. Armistead was every bit as surprised as she was. It could mean only one thing.

They were not alone. Someone else was in the house!

CHAPTER 72

Nikki backed herself into a corner of the closet and tripped over some shoes. The resulting noise, though small, sounded like an explosion. She waited a second, expecting Armistead to come bolting through the open closet door. Nothing.

The next noise she heard was the sound of glass breaking in the driveway. She strained to hear more, but only silence followed.

She reached into her back right pocket, pulled out her switchblade, and flipped it open, nearly slicing her hand. She started working her way toward the closet door. It was pitch black, so she felt her way along the clothes till she got to the doorframe. The house was as quiet as it was dark. Not a sound came from the bedroom.

Nikki mustered enough courage to slip out into the master bedroom, hugging the wall. She glanced toward the open door and saw no light from the hallway, no light from downstairs—the entire house was dark. She scanned the room and saw nothing but stationary shadows of unknown objects. Either Armistead had turned off every light in the house, or someone had gotten to the fuse box.

What could it mean? Perhaps Armistead was hiding in this room, watching her. Or maybe he was standing outside the bedroom door, biding his time, waiting for her to exit so he could blow her away. But then she heard another noise, a few steps that sounded like they were coming from the front foyer. Now was her chance! Bolt through the door, make a sharp left, fly down the flight of back steps, and exit through the back door of the family room.

There was no more time for indecision. In the darkness Nikki said a desperate little prayer, promising God if He got her out of this mess she would totally change, she would, well, she'd think of something important she could do later. Then she darted quickly out the bedroom door and turned hard to the left.

He grabbed her from behind. With one huge hand he covered her face, digging his fingers into her jaw, and covering her mouth with the palm of his hand. He wrapped his other arm around her chest, pinning her arms to her side, stopping her cold. The strength! She kicked and squirmed, but he had her in a death grip. Her switchblade dropped to the floor.

He quickly dragged her back into the bedroom, his hot and putrid breath moist on the back of her neck. Her scream became a muffled and pitiful groan. She twisted hard, but he wrenched her closer. She tried biting the hand but could not. He squeezed her tighter still, constricting her breath.

She trembled.

"Shut up!" he whispered, coarse and deep. Her eyes grew wide with fear. He dragged her toward the closet, overpowering her efforts to resist.

She felt nauseous and terrified, ready to pass out because he was squeezing her so hard. But something wasn't right. She had been so scared at first, she hadn't noticed. The course and powerful hands, the deep baritone voice, the smell of body odor, not cologne…

"I'm here to help," whispered Buster Jackson. "And if you quit squirming and shut up, I'll let you go."

Nikki nodded and felt the hands release her. She turned to face her sweaty assailant. Over the sound of her labored breathing, she could hear more footsteps—this time from the upstairs hallway.

"I followed you here from McDonald's," whispered Buster. "When I saw Armistead come back to his crib, I knew you were in deep trouble. I took out the fuse box"—Buster smiled his big gold-toothed smile—"yanked it out the wall. And I also yanked the doc's cell phone from his car on the way in." Buster reached into the front pocket of his baggy jeans, producing the phone. "Had to bust through a window to get it."

Despite Nikki's terror, this brought a quick and uneasy smile. "It was already unlocked, Buster. Otherwise, the alarm would have sounded."

Judging by the dumbfounded look on his face, this piece of information caught Buster off guard. "I knew that," he whispered.

Nikki heard another noise in the hallway and nodded toward the closet. They slipped in just as the flashlight beam hit the bedroom.

Buster moved right next to Nikki, touching his lips to her ears.

"When I make my move…get out. Don't look back, dog."

Nikki shook her head and turned to look in his eyes. "I'm staying with you."

Buster took his huge hand and grabbed Nikki's jaw, squeezing so hard the pain shot through her like a knife. "No."

Nikki nodded her head quickly, and Buster released her. This guy scared her. The look in his eyes, the way he so quickly resorted to force.

"Promise me you won't hurt him," Nikki whispered. Buster said nothing.

"Promise me," she demanded.

He stared at her, jaw clenched, bloodshot eyes narrowed.

She folded her arms. "Then I'm not leaving."

Buster grunted his frustration, rocking nervously from one foot to another. She watched those hooded eyes grow hard and cold, an executioner's look.

"Promise me," she insisted.

She saw Armistead's flashlight darting around the bedroom. A few more seconds and he would be checking in the closet. *Why do I care if Buster hurts Armistead? The man certainly deserves whatever he has coming.* But something deep inside her knew this was the right thing to do, and so she stepped in front of Buster, feet planted shoulder width apart. *I'm not moving.* Nikki the mule.

The light flashed closer.

"Promise me."

Buster grabbed the outside of Nikki's arms, then picked her up and moved her like a mannequin to a spot behind him. "I promise," he snorted.

"Here," Nikki shoved one of her cards in the back pocket of Buster's jeans. "Call me."

Just then she heard Armistead in the bedroom punching the numbers on his phone. He must have noticed that the receiver had been taken off the hook.

"He's calling the police!" she whispered to Buster.

Buster quickly stepped to the door of the closet and threw Armistead's cell phone across the room. When the flashlight pivoted in that direction, Buster bolted from the closet and headed straight toward Armistead. Nikki followed close behind.

Buster lowered his head and landed his shoulder squarely against Armistead's back, sending him crashing through the nightstand and into the wall, sandwiched between Buster and the dry wall, the flashlight falling on the floor. Nikki stood for a second, frozen in the shadows.

"Go!" barked Buster.

She wanted to stay, see this through, but she knew they would get in enormous trouble with the cops. Why should they both take the fall? She would owe Buster big time. She would make sure he got treated fairly. But in that split second of decision making, self-preservation won out. This was her chance! Her only chance!

She sprinted from the room, down the back stairs, and toward the rear door of the house. She heard scuffling and muted cursing from the master bedroom as she crossed the family room, then a sickening gurgle sound. She unlocked the back door, then hesitated for a second. Should she go back and make sure Buster didn't do anything drastic? Had he already done it? Did Buster need her help?

The gun! She hadn't heard any gunshots. If Armistead had struggled free and picked up his gun, she would have heard some shots. As long as no gun was involved, Buster would overpower him. What worried her was that she hadn't heard anybody say anything.

"You okay?" she yelled.

"Get out!" the big man yelled.

Nikki opened the back door and sprinted across the patio surrounding the pool. She flew through the gate and ran across Armistead's yard and the yards of neighboring houses. She was exhausted, but she never stopped until she reached her car. She tried to catch her breath but could not, looked to the right and left, then unlocked her car door and hopped in.

Nikki was nearly back to her condo before she started breathing anything close to normal. Her heart still pounded like it would explode inside her chest, and she didn't remember much about the drive home. All she could think about was Buster and Armistead, the anger she had seen in Buster's eyes, and the gun she had seen in Armistead's hand. She went inside her condo and took a long hot shower, with her cell phone just within reach, wondering the whole time if she should call the police. She eventually talked herself into lying down on the bed, but she had no desire to sleep.

She picked up her cell phone four times to dial 911. Each time her trembling fingers stopped short. She tried to call Charles twice, but couldn't bring herself to do that, either. After she put the phone down for the last time, she lay back down in bed, and a wave of exhaustion flooded her body. Her limbs felt like they weighed a thousand pounds, and her swirling mind finally slowed. When it came, the elusive sleep hit hard. But with it came relentless nightmares that raced nonstop through her mind until they were interrupted by the sound of her phone ringing in the darkness more than three hours later.

CHAPTER 73

Buster Jackson was almost to Williamsburg, heading west on I-64, before he pulled off the interstate to find a pay phone. He had been making good time, but he had also been carefully staying within five miles of the posted speed limits. He could not afford to be pulled over. A black man in a nice car registered to someone else would invite a search. Buster knew a thing or two about racial profiling.

He found an exit with a gas station at the end of the ramp. He kept mulling over the blur of events in his mind. His sudden move on Armistead, then dragging the doctor to his feet and slamming him against the wall. Buster had wedged his forearm against Armistead's neck, pinned him to the wall with it, actually lifting the doctor off his feet.

Buster wheeled right and pulled into the parking lot, his thoughts fixed on the bugging eyes of Armistead, the gurgle coming from the doctor's lying throat, Armistead's muffled pleas for mercy. It was ironic that this man, who had shown no mercy to Thomas at trial, would be begging for mercy himself. Most vivid of all, Buster remembered the feeling of Armistead's body going limp.

He jumped out of the car and hustled over to the outdoor pay phone, never taking his eyes from the vehicle. He reached into his pocket and pulled out Nikki's card. He called her collect.

She answered on the first ring.

"Hello."

"I have a collect call from a Buster Jackson. Will you accept the charge?"

"Yeah…sure."

"Nikki Moreno?"

"Buster!" Her voice was crisp, wide-awake. "Where are you? What happened?"

"Can't say," he glanced around to make sure nobody was listening. "But the doc is ready to sing. Take a subpoena to his crib tomorrow morning. If he doesn't come to the door right away, go ahead and enter. You're good at that." Buster chuckled. "Tell Pops his homey came through."

Buster did not wait for a response. He heard Nikki calling his name through the receiver, but he placed the phone back on the hook.

He glanced around nervously for the third time since he had pulled into the parking lot. He was thirsty, but he would not go inside, he would not allow a convenience-store clerk to ID him.

He walked toward the car and watched a minivan pull in next to the Lexus. He saw a father stumble from the driver's seat, a mother rubbing her eyes in the passenger's seat, and a few kids snoozing in the back.

He wondered how they would feel if they knew that they had just parked next to a car with a dead man in the trunk.

CHAPTER 74

Nikki was still awake when the sun came up Monday morning. She missed shaking the little guys out of bed, missed the sweet disposition of Stinky, even missed the morning wars with Tiger. She got ready quickly—a short miniskirt and white blouse for court, hair pulled back in a simple clip—and rushed into the law offices of Carson & Associates. She typed up a witness subpoena, thankful that the courts now allowed lawyers to do this on their own, so long as they filed a copy with the clerk. She signed Charles's name. The subpoena commanded Armistead to appear in court for the ten o'clock sentencing hearing or risk contempt of court.

By the time she pulled into the Woodard's Mill subdivision, it was nearly eight o'clock. Her hands became moist on the wheel as the possibilities raged through her mind. She hoped for the best—that Buster had somehow talked Armistead into confessing the truth, whatever that might be. But she also contemplated the worst—finding Armistead dead in the master bedroom. But if that were the case, why would Buster call her and tell her to subpoena Armistead to court? Maybe Buster was just trying to protect Nikki, give her a legitimate reason to go to the Armistead house and get her fingerprints on things. That way the cops wouldn't ask a thousand questions if Armistead was dead and Nikki's prints were everywhere.

No, she didn't think Buster was that sophisticated.

She pulled into the long tree-lined drive and parked directly in front of the three-car garage. She noticed that Armistead's car was gone. Just a few hours ago she had been here and endured one of the longest nights of her life. It looked so different in the daylight. So...peaceful.

As she walked toward the front door her skin felt clammy. It was quiet, eerily quiet. She climbed the steps and rang the doorbell, just as she had done last night. It didn't work. Then she remembered what Buster had done to the fuses. She knocked loudly.

After a few minutes, it was obvious there would be no answer. The silence mocked her hopes that Armistead would somehow appear, ready to testify. She took a deep breath and pulled the key out of her pocket, reaching down to insert it in the door. Just to be sure, she first checked the knob. It turned and the door flung open.

Not a good sign. If Buster had killed Armistead and wanted Nikki to have an alibi for having her fingerprints everywhere, then he would have left the door unlocked so she could enter without having to explain why she had a key. It was all adding up to a scenario that Nikki didn't like.

"Anybody home?" she called from the marble foyer. "I'm serving a court subpoena."

No answer.

She planned to retrace her steps from the night before, purposefully touching things she had touched the previous night. That way she would have a truthful explanation for her prints. She started in the study. Everything seemed to be the way she had left it except—

"Oh, my gosh," she murmured, putting her hands over her mouth. She was staring at Armistead's desk, looking at a neat pile of paper, the top page a handwritten memorandum addressed "To Whom It May Concern."

She started reading and groaned. Her hands trembled. "You promised," she cried. She quickly finished the first page, cursing Buster Jackson as she read. "You promised," she said again. "You promised!"

She slumped into a chair, every bit of her energy sapped by this letter, and pulled out her cell phone.

"Charles Arnold."

"He's dead," said Nikki. "Armistead is dead."

CHAPTER 75

At 10:00 a.m., while Silverman finished his introductory remarks, Charles mouthed a silent prayer. He was seated with Thomas at the defense table, with Theresa and the kids in the front row immediately behind them. Nikki had not yet arrived.

Things were happening so fast, spinning so far out of control, that Charles hardly had a chance to think things through. He was going on instincts, gambling instincts. He would sort it all out later.

Charles rose to his feet, even though it was time for the prosecution to present evidence on the issue of sentencing.

Silverman looked at him quizzically. "Mr. Arnold?"

"Judge, I don't want to delay these proceedings. But new evidence has emerged this past weekend that changes everything. On the basis of that new evidence"—he paused and glanced toward the Barracuda—"which clearly demonstrates prosecutorial misconduct, we would move for a new trial."

When Charles had begun speaking, there had been the usual rustling and murmuring that filled a courtroom as the proceedings begin. But suddenly the courtroom was stilled, the charges of prosecutorial misconduct captured everyone's attention.

Especially the attention of the Barracuda, who was predictably on her feet. "Does the desperation of defense counsel know no bounds?" she asked. "*This* is ridiculous."

Silverman glared at Charles. "Those are serious charges, Mr. Arnold. The court does not take them lightly."

"And I don't make them lightly, Your Honor. We need less than half an hour, but justice requires that the court hear this evidence."

"*What* evidence?" demanded the Barracuda. Silverman cut her off with a scathing look.

"Half an hour," said Silverman. "No more. And if you don't have some strong evidence, Mr. Arnold, you will be risking contempt. This is not the forum for taking cheap shots at the commonwealth's attorney."

"Yes, Your Honor. Thank you, Your Honor."

Charles relaxed slightly and blew out a breath, knowing he was in too deep to turn back now.

"Well?" said Silverman.

"The defense calls Lieutenant Gary Mitchell."

Mitchell, the African American police officer who had testified in the racial profiling case against Buster Jackson, rose slowly in the back of the courtroom and made his way toward the witness stand. He looked the same as he had a few weeks before—somewhat stooped, a man whose body showed every one of its fifty-five years. Wrinkles lined his droopy face and pulled hard at the corners of his mouth and eyes. Charles had called him on the phone nearly two hours earlier because he sensed that Mitchell was a man of integrity, a police officer he could trust.

"Please state your name for the record," began Charles.

"Lieutenant Gary Mitchell, Virginia Beach Police Department."

No sense wasting time on preliminaries, thought Charles.

"Have you recently received any reports concerning a possible suicide by Dr. Sean Armistead?"

There was a gasp from the prosecution table and a general stir from the courtroom. Silverman leaned forward.

"Yes," said Mitchell simply.

"By whom and when?" asked Charles.

"At about 8:15 this morning. By you."

The Barracuda scoffed. Spectators couldn't resist nudging each other and whispering. Silverman banged his gavel and called for order.

"What were the circumstances, as reported to you, that caused you to investigate a possible suicide?"

"Objection," said the Barracuda. "This is bush league."

"Is that an objection?" asked Silverman. "Bush league?"

"It's also hearsay," griped the Barracuda. "Defense counsel can't put a police officer on the stand to regurgitate what defense counsel said on the phone."

"I agree," said Silverman.

"I'll rephrase," said Charles, coming out from behind counsel table and moving toward the front of the courtroom. "To your personal knowledge, did somebody discover a suicide note from Dr. Armistead?"

"Yes. Your paralegal, Ms. Nikki Moreno, was apparently trying to serve a subpoena on Armistead this morning—"

"Objection," stated the Barracuda, sounding frustrated. "We're right back into hearsay again."

"Sustained," ruled Silverman.

"Were you *given* a suicide note?" asked Charles.

"Yes."

"By whom?"

"Nikki Moreno."

Charles looked at the Barracuda and smirked. So much for hearsay objections.

"Did the note cause you to look anywhere for a body?"

"Yes, it did."

"Where?"

"Well," said Mitchell, shifting in his seat. "I didn't actually look myself. But the note gave us a probable location for the body, so we called the state police and asked them to look."

"And where was that?" asked Charles.

"Along the Blue Ridge Parkway. In the same spot where Dr. Armistead's wife previously committed suicide. My understanding is that it's the same spot where they were initially engaged."

The courtroom buzzed as reporters and spectators digested this juicy piece of information.

"Was the body found?"

Mitchell nodded his head, at first slowly, then more rapidly. "At 9:18 this morning, the body was located in the driver's seat of Dr. Armistead's car at the bottom of a sharp drop-off from a scenic lookout spot on the parkway. The car caught fire, so we're using dental records to confirm the identification."

The Barracuda went white. Silverman watched Mitchell intently, soaking in every word.

"Was it the same spot where Dr. Armistead's wife had died?"

"Yes sir. It was."

Charles allowed the courtroom to absorb this news, then he turned and walked back to his counsel table. He grabbed three thick piles of documents. He took one pile—comprised of originals—and gave it to the witness. He placed the second pile on the Barracuda's table. The third pile he kept as his own copy.

"Can you please explain to the court what these papers are?"

"This is what Dr. Armistead left behind. It's more or less a suicide note with numerous attached exhibits."

Charles watched the Barracuda out of the corner of his eye. She was thumbing rapidly through the documents, doing her best to look unfazed.

"What is the first page entitled?" asked Charles.

"Well," replied Mitchell, "it's addressed 'To Whom It May Concern,' but it is actually entitled 'Dying Declaration of Dr. Sean Armistead.'"

"And did you personally go to the Armistead house and compare the handwriting on this note with other samples of Armistead's handwriting?"

"I did."

"What did you find?"

The Barracuda rose to object but then apparently thought better of it and sat back down. It was well-settled law that lay witnesses could give opinions about the source of handwriting.

"It was definitely his."

Charles then placed his copy of the documents on his counsel table and went up to the witness box to retrieve the originals. He walked deliberately to the judge's bench and placed the originals in front of Silverman. "With the court's permission," he said, "I would like to have this set of documents entered into evidence as the dying declaration of Dr. Armistead. Then I would like to read several excerpts."

The Barracuda stood to object. But Silverman didn't let her get the first word out. "You know the law on this counsel. The exhibit will be admitted."

Charles returned to his counsel table and began slowly reading from the document.

"I, Sean Armistead, intend this document to be a dying declaration and thereby admissible in the court case of Commonwealth versus Thomas Hammond. I have attached supporting documents that substantiate all the claims I am about to make and sincerely hope that they will be admitted into evidence as part of the case.

"I must begin by apologizing to Thomas and Theresa Hammond, the Hammond children, as well as my own lover and wife, Erica Armistead, for so completely ruining their lives by my selfish actions. I pray that the Hammond family will find it in their hearts to forgive me and that my Maker will forgive me for what I have done to my own wife.

"Second, let there be no mistake about my testimony in the Hammond case—it was perjury—"

The courtroom erupted, and Silverman had to use his gavel. Undeterred, Charles continued reading.

"I lied about Theresa Hammond coming to me after her son died and telling me that he had been sick for five or six days. That never happened. As far as I know, he was only sick for three days.

"I also lied about why I didn't transfer Joshua to Norfolk Children's Hospital. It was exactly as Mr. Arnold implied during his cross-examination. I didn't transfer the patient because I didn't want the doctors at that hospital to second-guess my decisions. My refusal to transfer may have cost Joshua his life.

"I lied because I was blackmailed by Deputy Commonwealth's Attorney Rebecca Crawford…"

A collective gasp filled the courtroom. At least one person sitting behind the prosecution table, totally blown away by the revelation, blurted out, "I can't believe this."

Charles paused and looked at the Barracuda, surprised to see her as composed as ever, staring at the paper without emotion, as if she were following along and reading about someone else.

"It wounds me to admit this, but I had an affair with Ms. Crawford after my wife became ill with Parkinson's. When Erica found out about it, she confronted Ms. Crawford and then went into a deep depression, eventually committing suicide at the same spot on the Blue Ridge Parkway where we were first engaged. When I found out, I immediately called Ms. Crawford and asked her to come to my house. After first talking to the Chesapeake police, I then talked to Ms. Crawford. She told me that the police knew I was having an affair but did not know with whom. She convinced me to lie to the police and tell them that I was having an affair with a coworker.

"After I went on the record with that lie, things deteriorated between Ms. Crawford and me. More and more, I came to see that she was just using me and protecting herself. When I confronted her, she said she would expose my lie and indict me for murder if I didn't protect our secret and comply with her new demands. She assured me that any jury in the world would convict me if they found out my wife died under mysterious circumstances and then I lied about an affair to the police. In exchange for whitewashing the investigation, Ms. Crawford demanded that I pay four hundred thousand dollars to her election campaign. She said she planned to announce later this summer that she would be running for commonwealth's attorney. She also demanded that I give perjured testimony to help convict Thomas and Theresa Hammond and thereby improve Ms. Crawford's chances of getting elected.

"I channeled the money for the election campaign through a bogus company named the Virginia Insurance Reciprocal. I had voluntarily made several deposits to that same company for the benefit of Ms. Crawford during our affair and before Erica died. I have included bank statements for that company. If you investigate the accounts that received the wire transfers from the Virginia Insurance Reciprocal account, you will find that they are tied to Ms. Crawford.

"To confirm the affair with Ms. Crawford, I have attached an itinerary for an alleged business trip to the Bahamas. It was really a one-week vacation with Ms. Crawford. The attached plane ticket receipt will confirm my itinerary. The airlines can confirm that she was on the same flight.

"If any further confirmation of the affair is necessary, check with the waiters at the Beach Grill, our favorite hangout. I always used cash, so there are no credit card receipts, but the waiters will remember us. We went there several times a week and always left big tips.

"I hope this statement is sufficient to undo the damage I have done in the Hammond case. I realize there is no way to undo the damage I did to Erica. I have no excuses and make none. I know it won't make things better, but after signing this note, I, too, will take a final trip to the Blue Ridge Parkway. Erica deserved better than me, and I can never forgive myself for what I've done."

Charles finished reading and glanced around the courtroom. He looked first at his own client, big Thomas Hammond, sitting at counsel table, hands folded, eyes closed, as if praying. Those in the gallery looked stunned, as if they had just witnessed the suicide themselves. The Barracuda was the only one in the courtroom moving to any discernible degree, scratching and marking her copy of the declaration.

"And then he signed it at the end," said Charles.

Silverman stroked his chin and surveyed the courtroom, looking slightly dazed himself. In all his years on the bench, he had undoubtedly never had anything that remotely prepared him for this. He finally noticed that Lieutenant Mitchell was still on the stand. "May the witness step down?" Silverman asked.

"Yes," said Charles.

"No objection," mumbled the Barracuda.

"Do you have any other witnesses?" After such a shocking revelation, the judge seemed to take some solace in the ordinary procedural rules that still governed in the courtroom.

"Just one," said Charles. "Rebecca Crawford."

CHAPTER 76

The Barracuda's mind raced wildly. It was sheer will and years of professional training that allowed her to keep her emotions in check while her world crumbled around her. A good lawyer was always part actor, never allowing her true emotions to come out, only what the role required. And right now the role required dignity...and indignation.

"That's outrageous," she stood and hissed. "Armistead can say anything he wants in his dying declaration because he doesn't have the guts to stick around and defend his fabrications under cross-examination on the witness stand. So now, to add insult to injury, the defendant wants to call me as a witness?" She sneered. "Fat chance."

"Are you refusing to take the stand?" Silverman asked. "I will not make you testify, but if you don't"—he held his palms up—"I'll have to take this evidence at face value."

The Barracuda marched to the well of the courtroom, directly in front of the judge's bench, and raised her right arm. "Give me the oath," she demanded, "so I can deal with Mr. Arnold's pack of lies."

Within seconds, she had settled into the witness stand, staring out at her adversary.

"Good morning," said Charles, smiling.

"Good morning," spit the Barracuda. *You jerk.*

"Let's get right down to it," Charles said. "This four hundred thousand dollars paid by Dr. Armistead—under the guise of the Virginia Insurance Reciprocal—any chance that some of that money went to your account or an account you control?"

She hated his smug look, the condescending nature of his question. But she forced herself not to focus on the anger. She needed to think clearly, quickly. The accounts could be subpoenaed. There was no use denying it.

"Yes."

Charles waited, looking like there must surely be something more, some further explanation.

"That's it? Yes?" he asked incredulously.

"Yes, the money went into an account that would ultimately be controlled by my election campaign." She tried to sound indignant. "We were trying to keep it confidential because I had not yet announced my intention to run for commonwealth's attorney. Still haven't...before *this*."

Charles just smiled and crossed his arms. She wanted to strangle him, choke that arrogant attitude right out of him.

"That's it?" Charles asked. "That's your full explanation? The man's wife dies, and he just says, 'Hey, now that my wife's dead, I think I'll donate a few hundred thousand as a campaign donation for a woman who has not yet announced her candidacy?'"

"When Dr. Armistead's wife committed suicide," the Barracuda replied acidly, "he went through a time of soul-searching and reprioritizing. He decided to put some of the money that he and Erica had accumulated to good use."

Charles still had that quizzical look on his face, the knit brow of disbelief. The Barracuda decided to lay it on a little thicker.

"When you see a young patient die on your watch," she continued, "because his parents won't even bring him to the hospital, you realize how important it is to have someone in the commonwealth's attorney's office who will enforce the laws."

"Indeed," said Charles. "Indeed." He took a few steps, never taking his eyes from her.

"Did you have an affair with him?" Charles asked.

"Absolutely not."

"Did he ever call you on your cell phone?"

"Of course, he was a witness in this case."

"Did he call you often?"

The Barracuda shrugged. *What did he know? What documents did he have?* "Often enough to be ready for his testimony."

"Do you have your cell phone with you now?" Charles asked.

The Barracuda looked at Silverman. The judge simply returned her stare.

"Well?" Charles prodded.

"It's in my briefcase, but it's turned off. We *are* in court," the Barracuda said snidely.

"Do you have a phone mail message that plays when the phone's off?"

"Of course."

Charles shuffled through the documents left behind by Armistead. He grabbed three near the bottom, took his own cell phone out of his briefcase, and turned on the power. "Is this all right, Judge?"

Silverman nodded.

While Charles played his little game, the Barracuda noticed the back door of the courtroom open. Nikki entered somewhat clumsily, wheeling a stand containing a television and VCR player down the aisle. *What now?* wondered the Barracuda. *Is this a bluff?* She calculated the odds of Charles Arnold actually having videotaped evidence. *Of what?*

"Can you identify these documents for the record?" Charles asked, holding them out with his left hand while holding his cell phone with his right.

"They appear to be cell phone bills," the Barracuda responded.

"It appears that Dr. Armistead was on a plan that gave him a certain number of hours a month. Would you agree?"

The Barracuda snatched the documents and glanced them over with as much contempt as she could muster. "If you say so."

"But in this particular month, February of this year, he exceeded those minutes. Do you see that?"

"Yes."

"And can you read for us, from this list of phone calls, the one number that appears most often?" Charles held up his own cell phone, preparing to dial.

"Let's skip the dramatics," the Barracuda snapped. "That's my cell phone number, and you know it. You don't need to complete your cute little demonstration."

"Would you care to explain to the court why Dr. Armistead was calling you so often in February of this year, months before young Joshua died?"

The Barracuda paused for a second but knew she had to come up with something quick. Innocent witnesses, those telling the truth, don't pause to think things over. But things were coming at her too fast, one after the other. The good news was that Armistead wasn't around to refute anything she would say. "I consulted him about medical issues in other cases."

"So he called you at eleven thirty at night on February 14? And twelve thirty at night on February 16? And nearly midnight on February 20?"

The Barracuda felt her face getting warm. One lie leading to another. This pompous defense attorney having fun at her expense. She so desperately wanted to strike back. Instead, she used every ounce of self-control she could muster to keep her emotions in check.

"Unlike lawyers in private practice, commonwealth's attorneys are not on the clock. Armistead was busy during the day at the hospital, and he was helping me with complex medical issues in some cases. I told him he could call anytime."

Charles crossed his arms and smirked. He waited again, as if there must be more to her answer than that.

"Mr. Arnold," inquired Judge Silverman, "anything else?"

"Sorry, Your Honor. I wanted to make sure she was finished." Charles looked over at Nikki who nodded back.

"Did you ever meet Dr. Armistead at the Beach Grill?"

"Once or twice on business, but nothing romantic, as Armistead claimed."

"Did you know," asked Charles slowly and deliberately, "that the Beach Grill has a security camera that periodically records its patrons?"

He was bluffing; he had to be. The Barracuda thought hard about the surroundings at the Beach Grill. *Was there a camera above the bar area?* She didn't remember one. She would take her chances. What did she have to lose?

"I am not aware of that. In fact, I doubt it's true."

The Barracuda watched as Nikki turned and whispered to a young man in the front row. The Barracuda thought she had seen him before. But where? *A waiter? A bartender?* It was so hard to remember. The Barracuda had always been too busy to notice those types of people.

Charles wheeled the VCR into the middle of the courtroom. "Can you see, Judge?" he asked.

Silverman nodded.

Charles turned again to the witness. "Did you ever hold hands with Dr. Armistead at the Beach Grill?"

Of course, she thought. It had been so much fun to flaunt their tryst, to tempt the fates. Now she was kicking herself. Arnold was probably bluffing. But if he wasn't, she would be guilty of perjury, on the spot, something the videotape would prove beyond reasonable doubt.

Charles crossed his arms and waited. The Barracuda looked deep into his eyes. She had made a career of being able to tell when people were lying. But there was no hint from him, nothing she could read. It was a huge risk, a possible perjury conviction. And for what? So that Thomas Hammond might spend a few years in jail.

She looked up at Silverman. "I'm invoking my Fifth Amendment rights and refusing to answer that question."

"Did you have a few beers with him?" asked Charles.

"I invoke the Fifth."

"Did you kiss him?" asked Charles.

The Barracuda snorted. "I invoke the Fifth."

"Did you conspire with him to give false testimony in this case?"

"The game's over, Mr. Arnold. I will no longer answer your misleading, insulting questions. I...take...the...Fifth." The Barracuda spat out the words, demonstrating her contempt.

"And did you plan to murder Erica Armistead if she did not commit suicide?"

She hated not answering this question, her blood beginning to boil. She knew how it would look. But the time for looking good was over. Now she was thinking self-preservation. How many times had she goaded witnesses into answering questions that resulted in indictments. "Is there something about this you don't understand, Mr. Arnold? I'm taking the Fifth."

"No, Ms. Crawford," Charles responded. "I think I understand perfectly." Then, turning to the judge, "Nothing further."

Charles wheeled the VCR unit off to the side of the courtroom and returned to his seat. The Barracuda watched for a moment in seething silence, then stood and stepped down from the witness stand, heading back toward her seat at counsel table.

"Ms. Crawford." Judge Silverman's voice had a steely edge to it. She wheeled around to face his wrath.

She had practiced in front of him for years, but she had never seen him like this. He was pointing at her, his hand shaking. "I have served this court a long time," he said, "and I thought I had seen it all. But I have n-never... *ever*...seen such a blatant disregard for the rule of law, such totally unethical and...*abhorrent* behavior." Silverman sat up on his seat and leaned forward, as if he were ready to come over the bench and strangle the Barracuda with his bare hands.

"You, ma'am, have been entrusted by this court with enforcing the law. But in light of your apparent conduct in this case, that role will now fall to me. I am hereby issuing, sua sponte, a bench warrant charging you with obstruction of justice.

"Deputies," he called out, "I remand Ms. Crawford to custody in a separate holding cell from the other prisoners. I will set the arraignment for 2:00 p.m. this afternoon, which ought to give Ms. Crawford sufficient time to retain a good lawyer."

Two deputies approached and attempted to grab the Barracuda by each arm. She brushed them off, thrust her chin in the air, and began walking from the well of the courtroom under her own volition with a deputy on each side. As she passed Charles, seated at counsel table, she refused to even look at him.

"No hard feelings?" he whispered, just loud enough for her to hear. "Or doesn't it really work that way?"

CHAPTER 77

Tiger couldn't believe his eyes.

"Are they taking her to jail?" he asked his mommy. He meant to whisper, but he was so excited that it actually came out pretty loud.

"Shh," said Theresa. "I think so."

"*Yes!*" said Tiger, once again a little louder than he intended. He felt the eyes of the spectators throughout the courtroom staring at him. "Sorry," he whispered, though he really wasn't.

It had been such a strange and wonderful day. He had not understood everything that had happened, but he had sensed it was going good. Plus he had learned a brand-new strategy for staying out of trouble. It had dawned on him at the end of the Barracuda's testimony.

"What's that mean?" he asked his mom, when the Barracuda took the Fifth.

"In America," explained Theresa, "you don't have to answer questions that might incriminate you—get you in trouble. It's called taking the Fifth."

Wow! Tiger thought to himself. *Why hadn't anybody told him about this before? "Take a fif." He'd have to remember that!* The budding young constitutional lawyer had a feeling he'd be making good use of that rule in the days to come.

But first, there was still one matter of unfinished business.

Even though everyone had been telling Tiger all weekend that he should just pray for a short prison sentence for his daddy, he had secretly disobeyed. Every night and every morning, silently, Tiger had prayed that his daddy would get out of jail altogether and just come home. It was exciting to see the Mean Lady heading off for jail, but it was not the same as having his dad come home. He was still praying for his dad to get out, even as the deputies escorted the Mean Lady from the courtroom.

"Will the defendant please rise," the judge said. His dad rose. Mr. Charles stood by his daddy's side.

"The declaration of Dr. Armistead makes it clear to this court that your conviction was based on false testimony," said the judge. "The death of Dr. Armistead makes it equally obvious that the commonwealth could not prove its case in a new trial. Accordingly, Mr. Hammond, I am setting aside the jury verdict on the basis of prosecutorial misconduct. You are a free man, Mr. Hammond. Free to go."

"Court adjourned," announced Judge Silverman, banging that little hammer of his one more time.

Tiger's daddy turned and gave Mr. Charles a bear hug. His mommy jumped out of her seat and hugged his daddy.

"What's that mean? What's that mean?" yelled Tiger, jumping up and down.

Just then Miss Nikki came over and swooped him up in one arm, throwing her other arm around Stinky. She swung him around in a circle. "It means your daddy's coming home!"

Tiger squeezed Miss Nikki's neck, hard as he could, then jumped down and ran into his daddy's arms. His dad had tears running down his cheeks, and he hugged Tiger like he would never let him go.

Then Tiger, smiling his toothy little grin while cradled in his daddy's arms, looked over his daddy's shoulder and saw a mean-looking deputy who had carted his daddy away to jail so many times before.

"Let's get outta here, Dad," said a suddenly worried Tiger.

"Good idea," said his dad, smiling through the tears. "Let's go home."

———— ✦⊰⊱✦ ————

Nikki grabbed Charles by the arm, turned him around, and kissed him on the cheek. "Nice job, handsome," she gushed.

"Thanks, Nikki. I couldn't have done it without you."

"I know."

Charles gave her a spontaneous hug, then felt a little self-conscious and let her go. They both stood there for a second and smiled.

"By the way," Charles dropped his voice. "What *was* on that videotape, anyway?"

"You don't want to know," answered Nikki.

"I was afraid of that," said Charles. Then he gave her another hug.

CHAPTER 78

Twenty-four hours later Nikki was sitting in Charles's office, searching for just the right words. She had waited outside his con law class, then followed him upstairs. This couldn't wait any longer. It was now Tuesday morning, and Nikki had hardly slept since Sunday night. She hated to involve Charles, but she didn't know where else to turn. Her conscience was killing her. And she needed a good lawyer.

Armistead had died as a result of Nikki's breaking-and-entering scheme. She didn't know the details, but she was pretty sure that Virginia law would treat her as if she had killed Armistead with her own hands. *But who would know?* Only she and Buster. And now Charles.

Nikki stared at her hands and rubbed them together. Charles had been unusually subdued himself, and she noticed the dark circles under his eyes that matched the ones she had confronted in her own mirror that morning. Something was eating him too.

He slouched down in his chair a little, spreading his long legs out in front of him and crossing them at the ankles. He picked up the Nerf basketball from his desk and tossed it to her. "Here," he said. "Makes it easier to think."

Nikki took a shot that missed by a foot. "Not a good sign," she said.

"Talk to me, girl." Charles sat up a little straighter and leaned forward. "Whatever it is, I'm on your side."

This was so hard. Would he condemn her? Forgive her like the woman at the well? Nikki thought about that night on the boardwalk, the street sermon, the chalk, Charles asking for forgiveness.

Now it was her turn to ask. "I know what happened to Armistead," she said softly. She paused to take a deep breath before continuing.

"Me too," injected Charles before she could speak again.

"Huh?"

Charles sighed and reached in a desk drawer. He tossed a document in Nikki's direction. "This came today. In the mail."

Nikki picked it up and started reading.

"It's a will," explained Charles. "The last will and testament of Dr. Sean Armistead."

"He mailed it before he died?"

"He mailed it," replied Charles. "Chesapeake postmark. Monday's date. Meaning it could have been dropped in the mail Sunday night or mailed by somebody else Monday or…"

Charles stood and shook his head. He fetched his Nerf ball and took a shot. All net. "It's all in the follow-through," he said.

"Or what?" asked Nikki, leaning forward.

"Or Armistead might have mailed it himself on Monday."

Nikki shook her head to clear her thoughts. *Armistead died Sunday night, didn't he?* Charles took another shot and continued talking.

"The will is pretty interesting. Names me as the executor and instructs me to keep the bequests as confidential as possible." This time Charles missed. Nikki grabbed the ball from the floor and tossed it back to him.

"So, Nikki, I'm telling you these things in strictest confidence, okay? I was debating whether I should say anything at all, but this document"— Charles stopped for a moment, a pained expression on his face—"it's like fingers around my neck, choking me. I've got to talk to someone about it."

Nikki nodded. She would have promised him anything to find out what the will said. In fact, she would have strangled it out of him herself if he had refused to tell her.

"Armistead leaves fifty thousand each to Tiger and Stinky to be used for their college education. He leaves twenty-five K to Thomas Hammond to compensate him for time spent in jail. He leaves five hundred thousand— half a million bucks—to fund a ministry to drug dealers in New York City that will be associated with the Baptist Ministry Center on the lower east side of Manhattan. He specifically instructs that I should be the one responsible for hiring and firing anybody who works at the center under this new program. The rest of his estate—and there will be a lot left—he gives to Parkinson's research." Charles interrupted his Nerf basketball shots to look at Nikki.

She scrunched up her brow, her head suddenly aching with all this stuff. "I get the Parkinson's research, since it's the disease that ravaged his wife. But the drug ministry? I don't get that."

"Maybe this will help," explained Charles. He dug into the same drawer and handed two other documents to Nikki. "Armistead not only sent his handwritten will to me, but he also sent an accompanying letter and an irrevocable trust agreement. The letter instructs me, if I should find it impossible to prove his death, to distribute his money the same way under this living irrevocable trust agreement as he specified in his will."

The tension in Nikki's head and neck increased. Charles was placing this puzzle in front of her, piece by piece, but she couldn't quite see how it fit together, didn't quite have that big picture yet from the front of the puzzle box. She had always prided herself on being the first to figure these scams out, but this one...

"Buster Jackson once told me that when he got out of jail, he wanted to start a ministry for drug addicts," Charles continued, shooting baskets again. "'Get them clean, get them jobs, get them saved,' is the way Buster phrased it. And one more thing, the name of the ministry project in New York City, according to the will, is to be the Lazarus Fund. Get it? The Lazarus Fund."

"I *don't* get it," said Nikki. A will, an irrevocable *living* trust, a biblical allusion. What was going on? And now Charles was tying Buster to the death of Armistead. Maybe Charles knew more than he was letting on.

"Buster and I once had a knock-down-drag-out argument on the biblical story of Lazarus," explained Charles. "Lazarus is the guy Christ raised from the dead. Buster didn't believe it at first, but I think I talked him into it."

"Okay," said Nikki, trying hard to follow.

"So here's the big picture," said Charles, stopping the constant motion of shooting baskets and leaning on the desk. "Armistead leaves a document he calls a dying declaration that ends up clearing Thomas Hammond in court. The concept of a dying declaration just happens to be something I told Buster about in a Bible study at the jail one night. Then Armistead leaves a will, or an irrevocable trust that works even if he's not dead, in which he leaves a bunch of money for a drug ministry in New York City, and then gives me the power to hire the people to work in that ministry—people like Buster. And then, to top it all off, they name the project the Lazarus Project, which seems like a clear signal to me that Armistead, who we thought was dead, is still alive."

Nikki's jaw dropped open. It suddenly began making sense. The big picture coming into focus. She was stunned. Elated. Buster had kept his word. She was off the hook!

"It all makes sense!" exclaimed Nikki. "The Monday postmark...everything." She watched Charles shrug and miss another shot. Her own heart, lightened by this theory, suddenly went out to this guy. "But Charles, if the Barracuda is behind bars and Armistead is still alive, why are you moping around like you just lost your best friend?"

"For starters," said Charles, plopping back down in his chair. "I got my client off by being an unwitting participant in a fraud on the court. Though everything in the dying declaration was technically true, even the title of it is grossly misleading."

"But that's not your fault," protested Nikki. "You couldn't have known..."

"That's where you're wrong," said Charles earnestly. "In a way, it is my fault. Buster got saved in jail and needed someone to disciple him, someone to help him grow as a Christian. I mean, a man with any kind of spiritual maturity wouldn't feel like he had to game the system to make it work. He'd trust God instead. But I was so skeptical of Buster, and so busy trying to make new converts on the streets, that I missed the opportunity to teach the one convert God had dumped right in my lap. I basically forgot that God called me to make disciples, not just converts." He slumped in his chair, eyes downcast. "That's my failure, not Buster's."

Though she would never understand it, for some reason this confession affected Nikki in a way that no sermon, argument, or emotional appeal for Christianity ever could. She found it hard to resist this level of vulnerability. Here was authentic spirituality—a man who cared more about integrity and relationship than he did about the outcome of a high-profile case. Sure, he wanted to win, but he wanted to win the right way.

But it also seemed that Charles was beating himself up pretty hard. Buster was a free man, not some kind of robot who did whatever Charles programmed him to do. "Charles, you may have a few faults, most of which I've already pointed out to you"—this brought a quick hint of a smile to his face—"but lack of spiritual intensity is not among them. I've never met anyone as focused as you on turning others into followers of Christ." She tossed him the Nerf ball and watched as he leaned back in his chair and started bouncing it off the wall.

"Thanks," he said, but Nikki could tell he didn't find much solace in her words. A couple of tosses later, he said, "That's my theory, Nikki. Now what's yours?"

"Oh, nothing quite that elaborate," shrugged Nikki. She could feel her cheeks burning. She smiled nervously as she tried to appear casual. "I actually thought that Armistead might really be dead." No sooner were the words out of her mouth than a troubling thought hit her. She suddenly realized why Charles was so distraught about what Buster might have done.

"If Armistead is still alive, whose body was that in his car?" Nikki asked.

Charles stopped tossing the ball—frozen in time and space. She saw a troubled look grab his face, as if he had been wrestling with this same question for a long time but couldn't quite figure it out, as if he had just completed a complex puzzle only to discover a couple of pieces still missing.

"You tell me," said Charles. "You tell me."

CHAPTER 79

They had been driving for hours and were now on the outskirts of New York City. Buster had bought the car they were riding in—a late model Oldsmobile with more than a hundred thousand miles on it—as soon as he had been released from jail. He bought it from a former "business acquaintance" with a promise to pay later. Buster's credit was not so hot, so he couldn't afford a car with tinted windows. This car didn't even have power windows.

Buster was driving, and the radio was blaring hip-hop.

"You think the rev got our package yet?" asked Buster, raising his voice to be heard over the radio.

"Either today or tomorrow."

"Tight."

Buster drove on without talking, jammin' to the music, replaying the whirlwind events of the last few days in his mind. He had been out of jail less than a week and had already committed enough crimes to revoke his probation forever. First, he had trespassed in Armistead's house on Sunday night and assaulted the doctor. That same night, he and Armistead had retrieved the corpse—probably another felony of some type or another—then Buster broke into the dentist's office to switch the dental records, undoubtedly another serious penal violation. So much for making like Mother Teresa.

Buster thought about the drive to the Blue Ridge Parkway. Buster had made Armistead drive the Olds, while Buster followed close behind in Armistead's Lexus, the corpse stashed safely in the trunk. When they arrived at Lookout Peak, they placed the corpse in the driver seat, pushed Armistead's car over the cliff, then climbed to the bottom where the car had landed. They doused the car in gasoline and started a huge fire. The body had been burned beyond recognition. They drove back to a hotel in Suffolk, Virginia, where they both stayed on Monday so they could monitor the trial on the local news. Next they started their nonstop trip to New York today—Tuesday.

The plan was working perfectly. He and Thomas were free; the Barracuda was not. Life was good.

"Can I ask you something?" Sean Armistead reached over and turned down the radio. Buster cast him a dirty look that Armistead didn't seem to notice. *Why do these white boys always have to turn down the tunes when they talk?*

"Why did you spare me on Sunday night?" Armistead asked.

Buster thought for a moment—not easy to do in the silence—his eyes glued to the road. He re-created the events of that night in his mind. "I looked in your eyes, Doc, just before your body made like a rag doll, and I saw fear. I saw your eyes beggin' for forgiveness, the same way I did when I knelt by the side of the road and gave my life to Christ. I didn't deserve no mercy, and the thief on the cross didn't deserve it either, Doc, but that didn't stop Christ. I figured if Christ had mercy on me, I better have some on you. Christians don't return hate for hate, Doc." He paused and flashed a gold-toothed grin. "Guess God took my forearm off your neck."

There was another prolonged silence. "You cool with that?" asked Buster.

"Yeah, Buster," replied Armistead. "I'm cool with that."

You'd better be, thought Buster. Mercy did not come easy to him. Still, he was working on it, resisting the urge to finish the work he had started Sunday night. Christians don't return hate for hate, he kept telling himself.

"Whatcha gonna do when we hit the city, Doc—now that you're a dead man and all?"

"I'll probably just see if I can get a new ID somehow and start life over. I might be able to still get my hands on some money from one of those Virginia Insurance Reciprocal accounts. And then"—Armistead paused, looking out the window—"I've just got to get alone for a while and think through some things."

"Tight," said Buster, turning the radio back up loud enough so the cars in the other lane could appreciate it. The whole interior throbbed.

Armistead reached over and turned the volume back down. Buster thought for a moment about breaking his hand. "One more thing," said Armistead.

408 . RANDY SINGER

"Better be good, Doc. That's my song."

"I've been trying to get up the nerve to ask you this the whole trip." Armistead fidgeted a little in his seat, then just spat it out. "Who was it we burned up in my car?"

Before Buster answered, he thought about A-town and smiled. God was so cool. If A-town hadn't bragged to Buster about where he had stashed his murder victim, if the Barracuda hadn't double-crossed Buster when he tried to reveal the location of the victim's body, if the victim hadn't been about the same size as Armistead, if A-town hadn't told Buster about where he hid the dude's dental records so Buster could make the switch—there were a lot of variables. Only God could make them all work out.

"Let's just say," Buster replied coyly, "that it helps to know where the bodies are buried."

Then Buster laughed—a big, baritone, gold-toothed laugh. And Dr. Sean Armistead, though he probably failed to see the humor, laughed right along with him.

CHAPTER 80

It is, thought Thomas, *just as I remembered it, yet it will never be the same.* He slumped down on the living room couch and stared at Theresa sitting in the recliner. The trailer felt at once comfortable yet depressing. Reminders of Joshie permeated every square inch.

It was now four days after the miraculous acquittal, and Thomas and Theresa had just won the battle of the bedtime. Tiger, rambunctious to the end, had finally put his head down on the pillow and stopped squirming. Though he only had a twin-sized mattress, Stinky had insisted on lying down with Tiger as she had for the past four nights. At some point in time, Stinky would have to go back to sleeping in her own room, but that was not a battle either Thomas or Theresa were ready to fight just yet.

Even before the kids came home for good, Theresa had wisely taken the steps necessary for the family to try and get on with life. The room that Tiger had previously shared with Joshie was now just Tiger's room. Theresa had packed all of Joshie's stuff neatly away. And Tiger had wasted no time junking the room up.

"What're you looking at?" asked Theresa, as she turned her attention from the television to Thomas.

"Nothin'," he lied. He couldn't take his eyes off her. He had put her through so much and wondered if she would ever forgive him.

"Yes, you were."

"I swear." Thomas held up his hand, as if taking an oath. Then he slowly stood up, walked over to the recliner, and tentatively reached out to massage Theresa's shoulders.

"I'm sorry," he whispered. "For everything."

Theresa placed her hand on top of his. "I don't blame you," she said, her voice so soft that Thomas could barely hear the words. "But I don't think I can ever stop blaming myself."

The blunt honesty of her reply paralyzed Thomas. It made him heartsick to think that Theresa shouldered his blame. What choice did she have when Joshie got sick? How he wished that he could just return to the first day of the sickness. He would seek medical help immediately, save Joshie's life, and allow Theresa to smile again.

Thomas loved this woman, after all these years, as much as the day they were married. Maybe more, after what they'd just been through. Together they would survive. But somehow he just couldn't find the words to comfort her, the words he knew she needed to hear. He had never been good at speech makin'.

"Daddy," whined Tiger from his bedroom. "Daddy!"

Thomas grunted. "That kid's got the worst timin' I ever saw."

"Wanna trade him in?" asked Theresa.

Thomas didn't answer. He was already on his way to the small bedroom.

"Will you lay down wif me," Tiger asked, "and tell me the story of Abe-ham?"

"Shh," said Thomas, holding his finger to his lips. "Your sister's sleeping."

Stinky's bright blue eyes popped open. "No, I'm not," she said cheerily. "Please! Pretty please!"

"Okay, okay," Thomas said as he lay down on the floor next to the bed. He acted like he was doing them a big favor. But in truth, there was nothing in the world that he would rather be doing. For the next ten minutes, he told the story of Abraham and Isaac, of the faith of an earthly father and the provision of a heavenly one. But then, as he got to the most exciting part, the moment when Abraham was raising his knife to slay his own son, the moment when God stayed Abraham's hand and provided a ram for the sacrifice instead of Isaac, a funny thing happened. Thomas's words started coming out slower and slower, and then they started to slur, and then he wasn't making any sense at all. And then, right in midsentence, he stopped talking altogether and started to snore.

✦

Stinky nudged Tiger with her elbow and started to giggle. This, of course, got Tiger started too, and pretty soon the kids were both giggling like crazy.

When they had giggled themselves out, Tiger sat up on his elbow and looked down at his dad. "Should we wake him up?" Tiger asked.

"No," said Stinky, "let him sleep. He's had a long day."

"Me too," Tiger said as he plopped his head back down on the pillow. He reached over the side of the bed and placed his hand on his daddy's chest. Then Tiger closed his eyes and started thinking his happy thoughts.

CHAPTER 81

Denita sat at the desk in her study, paying bills. One eye was on the clock, the other on her cell phone. Friday night. This was supposed to have been the big day when Senator Crafton and a few other heavyweights met with the president to finalize the deal. Denita had talked to Catherine Godfrey at least five times yesterday just to make sure they had all their ducks in a row. Catherine had promised to call back today, no later than five o'clock.

She was already three hours late.

Denita thought about calling Godfrey again, leaving another message. But what good would that do? Instead, she stared at the phone and cursed under her breath. What could have gone wrong? What could possibly have taken so long?

She thought about her one Achilles heel—the RU-486. But she wouldn't allow herself to dwell there. That was history. And with Charles pledged to silence, it was history that had never happened.

The phone rang, and Denita nearly jumped out of her skin. She answered it immediately, forgetting that she had planned on letting it ring a few times so she wouldn't look too anxious.

"Congratulations," said the voice of Catherine Godfrey. "They all liked the deal...Your Honor."

Your Honor. Those words sounded so sweet. And oh, how she had earned them. *Your Honor.* The fulfillment of a lifelong ambition.

"Thank God," sighed Denita. She could hear the party in the background on the other end of the phone. "What took you so long?" she asked.

Catherine made up a few weak excuses, then explained the process from here on out, and assured Denita that the rest was just a formality.

"Okay," said Denita, though she still found it hard to believe. "You sure the Senator will never know?"

Catherine blew out an impatient breath. "He trusts me, Denita. How many times have we been through this? Everything about the RU-486 deal is buried—it's just you, me…" she hesitated, her point not lost on Denita, "and Charles."

"Then it's over," promised Denita. "I know Charles. And despite his many shortcomings, the guy is a man of his word."

"Good," Catherine said. "Because I still intend to start Georgetown Law School in the fall."

It was, Denita knew, a tacit reference to their deal. And the silence on the phone indicated that Catherine was waiting for some confirmation.

"Georgetown Law School," said Denita. "I'll bet their graduates make great judicial law clerks."

"Yeah," Catherine quickly responded. "But I hear those jobs are hard to come by."

Denita chuckled, because it seemed like the proper thing to do. Then Catherine added, almost as an afterthought, "What do you think really turned him around on this?"

Denita smiled and looked down at the pile of bills in front of her. She flipped through the top few, pulling out the one monthly bill for a service she had just canceled. The Westside Florist Shop. It had been expensive to pay them each of the past three months to deliver flowers and plant a few roses in the cemetery. But it had saved her the trip. And she wouldn't have to worry about it any more. In many respects, it had been the best money she had ever spent.

"It was the flowers," said Denita, her smile widening. "Definitely the flowers."

———— ⊷≡⊶ ————

The Oakley sunglasses were probably overkill, Charles decided. He was about two blocks from his "pulpit," the corner of Atlantic Avenue and Virginia Beach Boulevard, wheeling his beloved green trash can down the sidewalk. He would be in his element soon, holding forth for the tourists, and he didn't want to be recognized as a lawyer. The media blitz following court on Monday had made him a minicelebrity, his face splashed all over local television. He therefore decided, as a precaution, to don the sunglasses so he could preach in anonymity, rising or falling with the merits of his argument, not the status of his fame.

He realized several blocks ago that there was no fame. Tourists and locals walked by as they always did, either ignoring him or looking at him like he was crazy. He would have ditched the Oakleys, but the sun was still low in the sky, and they did add an extra layer of cool.

It was the height of tourist season, and the hip-hop band was gettin' down. A large and bemused crowd stood gawking at the whirlwind of spinning, jumping, and angry lyrics that the band had unleashed. Charles smiled his electric white smile and strained against his load.

It was good to be home.

He hadn't been out here in what—two weeks? He started to feel the energy, the adrenaline that flowed when he was on a mission to save some souls. And this time, to make disciples. He promised himself that the next time God dropped a convert in his lap, Charles would do whatever it took to disciple that person. But still, after the events of the last few weeks, he also couldn't shake this gnawing feeling in the pit of his stomach, a constant reminder that he was very much alone.

He had reconciled himself to the fact that it was really over with Denita. They had been divorced for years. She now had an engagement ring. There was no turning the clock back on that relationship. At least they had parted this time on good terms, even tender terms, something that he hadn't experienced with Denita in years.

He would think about her often. And pray for her every night. But that chapter in his life was over.

He was also trying to reconcile himself to just being friends with the enigmatic Nikki Moreno, but that was considerably harder. He thought about her even more than Denita. He had been out here on the street dozens of times, had seen dozens of lives changed, but the one lingering memory was that special night two weeks ago, that night of magic with Nikki Moreno. He would never forget the sidewalk chalk, her vulnerable sharing about her past, their walk on the beach. Even as he approached the spot where he had apologized that night, his mind brought her into sharp relief. The haunting brown eyes, the beautiful olive skin, that spirited laughter. The alluring sound of her high-energy voice.

"Mind if I tag along, handsome?"

Charles whirled around, nearly dropping the trash can, half expecting there would be nobody there.

But it really was Nikki! More beautiful than he even remembered. He tried to play it cool but failed miserably…and broke into a huge smile.

"Nikki!" he exclaimed.

She spread her arms, as if to say "the one and only" and smiled her mischievous smile. "Need some company?"

Without thinking, Charles stepped forward and gave her a fierce hug, then caught himself and took a step back. "You bet," he said. "Could always use another heckler."

"Maybe you can find one," Nikki said. "But tonight, I'm coming to listen."

Charles paused for a beat, stunned and excited. Then he began nodding, as if he expected this all along. "C'mon," he said, "let's go do church."

He turned and started wheeling the trash can again, this time with Nikki by his side.

"So what're you preaching about tonight, handsome?"

Handsome. He loved it when she called him that. "I think I'll probably just tell a little story about two thieves on a cross." He glanced sideways at Nikki, his eyes shielded by the shades. He tried to hide his excitement, but the electricity was coursing through his veins. *This could be her night. He sure wouldn't mind discipling this one.*

"I think you'll probably like it," he said.

<hr />

Buster was coming at him with a knife, the gold tooth gleaming. As Buster raised his knife to strike, he broke into heinous laughter, and the gold-toothed grin became the dastardly smile of the Barracuda. "Answer the question!" she screamed. "Answer the question!"

Thomas sat straight up, his wide eyes taking stock of the room. It was not his jail cell but Tiger's room. Thomas was sitting next to Tiger's bed, the light in the room was still on, but the kids were sleeping soundly. *How long had he slept? One hour? Two?*

Thomas stood to leave the room but first bent over to kiss the kids. Stinky had her arm thrown over Tiger's neck. Tiger's arm was dangling off the bed and toward the floor where Thomas had been sleeping. He kissed them both on the cheek. They were angels. When they were sleeping.

Thomas walked groggily out to the living room and thought again about the words that Charles had spoken after the first day of trial. Faith, hope, and most importantly…love. He found Theresa, still awake, curled up on a corner of the sofa and reading. He sat down next to her, and she leaned against his chest.

"How long I been sleeping?" he asked, yawning.

"Couple hours."

He tilted his head sideways and looked at the woman. "What're you still doing up?"

"I was hoping you'd come back out." Theresa paused, searching for the right words. "I've got something to tell ya."

"Okay," said Thomas. He drew her closer, sensing her emotional struggle.

"I didn't want to tell you this with all this stuff going on," Theresa said softly. "And I didn't know what I'd do if you didn't get out of jail…" She stopped midsentence, choking back tears. Thomas just held her, waiting for the emotions to pass.

He felt her take a deep breath. And then she said, "Thomas, I'm pregnant."

Thomas squeezed her closer, then kissed the top of her head. "How long?" he asked.

"Two months."

"Praise God," Thomas said. He paused. "Better get you to a doctor. Get checked out."

"Thanks," she whispered.

He looked down at this wonderful woman in his arms.

They had both been deeply wounded by the loss of Joshie, and it showed. *Time,* thought Thomas, *and the promise of a new child would help them heal.* Today had been particularly hectic, and Theresa was looking tired. Her black hair was unwashed and stringy. Her eyes were red and puffy, partly from thinking of Joshie, partly from joy for the child within her. The tears were beginning to flow. Her skin was blotched with red marks where she had clawed at her neck, anxiously waiting for an opportunity to share this news with her husband.

To someone who didn't know her, she might not look so great. But she was carrying *his* baby, and she was the world's best mother and wife. Others could think what they wanted, see what they wanted. But he knew the truth. He could see more than skin-deep. And to him, she was the most gorgeous creature God had ever created. No doubt about it.

To him, she simply looked beautiful.

Acknowledgments

Some writers are so creative that they turn an acknowledgments page into a work of art. Not this one. I like to save those rare bursts of creativity for the story.

So this page is a simple thanks to the many people who have made this book better by their touch. And for those I have forgotten, this page is both your thanks and my apology.

A big thank you (and thunderous applause):

To Carolyn Curtis and to Keith, Karen, and Charlotte Singer, who plowed through the first ragged manuscript and helped smooth it out without grimacing (too much). Thanks for giving me the encouragement to stay after it. To the members of the Singer clan who let these characters move in with us for the last three years. Thanks, guys. I love you so much.

To Michael Garnier, Mary Hartman, Robin Pawling, and Rosalyn Singer, thanks for scrutinizing the final draft and deftly suggesting ways to better the story and make the characters as realistic as possible.

To the forgiving team at WaterBrook Press, thanks for your faith in the power of fiction. No author could ask for a better publishing team than Steve Cobb, Don Pape, Dudley Delffs, Brian McGinley, Ginia Hairston, Laura Wright, and company. If only my speeches could be as carefully edited as my stories.

To those who believed in this book and brought their own creativity to bear on the marketing and promotion—Martin Coleman, Wolfgang Schumacher, Jeff Griswold, Trish Ragsdale, Aaron Harris, Richard Smith, Jay Jessup, Martin King, and their respective teams—you guys amaze me.

To young Darr Smith. When I close my eyes and think of the little boy named "Tiger" in this book, your inquisitive face and indomitable spirit come to mind. And to the real life Charles Arnold, thanks for teaching me the challenges and rewards of street preaching. May God bless you on every corner.

About the Author

Randy Singer's previous books include *Directed Verdict,* which won the 2003 Christy Award for best Christian suspense novel. A veteran trial lawyer, he serves as chief counsel for the North American Mission Board and on the Board of Legal Advisors for the American Center for Law and Justice. Formerly, he was a law school professor and head of the trial section in a large Virginia firm. Randy lives in Atlanta, Georgia, with his wife, Rhonda, and their two children.

Page-Turning Courtroom Thrillers by Award-Winning Author Randy Singer

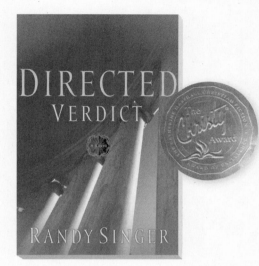

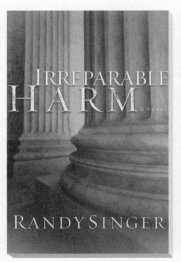

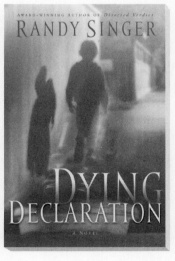

Available in bookstores everywhere.